Praise for t~~~~
and ~~~~

"Karin Slaughter keep~~~~
last."

"Simply the best bool~~~~
utterly gripping—ye~~~~ written with a tenderness and empathy
that will break your heart."

—Kathryn Stockett, author of *The Help*

"This is a great writer at the peak of her powers. Karin Slaughter
is at her nail-biting, heart-stopping, emotionally draining best."

—Peter James

"Simply one of the best thriller writers working today. I'd follow
her anywhere."

—Gillian Flynn

"Every Karin Slaughter novel is a cause for celebration."

—Kathy Reichs

"Fiction doesn't get any better than this."

—Jeffery Deaver

"Her characters, plot, and pacing are unrivaled among thriller
writers, and if you haven't yet read her, this is the moment."

—Michael Connelly

"Enter the world of Karin Slaughter. Just be forewarned: there's no
going back."

—Lisa Gardner

"A fearless writer. One of the boldest thriller writers working
today."

—Tess Gerritsen

"A hold-your-breath, pedal-to-the-metal thriller."

—Lee Child on *Pretty Girls*

"A hell-raising thriller."

—*New York Times Book Review* on *Pretty Girls*

THE GOOD DAUGHTER

THE GOOD
DAUGHTER

A Novel

KARIN
SLAUGHTER

𝒲𝓂

WILLIAM MORROW

An Imprint of HarperCollins*Publishers*

Excerpt from letter "To A"—Flannery O'Connor. Copyright © 1979 by Regina O'Connor, reprinted by permission of the Mary Flannery O'Connor Charitable Trust via Harold Matson Co., Inc. All rights reserved.

Dr. Seuss quotation from an interview in the *L.A. Times* reproduced by kind permission of the Dr. Seuss Estate.

A hardcover edition of this book was published in 2017 by William Morrow, an imprint of HarperCollins Publishers.

FIRST WILLIAM MORROW PAPERBACK EDITION PUBLISHED 2019.

Designed by Leah Carlson-Stanisic
Photograph by Jetrel/Shutterstock, Inc.

Library of Congress Cataloging-in-Publication Data has been applied for.

ISBN 978-0-06-269629-8

19 20 21 22 23   LSC   10 9 8 7 6 5 4 3 2 1

"... what you call my struggle to submit ... is not struggle to submit but a struggle to accept and with passion. I mean, possibly, with joy. Picture me with my ground teeth stalking joy—fully armed too as it's a highly dangerous quest."

—FLANNERY O'CONNOR

THE GOOD DAUGHTER

WHAT HAPPENED TO SAMANTHA

Samantha Quinn felt the stinging of a thousand hornets inside her legs as she ran down the long, forlorn driveway toward the farm-house. The sound of her sneakers slapping bare earth bongoed along with the rapid thumps of her heart. Sweat had turned her ponytail into a thick rope that whipped at her shoulders. The twigs of delicate bones inside her ankles felt ready to snap.

She ran harder, choking down the dry air, sprinting into the pain.

Up ahead, Charlotte stood in their mother's shadow. They all stood in their mother's shadow. Gamma Quinn was a towering fig-ure: quick blue eyes, short dark hair, skin as pale as an envelope, and with a sharp tongue just as prone to inflicting tiny, painful cuts in inconvenient places. Even from a distance, Samantha could see the thin line of Gamma's disapproving lips as she studied the stopwatch in her hand.

The ticking seconds echoed inside Samantha's head. She pushed herself to run faster. The tendons cording through her legs sent out a high-pitched wail. The hornets moved into her lungs. The plastic baton felt slippery in her hand.

Twenty yards. Fifteen. Ten.

Charlotte locked into position, turning her body away from Sa-mantha, looking straight ahead, then started to run. She blindly stretched her right arm back behind her, waiting for the snap of the baton into the palm of her hand so that she could run the next relay.

This was the blind pass. The handoff took trust and coordina-tion, and just like every single time for the last hour, neither one of them was up to the challenge. Charlotte hesitated, glancing back. Samantha lurched forward. The plastic baton skidded up Charlotte's wrist, following the red track of broken skin the same as it had twenty times before.

Charlotte screamed. Samantha stumbled. The baton dropped. Gamma let out a loud curse.

"That's it for me." Gamma tucked the stopwatch into the bib pocket of her overalls. She stomped toward the house, the soles of her bare feet red from the barren yard.

Charlotte rubbed her wrist. "Asshole."

"Idiot." Samantha tried to force air into her shaking lungs. "You're not supposed to look back."

"You're not supposed to rip open my arm."

"It's called a blind pass, not a freak-out pass."

The kitchen door slammed shut. They both looked up at the hundred-year-old farmhouse, which was a sprawling, higgledy-piggledy monument to the days before licensed architects and building permits. The setting sun did nothing to soften the awkward angles. Not much more than an obligatory slap of white paint had been applied over the years. Tired lace curtains hung in the streaked windows. The front door was bleached a driftwoody gray from over a century of North Georgia sunrises. There was a sag in the roofline, a physical manifestation of the weight that the house had to carry now that the Quinns had moved in.

Two years and a lifetime of discord separated Samantha from her thirteen-year-old little sister, but she knew in this moment at least that they were thinking the same thing: *I want to go home*.

Home was a red-brick ranch closer to town. Home was their childhood bedrooms that they had decorated with posters and stickers and, in Charlotte's case, green Magic Marker. Home had a tidy square of grass for a front yard, not a barren, chicken-scratched patch of dirt with a driveway that was seventy-five yards long so that you could see who was coming.

None of them had seen who was coming at the red-brick house.

Only eight days had passed since their lives had been destroyed, but it felt like forever ago. That night, Gamma, Samantha, and Charlotte had walked up to the school for a track meet. Their father was at work because Rusty was always at work.

Later, a neighbor recalled an unfamiliar black car driving slowly up the street, but no one had seen the Molotov cocktail fly through the bay window of the red-brick house. No one had seen the smoke billowing out of the eaves or the flames licking at the roof. By the time an alarm was raised, the red-brick house was a smoldering black pit.

Clothes. Posters. Diaries. Stuffed animals. Homework. Books. Two goldfish. Lost baby teeth. Birthday money. Purloined lipsticks. Secreted cigarettes. Wedding photos. Baby photos. A boy's leather jacket. A love letter from that same boy. Mix tapes. CDs and a computer and a television and home.

"Charlie!" Gamma stood on the stoop outside the kitchen doorway. Her hands were on her hips. "Come set the table."

Charlotte turned to Samantha and said, "Last word!" before she jogged toward the house.

"Dipshit," Samantha muttered. You didn't get the last word on something just by saying the words *"last word."*

She moved more slowly toward the house on rubbery legs, because she wasn't the moron who couldn't reach back and wait for a baton to be slapped into her hand. She did not understand why Charlotte could not learn the simple handoff.

Samantha left her shoes and socks beside Charlotte's on the kitchen stoop. The air inside the house was dank and still. *Unloved*, was the first adjective that popped into Samantha's head when she walked through the door. The previous occupant, a ninety-six-year-old bachelor, had died in the downstairs bedroom last year. A friend of their father was letting them live in the farmhouse until things were worked out with the insurance company. *If* things could be worked out. Apparently, there was a disagreement as to whether or not their father's actions had invited arson.

A verdict had already been rendered in the court of public opinion, which is likely why the owner of the motel they'd been staying at for the last week had asked them to find other accommodations.

Samantha slammed the kitchen door because that was the only way to make sure it closed. A pot of water sat idle on the olive-green stove. A box of spaghetti lay unopened on the brown laminate counter. The kitchen felt stuffy and humid, the most unloved space in the house. Not one item in the room lived in harmony with the others. The old-timey refrigerator farted every time you opened the door. A bucket under the sink shivered of its own accord. There was an embarrassment of mismatched chairs around the trembly chipboard table. The bowed plaster walls were spotted white where old photos had once hung.

Charlotte stuck out her tongue as she tossed paper plates onto the table. Samantha picked up one of the plastic forks and flipped it into her sister's face.

Charlotte gasped, but not from indignation. "Holy crap, that was amazing!" The fork had gracefully somersaulted through the air and wedged itself between the crease of her lips. She grabbed the fork and offered it to Samantha. "I'll wash the dishes if you can do that twice in a row."

Samantha countered, "You toss it into my mouth once, and I'll wash dishes for a week."

Charlotte squinted one eye and took aim. Samantha was trying not to dwell on how stupid it was to invite her little sister to throw a fork in her face when Gamma walked in carrying a large cardboard box.

"Charlie, don't throw utensils at your sister. Sam, help me look for that frying pan I bought the other day." Gamma dropped the box onto the table. The outside was marked EVERYTHING $1 EA. There were dozens of partially unpacked boxes scattered through the house. They created a labyrinth through the rooms and hallways, all filled with thrift store donations that Gamma had bought for pennies on the dollar.

"Think of the money we're saving," Gamma had proclaimed, holding up a faded purple Church Lady T-shirt that read *"Well, Isn't That SPE-CIAL?"*

At least that's what Samantha thought the shirt said. She was too busy hiding in the corner with Charlotte, mortified that their mother expected them to wear other people's clothes. Other people's socks. Even other people's underwear until thank God their father had put his foot down.

"For Chrissakes," Rusty had yelled at Gamma. "Why not just sew us all up in sackcloth and be done with it?"

To which Gamma had seethed, "Now you want me to learn how to *sew?*"

Her parents argued about new things now because there were no longer any old things to argue about. Rusty's pipe collection. His hats. His dusty law books splayed all over the house. Gamma's journals and research papers with red lines and circles and notations. Her Keds kicked off by the front door. Charlotte's kites. Samantha's hair clips. Rusty's mother's frying pan was gone. The green crockpot Gamma and Rusty had gotten for a wedding present was gone. The burnt-smelling toaster oven was gone. The owl kitchen clock with the eyes that went back and forth. The hooks where they left their jackets. The wall that the hooks were mounted to. Gamma's station wagon, which stood like a dinosaur fossil in the blackened cavern that had once been the garage.

The farmhouse contained five rickety chairs that had not been sold in the bachelor farmer's estate sale, an old kitchen table that was too cheap to be called an antique and a large chifforobe wedged into a small closet that their mother said they'd have to pay Tom Robinson a nickel to bust up.

Nothing hung in the chifforobe. Nothing was folded into the keeping room drawers or placed on high shelves in the pantry.

They had moved into the farmhouse two days ago, but hardly any boxes had been unpacked. The hallway off the kitchen was a maze of mislabeled containers and stained brown paper bags that could not be emptied until the cabinets were cleaned, and the cabinets would not be cleaned until Gamma forced them to do it. The mattresses upstairs rested on bare floors. Overturned crates held cracked lamps to read by and the books that they read were not treasured possessions but on loan from the Pikeville public library.

Every night, Samantha and Charlotte hand-washed their running shorts and sports bras and ankle socks and Lady Rebels Track & Field T-shirts because these were among their few, precious possessions that had escaped the flames.

"Sam." Gamma pointed to the air conditioner in the window. "Turn that thing on so we can get some air moving in here."

Samantha studied the large, metal box before finding the ON button. Motors churned. Cold air with a tinge of wet fried chicken hissed through the vent. Samantha stared out the window at the side yard. A rusted tractor was near the dilapidated barn. Some unknown farming implement was half-buried in the ground beside it. Her father's Chevette was caked in dirt, but at least it wasn't melted to the garage floor like her mother's station wagon.

She asked Gamma, "What time are we supposed to pick up Daddy from work?"

"He'll get a ride from somebody at the courthouse." Gamma glanced at Charlotte, who was happily whistling to herself as she tried to fold a paper plate into an airplane. "He has that case."

That case.

The words bounced around inside Samantha's head. Her father always had a case, and there were always people who hated him for it. There was not one low-life *alleged* criminal in Pikeville, Georgia, that Rusty Quinn would not represent. Drug dealers. Rapists. Murderers. Burglars. Car jackers. Pedophiles. Kidnappers. Bank robbers. Their case files read like pulp novels that always ended the same, bad way. Folks in town called Rusty the Attorney for the Damned, which was also what people had called Clarence Darrow, though to Samantha's knowledge, no one had ever firebombed Clarence Darrow's house for freeing a murderer from death row.

That was what the fire had been about.

Ezekiel Whitaker, a black man wrongly convicted of murdering a white woman, had walked out of prison the same day that a burning bottle of kerosene had been thrown through the Quinns' bay window. In case the message wasn't clear enough, the arsonist had also spray-painted the words NIGGER LOVER on the mouth of the driveway.

And now, Rusty was defending a man who'd been accused of kidnapping and raping a nineteen-year-old girl. White man, white girl, but still, tempers were running high because he was a white man from a trashy family and she was a white girl from a good one. Rusty and Gamma never openly discussed the case, but the details of the crime were so lurid that whispers around town had seeped in under the front door, mingled through the air vents, buzzed into their ears at night when they were trying to sleep.

Penetration with a foreign object.

Unlawful confinement.

Crimes against nature.

There were photographs in Rusty's files that even nosy Charlotte knew better than to seek out, because some of the photos were of the girl hanging in the barn outside her family's house because what the man had done to her was too horrible to live with, so she had taken her own life.

Samantha went to school with the dead girl's brother. He was two years older than Samantha, but like everyone else, he knew who her father was, and walking down the locker-lined hallway was like walking through the red-brick house while the flames stripped away her skin.

The fire hadn't only taken her bedroom and her clothes and her purloined lipsticks. Samantha had lost the boy to whom the leather jacket had belonged, the friends who used to invite her to parties and movies and sleepovers. Even her beloved track coach who'd trained Samantha since sixth grade had started making excuses about not having enough time to work with her anymore.

Gamma had told the principal that she was keeping the girls out of school and track practice so that they could help unpack, but Samantha knew that it was because Charlotte had come home crying every day since the fire.

"Well, shit." Gamma closed the cardboard box, giving up on the frying pan. "I hope you girls don't mind being vegetarian tonight."

Neither of them minded because it didn't really matter. Gamma was an aggressively terrible cook. She resented recipes. She was openly hostile toward spices. Like a feral cat, she instinctively bristled against any domestication.

Harriet Quinn wasn't called Gamma out of a precocious child's inability to pronounce the word "Mama," but because she held two doctorates, one in physics and one in something equally brainy that Samantha could never remember but, if she had to guess, had to do with gamma rays. Her mother had worked for NASA, then moved to Chicago to work at Fermilab before returning to Pikeville to take care of her dying parents. If there was a romantic story about how Gamma had given up her promising scientific career to marry a small-town lawyer, Samantha had never heard it.

"Mom." Charlotte plopped down at the table, head in her hands. "My stomach hurts."

Gamma asked, "Don't you have homework?"

"Chemistry." Charlotte looked up. "Can you help me?"

"It's not rocket science." Gamma dumped the spaghetti noodles into the pot of cold water on the stove. She twisted the knob to turn on the gas.

Charlotte crossed her arms low on her waist. "Do you mean, it's not rocket science, so I should be able to figure it out on my own, or do you mean, it's not rocket science, and that is the only science that you know how to perform, and so therefore you cannot help me?"

"There were too many conjunctions in that sentence." Gamma used a match to light the gas. A sudden *whoosh* singed the air. "Go wash your hands."

"I believe I had a valid question."

"Now."

Charlotte groaned dramatically as she stood from the table and loped down the long hallway. Samantha heard a door open, then close, then another open, then close.

"Fudge!" Charlotte bellowed.

There were five doors off the long hallway, none of them laid out in any way that made sense. One door led to the creepy basement. One led to the chifforobe. One of the middle doors inexplicably led to the tiny downstairs bedroom where the bachelor had died. Another led to the pantry. The remaining door led to the bathroom, and even after two days, none of them could quite retain the location in their long-term memory.

"Found it!" Charlotte called, as if they had all been breathlessly waiting.

Gamma said, "Grammar aside, she's going to be a fine lawyer one day. I hope. If that girl doesn't get paid to argue, she's not going to get paid at all."

Samantha smiled at the thought of her sloppy, disorganized sister wearing a blazer and carrying a briefcase. "What am I going to be?"

"Anything you want, my girl, just don't do it here."

This theme was coming up more often lately: Gamma's desire for Samantha to move out, to get away, to do anything but whatever it was that women did here.

Gamma had never fit in with the Pikeville mothers, even before Rusty's work had turned them into pariahs. Neighbors, teachers, people in the street, all had an opinion about Gamma Quinn, and it was seldom a positive one. She was too smart for her own good. She was a difficult woman. She didn't know when to keep her mouth shut. She refused to fit in.

When Samantha was little, Gamma had taken up running. As with everything else, she had been athletic before it was popular, running marathons on the weekends, doing her Jane Fonda tapes in front of the television. It wasn't just her athletic prowess that people found off-putting. You could not beat her at chess or Trivial Pursuit or even Monopoly. She knew all the questions on *Jeopardy*. She knew when to use *who* or *whom*. She could not abide misinformation. She disdained organized religion. In social situations, she had the strange habit of spouting obscure facts.

Did you know that pandas have enlarged wrist bones?

Did you know that scallops have rows of eyes along their mantles?

Did you know that the granite inside New York's Grand Central Terminal gives off more radiation than what's deemed acceptable at a nuclear power plant?

If Gamma was happy, if she enjoyed her life, if she was pleased with her children, if she loved her husband, were stray, unmatched pieces of information in the thousand-piece puzzle that was their mother.

"What's taking your sister so long?"

Samantha leaned back in the chair and looked down the hall. All five doors were still closed. "Maybe she flushed herself down the toilet."

"There's a plunger in one of those boxes."

The phone rang, a distinct jangling of a bell inside the old-fashioned rotary telephone on the wall. They'd had a cordless phone in the red-brick house, and an answering machine to screen all the calls that came in. The first time Samantha had ever heard the word *fuck* was on the answering machine. She was with her friend Gail from across the street. The phone was ringing as they walked through the front door, but Samantha had been too late to answer, so the machine had done the honors.

"Rusty Quinn, I will fuck you up, son. Do you hear me? I will fucking kill you, and rape your wife, and skin your daughters like I'm dressing a fucking deer, you fucking bleeding heart piece of shit."

The phone rang a fourth time. Then a fifth.

"Sam." Gamma's tone was stern. "Don't let Charlie answer that."

Samantha stood from the table, leaving unsaid the "what about me?" She picked up the receiver and pressed it to her ear. Automatically, her chin tucked in, her jaw set, waiting for a punch. "Hello?"

"Hey there, Sammy-Sam. Lemme speak to your mama."

"Daddy." Samantha sighed out his name. And then she saw Gamma give a tight shake of her head. "She just went upstairs to take a bath." Samantha realized too late that this was the same excuse she had given hours ago. "Do you want me to have her call you?"

Rusty said, "I feel our Gamma has been overly attentive to hygiene lately."

"You mean since the house burned down?" The words slipped out before Samantha could catch them. The insurance agent at Pikeville Fire and Casualty wasn't the only person who blamed Rusty Quinn for the fire.

Rusty chuckled. "Well, I appreciate you holding that back as long as you did." His lighter clicked into the phone. Apparently, her father had forgotten about swearing on a stack of Bibles that he would quit smoking. "Now, listen, hon, tell Gamma when she gets out of the *tub* that I'm gonna have the sheriff send a car over."

"The sheriff?" Samantha tried to convey her panic to Gamma, but her mother kept her back turned. "What's wrong?"

"Nothing's wrong, sugar. It's just that they never caught that bad old fella who burned down the house, and today, another innocent man has gone free, and some people don't like that, either."

"You mean the man who raped that girl who killed herself?"

"The only people who know what happened to that girl are her, whoever committed the crime, and the Lord God in heaven. I don't presume to be any of these people and I don't opine that you should, either."

Samantha hated when her father put on his country-lawyer-making-a-closing-argument voice. "Daddy, she hanged herself in a barn. That's a proven fact."

"Why is my life riddled with contrary females?" Rusty put his hand over the phone and spoke to someone else. Samantha could hear a woman's husky laugh. Lenore, her father's secretary. Gamma had never liked her.

"All right now." Rusty was back on the line. "You still there, honey?"

"Where else would I be?"

Gamma said, "Hang up the phone."

"Baby." Rusty blew out some smoke. "Tell me what you need me to do to make this better and I will do it immediately."

An old lawyer's trick; make the other person solve the problem. "Daddy, I—"

Gamma slammed her fingers down on the hook, ending the call.

"Mama, we were talking."

Gamma's fingers stayed hooked on the phone. Instead of explaining herself, she said, "Consider the etymology of the phrase 'hang up the phone.'" She pulled the receiver from Samantha's hand and hung it on the hook. "So, 'pick up the phone,' even 'off the hook,' starts to make sense. And of course you know the hook is a lever that, when depressed, opens up the circuit, indicating a call can be received."

"The sheriff's sending a car," Samantha said. "Or, I mean, Daddy's going to ask him to."

Gamma looked skeptical. The sheriff was no fan of the Quinns. "You need to wash your hands for dinner."

Samantha knew that there was no sense in trying to force further conversation. Not unless she wanted her mother to find a screwdriver and open the phone to explain the circuitry, which had happened with countless small appliances in the past. Gamma was the only mother on the block who changed the oil in her own car.

Not that they lived on a block anymore.

Samantha tripped on a box in the hallway. She grabbed her toes, holding on to them like she could squeeze out the pain. She had to limp the rest of the way to the bathroom. She passed her sister in the hallway. Charlotte punched her in the arm because that was the kind of thing Charlotte did.

The brat had closed the door, so Samantha had a false start before she found the bathroom. The toilet was low to the ground, installed back when people were shorter than they were now. The shower was a plastic corner unit with black mold growing inside the seams. A ball-peen hammer rested inside the sink. Black cast iron showed where the hammer had been repeatedly dropped into the bowl. Gamma had been the one to figure out why. The faucet was so old and rusted that you had to whack the tap handle to keep it from dripping.

"I'll fix that this weekend," Gamma had said, setting a reward for herself at the end of what would clearly be a difficult week.

As usual, Charlotte had left a mess in the tiny bathroom. Water pooled on the floor and flecked the mirror. Even the toilet seat was wet. Samantha reached for the roll of paper towels hanging on the wall, then changed her mind. From the beginning, the house had felt temporary, but now that her father had pretty much said he was sending the sheriff because it might get firebombed like the last one, cleaning seemed like a waste of time.

"Dinner!" Gamma called from the kitchen.

Samantha splashed water on her face. Her hair felt gritty. Streaks of red coated her calves and arms where clay had mixed in with her sweat. She wanted to soak in a hot bath, but there was only one bathtub in the house, claw-footed with a dark rust-colored ring around the lip from where the previous occupant had for decades sloughed the earth from his skin. Even Charlotte wouldn't get in the tub, and Charlotte was a pig.

"It feels too sad in here," her sister had said, slowly backing out of the upstairs bathroom.

The tub was not the only thing that Charlotte found unsettling. The spooky, damp basement. The creepy, bat-filled attic. The creaky closet doors. The bedroom where the bachelor farmer had died.

There was a photo of the bachelor farmer in the bottom drawer of the chifforobe. They had found it this morning on the pretense of cleaning. Neither dared to touch it. They had stared down at the lonesome, round face of the bachelor farmer and felt overwhelmed by something sinister, though the photo was just a typical depression-era farm scene with a tractor and a mule. Samantha felt haunted by the sight of the farmer's yellow teeth, though how something could look yellow in a black-and-white photo was a mystery.

"Sam?" Gamma stood in the bathroom doorway, looking at their reflections in the mirror.

No one had ever mistaken them for sisters, but they were clearly mother and child. They shared the same strong jawline and high cheekbones, the same arch to their eyebrows that most people took for aloofness. Gamma wasn't beautiful, but she was striking, with dark, almost black hair and light blue eyes that sparkled with delight when she found something particularly funny or ridiculous. Samantha was old enough to remember a time when her mother took life a lot less seriously.

Gamma said, "You're wasting water."

Samantha tapped the faucet closed with the small hammer and dropped it back into the sink. She heard a car pulling up the driveway. The sheriff's man, which was surprising because Rusty rarely followed through on his promises.

Gamma stood behind her. "Are you still sad about Peter?"

The boy whose leather jacket had burned in the fire. The boy who had written Samantha a love letter, but would no longer look her in the eye when they passed each other in the school hallway.

Gamma said, "You're pretty. Do you know that?"

Samantha saw her cheeks blush in the mirror.

"Prettier than I ever was." Gamma stroked Samantha's hair back with her fingers. "I wish that my mother had lived long enough to meet you."

Samantha rarely heard about her grandparents. From what she

could gather, they had never forgiven Gamma for moving away to go to college. "What was Grandma like?"

Gamma smiled, her mouth awkwardly navigating the expression. "Pretty like Charlie. Very clever. Relentlessly happy. Always bubbling up with something to do. The kind of person that people just *liked*." She shook her head. With all of her degrees, Gamma still had not deciphered the science of likability. "She had streaks of gray in her hair before she turned thirty. She said it was because her brain worked so hard, but you know of course that all hair is originally white. It gets melanin through specialized cells called melanocytes that pump pigment into the hair follicles."

Samantha leaned back into her mother's arms. She closed her eyes, enjoying the familiar melody of Gamma's voice.

"Stress and hormones can leech pigmentation, but her life at the time was fairly simple—mother, wife, Sunday school teacher—so we can assume that the gray was due to a genetic trait, which means that either you or Charlie, or both, could have the same thing happen."

Samantha opened her eyes. "Your hair isn't gray."

"Because I go to the beauty parlor once a month." Her laughter tapered off too quickly. "Promise me you'll always take care of Charlie."

"Charlotte can take care of herself."

"I'm serious, Sam."

Samantha felt her heart tremble at Gamma's insistent tone. "Why?"

"Because you're her big sister and that's your job." She gripped both of Samantha's hands in her own. Her gaze was steady in the mirror. "We've had a rough patch, my girl. I won't lie and say it's going to get better. Charlie needs to know that she can depend on you. You have to put that baton firmly in her hand every time, no matter where she is. You find her. Don't expect her to find you."

Samantha felt her throat clench. Gamma was talking about

something else now, something more serious than a relay race. "Are you going away?"

"Of course not." Gamma scowled. "I'm only telling you that you need to be a useful person, Sam. I really thought you were past that silly, dramatic teenager stage."

"I'm not—"

"Mama!" Charlotte yelled.

Gamma turned Samantha around. She put her calloused hands on either side of her daughter's face. "I'm not going anywhere, kiddo. You can't get rid of me that easily." She kissed her nose. "Give that faucet another whack before you come to supper."

"Mom!" Charlotte screamed.

"Good Lord," Gamma complained as she walked out of the bathroom. "Charlie Quinn, do not shriek at me like a street urchin."

Samantha picked up the little hammer. The slim wooden handle was perpetually wet, like a dense sponge. The round head was rusted the same red as the front yard. She tapped the faucet and waited to make sure no more water dripped out.

Gamma called, "Samantha?"

Samantha felt her brow furrow. She turned toward the open door. Her mother never called her by her full name. Even Charlotte had to suffer through being called Charlie. Gamma had told them that one day they would appreciate being able to pass. She'd gotten more papers published and funding approved by signing her name as Harry than she'd ever gotten by signing it as Harriet.

"Samantha." Gamma's tone was cold, more like a warning. "Please ensure the faucet valve is closed and quickly make your way into the kitchen."

Samantha looked back at the mirror, as if her reflection could explain to her what was going on. This was not how her mother spoke to them. Not even when she was explaining the difference between a Marcel handle and the spring-loaded lever on her curling iron.

Without thinking, Samantha reached into the sink and wrapped her hand around the small hammer. She held it behind her back as she walked up the long hall toward the kitchen.

All of the lights were on. The sky had grown dark outside. She pictured her running shoes alongside Charlotte's on the kitchen stoop, the plastic baton left somewhere in the yard. The kitchen table laid with paper plates. Plastic forks and knives.

There was a cough, deep, maybe a man's. Maybe Gamma's, because she coughed that way lately, like the smoke from the fire had somehow made its way into her lungs.

Another cough.

The hair on the back of Samantha's neck prickled to attention.

The back door was at the opposite end of the hall, a halo of dim light encircling the frosted glass. Samantha glanced behind her as she continued up the hall. She could see the doorknob. She pictured herself turning it even as she walked farther away. Every step she took, she asked herself if she was being foolish, or if she should be concerned, or if this was a joke because her mother used to love to play jokes on them, like sticking plastic googly eyes on the milk jug in the fridge or writing "help me, I'm trapped inside a toilet paper factory!" on the inside of the toilet paper roll.

There was only one phone in the house, the rotary dial in the kitchen.

Her father's pistol was in the kitchen drawer.

The bullets were somewhere in a cardboard box.

Charlotte would laugh at her if she saw the hammer. Samantha tucked it down the back of her running shorts. The metal was cold against the small of her back, the wet handle like a curling tongue. She lifted her shirt to cover the hammer as she walked into the kitchen.

Samantha felt her body go rigid.

This wasn't a joke.

Two men stood in the kitchen. They smelled of sweat and beer and nicotine. They wore black gloves. Black ski masks covered their faces.

Samantha opened her mouth. The air had thickened like cotton, closing her throat.

One was taller than the other. The short one was heavier. Bulkier. Dressed in jeans and a black button-up shirt. The tall one wore a faded white concert T-shirt, jeans, and blue hightop sneakers with the red laces untied. The short one felt more dangerous but it was hard to tell because the only thing Samantha could see behind the masks was their mouths and eyes.

Not that she was looking at their eyes.

Hightop had a revolver.

Black Shirt had a shotgun that was pointed directly at Gamma's head.

Her hands were raised in the air. She told Samantha, "It's okay."

"No it ain't." Black Shirt's voice had the gravelly shake of a rattlesnake's tail. "Who else is in the house?"

Gamma shook her head. "Nobody."

"Don't lie to me, bitch."

There was a tapping noise. Charlotte was seated at the table, trembling so hard that the chair legs thumped against the floor like a woodpecker tapping a tree.

Samantha looked back down the hall, to the door, the dim halo of light.

"Here." The man in the blue hightops motioned for Samantha to sit beside Charlotte. She moved slowly, carefully bending her knees, keeping her hands above the table. The wooden handle of the hammer thunked against the seat of the chair.

"What's that?" Black Shirt's eyes jerked in her direction.

"I'm sorry," Charlotte whispered. Urine puddled onto the floor. She kept her head down, rocking back and forth. "I'm-sorry-I'm-sorry-I'm-sorry."

Samantha took her sister's hand.

"Tell us what you want," Gamma said. "We'll give it to you and then you can leave."

"What if I want that?" Black Shirt's beady eyes were trained on Charlotte.

"Please," Gamma said. "I will do whatever you want. Anything."

"Anything?" Black Shirt said it in a way that they all understood what was being offered.

"No," Hightop said. His voice was younger-sounding, nervous or maybe afraid. "We didn't come for that." His Adam's apple jogged beneath the ski mask as he tried to clear his throat. "Where's your husband?"

Something flashed in Gamma's eyes. Anger. "He's at work."

"Then why's his car outside?"

Gamma said, "We only have one car because—"

"The sheriff . . ." Samantha swallowed the last word, realizing too late that she shouldn't have said it.

Black Shirt was looking at her again. "What's that, girl?"

Samantha put down her head. Charlotte squeezed her hand. The sheriff, she had started to say. The sheriff's man would be here soon. Rusty had said they were sending a car, but Rusty said a lot of things that turned out to be wrong.

Gamma said, "She's just scared. Why don't we go into the other room? We can talk this out, figure out what you boys want."

Samantha felt something hard bang against her skull. She tasted the metal fillings in her teeth. Her ears were ringing. The shotgun. He was pressing the barrel to the top of her head. "You said something about the sheriff, girl. I heard you."

"She didn't," Gamma said. "She meant to—"

"Shut up."

"She just—"

"I said shut the fuck up!"

Samantha looked up as the shotgun swiveled toward Gamma.

Gamma reached out, but slowly, as if she was pushing her hands through sand. They were all suddenly trapped in stop-motion, their movements jerky, their bodies turned to clay. Samantha watched as one by one, her mother's fingers wrapped around the sawed-off shotgun. Neatly trimmed fingernails. A thick callous on her thumb from holding a pencil.

There was an almost imperceptible *click*.

A second hand on a watch.

A door latching closed.

A firing pin tapping against the primer in a shotgun shell.

Maybe Samantha heard the click or maybe she intuited the sound because she was staring at Black Shirt's finger when he pulled back the trigger.

An explosion of red misted the air.

Blood jetted onto the ceiling. Gushed onto the floor. Hot, ropey red tendrils splashed across the top of Charlotte's head and splattered onto the side of Samantha's neck and face.

Gamma fell to the floor.

Charlotte screamed.

Samantha felt her own mouth open, but the sound was trapped inside of her chest. She was frozen now. Charlotte's screams turned into a distant echo. Everything drained of color. They were suspended in black and white, like the bachelor farmer's picture. Black blood had aerosoled onto the grille of the white air conditioner. Tiny flecks of black mottled the glass in the window. Outside, the night sky was a charcoal gray with a lone pinlight of a tiny, distant star.

Samantha reached up with her fingers to touch her neck. Grit. Bone. More blood because everything was stained with blood. She felt a pulse in her throat. Was it her own heart or pieces of her mother's heart beating underneath her trembling fingers?

Charlotte's screams amplified into a piercing siren. The black blood turned crimson on Samantha's fingers. The gray room blossomed back into vivid, blinding, furious color.

Dead. Gamma was dead. She was never again going to tell Samantha to get away from Pikeville, to yell at her for missing an obvious question on a test, for not pushing herself harder in track, for not being patient with Charlotte, for not being useful in her life.

Samantha rubbed together her fingers. She held a shard of Gamma's tooth in her hand. Vomit rushed into her mouth. She was blinded by tears. Grief vibrated like a harp string inside her body.

In the blink of an eye, the world had turned upside down.

"Shut up!" Black Shirt slapped Charlotte so hard that she nearly fell out of the chair. Samantha caught her, clinging to her. They were both sobbing, shaking, screaming. This couldn't be happening. Their mother couldn't be dead. She was going to open her eyes. She was going to explain to them the workings of the cardiovascular system as she slowly put her body back together.

Did you know that the average heart pumps five liters of blood per minute?

"Gamma," Samantha whispered. The shotgun blast had opened up her chest, her neck, her face. The left side of her jaw was gone. Part of her skull. Her beautiful, complicated brain. Her arched, aloof eyebrow. No one would explain things to Samantha anymore. No one would care whether or not she understood. "Gamma."

"Jesus!" Hightop furiously slapped at his chest, trying to brush off the chunks of bone and tissue. "Jesus Christ, Zach!"

Samantha's head snapped around.

Zachariah Culpepper.

The two words flashed neon in her mind. Then: *Grand theft auto. Animal cruelty. Public indecency. Inappropriate contact with a minor.*

Charlotte wasn't the only one who read their father's case files. For years, Rusty Quinn had saved Zach Culpepper from doing serious time. The man's unpaid legal bills were a constant source of tension between Gamma and Rusty, especially since the house had burned down. Over twenty thousand dollars was owed, but Rusty refused to go after him.

"Fuck!" Zach had clearly seen Samantha's flash of recognition. "Fuck!"

"Mama . . ." Charlotte hadn't realized that everything had changed. She could only stare at Gamma, her body shaking so hard that her teeth chattered. "Mama, Mama, Mama . . ."

"It's all right." Samantha tried to stroke her sister's hair but her fingers snagged in the braids of blood and bone.

"It ain't all right." Zach wrenched off his mask. He was a hard-looking man. Acne scars pocked his skin. A spray of red circled his mouth and eyes where the blowback from the shotgun had painted his face. "God dammit! What'd you have to use my name for, boy?"

"I d-didn't—" Hightop stammered. "I'm sorry."

"We won't tell." Samantha looked down, as if she could pretend she hadn't seen his face. "We won't say anything. I promise."

"Girl, I just blew your mama to bits. You really think you're walking out of here alive?"

"No," Hightop said. "That's not what we came for."

"I came here to erase some bills, boy." Zach's steely gray eyes turreted around the room like a machine gun. "Now I'm thinking it's me that Rusty Quinn's gotta pay."

"No," Hightop said. "I told you—"

Zach shut him up by jamming the shotgun into his face. "You ain't seein' the big picture here. We gotta get outta town, and that takes a hell of a lot of money. Everybody knows Rusty Quinn keeps cash in his house."

"The house burned down." Samantha heard the words before she registered that they were coming from her own mouth. "Everything burned down."

"Fuck!" Zach screamed. "Fuck!" He grabbed Hightop by the arm and dragged him into the hallway. He kept the shotgun pointed in their direction, his finger on the trigger. There was furious whispering back and forth that Samantha could clearly hear, but her brain refused to process the words.

"No!" Charlotte fell to the floor. A trembling hand reached

down to hold their mother's. "Don't be dead, Mama. Please. I love you. I love you so much."

Samantha looked up at the ceiling. Red lines crisscrossed the plaster like silly string. Tears flooded down her face, soaked into the collar of her only shirt that had been saved from the fire. She let the grief roll through her body before she forced it back out. Gamma was gone. They were alone in the house with her murderer and the sheriff's man was not going to come.

Promise me you'll always take care of Charlie.

"Charlie, get up." Samantha pulled at her sister's arm, eyes averted because she couldn't look at Gamma's ripped-open chest, the broken ribs that stuck out like teeth.

Did you know that shark teeth are made of scales?

Sam whispered, "Charlie, get up."

"I can't. I can't let—"

Sam wrenched her sister back into the chair. She pressed her mouth to Charlie's ear and said, "Run when you can." Her voice was so quiet that it caught in her throat. "Don't look back. Just run."

"What're you two saying?" Zach jammed the shotgun against Sam's forehead. The metal was hot. Pieces of Gamma's flesh had seared onto the barrel. She could smell it like meat on the grill. "What did you tell her to do? Make a run for it? Try to get away?"

Charlotte squeaked. Her hand went to her mouth.

Zach asked, "What'd she tell you to do, baby doll?"

Sam's stomach roiled at the way his tone softened when he talked to her sister.

"Come on, honey." Zach's gaze slithered down to Charlie's small chest, her thin waist. "Ain't we gonna be friends?"

Sam stuttered out, "S-stop." She was sweating, shaking. Like Charlie, she was going to lose control of her bladder. The round barrel of the gun felt like a drill burrowing into her skull.

Still, she said, "Leave her alone."

"Was I talking to you, bitch?" Zach pressed the shotgun against Sam's head until her chin pointed up. "Was I?"

Sam gripped her hands into tight fists. She had to stop this. She had to protect Charlotte. "You leave us alone, Zachariah Culpepper." She was shocked by her own defiance. She was terrified, but every ounce of terror was tinged with an overwhelming rage. He had murdered her mother. He was leering at her sister. He had told them both that they weren't walking out of here. She thought of the hammer tucked in the back of her shorts, pictured it lodging into Zach's brain. "I know exactly who you are, you fucking pervert."

He flinched at the word. Anger contorted his features. His hands gripped the shotgun so hard that his knuckles turned white, but his voice was calm when he told her, "I'm gonna peel off your eyelids so you can watch me slice out your sister's cherry with my knife."

Her eyes locked with his. The silence that followed the threat was deafening. Sam couldn't look away. Fear ran like razor blades through her heart. She had never in her life met someone so utterly, soullessly evil.

Charlie began to whimper.

"Zach," Hightop said. "Come on, man." He waited. They all waited. "We had a deal, all right?"

Zach didn't move. None of them moved.

"We had a deal," Hightop repeated.

"Sure," Zach broke the silence. He let Hightop take the shotgun from his hands. "A man's only as good as his word."

He started to turn away, but then changed his mind. His hand shot out like a whip. He grabbed Sam's face, fingers gripping her skull like a ball, slamming her back so hard that the chair fell away and her head clanged into the front of the sink.

"You think I'm a pervert now?" His palm crushed her nose. His fingers gouged into her eyes like hot needles. "You got something else to say about me?"

Samantha opened her mouth, but she had no breath to form a scream. Pain ripped through her face as his fingernails cut into her eyelids. She grabbed his thick wrist, blindly kicked out at him, tried to scratch him, to punch him, to stop the pain. Blood wept down her cheeks. Zach's fingers shook, pressing so hard that Sam could feel her eyeballs flex back into her brain. His fingers curled as he tried to rip off her eyelids. She felt his nails scrape against her bare eyeballs.

"Stop it!" Charlie screamed. "Stop!"

The pressure stopped just as suddenly as it had started.

"Sammy!" Charlie's breath was hot, panicked. Her hands went to Sam's face. "Sam? Look at me. Can you see? Look at me, please!"

Carefully, Sam tried to open her eyelids. They were torn, almost shredded. She felt like she was looking through a piece of old lace.

Zach said, "What the fuck is this?"

The hammer. It had fallen out of her shorts.

Zach picked it up off the floor. He examined the wooden handle, then gave Charlie a meaningful look. "Wonder what I can do with this?"

"Enough!" Hightop grabbed the hammer and threw it down the hallway. They all listened to the metal head skip across the hardwood floor.

Zach said, "Just having a little fun, brother."

"Both of you stand up," Hightop said. "Let's get this over with."

Charlie stayed on the floor. Sam blinked away blood. She could barely see to move. The overhead light was like hot oil in her eyes.

"Help her up," Hightop told Zach. "You promised, man. Don't make this worse than it has to be."

Zach yanked Sam's arm so hard that it almost left the socket. She struggled to her feet, steadying herself against the table. Zach pushed her toward the door. She bumped into a chair. Charlie reached for her hand.

Hightop opened the door. "Go."

They had no choice but to move. Charlie went first, shuffling sideways to help Sam down the stairs. Outside the bright lights of the kitchen, her eyes stopped throbbing as hard. There was no adjusting to the darkness. Shadows kept falling in and out of her gaze.

They should have been at track practice right now. They had begged Gamma to let them skip for the first time in their lives and now their mother was dead and they were being led out of the house at gunpoint by the man who had come here to erase his legal bills with a shotgun.

"Can you see?" Charlie asked. "Sam, can you see?"

"Yes," Sam lied, because her vision was strobing like a disco ball, except instead of flashes of light, she was seeing flashes of gray and black.

"This way," Hightop said, leading them not toward the old pickup truck in the driveway, but into the field behind the farmhouse. Cabbage. Sorghum. Watermelons. That's what the bachelor farmer had grown. They had found his seed ledger in an otherwise empty upstairs closet. His three hundred acres had been leased to the farm next door, a thousand-acre spread that had been planted at the start of spring.

Sam could feel the freshly planted soil under her bare feet. She leaned into Charlie, who held tight to her hand. With her other hand, Sam reached out blindly, unreasonably afraid that she would run into something in the open field. Every step away from the farmhouse, away from the light, added one more layer of darkness to her vision. Charlie was a blob of gray. Hightop was tall and skinny, like a charcoal pencil. Zach Culpepper was a menacing black square of hate.

"Where are we going?" Charlie asked.

Sam felt the shotgun press into her back.

Zach said, "Keep walking."

"I don't understand," Charlie said. "Why are you doing this?"

Her voice was directed toward Hightop. Like Sam, she understood that the younger man was the weaker one, but that he was also somehow in charge.

Charlie asked, "What did we do to you, mister? We're just kids. We don't deserve this."

"Shut up," Zach warned. "Both of you shut the fuck up."

Sam squeezed Charlie's hand even tighter. She was almost completely blind now. She was going to be blind forever, except forever wasn't that much longer. At least not for Sam. She made her hand loosen around Charlie's. She quietly willed her sister to take in their surroundings, to stay alert for the chance to run.

Gamma had shown them a topographical map of the area two days ago, the day they had moved in. She was trying to sell them on country life, pointing out all the areas they could explore. Now, Sam mentally flipped through the highlights, searching for an escape route. The neighbor's acreage went past the horizon, a clear open plane that would likely lead to a bullet in Charlie's back if she ran in that direction. Trees bordered the far right side of the property, a dense forest that Gamma warned was probably filled with ticks. There was a creek on the other side of the forest that fed into a tunnel that snaked underneath a weather tower and led to a paved but rarely used road. An abandoned barn half a mile north. Another farm two miles east. A swampy fishing hole. Frogs would be there. Butterflies would be over here. If they were patient, they might see deer in this field. Stay away from the road. Leaves three, quickly flee. Leaves five, stay and thrive.

Please flee, Sam silently begged Charlie. *Please don't look back to make sure I'm following you.*

Zach said, "What's that?"

They all turned around.

"It's a car," Charlie said, but Sam could only make out the sparkling headlights slowly traveling down the long driveway to the farmhouse.

The sheriff's man? Someone driving their father home?

"Shit, they're gonna make my truck in two seconds." Zach pushed them toward the forest, using the shotgun like a cattle prod to make them walk faster. "Y'all keep moving or I'll shoot you right here."

Right here.

Charlie stiffened at the words. Her teeth started to chatter again. She had finally made the connection. She understood that they were walking to their deaths.

Sam said, "There's another way out of this."

She was talking to Hightop, but Zach was the one who snorted.

Sam said, "I'll do whatever you want." She heard Gamma's voice speaking the words alongside her. "Anything."

"Shit," Zach said. "You don't think I'm gonna take what I want anyways, you stupid bitch?"

Sam tried again. "We won't tell them it was you. We'll say you had your masks on the entire time and—"

"With my truck in the driveway and your mama dead in the house?" Zach huffed a snort. "Y'all Quinns think you're so fucking smart, can talk your way outta anything."

"Listen to me," Sam begged. "You've got to leave town anyway. There's no reason to kill us, too." She turned her head toward Hightop. "Please, just think about it. All you have to do is tie us up. Leave us somewhere they won't find us. You're going to have to leave town either way. You don't want more blood on your hands."

Sam waited for a response. They all waited.

Hightop cleared his throat before finally saying, "I'm sorry."

Zach's laughter had an edge of triumph.

Sam couldn't give up. "Let my sister go." She had to stop speaking for a moment so she could swallow the saliva in her mouth. "She's thirteen. Just a kid."

"Don't look like no kid to me," Zach said. "Got them nice high titties."

"Shut up," Hightop warned. "I mean it."

Zach made a sucking noise with his teeth.

"She won't tell anyone," Sam had to keep trying. "She'll say it was strangers. Won't you, Charlie?"

"Black fella?" Zach asked. "Like the one your daddy got off for murder?"

Charlie spat out, "You mean like he got you off for showing your wiener to a bunch of little girls?"

"Charlie," Sam begged. "Please, be quiet."

"Let her speak," Zach said. "I like it when they got a little fight in 'em."

Charlie went quiet. She stayed silent as they headed into the woods.

Sam followed closely, racking her brain for an appeal that would persuade the gunmen that they didn't have to do this. But Zach Culpepper was right. His truck back at the house changed everything.

"No," Charlie whispered to herself. She did this all of the time, vocalizing an argument she was having in her head.

Please run, Sam silently begged. *It's okay to go without me.*

"Move." Zach shoved the shotgun into her back until Sam walked faster.

Pine needles dug into her feet. They were going deeper into the forest. The air got cooler. Sam closed her eyes, because it was pointless trying to see. She let Charlie guide her through the woods. Leaves rustled. They stepped over fallen trees, walked into a narrow stream that was probably run-off from the farm to the creek.

Run, run, run, Sam silently prayed to Charlie in her head. *Please run.*

"Sam . . ." Charlie stopped walking. Her arm gripped Sam around the waist. "There's a shovel. A shovel."

Sam didn't understand. She touched her fingers to her eyelids. Dried blood had caked them shut. She pushed gently, coaxing open her eyes.

Soft moonlight cast a blue glow on the clearing in front of them. There was more than a shovel. A mound of freshly turned earth was piled beside an open hole in the ground.

One hole.

One grave.

Her vision tunneled on the gaping, black void as everything came into focus. This wasn't a burglary, or an attempt to intimidate away a bunch of legal bills. Everyone knew that the house burning down had put the Quinns in dire financial straits. The fight with the insurance company. The eviction from the hotel. The thrift store purchases. Zachariah Culpepper had obviously assumed that Rusty was going to replenish his bank account by forcing nonpaying clients to settle their bills. He wasn't that far off. Gamma had screamed at Rusty the other night about how the twenty thousand dollars Culpepper owed them would go a long way toward making the family solvent again.

Which meant that all of this boiled down to money.

And worse, stupidity, because the outstanding bills would not have died with her father.

Sam felt the reverberations of her earlier rage. She bit her tongue so hard that blood seeped into her mouth. There was a reason Zachariah Culpepper was a lifelong con. As with all of his crimes, the plan was a bad one, poorly executed. Every single blunder had led them to this place. They had dug a grave for Rusty, but since Rusty was late because he was always late, and since today was the one day they had been allowed to skip track practice, now it was meant for Charlie and Sam.

"All right, big boy. Time for you to do your part." Zach rested the butt of the shotgun on his hip. He pulled a switchblade out of his pocket and slapped it open with one hand. "The guns'll be too loud. Take this. Right across the throat like you'd do with a pig."

Hightop did not take the knife.

Zach said, "Come on, like we agreed. You do her. I'll take care of the little one."

Hightop still did not move. "She's right. We don't have to do this. The plan wasn't ever to hurt the women. They weren't even supposed to be here."

"Say what now?"

Sam grabbed Charlie's hand. They were distracted. She could run.

Hightop said, "What's done is done. We don't have to make it worse by killing more people. Innocent people."

"Jesus Christ." Zach closed the knife and shoved it back into his pocket. "We went over this in the kitchen, man. Ain't like we gotta choice."

"We can turn ourselves in."

Zach gripped the shotgun. "Bull. Shit."

"I'll turn myself in. I'll take the blame for everything."

Sam pushed against Charlie, letting her know it was time to move. Charlie didn't move. She held tight.

"The hell you will." Zach thumped Hightop in the chest. "You think I'm gonna go down on a murder charge 'cause you grew a fucking conscience?"

Sam let go of her sister's hand. She whispered, "Charlie, run."

"I won't tell," Hightop said. "I'll say it was me."

"In my got-damn truck?"

Charlie tried to take Sam's hand again. Sam pulled away, whispering, "Go."

"Motherfucker." Zach raised the shotgun, pointing it at Hightop's chest. "This is what's gonna happen, son. You're gonna take my knife and you're gonna slice open that bitch's throat, or I will blow a hole in your chest the size of Texas." He stamped his foot. "Right now."

Hightop slung up the revolver, pointing it at Zach's head. "We're gonna turn ourselves in."

"Get that fucking gun outta my face, you pansy-ass piece of shit."

Sam nudged Charlie. She had to move. She had to get out of here. There would only be one chance. She practically begged her sister, "Go."

Hightop said, "I'll kill you before I kill them."

"You ain't got the balls to pull that trigger."

"I'll do it."

Charlie still wouldn't budge. Her teeth were chattering again.

"Run," Sam pleaded. "You have to run."

"Rich boy piece of shit." Zach spat on the ground. He went to wipe his mouth, but only as a distraction. He reached out for the revolver. Hightop had anticipated the move. He backhanded the shotgun. Zach was thrown off balance. He couldn't keep his footing. He fell back, arms flailing.

"Run!" Sam shoved her sister away. *"Charlie, go!"*

Charlie turned into a blur of motion. Sam started to follow, leg raised, arm bent—

Another explosion.

A flash of light from the revolver.

A sudden vibration in the air.

Sam's head jerked so violently that her neck cracked. Her body followed in a wild twist. She spun like a top, falling into darkness the same way Alice fell into the rabbit hole.

Do you know how pretty you are?

Sam's feet hit the ground. She felt her knees absorb the shock.

She looked down.

Her toes were spread flat against a water-soaked hardwood floor.

She looked up to find her reflection staring back from a mirror.

Inexplicably, Sam was at the farmhouse standing at the bathroom sink.

Gamma stood behind her, strong arms wrapped around Sam's waist. Her mother looked younger, softer, in the mirror. Her eyebrow was arched up as if she'd heard something dubious. This was the woman who'd explained the difference between fission and fusion to a stranger at the grocery store. Who'd devised complicated scavenger hunts that took up all of their Easters.

What were the clues now?

"Tell me," Sam asked her mother's reflection. "Tell me what you want me to do."

Gamma's mouth opened, but she did not speak. Her face began to age. Sam felt a longing for the mother she would never see grow old. Fine lines spread out from Gamma's mouth. Crow's feet around her eyes. The wrinkles deepened. Streaks of gray salted her dark hair. Her jawline grew fuller.

Her skin began to peel away.

White teeth showed through an open hole in her cheek. Her hair turned into greasy white twine. Her eyes grew desiccated. She wasn't aging.

She was decomposing.

Sam struggled to get away. The smell of death enveloped her: wet earth, fresh maggots burrowing underneath her skin. Gamma's hands clamped around her face. She made Sam turn around. Fingers reduced to dry bone. Black teeth honed into razor blades as Gamma opened her mouth and screamed, *"I told you to get out!"*

Sam gasped awake.

Her eyes slit open onto an impenetrable blackness.

Dirt filled her mouth. Wet soil. Pine needles. Her hands were in front of her face. Hot breath bounced against her palms. There was a sound—

Shsh. Shsh. Shsh.

A broom sweeping.

An ax swinging.

A shovel dropping dirt into a grave.

Sam's grave.

She was being buried alive. The weight of the soil on top of her was like a metal plate.

"I'm sorry." Hightop's voice caught around the words. "Please, God, please forgive me."

The dirt kept coming, the weight turning into a vise that threatened to press the breath right out of her.

Did you know that Giles Corey was the only defendant in the Salem witch trials who was pressed to death?

Tears filled Sam's eyes, slid down her face. A scream got trapped inside her throat. She couldn't panic. She couldn't start yelling or flailing because they would not help her. They would shoot her again. Begging for her life would only speed up the taking of her life.

"Don't be silly," Gamma said. *"I thought you were past that teenager stage."*

Sam inhaled a shaky breath.

She startled as she realized that air was entering her lungs.

She could breathe!

Her hands were cupped to her face, creating an air pocket inside the dirt. Sam tightened the seal between her palms. She forced her breaths to slow in order to preserve what precious air she had left.

Charlie had told her to do this. Years ago. Sam could picture her sister in her Brownie uniform. Arms and legs like tiny sticks. Her creased yellow shirt and brown vest with all the patches she had earned. She had read aloud from her *Adventure* handbook at the breakfast table.

" 'If you find yourself caught in an avalanche, do not cry out or open your mouth,' " Charlie had read. " 'Put your hands in front of your face and try to create an airspace as you are coming to a stop.' "

Sam stuck out her tongue, trying to see how far away her hands were. She guessed a quarter of an inch. She flexed her fingers, trying to elongate the pocket of air. There was nothing to move into. The dirt was packed tightly around her hands, almost like cement.

She tried to glean the position of her body. She wasn't flat on her back. Her left shoulder was pressed to the ground, but she wasn't fully lying on her side, either. Her hips were turned at an angle to her shoulders. Cold seeped into the back of her running shorts. Her right knee was bent, her left leg was straight.

Torso twist.

A runner's stretch. Her body had fallen into a familiar position.

Sam tried to shift her weight. She couldn't move her legs. She tried her toes. Her calf muscles. Her hamstrings.

Nothing.

Sam closed her eyes. She was paralyzed. She would never walk again, run again, move again without assistance. Panic rushed into her chest like a swarm of mosquitos. Running was all that she had. It was who she was. What was the point of trying to survive if she could never use her legs again?

She pressed her face into her hands so that she wouldn't cry out.

Charlie could still run. Sam had watched her sister bolt toward the forest. It was the last thing she'd seen before the revolver went off. Sam conjured into her mind the image of Charlie sprinting, her spindly legs moving impossibly fast as she flew forward, away, never hesitating, never stopping to look back.

Don't think about me, Sam begged, the same thing she had told her sister a million times before. *Just concentrate on yourself and keep running.*

Had Charlie made it? Had she found help? Or had she looked over her shoulder to see if Sam was following and instead found Zachariah Culpepper's shotgun jammed into her face?

Or worse.

Sam forced the thought from her mind. She saw Charlie running free, getting help, bringing the police back to the grave because she had their mother's sense of direction and she never got lost and she would remember where her sister was buried.

Sam counted out the beats of her heart until she felt them slow to a less frantic pace.

And then she felt a tickle in her throat.

Everything was filled with dirt—her ears, nose, mouth, lungs. She couldn't stop the cough that wanted to come out of her mouth. Her lips opened. The reflexive intake of air pulled more dirt into her nose. She coughed again, then again. The third time was so hard that she felt her stomach cramp as her body strained to pull itself into a ball.

Sam felt a jolt in her heart.

Her legs had twitched.

Panic and fear had cut off the vital connections between her brain and her musculature. She had not been paralyzed; she had been terrified, some ancient fight or flight mechanism pushing her out of her own body until she could understand what was happening. Sam felt elation as sensation slowly returned to her lower body. It was as if she was walking into a pool of water. At first, she could feel her toes spreading through the thick earth. Then her ankles were able to bend. Then she felt the tiniest amount of movement in her ankles.

If she could move her feet, what else could she move?

Sam flexed her calves, warming them up. Her quads started to fire. Her knees tensed. She concentrated on her legs, telling herself that they could move until her body sent back the message that yes, her legs could move.

She was not paralyzed. She had a chance.

Gamma always said that Sam had learned how to run before she'd learned how to walk. Her legs were the strongest part of her body.

She could kick her way out.

Sam worked her legs, making infinitesimal motions back and forth, trying to burrow through the heavy layer of dirt. Her breath grew hot in her hands. A dense fog clouded out the panic in her brain. Was she using up too much air? Did it matter? She kept losing track of what she was doing. Her lower body was moving back and forth and sometimes she found herself thinking she was lying on the deck of a tiny boat rocking on the ocean and then she would come to, would realize that she was trapped underground and struggle to move faster, harder, only to be lulled back onto the boat again.

She tried to count: *One Mississippi, two Mississippi, three Mississippi* . . .

Her legs cramped. Her stomach cramped. Everything cramped. Sam made herself stop, if only for a few seconds. The rest was almost as painful as the effort. Lactic acid boiled off her spent muscles, causing her stomach to churn. Her vertebrae had twisted into overtightened bolts that pinched the nerves and shot an electric pain into her neck and legs. Every breath was caught in her hands like a trapped bird.

" 'There is a fifty percent chance of survival,' " Charlie had read from her *Adventure* book. " 'But only if the victim is found within one hour.' "

Sam didn't know how long she'd been in the grave. Like losing the red-brick house, like watching her mother die, that had been a lifetime ago.

She tightened her stomach muscles and tried a sideways push-up. Her arm tensed. Her neck strained. The earth pressed back, grinding her shoulder into the wet soil.

She needed more room.

Sam tried to rock her hips. There was an inch of space at first, then two inches, then she could move her waist, her shoulder, her neck, her head.

Was there suddenly more space between her mouth and her hands?

Sam stuck out her tongue again. She felt the tip brush against the gap between her two palms. That was half an inch, at least.

Progress.

She worked on her arms next, shifting them up and down, up and down. There were no inches this time. Centimeters, then millimeters of dirt shifted. She had to keep her hands in front of her face so she could breathe. But then she realized that she had to dig with her hands.

One hour. That was all Charlie had given her. Sam's time had to be running out. Her palms were hot, bathed in condensation. Her brain was awash in dizziness.

Sam took a last, deep breath.

She pushed her hands away from her face. Her wrists felt like they were going to break as she twisted her hands around. She pressed together her lips, gritted her teeth, and clawed at the ground, furiously trying to dislodge the dirt.

And still the earth pushed back.

Her shoulders ignited in pain. Trapezoids. Rhomboids. Scapulae. Hot irons pierced her biceps. Her fingers felt like they were going to snap. Her nails chipped off. The skin on her knuckles peeled away. Her lungs were going to collapse. She couldn't keep holding her breath. She couldn't keep fighting. She was tired. She was alone. Her mother was dead. Her sister was gone. Sam started to yell, first in her head, then through her mouth. She was so angry—furious at her mother for grabbing the shotgun, livid with her father for bringing this hell to their doorstep, pissed at Charlie for not being stronger, and fucking apoplectic that she was going to die in this God damn grave.

Shallow grave.

Cool air wrapped around her fingers.

She had broken through the soil. Less than two feet separated Sam from life and death.

There was no time to rejoice. She had no air in her lungs, no hope unless she could keep digging.

She flicked away debris with her fingers. Leaves. Pinecones. Her murderer had tried to hide the freshly dug earth but he hadn't counted on the girl inside climbing her way out. She grabbed a handful of dirt, then another, then kept going until she was able to clench her abdominal muscles one last time and leverage herself up.

Sam gagged on the sudden rush of fresh air. She spat out dirt and blood. Her hair was matted. She touched her fingers to the side of her scalp. Her pinky slipped into a tiny hole. The bone was smooth inside the circle. This was where the bullet had gone in. She had been shot in the head.

She had been shot in the head.

Sam took away her hand. She dared not wipe her eyes. She squinted into the distance. The forest was a blur. She saw two fat dots of light floating like lazy bumblebees in front of her face.

She heard the trickling of water, echoing, like through an access tunnel that snaked underneath a weather tower and led to a paved road.

Another pair of lights floated by.

Not bumblebees.

Headlights.

CHAPTER ONE

Charlie Quinn walked through the darkened halls of Pikeville middle school with a gnawing sense of trepidation. This wasn't an early morning walk of shame. This was a walk of deeply held regret. Fitting, since the first time she'd had sex with a boy she shouldn't have had sex with was inside this very building. The gymnasium, to be exact, which just went to show that her father had been right about the perils of a late curfew.

She gripped the cell phone in her hand as she turned a corner. The wrong boy. The wrong man. The wrong phone. The wrong way because she didn't know where the hell she was going. Charlie turned around and retraced her steps. Everything in this stupid building looked familiar, but nothing was where she remembered it was supposed to be.

She took a left and found herself standing outside the front office. Empty chairs were waiting for the bad students who would be sent to the principal. The plastic seats looked similar to the ones in which Charlie had whiled away her early years. Talking back. Mouthing off. Arguing with teachers, fellow students, inanimate objects. Her adult self would've slapped her teenage self for being such a pain in the ass.

She cupped her hand to the window and peered inside the dark office. Finally, something that looked how it was supposed to look. The high counter where Mrs. Jenkins, the school secretary, had held court. Pennants drooping from the water-stained ceiling. Student artwork taped to the walls. A lone light was on in the back. Charlie wasn't about to ask Principal Pinkman for directions to her booty call. Not that this was a booty call. It was more of a *"Hey, girl, you picked up the wrong iPhone after I nailed you in my truck at Shady Ray's last night"* call.

There was no point in Charlie asking herself what she had been thinking, because you didn't go to a bar named Shady Ray's to think.

The phone in her hand rang. Charlie saw the unfamiliar screen saver of a German shepherd with a Kong toy in its mouth. The caller ID read SCHOOL.

She answered, "Yes?"

"Where are you?" He sounded tense, and she thought of all the hidden dangers that came from screwing a stranger she'd met in a bar: incurable venereal diseases, a jealous wife, a murderous baby mama, an obnoxious Alabama affiliation.

She said, "I'm in front of Pink's office."

"Turn around and take your second right."

"Yep." Charlie ended the call. She felt herself wanting to puzzle out his tone of voice, but then she told herself that it didn't matter because she was never going to see him again.

She walked back the way she'd come, her sneakers squeaking on the waxed floor as she made her way down the dark hallway. She heard a snap behind her. The lights had come on in the front office. A hunched old woman who looked suspiciously like the ghost of Mrs. Jenkins shuffled her way behind the counter. Somewhere in the distance, heavy metal doors opened and closed. The beep-whir of the metal detectors swirled into her ears. Someone jangled a set of keys.

The air seemed to contract with each new sound, as if the school was bracing itself for the morning onslaught. Charlie looked at the large clock on the wall. If the schedule was still the same, the first homeroom bell would ring soon, and the kids who had been dropped off early and warehoused in the cafeteria would flood the building.

Charlie had been one of those kids. For a long time, whenever she thought of her father, her mind conjured up the scene of his arm leaning out of the Chevette's window, freshly lit cigarette between his fingers, as he pulled out of the school parking lot.

She stopped walking.

The room numbers finally caught her attention, and she knew immediately where she was. Charlie touched her fingers to a closed wooden door. Room three, her safe haven. Ms. Beavers had retired eons ago, but the old woman's voice echoed in Charlie's ears: "They'll only get your goat if you show them where you keep your hay."

Charlie still didn't know what that meant, exactly. You could extrapolate that it had something to do with the extended Culpepper clan, who had bullied Charlie relentlessly when she'd finally returned to school.

Or, you could take it that, as a girls' basketball coach named Etta Beavers, the teacher knew what it felt like to be taunted.

There was no one who could give Charlie advice on how to handle the present situation. For the first time since college, she'd had a one-night stand. Or a one-night sit, if it boiled down to the exact position. Charlie wasn't the type of person who did that sort of thing. She didn't go to bars. She didn't drink to excess. She didn't really make hugely regrettable mistakes. At least not until recently.

Her life had started to unspool back in August of last year. Charlie had spent almost every waking hour since then raveling out mistake after mistake. Apparently, the new month of May was not going to see any improvement. The blunders were now starting before she even got out of bed. This morning, she'd been wide awake on her back, staring up at the ceiling, trying to convince herself that what had happened last night had not happened at all when an unfamiliar ringtone had come from her purse.

She had answered because wrapping the phone in aluminum foil, throwing it into the dumpster behind her office and buying a new phone that would restore from her old phone backup did not occur to her until after she had said hello.

The short conversation that followed was of the kind you would expect between two total strangers: *Hello, person whose name I must have asked for but now can't recall. I believe I have your phone.*

Charlie had offered to meet the man at his work because she didn't want him to know where she lived. Or worked. Or what kind of car she drove. Between his pickup truck and his admittedly exquisite body, she'd thought he'd tell her he was a mechanic or a farmer. Then he'd said that he was a teacher and she'd instantly flashed up a *Dead Poets Society* kind of thing. Then he'd said he taught middle school and she'd jumped to the unfounded conclusion that he was a pedophile.

"Here." He stood outside an open door at the far end of the hall.

As if on cue, the overhead fluorescents popped on, bathing Charlie in the most unflattering light possible. She instantly regretted her choice of ratty jeans and a faded, long-sleeved Duke Blue Devils basketball T-shirt.

"Good Lord God," Charlie muttered. No such problems at the end of the hall.

Mr. I-Can't-Remember-Your-Name was even more attractive than she remembered. The standard button-down-with-khakis uniform of a middle-school teacher couldn't hide the fact that he had muscles in places that men in their forties had generally replaced with beer and fried meat. His scraggly beard was more of a five o'clock shadow. The gray at his temples gave him a wizened air of mystery. He had one of those dimples in his chin that you could use to open a bottle.

This was not the type of man Charlie dated. This was the exact type of man that she studiously avoided. He felt too coiled, too strong, too unknowable. It was like playing with a loaded gun.

"This is me." He pointed to the bulletin board outside his room. Small handprints were traced onto white butcher paper. Purple cut-out letters read MR. HUCKLEBERRY.

"Huckleberry?" Charlie asked.

"It's Huckabee, actually." He held out his hand. "Huck."

Charlie shook his hand, too late realizing that he was asking for his iPhone. "Sorry." She handed him the phone.

He gave her a crooked smile that had probably sent many a young girl into puberty. "Yours is in here."

Charlie followed him into the classroom. The walls were adorned with maps, which made sense because he was apparently a history teacher. At least if you believed the sign that said MR. HUCKLEBERRY LOVES WORLD HISTORY.

She said, "I may be a little sketchy on last night, but I thought you said you were a Marine?"

"Not anymore, but it sounds sexier than middle-school teacher." He gave a self-deprecating laugh. "Joined up when I was seventeen, took my retirement six years ago." He leaned against his desk. "I was looking for a way to keep serving, so I got my master's on a GI bill and here we are."

"I bet you get a lot of tear-stained cards on Valentine's Day." Charlie would've failed history every single day of her life if her teacher had looked like Mr. Huckleberry.

He asked, "Do you have kids?"

"Not that I know of." Charlie didn't return the question. She assumed that someone with kids wouldn't use a photo of his dog as his screen saver. "You married?"

He shook his head. "Didn't suit me."

"It suited me." She explained, "We've been officially separated for nine months."

"Did you cheat on him?"

"You'd think so, but no." Charlie ran her finger along the books on the shelf by his desk. Homer. Euripides. Voltaire. Brontë. "You don't strike me as the *Wuthering Heights* type."

He grinned. "Not much talking in the truck."

Charlie started to return the grin, but regret pulled down the corners of her mouth. In some ways, this easy, flirty banter felt like more of a transgression than the physical act of sex. She bantered with her husband. She asked inane questions of her husband.

And last night, for the first time in her married life, she had cheated on her husband.

Huck seemed to sense her mood shift. "It's obviously none of my business, but he's nuts for letting you go."

"I'm a lot of work." Charlie studied one of the maps. There were blue pins in most of Europe and some of the Middle East. "You go to all of these places?"

He nodded, but didn't elaborate.

"Marines," she said. "Were you a Navy SEAL?"

"Marines can be SEALs but not all SEALs are Marines."

Charlie was about to tell him that he hadn't answered the question, but Huck spoke first.

"Your phone started ringing at o'dark thirty."

Her heart flipped in her chest. "You didn't answer?"

"Nah, it's much more fun trying to figure you out from your caller ID." He pushed himself up on the desk. "B2 called around five this morning. I'm assuming that's your hook-up at the vitamin shop."

Charlie's heart flipped again. "That's Riboflavin, my spin-class instructor."

He narrowed his eyes, but he didn't push her. "The next call came at approximately five fifteen, someone who showed up as Daddy, who I deduce by the lack of the word *sugar* in front of the name is your father."

She nodded, even as her mother's voice silently stressed that it was *whom*. "Any other clues?"

He pretended to stroke a long beard. "Beginning around five thirty, you got a series of calls from the county jail. At least six, spaced out about five minutes apart."

"You got me, Nancy Drew." Charlie held up her hands in surrender. "I'm a drug trafficker. Some of my mules got picked up over the weekend."

He laughed. "I'm halfway believing you."

"I'm a defense lawyer," she admitted. "Usually people are more receptive to drug trafficker."

Huck stopped laughing. His eyes narrowed again, but the playfulness had evaporated. "What's your name?"

"Charlie Quinn."

She could've sworn he flinched.

She asked, "Is there a problem?"

His jaw was clenched so hard the bone jutted out. "That's not the name on your credit card."

Charlie paused, because there was a lot wrong with that statement. "That's my married name. Why were you looking at my credit card?"

"I wasn't looking. I glanced at it when you put it down on the bar." He stood up from the desk. "I should get ready for school."

"Was it something I said?" She was trying to make a joke out of it, because of course it was something she'd said. "Look everybody hates lawyers until they need one."

"I grew up in Pikeville."

"You're saying that like it's an explanation."

He opened and closed the desk drawers. "Homeroom's about to start. I need to do my first-period prep."

Charlie crossed her arms. This wasn't the first time she'd had this conversation with longtime Pikeville residents. "There's two reasons for you to be acting like you're acting."

He ignored her, opening and closing another drawer.

She counted out the possibilities on her fingers. "Either you hate my father, which is okay, because a lot of people hate him, or—" She held up her finger for the more likely excuse, the one that had put a target on Charlie's back twenty-eight years ago when she'd returned to school, the one that still got her nasty looks in town from the people who supported the extended, inbred Culpepper clan. "You think I'm a spoiled little bitch who helped frame Zachariah Culpepper and his innocent baby brother so my dad could get his hands on some pissant life insurance policy and their shitty little trailer. Which he never did, by the way. He could've sued them for the twenty grand they owed in legal bills, but he didn't. Not to mention I could pick those fuckers out of a lineup with my eyes closed."

He was shaking his head before she even finished. "None of those things."

"Really?" She had pegged him for a Culpepper truther when he'd told her that he'd grown up in Pikeville.

On the other hand, Charlie could see a career-Marine hating Rusty's kind of lawyering right up until that Marine got caught with a little too much Oxy or a lot too much hooker. As her father always said, a Democrat is a Republican who's been through the criminal justice system.

She told Huck, "Look, I love my dad, but I don't practice the same kind of law that he does. Half my caseload is in juvenile court, the other half is in drug court. I work with stupid people who do stupid things, who need a lawyer to keep the prosecutor from overcharging them." She held out her hands in a shrug. "I just level the playing field."

Huck glared at her. His initial anger had escalated to furious in the blink of an eye. "I want you to leave my room. Right now."

His hard tone made Charlie take a step back. For the first time, it occurred to her that no one knew she was at the school and that Mr. Huckleberry could probably break her neck with one hand.

"Fine." She snatched her phone off his desk and started toward the door. Even as Charlie was telling herself she should shut up and go, she swung back around. "What did my father ever do to you?"

Huck didn't answer. He was sitting at his desk, head bent over a stack of papers, red ink pen in hand.

Charlie waited.

He tapped the pen on his desk, a drumbeat of a dismissal.

She was about to tell him where to stick the pen when she heard a loud crack echo down the hallway.

Three more cracks followed in quick succession.

Not a car backfiring.

Not fireworks.

A person who has been up close when a gun is fired into another human being never mistakes the sound of a gunshot for something else.

Charlie was yanked down to the floor. Huck threw her behind a filing cabinet, shielding her body with his own.

He said something—she saw his mouth move—but the only sound she could hear was the gunshots echoing inside her head. Four shots, each a distinctive, terrifying echo to the past. Just like before, her mouth went dry. Just like before, her heart stopped beating. Her throat closed. Her vision tunneled. Everything looked small, narrowed to a single, tiny point.

Huck's voice rushed back in. "Active shooter at the middle school," he whispered calmly into his phone. "Sounds like he's near the principal's—"

Another crack.

Another bullet fired.

Then another.

Then the homeroom bell rang.

"Jesus," Huck said. "There's at least fifty kids in the cafeteria. I have to—"

A blood-curdling scream broke off the rest of his words.

"Help!" a woman yelled. "Please, help us!"

Charlie blinked.

Gamma's chest exploding.

She blinked again.

Blood misting from Sam's head.

Charlie, run!

She was out the door before Huck could stop her. Her legs pistoned. Her heart pounded. Her sneakers gripped the waxy floor but in her mind, she could feel the earth moving against her bare feet, tree limbs slicing into her face, fear cinching a length of barbed wire around her chest.

"Help us!" the woman cried. "Please!"

Huck caught up with Charlie as she rounded the corner. He was nothing more than a blur as her vision tunneled again, this time to the three people at the end of the hallway.

A man's feet pointed up at the ceiling.

Behind him, to his right, a smaller set of feet splayed out.

Pink shoes. White stars on the soles. Lights that would flash when she walked.

An older woman knelt beside the little girl rocking back and forth, wailing.

Charlie wanted to wail, too.

Blood had sprayed the plastic chairs outside the office, splattered onto the walls and ceiling, jetted onto the floors.

There was a familiarity to the carnage that spread a numbness through Charlie's body. She slowed to a jog, then a brisk walk. She had seen this before. She knew that you could put it all in a little box and close it up later, that you could go on with your life if you didn't sleep too much, didn't breathe too much, didn't live too much so that death came back and snatched you away for the taking.

Somewhere, a set of doors banged open. Loud footsteps clumped through the hallways. Voices were raised. Screaming. Crying. Words were being shouted, but they were unintelligible to Charlie. She was underwater. Her body moved slowly, arms and legs floating against an exaggerated gravity. Her brain silently cataloged all of the things that she did not want to see.

Mr. Pinkman was on his back. His blue tie was tossed over his shoulder. Blood mushroomed from the center of his white dress shirt. The left side of his head was open, skin hanging like tattered paper around the white of his skull. There was a deep, black hole where his right eye should have been.

Mrs. Pinkman was not beside her husband. She was the screaming woman who had suddenly stopped screaming. She was cradling the child's head in her lap, holding a pastel blue sweater to the girl's neck. The bullet had ripped open something vital. Mrs. Pinkman's hands were bright red. Blood had turned the diamond on her wedding ring the color of a cherry pit.

Charlie's knees gave out.

She was on the floor beside the girl.

She was seeing herself lying on the ground in the forest.

Twelve? Thirteen?

Spindly little legs. Short black hair like Gamma. Long eyelashes like Sam.

"Help," Mrs. Pinkman whispered, her voice hoarse. "Please."

Charlie reached out her hands, not knowing where to put them. The little girl's eyes rolled up, then just as suddenly, she focused on Charlie.

"It's okay," Charlie told her. "You'll be okay."

"Go before this lamb, oh Lord," Mrs. Pinkman prayed. "Be not far from her. Make haste to help her."

You won't die, Charlie's brain begged. *You won't surrender. You will graduate high school. You will go to college. You will get married. You will not leave a gaping hole in your family where your love used to be.*

"Make haste to guide me, oh Lord my salvation."

"Look at me," Charlie told the girl. "You're going to be fine."

The girl was not going to be fine.

Her eyelids began to flutter. Her blue-tinged lips parted. Tiny teeth. White gums. The light pink tip of her tongue.

Slowly, the color began to drain from her face. Charlie was reminded of the way winter came down the mountain, the festive red and orange and yellow leaves turning umber, then brown, then starting to fall, so that by the time the cold reached its icy fingers into the foothills outside of town, everything was dead.

"Oh God," Mrs. Pinkman sobbed. "Little angel. Poor little angel."

Charlie couldn't remember taking the child's hand, but there were her little fingers caught between Charlie's bigger ones. So small and cold, like a lost glove on the playground. Charlie watched the fingers slowly release until the girl's hand fell slack to the floor.

Gone.

"Code Black!"

Charlie jerked at the sound.

"Code Black!" A cop was running up the hallway. He had his radio in one hand, a shotgun in the other. Panic cracked his voice. "Get to the school! Get to the school!"

For a brief second, the man made eye contact with Charlie. There was a spark of recognition, and then he saw the body of the dead child. Horror, then grief collapsed his features. The toe of his shoe caught a streak of blood. His feet slipped out from underneath him. He fell hard to the ground. His breath *oofed* out of his open mouth. The shotgun flew from his hand and skittered across the floor.

Charlie looked down at her own hand, the one that had held the child's. She rubbed together her fingers. The blood was sticky, not like Gamma's, which had felt slick like oil.

Bright white bone. Pieces of heart and lung. Cords of tendon and arteries and veins and life spilling out of her gaping wounds.

She remembered going back to the farmhouse after it was all over. Rusty had hired someone to clean, but they hadn't done a thorough job. Months later, Charlie was looking for a bowl at the back of one of the cabinets and she'd found a piece of Gamma's tooth.

"Don't!" Huck yelled.

Charlie looked up, shocked by what she saw. What she had missed. What at first she couldn't comprehend even though it was taking place less than fifty feet in front of her.

A teenage girl was sitting on the floor, her back to the lockers. Charlie's brain flashed up an image from before, the girl sneaking into the edge of her tunnel vision as Charlie ran up the hallway toward the carnage. Charlie had instantly recognized the girl's type: black clothes, black eyeliner. A Goth. No blood. Round face showing shock, not pain. *She's okay*, Charlie had thought, running past her to reach Mrs. Pinkman, to reach the child. But the Goth girl wasn't okay.

She was the shooter.

She had a revolver in her hand. Instead of picking off more victims, she was pointing the gun at her own chest.

"Put it down!" The cop was standing a few yards away, his shotgun jammed into his shoulder. Terror informed his every movement, from the way he was bouncing on the balls of his feet to the death grip he had on the weapon. "I said put it the fuck down!"

"She will." Huck knelt with his back to the girl, shielding her. His hands were up. His voice was steady. "It's okay, Officer. Let's stay calm here."

"Get out of my way!" The cop wasn't calm. He was amped up, ready to pull the trigger the moment he got a clean shot. "Get the fuck out of my way!"

"Her name is Kelly," Huck said. "Kelly Wilson."

"Fucking move, asshole!"

Charlie didn't watch the men. She watched the weapons.

Revolver and shotgun.

Shotgun and revolver.

She felt a wave pass through her body, the same kind of anesthesia that had numbed her so many times before.

"Move!" the cop screamed. He jerked the shotgun one way, then the other, trying to angle around Huck. "Get the fuck out of my way!"

"No." Huck stayed on his knees, his back to Kelly. His hands stayed in the air. "Don't do this, man. She's only sixteen years old. You don't want to kill a——"

"Move out of my way!" The cop's fear was like an electric current crackling the air. "Get on the floor!"

"Stop it, man." Huck moved with the shotgun, blocking him at every point. "She's not trying to shoot anybody but herself."

The girl's mouth opened. Charlie couldn't hear the words, but the cop obviously did.

"Did you hear that fucking bitch!" the cop screamed. "Let her do it or get the fuck out of my way!"

"Please," Mrs. Pinkman whispered. Charlie had almost forgotten about the woman. The principal's wife had her head in her hands, her eyes covered so she didn't have to see. "Please stop."

"Kelly." Huck's voice was calm. He reached his hand over his shoulder, palm up. "Kelly, give me the gun, sweetheart. You don't have to do this." He waited a few seconds, then said, "Kelly. Look at me."

Slowly, the girl looked up. Her mouth was slack. Her eyes were glassy.

"Front hallway! Front hallway!" Another cop rushed past Charlie. He went down on one knee, sliding across the floor, two-handing his Glock and screaming, "Put it down!"

"Please, God," Mrs. Pinkman sobbed into her hands. "Forgive this sin."

"Kelly," Huck said. "Hand me the gun. Nobody else has to get hurt."

"Down!" the second cop boomed. Hysteria pitched his voice up too high. Charlie could see his finger tense on the trigger. "Get down on the ground!"

"Kelly." Huck made his voice firm, like an angry parent. "I'm not asking anymore. Give me the gun right now." He shook his open hand in the air for emphasis. "I mean it."

Kelly Wilson began to nod. Charlie watched the teenager's eyes gradually come back into focus as Huck's words started to penetrate. Someone was telling her what to do, showing her a way out of this. Her shoulders relaxed. Her mouth closed. She blinked several times. Charlie intrinsically understood what the girl was going through. Time had stopped, and then someone, somehow, had found a key to wind it back up again.

Slowly, Kelly moved to put the revolver in Huck's hand.

The cop pulled the trigger anyway.

CHAPTER TWO

Charlie watched Huck's left shoulder jerk as the bullet ripped through his arm. His nostrils flared. His lips parted for breath. Blood wicked into the fibers of his shirt like a red iris. Still, he held onto the revolver that Kelly had placed in his hand.

Someone whispered, "Jesus Christ."

"I'm all right," Huck told the cop who had shot him. "You can holster your weapon, okay?"

The cop's hands shook so hard that he could barely hold on to his gun.

Huck said, "Officer Rodgers, holster your weapon and take this revolver."

Charlie felt rather than saw a swarm of police officers run past her. The air billowed around them like the cartoon swirls that came out of clouds, nothing more than thin, curved lines that indicated movement.

Then a paramedic was holding tightly to Charlie's arm. Then someone was shining a flashlight into her eyes, asking if she was hurt, if she was in shock, if she wanted to go to the hospital.

"No," Mrs. Pinkman said. Another paramedic was checking her for injuries. Her red shirt was soaked with blood. "Please. I'm fine."

No one was checking on Mr. Pinkman.

No one was checking on the little girl.

Charlie looked down at her hands. The bones inside the tips of her fingers were vibrating. The sensation slowly spread until she felt like she was standing an inch outside of her body, that every breath was a reverberation of another breath that she had previously taken.

Mrs. Pinkman cupped her hand to Charlie's cheek. She used her thumb to wipe away tears. Pain was etched into the deep wrinkles lining the woman's face. With anyone else, Charlie would've pulled away, but she leaned into Mrs. Pinkman's warmth.

They had been here before.

Twenty-eight years ago, Mrs. Pinkman was Miss Heller, living with her parents two miles away from the farmhouse. She was the one who'd answered the tentative knock at her door and found thirteen-year-old Charlie standing on the front porch, covered in sweat, streaked with blood, asking if they had any ice cream.

That was what people focused on when they told the story—not that Gamma had been murdered or that Sam had been buried alive, but that Charlie had eaten two bowls of ice cream before she'd told Miss Heller that something bad had happened.

"Charlotte." Huck grabbed her shoulder. She watched his mouth move as he repeated the name that wasn't her name anymore. His tie was undone. She saw the red splotches dotting the white bandage around his arm.

"Charlotte." He shook her again. "You need to call your dad. Now."

Charlie looked up, looked around. Time had moved on without her. Mrs. Pinkman was gone. The paramedics had disappeared. The only thing that remained the same was the bodies. They were still there, just a few feet away. Mr. Pinkman with his tie over his shoulder. The little girl with her pink jacket that was stained with blood.

"Call him," Huck said.

Charlie fumbled for the phone in her back pocket. He was right. Rusty would be worried. She needed to let him know that she was okay.

Huck said, "Tell him to bring the newspapers, the chief of

police, whoever he can get down here." He looked away. "I can't stop them on my own."

Charlie felt a tightness in her chest, her body telling her that she was trapped inside something dangerous. She followed Huck's gaze down the hallway.

He wasn't worried about Charlie.

He was worried about Kelly Wilson.

The teenager was facedown on the floor, both arms handcuffed tightly behind her back. She was petite, no more than Charlie's size, but she was pinned down the same as if she were a violent con. One cop had his knee pressed into her back, another kneeled on her legs and yet another was grinding the sole of his boot into the side of the girl's face.

These actions alone could be seen through the wide lens of admissible restraint, but that's not why Huck had told her to call Rusty. Five more cops stood in a circle around the girl. She hadn't heard them before but she could hear them clearly now. They were screaming, cursing, waving their arms around. Charlie knew some of these men, recognized them from high school or the courtroom or both. The expressions on their faces were all painted in the same shade of rage. They were furious about the deaths, livid about their own feelings of helplessness. This was their town. Their school. They had children who were students here, teachers, friends.

One of the cops punched a locker so hard that the hinge broke on the metal door. Others kept clenching and unclenching their hands. A few walked back and forth across the short length of the hall like animals in a cage. Maybe they *were* animals. One wrong word could spark a kick, then a punch, then batons would be pulled, guns would be drawn, and they would set upon Kelly Wilson like jackals.

"My girl's that age," someone hissed between gritted teeth. "They were in the same class."

Another fist slammed into another locker.

"Pink coached me up," someone said.

"He ain't never gonna coach nobody up never again."

Yet another locker door was kicked off its hinges.

"You—" Charlie's voice cracked before she could finish. This was dangerous. Too dangerous. "Stop," she said, then begged, "Please stop."

They either didn't hear her or didn't care.

"Charlotte," Huck said. "Don't get into this. Just—"

"Fucking bitch." The cop with his knee jammed into Kelly's back yanked a fistful of the girl's hair. "Why'd you do it? Why'd you kill 'em?"

"Stop," Charlie said. Huck's hand went to her arm, but she stood up anyway. "Stop," she repeated.

No one was listening. Her voice was too timid because every muscle in her body was telling her not to insert herself into this buzz saw of masculine fury. It was like trying to stop dogs from fighting, except the dogs had loaded guns.

"Hey," Charlie said, fear making her choke on the word. "Take her to the station. Put her in lock-up."

Jonah Vickery, an asshole jock she knew from high school, snapped out his metal baton.

"Jonah." Charlie's knees were so weak that she had to lean against the wall to keep from sliding to the floor. "You need to Mirandize her and—"

"Charlotte." Huck motioned for her to sit back down on the floor. "Don't get into this. Call your dad. He can stop this."

He was right. Cops were afraid of her father. They knew about his lawsuits, his public platform. Charlie tried to press the home button on the phone. Her fingers were too thick. Sweat had turned the dried blood into a thick paste.

"Hurry," Huck said. "They're going to end up killing her."

Charlie watched a foot swing into Kelly's side hard enough to make the girl's hips leave the ground.

Another metal baton snapped out.

Charlie finally managed to press the home button. A photo of

Huck's dog filled the screen. She didn't ask Huck for the code. It was too late to call Rusty. He wouldn't make it to the school in time. She tapped the camera icon, knowing it bypassed the lock screen. Two swipes later, the video was recording. She zoomed in on the girl's face. "Kelly Wilson. Look at me. Can you breathe?"

Kelly blinked. Her head looked like it was the size of a doll's compared to the black police-issue boot that was pressing into the side of her face.

Charlie said, "Kelly, look into the camera."

"God dammit," Huck cursed. "I said to—"

"You guys need to stop this." Charlie dragged her shoulder against the lockers as she walked closer to the lion's den. "Take her to the station. Photograph her. Fingerprint her. Don't let this blow back on—"

"She's filming us," one of the cops said. Greg Brenner. Another asshole jock. "Put it down, Quinn."

"She's a sixteen-year-old girl." Charlie kept recording. "I'll ride with her in the back of the car. You can arrest her and—"

"Make her stop," Jonah said. He was the one with his foot pressed against the face of a teenage girl. "She's worse than her fucking father."

"Give her a bowl of ice cream," Al Larrisy suggested.

Charlie said, "Jonah, get your boot off her head." She trained the camera onto each man's face. "There's a right way to do this. You all know that. Don't be the reason this case gets tossed."

Jonah pressed his foot down so hard that Kelly's jaw was forced open. Blood dribbled out where her braces had cut into her cheek. He said, "You see that dead baby over there?" He pointed up the hallway. "You see where her neck got blowed off?"

"What do you think?" Charlie asked, because she had the little girl's blood all over her hands.

"I think you care more about a fucking murderer than you do about two innocent victims."

"That's enough." Greg tried to grab the phone. "Turn it off."

Charlie turned away so she could keep filming. "Put us both in the car," she said. "Take us to the station and—"

"Give me that." Greg reached for the phone again.

Charlie tried to feint away, but Greg was too fast. He snatched the phone out of her hand and threw it to the ground.

Charlie leaned down to retrieve it.

"Leave it," he ordered.

Charlie kept reaching for the phone.

Without warning, the point of Greg's elbow cracked against the bridge of her nose. Her head snapped back, banging into the locker. The pain was like a bomb had gone off inside of her face. Charlie's mouth opened. She coughed out blood.

No one moved.

No one spoke.

Charlie cupped her hands to her face. Blood poured from her nose like a faucet. She felt stunned. Greg *looked* stunned. He held up his hands as if to say he didn't mean it. But the damage had already been done. Charlie staggered sideways. She tripped over her own feet. Greg reached out to catch her. He was too late.

The last thing she saw was the ceiling spinning over her head as she hit the ground.

CHAPTER THREE

Charlie sat on the floor of the interview room with her back wedged into the corner. She had no idea how much time had passed since she'd been hauled off to the police station. An hour at least. Her wrists were still handcuffed. Toilet paper was still shoved up her broken nose. Stitches prickled the back of her scalp. Her head was pounding. Her vision was blurry. Her stomach was churning. She had been photographed. She had been fingerprinted. She was still wearing the same clothes. Her jeans were dotted with dark red splotches. The same pattern riddled her Duke Blue Devils T-shirt. Her hands were still caked with dried blood, because the cell where they had let her use the toilet only had a trickle of cold, brown water coming out of the filthy sink faucet.

Twenty-eight years ago, she had begged the nurses at the hospital to let her take a bath. Gamma's blood was seared to her skin. Everything was sticky. Charlie had not completely submerged herself in water since the red-brick house had burned down. She'd wanted to feel the warmth envelop her, to watch the blood and bone float away like a bad dream fading from her memory.

Nothing ever truly faded. Time only dulled the edges.

Charlie let out a slow breath. She rested the side of her head against the wall. She closed her eyes. She saw the dead little girl in the school hallway, the way her color had drained like winter, the way her hand had fallen from Charlie's hand the same way that Gamma's hand had fallen away.

The little girl would still be in the cold hallway at school—her body, at least, along with Mr. Pinkman's. Both still dead. Both still exposed to one more final injustice. They would be left out in the open, uncovered, unprotected, while people traipsed back and forth around them. That was how homicides worked. No one moved anything, not even a child, not even a beloved coach, until every inch of the crime scene was photographed, cataloged, measured, diagrammed, investigated.

Charlie opened her eyes.

This was all such sad, familiar territory: the images she couldn't get out of her head, the dark places that her brain kept going to over and over again like car wheels wearing down a gravel road.

She breathed through her mouth. Her nose had a painful pulse. The paramedic had said it wasn't broken, but Charlie didn't trust any of them. Even while her head was being sutured, the cops were scrambling to cover for each other, articulating their reports, all of them agreeing that Charlie had been hostile, that she had knocked herself against Greg's elbow, that the phone had been broken when she accidentally stepped on it.

Huck's phone.

Mr. Huckleberry had repeatedly made that point that the phone and its contents belonged to him. He'd even shown them the screen so that they could watch the video being deleted.

While it was happening, it had hurt too much to shake her head, but Charlie did so now. They had shot Huck, unprovoked, and he was taking up for them. She had seen this kind of behavior in almost every police force she had ever dealt with.

No matter what, these guys always, always covered for each other.

The door opened. Jonah came in. He carried two folding chairs, one in each hand. He winked at Charlie, because he liked her better now that she was in his custody. He'd been the same kind of sadist in high school. The uniform had only codified it.

"I want my father," she said, the same thing she said every time someone entered the room.

Jonah winked again as he unfolded the chairs on either side of the table.

"I have a legal right to counsel."

"I just talked to him on the phone." This came not from Jonah, but from Ben Bernard, an assistant district attorney for the county. He barely glanced at Charlie as he tossed a folder onto the table and sat down. "Take the cuffs off her."

Jonah asked, "You want me to hook her leash to the table?"

Ben smoothed down his tie. He looked up at the man. "I said to take those fucking handcuffs off my wife *right now.*"

Ben had raised his voice to say this, but he hadn't yelled. He never yelled, at least not in the eighteen years that Charlie had known him.

Jonah swung his keys around his fingers, making it clear that he was going to do this in his own time, of his own volition. He roughly unlocked the cuffs and stripped them from Charlie's wrists, but the joke was on him because she was so numb that she didn't feel any of it.

Jonah slammed the door when he left the room.

Charlie listened to the slam echo off the concrete walls. She stayed seated on the floor. She waited for Ben to say something jokey, like nobody puts baby in a corner, but Ben had two homicide victims at the middle school, a suicidal teenage murderer in custody and his wife was sitting in a corner covered in blood, so instead she took consolation in the way he lifted his chin to indicate that she should sit in the chair across from him.

She asked, "Is Kelly all right?"

"She's on suicide watch. Two female officers, around the clock."

"She's sixteen," Charlie said, though they both knew that Kelly Wilson would be direct filed as an adult. The teenager's only saving grace—literally—was that minors were no longer eligible for the death penalty. "If she asked for a parent, that can be construed as the equivalent of asking for a lawyer."

"Depends on the judge."

"You know Dad will get a change of venue." Charlie knew her father was the only lawyer in town who would take the case.

The overhead light flashed off Ben's glasses as he nodded toward the chair again.

Charlie pushed herself up against the wall. A wave of dizziness made her close her eyes.

Ben asked, "Do you need medical treatment?"

"Somebody already asked me that." Charlie didn't want to go to a hospital. She probably had a concussion. But she could still walk as long as she kept some part of her body in contact with something solid. "I'm fine."

He said nothing, but the silent, "of course you're fine, you're always fine," reverberated around the room.

"See?" She touched the wall with the tips of her fingers, an acrobat on a wire.

Ben didn't look up. He adjusted his glasses. He opened the file folder in front of him. There was a single form inside. Charlie's eyes wouldn't focus to read the words, even when he began writing in his big, blocky letters.

She asked, "With what offense have I been charged?"

"Obstruction of justice."

"That's a handy catchall."

He kept writing. He kept not looking at her.

She asked, "You already saw what they did to me, didn't you?"

The only sound Ben made was his pen scratching across the paper.

"That's why you won't look at me now, because you already looked at me through that." She nodded toward the two-way mirror. "Who else is there? Coin?" District Attorney Ken Coin was Ben's boss, an insufferable dickslap of a man who saw everything in black and white and, more recently, brown, because of the housing boom that had brought an influx of Mexican immigrants up from Atlanta.

Charlie watched the reflection of her raised hand in the mirror, her middle finger extending in a salute to DA Coin.

Ben said, "I've taken nine witness statements that said you were inconsolable at the scene, and in the course of being comforted by Officer Brenner, your nose met with his elbow."

If he was going to talk to her like a lawyer, then she was going to be a lawyer. "Is that what the video on the phone showed, or do I need to get a subpoena for a forensic examination of any deleted files?"

Ben's shoulder went up in a shrug. "Do what you have to do."

"All right." Charlie braced her palms on the table so that she could sit. "Is this the part where you offer to drop the bogus obstruction charge if I don't file an excessive force complaint?"

"I already dropped the bogus obstruction charge." His pen moved down to the next line. "You can file as many complaints as you want."

"All I want is an apology."

She heard a sound behind the mirror, something close to a gasp. In the past twelve years, Charlie had filed two very successful lawsuits against the Pikeville Police force on behalf of her clients. Ken Coin had probably assumed she was sitting in here counting all of the money she was going to make off the city instead of grieving for the child who had died in her arms, or mourning the loss of the principal who had given her detention instead of kicking her out of school when they both knew that Charlie deserved it.

Ben kept his head bent down. He tapped his pen against the table. She tried not to think about Huck doing the same thing at his school desk.

He asked, "Are you sure?"

Charlie waved toward the mirror, hoping Coin was there. "If you guys could just admit when you did something wrong, then when you said that you did something right, people would believe you."

Ben finally looked at her. His eyes tracked across her face, taking in the damage. She saw the fine lines around his mouth when he frowned, the deep furrow in his brow, and wondered if he had ever noticed the same signs of age in her face.

They had met in law school. He had moved to Pikeville in order to be with her. They had planned on spending the rest of their lives together.

She said, "Kelly Wilson has a right to—"

Ben held up his hand to stop her. "You know that I agree with everything you're going to say."

Charlie sat back in the chair. She had to remind herself that neither she nor Ben had ever bought into Rusty and Ken Coin's "us against them" mentality.

She said, "I want a written apology from Greg Brenner. A real apology, not some bullshit, 'I'm sorry you feel that way' excuse like I'm a hysterical woman and he wasn't acting like a God damn Brownshirt."

Ben nodded. "Done."

Charlie reached for the form. She grabbed the pen. The words were a blur, but she had read enough witness statements to know where you were supposed to sign your name. She scrawled her signature near the bottom, then slid the form back toward Ben. "I'll trust you to keep your side of the bargain. Fill in the statement however you want."

Ben stared down at the form. His fingers hovered at the edge. He wasn't looking at her signature, but at the bloody brown fingerprints she'd left on the white paper.

Charlie blinked to clear her eyes. This was the closest they had come to touching each other in nine months.

"Okay." He closed the folder. He made to stand.

"It was just the two of them?" Charlie asked. "Mr. Pink and the little—"

"Yes." He hesitated before sitting back down in the chair. "One of the janitors locked down the cafeteria. The assistant principal stopped the buses at the street."

Charlie did not want to think about the damage that Kelly Wilson could have done if she had started firing the gun a few seconds after the bell instead of before.

Ben said, "They all have to be interviewed. The kids. Teachers. Staff."

Charlie knew the city wasn't capable of coordinating so many interviews, let alone putting together such a large case on its own. The Pikeville Police Department had seventeen full-time officers. Ben was one of six lawyers in the district attorney's office.

She asked, "Is Ken going to ask for help?"

"They're already here," Ben said. "Everybody just showed up. Troopers. State police. Sheriff's office. We didn't even have to call them."

"That's good."

"Yeah." He picked at the corner of the folder with his fingers. His lips twitched the way they always did when he chewed at the tip of his tongue. It was an old habit that wouldn't die. Charlie had once seen his mother reach across the dinner table and slap his hand to make him stop.

She asked, "You saw the bodies?"

He didn't answer, but he didn't have to. Charlie knew that Ben had seen the crime scene. She could tell by the somber tone in his voice, the slump in his shoulders. Pikeville had grown over the last two decades, but it was still a small town, the kind of place where heroin was a much larger concern than homicide.

Ben said, "You know it takes time, but I told them to move the bodies as soon as possible."

Charlie looked up at the ceiling to keep the tears in her eyes. He had awakened her dozens of times from her worst nightmare: a day in the life, Charlie and Rusty going about their mundane chores inside the old farmhouse, cooking meals and doing laundry and washing dishes while Gamma's body rotted against the cabinets because the police had forgotten to take her away.

It was probably the piece of tooth Charlie had found in the back of the cabinet, because what else had they missed?

Ben said, "Your car is parked behind your office. They locked down the school. It'll probably be closed for the rest of the week. There's already a news van up from Atlanta."

"Is that where Dad is, combing his hair?"

They both smiled a little, because they both knew that her father loved nothing more than to see himself on television.

Ben said, "He told you to hang tight. When I called him. That's what Rusty said—'Tell that girl to hang tight.'"

Which meant that Rusty wasn't going to ride to her rescue. That he assumed his tough daughter could handle herself in a room full of Keystone Kops while he rushed to Kelly Wilson's house and got her parents to sign his fee agreement.

When people talked about how much they hated lawyers, it was Rusty who came to mind.

Ben said, "I can have one of the squad cars take you to your office."

"I'm not getting in a car with any of those assholes."

Ben ran his fingers through his hair. He needed a trim. His shirt was wrinkled. His suit was missing a button. She wanted to think he was falling apart without her, but the truth was that he was always disheveled and Charlie was more likely to tease him about looking like a hipster hobo than to take out a needle and thread.

She said, "Kelly Wilson was in their custody. She wasn't resisting. The moment they cuffed her, they were responsible for her safety."

"Greg's daughter goes to that school."

"So does Kelly." Charlie leaned closer. "We're not living in

Abu Ghraib, okay? Kelly Wilson has a constitutional right to due process under the law. It's up to a judge and jury to decide, not a bunch of vigilante cops with hard-ons to beat down a teenage girl."

"I get it. We all get it." Ben thought she was grandstanding for the great Oz behind the mirror. "'A just society is a lawful society. You can't be a good guy if you act like a bad guy.'"

He was quoting Rusty.

She said, "They were going to beat the shit out of her. Or worse."

"So you volunteered yourself instead?"

Charlie felt a burning sensation in her hands. Without thinking, she was scratching at the dried blood, rolling it into tiny balls. Her fingernails were ten black crescents.

She looked up at her husband. "You said you took nine witness statements?"

Ben gave a single, reluctant nod. He knew why she was asking the question.

Eight cops. Mrs. Pinkman wasn't there when Charlie's nose was broken, which meant that the ninth statement had come from Huck, which meant that Ben had already talked to him.

She asked, "Do you know?" That was the only thing that mattered between them right now, whether or not Ben knew why she had been at the school this morning. Because if Ben knew, then everyone else knew, which meant that Charlie had yet again found another uniquely cruel way to humiliate her husband.

"Ben?" she asked.

He ran his fingers through his hair. He smoothed down his tie. He had so many tells that they could never play cards together, not even Go Fish.

"Babe, I'm sorry," she whispered. "I'm so, so sorry."

There was a quick knock before the door opened. Charlie held out hope that it was her father, but an older black woman wearing a navy pantsuit and white blouse walked into the room. Her short black hair was tufted with white. She had a large, banged-up-looking purse on her arm that was almost as big as the one that Charlie carried to work. A laminated ID hung on a lanyard around her neck, but Charlie couldn't read it.

The woman said, "I'm special agent in charge Delia Wofford with the Georgia Bureau of Investigation. You're Charlotte Quinn?" She reached out to shake Charlie's hand, but changed her mind when she saw the dried blood. "Have you been photographed?"

Charlie nodded.

"For godsakes." She opened her purse and pulled out a packet of Wet Wipes. "Use as many as you need. I can get more."

Jonah was back with another chair. Delia pointed to the head of the table, indicating that's where she wanted to sit. She asked Jonah, "Are you the jerk who wouldn't let this woman clean herself up?"

Jonah didn't know what to do with the question. He had probably never had to answer to any woman besides his mother, and that had been a long time ago.

"Close the door behind you." Delia waved Jonah off as she sat down. "Ms. Quinn, we'll get through this as quickly as possible. Do you mind if I record this?"

Charlie shook her head. "Knock yourself out."

She tapped some buttons on her phone to activate the recorder, then unpacked her bag, tossing notepads and books and papers onto the table.

The concussion made it impossible for Charlie to read anything in front of her, so she opened up the pack of Wet Wipes and got to work. She scrubbed between her fingers first, dislodging specks of black that floated like ashes from a roaring fire. The blood had seared itself into the pores. Her hands looked like an old woman's. She was suddenly overcome with exhaustion. She wanted to go home. She wanted a hot bath. She wanted to think about what had happened today, to examine all the pieces, then gather them up, put them in a box and place it high on a shelf so that she never had to deal with it again.

"Ms. Quinn?" Delia Wofford was offering her a bottle of water.

Charlie almost snatched it out of the woman's hand. She hadn't realized she was thirsty until that moment. Half of the water was gone before the logical part of her brain reminded her that it wasn't a good idea to drink so quickly on a sour stomach.

"Sorry." Charlie put her hand to her mouth to cover the noxious belch.

The agent had obviously endured worse. "Ready?"

"You're recording this?"

"Yes."

Charlie peeled another wipe out of the packet. "First, I want some information about Kelly Wilson."

Delia Wofford had enough years under her belt to not look as annoyed as she must have felt. "She's been examined by a doctor. She's under constant surveillance."

That's not what Charlie had meant, and the agent knew it. "There are nine factors you have to consider before ascertaining whether or not a juvenile's statement is—"

"Ms. Quinn," Delia interrupted. "Let's stop worrying about Kelly Wilson and start worrying about you. I'm sure you don't want to spend a second longer here than you absolutely have to."

Charlie would've rolled her eyes if not for the fear of making herself dizzy. "She's sixteen. She's not old enough to—"

"Eighteen."

Charlie stopped cleaning her hands. She stared at Ben, not Delia Wofford, because they had both agreed very early on in their marriage that a lie by omission was still a lie.

Ben stared back. His expression told her nothing.

Delia said, "According to her birth certificate, Kelly Wilson turned eighteen two days ago."

"You've—" Charlie had to look away from Ben because their

broken marriage took a back seat to a death warrant. "You've seen her birth certificate?"

Delia shuffled through a stack of folders until she found what she was looking for. She put a sheet of paper in front of Charlie. All Charlie could make out was a round, official-looking seal.

Delia said, "The school records back it up, but we were faxed this official copy from the Georgia Department of Health an hour ago." Her finger pointed to what must have been Kelly's birth date. "She turned eighteen at six twenty-three on Saturday morning, but you know the law gives her until midnight before she's officially an adult."

Charlie felt sick. *Two days.* Forty-eight hours meant the difference between life with a possibility of parole and death by lethal injection.

"She was held back a grade. That's probably where the confusion lies."

"What was she doing at the middle school?"

"There are still a great many unanswered questions." Delia dug around in her purse and found a pen. "Now, Ms. Quinn, for the record, are you willing to give a statement? It's your right to refuse. You know that."

Charlie could barely follow the agent's words. She placed her palm flat against her stomach, forcing it to calm. Even if by some miracle Kelly Wilson managed to avoid the death penalty, Georgia's Seven Deadly Sins law would make sure she never got out of prison.

Would that be so wrong?

There was no ambiguity here. Kelly had literally been caught holding the murder weapon in her hands.

Charlie looked at her own hands, still bloody from the little girl who had died in her arms. Died because Kelly Wilson had shot her. Murdered her. Just like she had murdered Mr. Pinkman.

"Ms. Quinn?" Delia glanced at her watch, but Charlie knew the woman was exactly where she needed to be.

Charlie also knew how the legal system worked. No one would tell the story of what happened this morning without an eye toward nailing Kelly Wilson to a cross. Not the eight cops who were there. Not Huck Huckabee. Maybe not even Mrs. Pinkman, whose husband had been murdered not ten yards from her classroom door.

Charlie said, "I agree to give a statement."

Delia had a legal pad in front of her. She twisted open her pen. "Ms. Quinn, first I want to tell you how sorry I am that you've been pulled into this. I'm aware of your family history. I'm sure it was difficult witnessing . . ."

Charlie rolled her hand, indicating she should move on.

"All right," Delia said. "This next bit I have to say. I want you to know that the door behind me is unlocked. You're not under arrest. You are not being detained. As I told you before, you're free to leave at any time, though as one of the few witnesses to today's tragedy, your voluntary statement could be instrumental in helping us put together what happened."

Charlie noted that the woman had not warned her that lying to a GBI agent could land her in prison. "You want me to help you build your case against Kelly Wilson."

"I just want you to tell me the truth."

"And I can only do that to the best of my knowledge." Charlie didn't realize that she was feeling hostile until she looked down and saw that her arms were crossed.

Delia rested her pen on the table, but the recorder was still going. "Ms. Quinn, let's put this out there that this is a very awkward situation for all of us."

Charlie waited.

Delia asked, "Would it help you speak more freely if your husband left the room?"

Charlie smoothed her lips together. "Ben knows why I was at the school this morning."

If Delia was disappointed that her ace had been played, she

didn't let on. She picked up the pen. "Let's start from that point, then. I know your car was parked in the faculty lot to the east of the main entrance. How did you enter the building?"

"The side door. It was propped open."

"Did you notice the door was open when you parked your car?"

"It's always open." Charlie shook her head. "I mean, it was when I was a student there. It's quicker from the parking lot to the cafeteria. I used to go to the . . ." Her voice trailed off, because it didn't matter. "I parked in the side lot and went through the side door, which I assumed from my previous time as a student would be open."

Delia's pen moved across the pad. She didn't look up when she asked, "You went directly to Mr. Huckabee's classroom?"

"I got turned around. I walked by the front office. It was dark inside, except Mr. Pinkman's light was on in the back."

"Did you see anyone?"

"I didn't see Mr. Pinkman, just that his light was on."

"What about anybody else?"

"Mrs. Jenkins, the school secretary. I think I saw her go into the office, but I was way down the hall by then. The lights came on. I turned around. I was about thirty yards away." Standing where Kelly Wilson had stood when she murdered Mr. Pinkman and the little girl. "I'm not sure it was Mrs. Jenkins who entered the office, but it was an older woman who looked like her."

"And that's the only person you saw, an older woman entering the office?"

"Yes. The doors were closed to the classrooms. Some teachers were inside, so I guess I saw them, too." Charlie chewed her lip, trying to get her thoughts together. No wonder her clients talked themselves into trouble. Charlie was a witness, not even a suspect, and she was already leaving out details. "I didn't recognize any of the teachers behind the doors. I don't know if they saw me, but it's possible they did."

"Okay, so you went to Mr. Huckabee's classroom next?"

"Yes. I was in his room when I heard the gunshot."

"*A* gunshot?"

Charlie wadded the Wet Wipes into a ball on the table. "Four gunshots."

"Rapid?"

"Yes. No." She closed her eyes. She tried to remember. Only a handful of hours had passed. Why did everything feel like it had happened an eternity ago? "I heard two shots, then two more? Or three and then one?"

Delia held her pen aloft, waiting.

"I don't remember the sequence," Charlie admitted, and she again reminded herself that this was a sworn statement. "To the best of my recollection, there were four shots, total. I remember counting them. And then Huck pulled me down." Charlie cleared her throat. She resisted the need to look at Ben, to gauge how he was taking this. "Mr. Huckabee pulled me down behind the filing cabinet, I assume for cover."

"Any more gunshots?"

"I—" She shook her head because again she was unsure. "I don't know."

Delia said, "Let's back up a little. It was only you and Mr. Huckabee in the room?"

"Yes. I didn't see anyone else in the hall."

"How long were you in Mr. Huckabee's room before you heard the shots?"

Again, Charlie shook her head. "Maybe two to three minutes?"

"So, you go into his classroom, two to three minutes pass, you hear these four gunshots, Mr. Huckabee pulls you down behind the filing cabinet, and then?"

Charlie shrugged. "I ran."

"Toward the exit?"

Charlie's eyes flicked toward Ben. "Toward the gunshots."

Ben silently scratched his jaw. This was one of their things, the way Charlie always ran toward danger when everyone else was running away.

"All right." Delia spoke as she wrote. "Was Mr. Huckabee with you when you ran toward the gunshots?"

"He was behind me." Charlie remembered sprinting past Kelly, leaping over her extended legs. This time, her memory showed Huck kneeling beside the girl. That made sense. He would've seen the gun in Kelly's hand. He would've been trying to talk the teenager into giving him the revolver the entire time that Charlie was watching the little girl die.

She asked Delia, "Can you tell me her name? The little girl?"

"Lucy Alexander. Her mother teaches at the school."

Charlie saw the girl's features come into focus. Her pink coat. Her matching backpack. Was her name monogrammed on the inside of her jacket or was that a detail that Charlie was making up?

Delia said, "We haven't released her name to the press, but her parents have been notified."

"She didn't suffer. At least, I don't think so. She didn't know she was . . ." Once again, Charlie shook her head, aware that she was filling in blanks with things that she wanted to be true.

Delia said, "So, you ran toward the gunshots, in the direction of the front office." She turned to a fresh page in her pad. "Mr. Huckabee was behind you. Who else did you see?"

"I don't remember seeing Kelly Wilson. I mean, I did remember later that I saw her, when I heard the cops shouting, but when I was running, well, before that, Huck caught up with me, he passed me at the corner, and then I passed him . . ." Charlie chewed her lip again. This meandering narrative was the kind of thing that drove her crazy when she talked to her clients. "I ran past Kelly. I thought she was a kid. A student." Kelly Wilson had been both of those things. Even at eighteen, she was tiny, the kind of girl who would always look like a kid, even when she was a grown woman with children of her own.

"I'm getting fuzzy on the timeline," Delia admitted.

"I'm sorry." Charlie tried to explain, "It screws with your head when you're in the middle of this kind of thing. Time turns from a straight line into a sphere, and it's not until later that you can hold it in your hand and look at all the different sides, and you think, *Oh, now I remember—this happened, then this happened, then* . . . It's only after the fact that you can pull it back into a straight line that makes sense."

Ben was studying her. She knew what he was thinking because she knew the inside of his head better than she did her own. With those few sentences, Charlie had revealed more about her feelings when Gamma and Sam had been shot than she had alluded to in sixteen years of marriage.

Charlie kept her focus on Delia Wofford. "What I'm saying is that I didn't remember seeing Kelly the first time until I saw her the second time. Like déjà vu, but real."

"I get it." Delia nodded as she resumed writing. "Go on."

Charlie had to think to find her place. "Kelly hadn't moved between the two times I saw her. Her back was to the wall. Her legs were straight out in front of her. The first time, when I was running up the hall, I remember glancing at her to make sure she was okay. To make sure she wasn't a victim. I didn't see the gun that time. She was dressed in black, like a Goth girl, but I didn't look at her hands." Charlie stopped to take a deep breath. "The violence seemed to be confined to the end of the hall, outside the front office. Mr. Pinkman was on the floor. He looked dead. I should've checked his pulse, but I went to the little girl, to Lucy. Miss Heller was there."

Delia's pen stopped. "Heller?"

"What?"

They stared at each other, both clearly confused.

Ben broke the silence. "Heller is Judith Pinkman's maiden name."

Charlie shook her aching head. Maybe she should've gone to the hospital after all.

"All right." Delia turned to another fresh page. "What was Mrs. Pinkman doing when you saw her at the end of the hallway?"

Again, Charlie had to think back to find her place. "She screamed," Charlie remembered. "Not then, but before. I'm sorry. I left that out. Before, when I was in Huck's room, after he pulled me behind the filing cabinet, we heard a woman screaming. I don't know if it was before or after the bell rang, but she screamed, 'Help us.'"

"Help *us*," Delia confirmed.

"Yes," Charlie said. That was why she had started running, because she knew the excruciating desperation of waiting for someone, anyone, who could help make the world right again.

"And so?" Delia said. "Mrs. Pinkman was where in the hallway?"

"She was kneeling beside Lucy, holding her hand. She was praying. I held Lucy's other hand. I looked into her eyes. She was still alive then. Her eyes were moving, her mouth opened." Charlie tried to swallow down the grief. She had spent the last few hours reliving the girl's death, but saying it out loud was too much. "Miss Heller said another prayer. Lucy's hand let go of mine and . . ."

"She passed?" Delia provided.

Charlie squeezed her hand shut. All these years later, she could still recall what it felt like to hold Sam's trembling fingers inside her own.

She wasn't sure which was harder to witness: a sudden, shocking death or the slow, deliberate way that Lucy Alexander had faded into nothing.

Each existed in its own realm of the unbearable.

Delia asked, "Do you need a moment?"

Charlie let her silence answer the question. She stared past

Ben's shoulder into the mirror. For the first time since they'd locked her in the room, she studied her reflection. She'd dressed down on purpose to go to the school, not wanting to send the wrong message. Jeans, sneakers, a too-big, long-sleeved T-shirt. The faded Duke Devil logo was spattered with blood. Charlie's face wasn't any better. The red discoloration around her right eye was turning into a proper bruise. She pulled the wads of tissue out of her nose. The skin tore like a scab. Tears welled in her eyes.

Delia said, "Take your time."

Charlie didn't want to take her time. "I heard Huck telling the cop to put down his gun. He had a shotgun." She remembered, "He tripped before. The cop with the shotgun. He stepped in some blood and . . ." She shook her head. She could still see the panic on the man's face, the breathless sense of duty. He had been terrified, but like Charlie, he had run toward the danger instead of away.

"I want you to look at these photographs." Delia rifled through her bag again. She spread three photos on the table. Headshots. Three white men. Three crew cuts. Three thick necks. If they hadn't been cops, they would've been mobsters.

Charlie pointed to the one in the middle. "That's who had the shotgun."

Delia said, "Officer Carlson."

Ed Carlson. He'd been a year ahead of Charlie at school. "Carlson was pointing the shotgun at Huck. Huck told him to take it easy, or something like that." She pointed to another photo. The name below said RODGERS, but Charlie had never met him. She said, "Rodgers was there, too. He had a pistol."

"A pistol?"

"A Glock 19," Charlie said.

"You know your weapons?"

"Yes." Charlie had spent the last twenty-eight years learning everything she could about every gun ever made.

Delia asked, "Officers Carlson and Rodgers were pointing their weapons at whom?"

"At Kelly Wilson, but Mr. Huckabee was on his knees in front of her, shielding her, so I guess that technically, they were pointing their weapons at him."

"And what was Kelly Wilson doing at this time?"

Charlie realized she hadn't mentioned the gun. "She had a revolver."

"Five shot? Six?"

"I would only be guessing. It looked older. Not snub-nosed, but—" Charlie stopped. "Was there another gun? Another shooter?"

"Why would you ask that?"

"Because you asked how many shots were fired, and you asked how many bullets were in the revolver."

"I wouldn't extrapolate from my questions, Ms. Quinn. At this point in the investigation, we can say with a high degree of certainty that there was not another gun and there was not another shooter."

Charlie pressed together her lips. Had she heard more than four gunshots in the beginning? Had she heard more than six?

Suddenly, she wasn't certain of anything.

Delia said, "You said that Kelly Wilson had the revolver. What was she doing with it?"

Charlie closed her eyes to give her brain a moment to reset back to the hallway. "Kelly was sitting on the floor like I said. Her back was to the wall. She had the revolver pointed at her chest, like this." Charlie clasped her hands together, miming the way the girl had held the gun with both hands, her thumb looped inside the trigger guard. "She looked like she was going to kill herself."

"Her left thumb was inside the trigger guard?"

Charlie looked at her hands. "Sorry, I'm only guessing. I'm left-handed. I don't know which thumb was inside the trigger guard, but one of them was."

Delia continued writing. "And?"

Charlie said, "Carlson and Rodgers were screaming for Kelly to put down the gun. They were freaked out. We were all freaked out. Except for Huck. I guess he's seen combat or . . ." She didn't speculate. "Huck had his hand out. He told Kelly to give him the revolver."

"Did Kelly Wilson make a statement at any time?"

Charlie wasn't going to validate that Kelly Wilson had spoken, because she didn't trust the two men who had heard her words to relay them truthfully.

She said, "Huck was negotiating Kelly's surrender. She was complying." Charlie's gaze went back to the mirror, where she hoped Ken Coin was about to piss himself. "Kelly placed the revolver in Huck's hand. She had completely relinquished it. That's when Officer Rodgers shot Mr. Huckabee."

Ben opened his mouth to speak, but Delia held up her hand to stop him.

"Where was he shot?" the agent asked.

"Here." Charlie indicated her bicep.

"What was Kelly Wilson's affect during this time?"

"She looked dazed." Charlie silently berated herself for answering the question. "That's just a guess. I don't know her. I'm not an expert. I can't speak to her state of mind."

"Understood," Delia said. "Was Mr. Huckabee unarmed when he was shot?"

"Well, he had the revolver in his hand, but sideways, the way Kelly had put it there."

"Show me?" She took a Glock 45 out of her purse. She dropped the clip, pulled on the slide to eject the cartridge, and placed the gun on the table.

Charlie didn't want to take the Glock. She hated guns, even though she practiced twice a month at the range. She was never, ever going to find herself in another situation where she didn't know how to use a gun.

Delia said, "Ms. Quinn, you don't have to, but it would be help-ful if you could show me the position of the revolver when it was placed in Mr. Huckabee's hand."

"Oh." Charlie felt like a giant lightbulb turned on over her head. She had been so overwhelmed by the murders that she hadn't processed the fact that there was a second investigation into the officer-involved shooting. If Rodgers had moved his gun an inch in the wrong direction, Huck could've been a third body lying in the front office hallway.

"It was like this." Charlie picked up the Glock. The black metal felt cold against her skin. She hefted it into her left hand, but that was wrong. Huck had reached back with his right. She put the gun in her open right palm, turned sideways, muzzle facing backward, the same way Kelly had with the revolver.

Delia already had her cell phone in her hands. She took sev-eral pictures, saying, "You don't mind?" when she knew full well it was too late if Charlie minded. "What happened to the revolver?"

Charlie placed the Glock on the table so that the muzzle pointed toward the back wall. "I don't know. Huck didn't really move. I mean, he flinched, I guess from the pain of a bullet shredding his arm, but he didn't fall down or anything. He told Rodgers to take the revolver, but I don't remember whether or not Rodgers took it, or if someone else did."

Delia's pen had stopped writing. "After Mr. Huckabee was shot, he told Rodgers to take the revolver?"

"Yes. He was very calm about it, but I mean, it was tense, be-cause nobody knew whether or not Rodgers was going to shoot him again. He still had his Glock pointed at Huck. Carlson still had his shotgun."

"But there wasn't another shot fired?"

"No."

"Could you see if anyone had their finger on a trigger?"

"No."

"And you didn't see Mr. Huckabee hand the revolver to anyone?"

"No."

"Did you see him put it anywhere on his person? On the ground?"

"I don't—" Charlie shook her head. "I was more concerned that he had been shot."

"Okay." She made a few more notes before looking up. "What do you remember next?"

Charlie didn't know what she remembered next. Had she looked down at her hands the same way she was looking down at them now? She could remember the sound of heavy breathing from Carlson and Rodgers. Both men had looked as terrified as Charlie had felt, sweating profusely, their chests heaving up and down under the weight of their bulletproof vests.

My girl's that age.

Pink coached me up.

Carlson hadn't buckled his bulletproof vest. The sides had flapped open as he ran into the school with his shotgun. He'd had no idea what he would find when he turned that corner; bodies, carnage, a bullet to the head.

If you've never seen anything like that before, it could break you.

Delia asked, "Ms. Quinn, do you need a moment?"

Charlie thought about the terrified look on Carlson's face when he slipped in the patch of blood. Had there been tears in his eyes? Was he wondering if the dead girl a few feet away from his face was his own child?

"I'd like to go now." Charlie didn't know that she was going to say the words until she heard them come out of her mouth. "I'm leaving."

"You should finish your statement." Delia smiled. "I'll only need a few more minutes."

"I'd like to finish it at a later date." Charlie gripped the table so she could stand. "You said that I'm free to go."

"Absolutely." Delia Wofford again proved unflappable. She handed Charlie one of her business cards. "I look forward to speaking with you again soon."

Charlie took the card. Her vision was still out of focus. Her stomach sloshed acid up into her throat.

Ben said, "I'll take you out the back way. Are you okay to walk to your office?"

Charlie wasn't sure about anything except that she had to get out of here. The walls were closing in. She couldn't breathe through her nose. She was going to suffocate if she didn't get out of this room.

Ben tucked her water bottle into his jacket pocket. He opened the door. Charlie practically fell into the hallway. She braced her hands against the wall opposite the door. Forty years of paint had turned the cinder blocks smooth. She pressed her cheek against the cold surface. She took a few deep breaths and waited for the nausea to pass.

"Charlie?" Ben said.

She turned back around. There was suddenly a river of people between them. The building was teeming with law enforcement. Muscle-bound men and women with big rifles strapped to their wide chests rushed back and forth. State troopers. Sheriff's deputies. Highway patrol. Ben was right; they had all shown up. She saw letters on the backs of their shirts. GBI. FBI. ATF. SWAT. ICE. BOMB SQUAD.

When the hall finally cleared, Ben had his phone in his hands. He was silent as his thumbs moved across the screen.

She leaned against the wall and waited for him to finish texting whoever he was texting. Maybe the twenty-six-year-old from his office. Kaylee Collins. The girl was Ben's type. Charlie knew this because, at that age, she had been her husband's type, too.

"Shit." Ben's thumbs swiped across the screen. "Gimme another second."

Charlie could've walked herself out of the police station. She could've walked the six blocks to her office.

But she didn't.

She studied the top of Ben's head, the way his hair grew from the crown like a spiral ham. She wanted to fold herself into his body. To lose herself in him.

Instead, Charlie silently repeated the phrases she had practiced in her car, in the kitchen, sometimes in front of the bathroom mirror:

I can't live without you.

The last nine months have been the loneliest of my life.

Please come home because I can't take it anymore.

I'm sorry.

I'm sorry.

I'm sorry.

"Plea deal on another case went south." Ben dropped the phone into his jacket pocket. It clinked against Charlie's half-empty water bottle. "Ready?"

She had no choice but to walk. She kept her fingertips to the wall, turning sideways as more cops in black tactical gear passed by. Their expressions were cold, unreadable. They were either going somewhere or coming back from something, their collective jaws set against the world.

This was a school shooting.

Charlie had been so focused on the *what* that she had forgotten the *where*.

She wasn't an expert, but she knew enough about these investigations to understand that every school shooting informed the next one. Columbine, Virginia Tech, Sandy Hook. Law enforcement agencies studied these tragedies in an effort to prevent, or at the very least understand, the next one.

The ATF would comb the middle school for bombs because others had used bombs before. The GBI would look for accomplices because sometimes, rarely, there were accomplices. Canine officers would hunt for suspicious backpacks in the halls. They would check every locker, every teacher's desk, every closet for explosives. Investigators would look for Kelly's diary or a hit list, diagrams of the school, stashes of weaponry, a plan of assault. Tech people would look at computers, phones, Facebook pages, Snapchat accounts. Everyone would search for a motive, but what motive could they find? What answer could an eighteen-year-old offer to explain why she had decided to commit cold-blooded murder?

That was Rusty's problem now. Exactly the kind of thorny, moral and legal issue that got him out of bed in the morning.

Exactly the kind of law that Charlie had never wanted to practice.

"Come on." Ben walked ahead of her. He had a long, loping stride because he always put too much weight on the balls of his feet.

Was Kelly Wilson being abused? That would be Rusty's first line of inquiry. Was there some sort of mitigating circumstance that would keep her off death row? She had been held back at least one year in school. Did that indicate a low IQ? Diminished capacity? Was Kelly Wilson capable of telling right from wrong? Could she participate in her own defense, as required by law?

Ben pushed open the exit door.

Was Kelly Wilson a bad seed? Was the explanation here the only explanation that would never make sense? Would Delia Wofford tell Lucy Alexander's parents and Mrs. Pinkman that the reason they lost their loved ones was because Kelly Wilson was bad?

"Charlie," Ben said. He was holding open the door. His iPhone was back in his hand.

Charlie shielded her eyes as she walked outside. The sunlight was as sharp as a blade. Tears rolled down her cheeks.

"Here." Ben handed her a pair of sunglasses. They belonged to her. He must have gotten them out of her car.

Charlie took the glasses but couldn't put them on her tender nose. She opened her mouth for air. The sudden heat was too much. She leaned down, hand braced on her knee.

"Are you going to be sick?"

"No," she said, then "maybe," then she threw up just enough to make a splatter.

Ben didn't step back. He managed to gather her hair away from her face without touching her skin. Charlie retched two more times before he asked, "All right?"

"Maybe." Charlie opened her mouth. She waited for more. A line of spit came out, but nothing else. "Okay."

He let her hair drop back around her shoulders. "The paramedic told me that you have a concussion."

Charlie couldn't lift her head, but she told him, "There's nothing they can do about it."

"They can monitor you for symptoms like nausea and blurred vision and headaches and forgetting names and not tracking when you're asked a simple question."

"They wouldn't know the names I was forgetting," she said. "I don't want to spend the night in a hospital."

"Stay at the HP." The higgledy-piggledy. Sam's name for the meandering farmhouse had stuck. Ben said, "Rusty can watch you."

"So I die from secondhand smoke instead of a brain aneurysm?"

"That's not funny."

Head still down, Charlie reached back for the wall. The feel of the solid concrete block gave her enough steadiness to risk standing up straight. She cupped her hand to her eyes. She remembered cupping her hand to the window of the front office this morning.

Ben handed her the water bottle. He had already taken the top off for her. She took a few slow sips and tried not to read too much into his thoughtfulness. Her husband was thoughtful with everybody.

She asked, "Where was Mrs. Jenkins when the shooting started?"

"In the file room."

"Did she see anything?"

"Rusty will find out everything during discovery."

"Everything," Charlie repeated. In the coming months, Ken Coin would be required by law to turn over any material in the investigation that could be reasonably interpreted as evidence. Coin's idea of "reasonable" was as fixed as a spider's web.

She asked Ben, "Is Mrs. Pinkman okay?"

He didn't bring up her "Heller" slip because that wasn't his way. "She's at the hospital. They had to sedate her."

Charlie should visit her, but she knew that she would find an excuse not to. "You let me think Kelly Wilson was sixteen years old."

"I thought you could figure it out by holding a sphere in your hand and pulling apart time."

Charlie laughed. "That was some next-level bullshit I laid down in there."

"There's some out here, too."

Charlie wiped her mouth with the back of her sleeve. She smelled dried blood again. Like everything else, she remembered the smell from before. She remembered the dark flecks falling like ash from her hair. She remembered that even after she'd bathed, even after she'd scrubbed herself raw, the odor of death had lingered.

She said, "You called me this morning."

Ben shrugged like it didn't matter.

Charlie poured the rest of the water onto her hands to clean them. "Have you talked to your mom and your sisters? They'll be worried."

"We talked." He did that shrug again. "I should go back in."

Charlie waited, but he didn't go back in. She grappled for a reason to make him stay. "How's Barkzilla?"

"Barky." Ben took the empty bottle. He screwed on the cap. He dropped it back into his jacket pocket. "How's Eleanor Roosevelt?"

"Quiet."

He tucked his chin into his chest, returning to silence. This was nothing new. Her normally articulate husband had not articulated much to her in the past nine months.

But he wasn't leaving. He wasn't nodding her along, urging her to go. He wasn't telling her that the only reason he wasn't asking her if she was okay was because she would say that she was okay even if she wasn't. Especially if she wasn't.

She asked, "Why did you call me this morning?"

Ben groaned. He leaned his head back against the wall.

Charlie leaned her head back against the wall, too.

She studied the sharp line of his jaw. This was her type—a lanky, laid-back nerd who could quote *Monty Python* as easily as the United States constitution. He read graphic novels. He drank a glass of milk every night before he went to bed. He loved potato salad, and *Lord of the Rings*, and model trains. He preferred fantasy football to the real kind. He could not put on weight if you force-fed him butter. He was six feet tall when he stood up straight, which didn't happen often.

She loved him so much that her heart literally hurt at the thought of never holding him again.

Ben said, "Peggy had this friend when she was fourteen. Her name was Violet."

Peggy was the bossiest of his three older sisters.

"She was killed in a car crash. She was on her bicycle. We went to the funeral. I don't know what my mom was thinking, taking me. I was too young to see that kind of thing. It was open casket. Carla held me up so I could see her." His throat worked. "I, like, lost my shit. Mom had to take me out into the parking lot. It gave me nightmares. I thought that was the worst thing that I would ever see. A dead kid. A dead little girl. But she was cleaned up. You couldn't see what had happened, that the car had hit her in the back. That she had bled to death, but inside. Not like the girl today. Not like what I saw at the school."

There were tears in his eyes. Each word out of his mouth broke another piece of Charlie's heart. She had to clench her fists to keep from reaching out to him.

Ben said, "Murder is murder. I can deal with that. Dealers. Gangbangers. Even domestic violence. But a kid? A little girl?" He kept shaking his head. "She didn't look like she was sleeping, did she?"

"No."

"She looked like she had been murdered. Like someone had fired a gun at her throat and the bullet ripped it open and she died a horrible, violent death."

Charlie looked up into the sun because she didn't want to see Lucy Alexander dying all over again.

Ben said, "The guy's a war hero. Did you know that?"

He was talking about Huck.

"He saved a platoon or something, but he won't talk about it because he's like fucking Batman or something." Ben pushed himself away from the wall, away from Charlie. "And this morning, he took a bullet in his arm. To save a murderer, whom he kept from getting murdered. And then he stood up for the guy who almost killed him. He lied in a sworn statement to keep another guy out of trouble. He's so fucking handsome, right?" Ben was angry now, but his voice was low, shrunken by the humiliation that came courtesy of his bitch wife. "A guy like that, you see him walking down the street, you don't know whether you want to fuck him or have a beer with him."

Charlie looked down at the ground. They knew she had done both.

"Lenore's here."

Rusty's secretary had pulled up to the gate in her red Mazda.

Charlie said, "Ben, I'm sorry. It was a mistake. An awful, awful mistake."

"Did you let him on top?"

"Of course not. Don't be ridiculous."

Lenore tapped the horn. She rolled down her window and waved. Charlie waved back, her hand splayed, trying to let Lenore know that she needed a minute.

"Ben—"

It was too late. Ben was already pulling the door closed behind him.

CHAPTER FOUR

Charlie sniffed her sunglasses as she walked toward Lenore's car. She knew she was acting like a foolish girl in a teen romance, but she wanted to smell Ben. What she got instead was a whiff of her own sweat tinged with vomit.

Lenore leaned across the car to push open the door. "You put those on your nose, sweetheart, not in front of it."

Charlie couldn't put anything on her nose. She tossed the cheap glasses onto the dashboard as she got in. "Did Daddy send you?"

"Ben texted me, but, listen, your dad wants us to fetch the Wilsons and bring them back to the office. Coin's trying to execute a search warrant. I brought your court clothes to change into."

Charlie had started shaking her head as soon as she heard the words "your dad wants." She asked, "Where's Rusty?"

"At the hospital with the Wilson girl."

Charlie huffed a laugh. Ben had really honed his deception skills. "How long before Dad figured out she wasn't being held at the station?"

"Over an hour."

Charlie put on her seat belt. "I was thinking how much Coin loves to play his games." She had no doubt the district attorney had put Kelly Wilson in the back of an ambulance for the trip to the hospital. By maintaining the illusion that she wasn't in police custody, he could argue that any statement she made absent counsel was voluntary. "She's eighteen years old."

"Rusty told me. The girl was practically catatonic at the hospital. He barely got her mama's phone number out of her."

"That's how she was when I saw her. Almost in a fugue state." Charlie hoped Kelly Wilson snapped out of it soon. At the moment, she was Rusty's most vital source of information. Until he received the discovery materials from Ken Coin—witness lists, police statements, investigators' notes, forensics—her father would be flying blind.

Lenore put her hand on the gear. "Where am I taking you?"

Charlie pictured herself at home, standing under a hot shower, surrounding herself with pillows in bed. And then she remembered that Ben wouldn't be there and said, "I guess to the Wilsons."

"They live on the backside of the Holler." Lenore put the car in gear. She made a wide U-turn and drove up the street. "There's no street address. Your dad sent me country directions—take a left at the old white dog, take a right at the crooked oak tree."

"That's good news for Kelly, I guess." Rusty could break a search warrant that didn't have the right address or at least a proper description of the house. The odds were against Ken Coin to come up with either. There were hundreds of rental houses and trailers up and down the Holler. No one knew exactly how many people lived there, what their names were or whether or not their children were attending school. The slumlords didn't bother with leases or background checks so long as the right amount of cash showed up every week.

Charlie asked, "How long do you think we have before Ken locates the house?"

"No idea. They brought in a helicopter from Atlanta an hour ago, but from what I can tell, it's on the other side of the mountain."

Charlie knew that she could find the Wilson house. She was in the Holler at least twice a month chasing down past-due legal bills. Ben had been horrified when she'd casually mentioned her nighttime excursions. Sixty percent of the crime in Pikeville was committed in or near Sadie's Holler.

Lenore said, "I packed a sandwich for you."

"I'm not hungry." Charlie looked at the clock on the dash: 11:52 AM. Less than five hours ago, she'd been looking inside the darkened front office at the middle school. Less than ten minutes after that, two people were dead, another was shot, and Charlie was about to get her nose broken.

Lenore said, "You should eat."

"I will." Charlie stared out the window. Sunlight strobed through the tall trees behind the buildings. The flickering light flashed images into her mind like an old-timey slideshow. Charlie allowed herself the rare indulgence of lingering on the ones of Gamma and Sam—running down the long driveway to the farmhouse, giggling over a thrown plastic fork. She knew what came later, so she fast-forwarded until Sam and Gamma were firmly back in the past and all that remained was the aftermath of this morning.

Lucy Alexander. Mr. Pinkman.

A little girl. A middle-school principal.

The victims didn't seem to have much in common except that they had been in the wrong place at the wrong time. If Charlie had to guess, she would assume that Kelly Wilson's plan was to stand in the middle of the hall, revolver out in front of her, and wait for the bell to ring.

Then little Lucy Alexander rounded the corner.

Pop.

Then Mr. Pinkman rushed out of his office.

Pop-pop-pop.

Then the bell had rung and, but for some quick-thinking staff, a sea of fresh victims would have rushed down that same hallway.

Goth. Loner. Held back a grade.

Kelly Wilson was the exact type of girl who got bullied. Alone at the lunch table, last to get picked during gym, attending the school dance with a boy who only wanted one thing.

Why had Kelly picked up a gun when Charlie hadn't?

Lenore said, "At least drink that Coke in the cooler. It'll help with the shock."

"I'm not in shock."

"I bet you think your nose isn't broken, either."

"Actually, I do think it's broken." Lenore's persistent mentions of Charlie's health finally made Charlie aware that her health wasn't that great. Her head was in a vise. Her nose had its own heartbeat. Her eyelids felt like they were weighed down with honey. She gave in for a few seconds, letting them close, welcoming the blankness.

Over the hum of the engine, she could hear Lenore's feet working the pedals as she shifted gears. She always drove barefooted with her high heels on the floor beside her. She tended toward short skirts and colored stockings. The look was too young for a seventy-year-old woman, but considering that Charlie currently had more hair on her legs than Lenore, she couldn't sit in judgment.

"You need to drink some of that Coke," Lenore said.

Charlie opened her eyes. The world was still there.

"Now."

Charlie was too exhausted to argue. She found the cooler wedged against the seat. She took out the Coke but left the sandwich. Instead of opening the bottle, she held it to the back of her neck. "Can I have some aspirin?"

"Nope. Raises the risk of bleeding."

Charlie would've welcomed a coma over the pain. There was something about the bright sun that had turned her head into a giant, ringing bell. "What's that thing you get in your ears?"

"Tinnitus," Lenore said. "I'll stop the car if you don't start drinking that Coke right now."

"And let the police get to the Wilson house before we do?"

"They'd have to leave out on this road, for one, and for two, even if they find the location of the house, and even if they have a judge standing by, it'll take at least half an hour to put the warrant together and three, shut the hell up and do what I tell you before I pop you on the leg."

Charlie used her T-shirt to twist off the cap. She sipped the Coke and watched downtown slip into the side mirror.

Lenore asked, "Did you throw up?"

"Pass." Charlie felt her stomach clench again. The world outside was too disorienting. She had to close her eyes to regain her equilibrium.

The slideshow popped into her head again: Lucy Alexander. Mr. Pinkman. Gamma. Sam. Charlie clicked through the images quickly like she was searching for a file on her computer.

What had she said to special agent Delia Wofford that might hurt Kelly Wilson's defense? Rusty would want to know. He would also want to know about the number and sequence of gunshots, the capacity of the revolver, what Kelly had whispered when Huck was begging her to give him the gun.

That last part would be crucial to Kelly Wilson's defense. If she had made an admission, if she had offered a glib comment or stated a grim motive for her crimes, then no amount of oratory flourish on Rusty's part would save her from the needle. Ken Coin would never turn such a high-profile prosecution over to the state. He had argued two capital cases before. No jury in Pikeville would refuse his request for death by lethal injection. Coin spoke with a particular authority. Back when he was a police officer, he'd executed a man with his own hands.

Twenty-eight years ago, Daniel Culpepper, Zachariah Culpepper's brother, had been sitting in his trailer watching television when Officer Ken Coin had rolled up in his squad car. It was eight thirty in the evening. Gamma's body had already been found at the farmhouse. Sam was bleeding her life away in the shallow stream that ran under the weather tower. Thirteen-year-old Charlie was sitting in the back of an ambulance begging the paramedics to let her go home. Officer Coin had kicked down the front door to Daniel Culpepper's trailer. The suspect had grabbed his gun. Coin had shot the nineteen-year-old seven times in the chest.

To this day, the majority of the Culpepper clan insisted on Daniel's innocence, but the evidence against the kid was incontrovertible. The revolver found in Daniel's hand was later identified as the same weapon that had been used to shoot Sam in the head. Daniel's blood-covered jeans and distinctive blue hightops were found smoldering in a burn barrel behind the trailer. Even his own brother said they both went to the HP to kill Rusty. They were worried they would lose their home over some stupid legal bill they assumed would come due after the Quinns lost everything in the fire. Charlie was left to survive the ordeal with the knowledge that her family's life had been reduced to the price of a used trailer.

Lenore said, "We're going past the school."

Charlie opened her eyes. Pikeville Middle School had been Pikeville Junior High when Charlie was a student. The building had sprawled over the years, hastily overbuilt to accommodate the twelve hundred students pulled in from the neighboring communities. The high school beside it was even larger, meant to house almost two thousand kids.

She saw the empty space where her car had been parked. Police tape cordoned off the lot. There were other cars that belonged to teachers scattered among the police cruisers, government sedans, ambulances, fire trucks, crime scene buses, the coroner's van. A news helicopter was flying low over the gymnasium. The scene felt surreal, like a director would yell "cut" and everyone would take lunch.

Charlie said, "Mrs. Pinkman had to be sedated."

"She's a good woman. She doesn't deserve this. Nobody does."

Charlie nodded because she couldn't talk past the glass in her throat. Judith Heller Pinkman had been a weird touchstone to Charlie over the years. They would see each other in the hall when Charlie finally went back to school. Miss Heller always smiled, but she didn't push Charlie, didn't force her to talk about the tragedy behind their connection. She kept her distance, which, in retrospect, took a kind of discipline that most people didn't possess.

Lenore asked, "I wonder how long the media attention will last?" She was looking up at the helicopter. "Two victims. That's quaint compared to most mass shootings."

"Girls don't kill. At least, not like this."

" 'I Don't Like Mondays.' "

"In general, or do you mean the Boomtown Rats' song?"

"The song." Lenore said, "It's based on a shooting. 1979. A sixteen-year-old girl took a sniper rifle to a playground. I forget how many she killed. When the cops asked her why she did it, she said, 'I don't like Mondays.' "

"Jesus," Charlie whispered, hoping like hell that Kelly Wilson hadn't been that callous when she had whispered whatever she'd said in the hallway.

And then Charlie wondered why she cared about Kelly Wilson, because the girl was a murderer.

Charlie was jarred by the sudden clarity of thought.

Take away all that had happened this morning—the fear, the deaths, the memories, the heartache—and Charlie was left with one simple truth: *Kelly Wilson had murdered two people in cold blood.*

Unbidden, Rusty's voice intruded: *So what?*

Kelly still had a right to a trial. She still had a right to the best defense she could find. Charlie had said as much to the angry group of cops who had wanted to beat the girl to death, but now, sitting in the car with Lenore, Charlie wondered if she had come to the girl's defense simply because no one else would.

Another personality flaw that had become a sore point in her marriage.

She reached into the back seat, this time for her court clothes. She found what Ben called her Amish shirt and what Charlie considered one step up from a burka. The Pikeville judges, all of them cranky old men, were an aggressively conservative lot. Female lawyers had to choose between wearing long skirts and chaste blouses or having every objection, every motion, every word out of their mouth overruled.

Lenore asked, "Are you okay?"

"No, not really." Letting out the truth took some of the pressure off of her chest. Charlie had always told Lenore things that she would never admit to anyone else. Lenore had known Rusty for over fifty years. She was a black hole into which all of the Quinn family secrets disappeared. "My head is killing me. My nose is broken. I feel like I threw up a lung. I can't even see to read, and none of that matters because I cheated on Ben last night."

Lenore silently shifted gears as she pulled onto the two-lane highway.

Charlie said, "It was okay while it lasted. I mean, he got the job done." She carefully peeled off her Duke T-shirt, trying not to bump her nose. "I woke up crying this morning. I couldn't stop. I just lay in bed for half an hour staring up at the ceiling and wanting to kill myself. And then the phone rang."

Lenore shifted again. They were leaving the Pikeville city limits. The wind off the mountains buffeted the compact sedan.

"I shouldn't have picked up the stupid phone. I couldn't even remember his name. He couldn't remember mine. At least he pretended not to. It was embarrassing and sordid and now Ben knows. The GBI knows. Everyone in his office knows."

Charlie said, "That's why I was at the school this morning, to meet the guy because I took his phone by mistake and he called and . . ." She put on her court shirt, a starched button-up with ruffles down the front to assure the judges that she was taking this woman thing seriously. "I don't know what I was thinking."

Lenore shifted into sixth. "That you were lonely."

Charlie laughed, though there was nothing funny about the truth. She watched her fingers as she buttoned the shirt. The buttons were suddenly too small. Or maybe it was that her hands were sweating. Or maybe it was that the tremble was back in her fingers, the vibration of bone that felt like a tuning fork had been struck against her chest.

"Baby," Lenore said. "Let it out."

Charlie shook her head. She didn't want to let it out. She wanted to hold it back, to put all the horrible images in their box, shove it onto a shelf, and never open it ever again.

But then a teardrop fell.

Then another.

Then Charlie was crying, then she was sobbing so hard that she doubled over, her head in her hands, because the grief was too much to carry.

Lucy Alexander. Mr. Pinkman. Miss Heller. Gamma. Sam. Ben.

The car slowed. The tires bumped against gravel as Lenore pulled to the side of the road. She rubbed Charlie's back. "It's okay, baby."

It wasn't okay. She wanted her husband. She wanted her useless asshole of a father. Where was Rusty? Why was he never there when she needed him?

"It's okay." Lenore kept rubbing Charlie's back and Charlie kept crying because it was never going to be all right.

From the moment Charlie had heard those first gunshots in Huck's room, the entirety of the most violent hour of her life had snapped back into her waking memory. She kept hearing the same words over and over again. Keep running. Don't look back. Into the woods. To Miss Heller's house. Up the school hallway. Toward the gunshots. But she was too late. Charlie was always too fucking late.

Lenore stroked back Charlie's hair. "Deep breaths, sweetheart."

Charlie realized she was starting to hyperventilate. Her vision blurred. Sweat broke out on her forehead. She made herself breathe until her lungs could take in more than a teaspoonful of air at a time.

"Take your time," Lenore said.

Charlie took a few more deep breaths. Her vision cleared, at least as much as it was going to. She took another series of breaths, holding them for a second, maybe two, to prove to herself that she could.

"Better?"

Charlie whispered, "Was that a panic attack?"

"Might still be one."

"Help me up." Charlie reached for Lenore's hand. The blood rushed from her head. Instinctively, she touched her aching nose, and the pain intensified.

Lenore said, "You really got whacked, sweetheart."

"You should see the other guy. Not a scratch on him."

Lenore didn't laugh.

Charlie said, "I'm sorry. I don't know what came over me."

"Don't be stupid. You know what came over you."

"Yeah, well," Charlie said, the two words she always said when she didn't want to talk about something.

Instead of putting the car in gear, Lenore's long fingers laced through Charlie's smaller ones. For all her miniskirts, she still had man hands, wide with knobby knuckles and lately, age spots. In many ways, Charlie had gotten more of her mothering from Lenore than Gamma. It was Lenore who showed her how to wear makeup, who took Charlie to the store to buy her first box of tampons, who warned her to never ever trust a man to take care of birth control.

Charlie said, "Ben texted you to pick me up. That's something, right?"

"It is."

Charlie opened the glove box and found some tissue. She couldn't blow her nose. She patted underneath. She squinted her eyes out the window, relieved that she could see things rather than shapes. Unfortunately, the view was the worst one possible. They were three hundred yards away from where Daniel Culpepper had been shot in his trailer.

Charlie said, "The really shitty thing is that I can't even say that today was the worst day of my life."

Lenore laughed this time, a husky, deep-throated acknowledgment that Charlie was right. She worked the gears and pulled back onto the highway. The going was smooth until she slowed for the turn onto Culpepper Road. Deep potholes gave way to gravel, which eventually turned into packed red clay. There was a subtle change in the temperature, maybe a few degrees, as they drove down the mountain. Charlie resisted the urge to shiver. Her trepidation felt like a thing she could hold in her hand. The hairs on the back of her neck rose up. She always felt this way when she came into the Holler. It wasn't only the sense of not belonging, but the knowledge that the wrong turn, the wrong Culpepper, and physical danger would no longer be an abstract concept.

"Shit!" Lenore startled when a pack of dogs rushed a chain-link fence. Their frenzied barking sounded like a thousand hammers pounding against the car.

"Redneck alarm," Charlie told her. You couldn't step foot in the Holler without a hundred dogs howling your arrival. The deeper in you went, the more young white men you'd see standing on their front porches, one hand holding their cell phone and the other under their shirt rubbing their belly. These young men were capable of work, but they eschewed the labor-intensive jobs for which they were qualified. They smoked dope all day, played video games, stole when they needed money, beat their girlfriends when they wanted Oxy, sent their kids to pick up their disability checks at the post office, and let their glorious life choices form the backbone of Charlie's legal practice.

She felt a flash of guilt for painting the entire Holler with the Culpepper brush. She knew that some good people lived here. They were hardworking, striving men and women whose only sin was to be poor, but Charlie could not help the knee-jerk reaction to the taint of proximity.

There had been six Culpepper girls of various ages who had made Charlie's life a living hell when she went back to school. They were flea-bitten, nasty bitches with long painted fingernails and filthy mouths. They bullied Charlie. They stole her lunch money. They ripped up her textbooks. One of them had even left a pile of shit in her gym bag.

To this day, the family insisted that Charlie had lied about seeing Zachariah with the shotgun. They figured she was guided by some glorious scheme on Rusty's part to lay claim to the meager life insurance policy and two-bedroom trailer that was up for grabs after Daniel had died and Zachariah was sent to prison. As if a man who had made it his life's work to see justice done would trade his morality for a few pieces of silver.

The fact that Rusty had never sued the family for a penny did nothing to temper their wild conspiracy theories. They continued to firmly believe that Ken Coin planted the abundance of evidence found at the trailer and on Daniel's person. That Coin murdered Daniel to kick-start his political career. That Coin's brother, Keith, helped alter evidence at the state lab.

Still, it was Charlie who was on the receiving end of the majority of their rage. She had identified the brothers. The lies had not only started at her lips, but she continued to insist they were true. Thus the murder of one Culpepper brother and the death-row confinement of another rested squarely on her shoulders.

They weren't entirely off the mark, at least not where Zachariah was concerned. Despite Rusty's scathing disapproval, thirteen-year-old Charlie had stood in front of a packed courtroom and asked the judge to sentence Zachariah Culpepper to death. She would've done the same at Daniel's trial if Ken Coin hadn't robbed her of the pleasure.

"What is that racket?" Lenore asked.

Charlie heard the chopping sound of a helicopter overhead. She recognized the logo from one of the Atlanta news stations.

Lenore handed Charlie her phone. "Read me the directions."

Charlie dialed in the passcode, which was her own birthday, and pulled up Rusty's text. Her father had graduated from the University of Georgia law school and was one of the best known trial lawyers in the state, but he couldn't spell for shit. "Left up here," she told Lenore, pointing to a track marked by a white flagpole with a large Confederate flag. "Then right at this trailer."

Charlie skimmed ahead, recognizing the route as one she had taken before. She had a client with a meth problem he financed by selling to other junkies with meth problems. He had tried to pay her in crystal once. Apparently, he lived two doors down from the Wilsons. She said, "Take a right up here, then another right at the bottom of the hill."

"I stuck your fee agreement in your purse."

Charlie felt her lips purse to ask why, but then she answered her own question. "Dad wants me to represent the Wilsons so it burns me as a witness against Kelly."

Lenore looked at her, then looked at her again. "How did you miss that twenty minutes ago?"

"I don't know," Charlie said, but she did know. Because she was traumatized. Because she ached for her husband. Because she was such an idiot that again and again she expected her father to be the kind of person who worried about his daughter the way he worried about pimps and gangbangers and murderers. "I can't do it. Any judge worth his salt would slap me so hard with a bar complaint I'd be in China before my license to practice was revoked."

"You won't have to chase chicken bones up and down the Holler once you settle your lawsuit." She nodded to her phone. "You need to take some pictures of your face while the bruises are fresh."

"I told Ben I'm not filing a lawsuit."

Lenore's foot slipped off the gas.

"All I want is a sincere apology. In writing."

"An apology isn't going to change anything." They had reached the bottom of the hill. Lenore took a sharp right. Charlie didn't have to wait long for the lecture that was brewing. "Assholes like Ken Coin preach about small government, but they end up spending twice as much on lawsuits as they would on training cops the right way in the first place."

"I know."

"The only way to make them change is to hit them in the pocketbook."

Charlie wanted to stick her fingers into her ears. "I'm going to get this from Dad. I don't need it from you. It's here."

Lenore hit the brakes. The car lurched. She backed up a few feet, then turned onto another dirt track. Weeds sprung up between the wheel grooves. They passed a yellow school bus parked under a weeping willow. The Mazda bumped over a ridge, then a cluster of small houses came into view. There were four in all, scattered around a wide oval. Charlie checked Rusty's text again, and matched the number to the house on the far right. There was no driveway, only the edge of the track. The house was made of painted chipboard. A large bay window blistered out in the front like a ripe pimple. Cinder blocks served as front steps.

Lenore said, "Ava Wilson drives a bus. She was at the school this morning when they locked down the building."

"Did someone tell her that Kelly was the shooter?"

"She didn't find out until Rusty called her cell."

Charlie was glad Rusty hadn't stuck her with making that phone call. "Is the father in the picture?"

"Ely Wilson. He works day labor down in Ellijay, one of those guys who waits outside the lumber yard every morning for some-body to put him to work."

"Have the police located him?"

"Not that we know of. The family only has one cell phone, and the wife has it."

Charlie stared at the sad-looking house. "So she's in there alone."

"Not for long." Lenore looked up as another helicopter hovered into view. This one was painted in the distinctive blue and silver stripes of the Georgia State Patrol. "They'll pop a Google map on the warrant and be here in half an hour."

"I'll be quick." Charlie went to get out of the car, but Lenore stopped her.

"Here." Lenore pulled Charlie's purse from the back seat. "Ben gave me this when he brought back your car."

Charlie wrapped her hand around the strap, wondering if she was holding the bag the same way Ben had. "That's something, right?"

"It is."

Charlie got out of the car and walked toward the house. She rummaged around in her purse for some breath mints. She had to settle for a handful of furry Tic Tacs stuck like lice into the seams of the front pocket.

She had learned the hard way that Holler people generally an-swered the door with some kind of weapon in their hands, so in-stead of traversing the cinder block front steps, she walked to the bay window. There were no curtains. Three pots of geraniums were underneath. There was a glass ashtray resting on the soil, but it was empty.

Inside, Charlie could see a petite, dark-haired woman sitting on the couch, transfixed by the image on the television. Everyone in the Holler had a giant, flat-screen TV that had apparently fallen off the same truck. Ava Wilson had the news on. The sound was up so high that the reporter's voice was audible from outside.

"*. . . new details coming in from our Atlanta affiliate . . .*"

Charlie went to the front door and knocked, three sharp raps.

She waited. She listened. She knocked a second time. Then a third.

"Hello?" she called.

Finally, the television was muted. She heard the shuffling of feet. A lock clicking back. A chain sliding. Another lock opening. The extra security was a joke considering a thief could punch his hand through the flimsy wall.

Ava Wilson blinked at the stranger outside her door. She was as small as her daughter, with the same almost childlike quality. She was wearing light blue pajamas with cartoon elephants on the pants. Her eyes were bloodshot. She was younger than Charlie, but shoots of gray ran through her dark brown hair.

"I'm Charlie Quinn," she told the woman. "My father, Rusty Quinn, is your daughter's attorney. He asked me to pick you up and take you to his office."

The woman did not move. She did not speak. This was what shock looked like.

Charlie asked, "Have the police spoken to you?"

"No, ma'am," she said, her Holler accent blending together the words. "Your daddy told me not to answer the phone unless I recognized the number."

"He's right." Charlie shifted on her feet. She could hear dogs barking in the distance. The sun was burning the top of her head. "Look, I know you're devastated about your daughter, but I need to prepare you for what's coming next. The police are on their way here right now."

"Are they bringing Kelly home?"

Charlie was thrown off by the hopefulness in Ava Wilson's voice. "No. They're going to search your house. They'll probably start in Kelly's room, then—"

"Will they take her some clean clothes?"

Again, Charlie was thrown. "No, they're going to search the house for weapons, any notes, computers—"

"We don't got a computer."

"Okay, that's good. Did Kelly do her schoolwork at the library?"

"She didn't do anything," Ava said. "She didn't kill . . ." Her voice trailed off. Her eyes glistened. "Ma'am, you gotta hear me. My baby didn't do what they're saying."

Charlie had dealt with her share of mothers who were convinced that their children were being framed, but there was no time to give Ava Wilson the speech about how sometimes good people did bad things. "Listen to me, Ava. The police are going to come in whether you let them or not. They'll remove you from the house. They'll do a thorough search. They might break things or find things you don't want them to find. I doubt they'll hold you in custody, but they might if they think you're going to alter evidence, so please don't do that. You cannot, please, hear me on this: you cannot say anything to them about Kelly or why she might have done this or what might have happened. They are not trying to help her and they are not her friends. Understand?"

Ava did not acknowledge the information. She just stood there.

The helicopter swooped lower. Charlie could see the pilot's face behind the bubbled glass. He was talking into the mic, probably giving the coordinates for the search warrant.

She asked Ava, "Can we go inside?"

The woman didn't move, so Charlie took her by the arm and led her into the house. "Have you heard from your husband?"

"Ely don't call until he's done working, from the payphone outside the lumber yard."

Which meant that Kelly's father would probably learn about his daughter's crimes from his car radio. "Do you have a suitcase or a small bag you can put some clothes in?"

Ava did not answer. Her eyes were fixed on the muted television.

The middle school was on the news. An aerial shot showed the top of the gymnasium, which was likely being used as a staging ground. The scroll at the bottom of the screen read: BOMB SQUAD SWEPT BUILDING FOR SUSPICIOUS DEVICES. TWO DEAD—8-YEAR-OLD STUDENT, HERO PRINCIPAL WHO TRIED TO SAVE HER.

Lucy Alexander was only eight years old.

"She didn't do this," Ava said. "She wouldn't."

Lucy's cold hand.

Sam's trembling fingers.

The sudden white waxiness of Gamma's skin.

Charlie wiped her eyes. She glanced around the room, fighting against the slideshow of horror that had returned to her head. The Wilson house was shabby, but tidy. A Jesus hung on a cross by the front door. The galley kitchen was right off the cramped living room. Dishes were drying in the rack. Yellow gloves were folded limply over the edge of the sink. The counter was cluttered, but there was order to it.

Charlie told Ava, "You're not going to be allowed back in the house for a while. You'll need a change of clothes, some toiletries."

"The toilet's right behind you."

Charlie tried again. "You need to pack some things." She waited to see if Ava understood. "Clothes, toothbrushes. Nothing else."

Ava nodded, but she either could not or would not look away from the television.

Outside, the helicopter lifted away. Charlie was burning through time. Coin had probably gotten his warrant signed by now. The search team would be en route from town, full lights and sirens.

She asked Ava, "Do you want me to pack some things for you?" Charlie waited for another nod. And waited. "Ava, I'm going to get some clothes for you, then we're going to wait outside for the police."

Ava clutched the remote in her hand as she sat on the edge of the couch.

Charlie opened kitchen cabinets until she found a plastic grocery bag. She slipped on one of the yellow dishwashing gloves from the sink, then walked past the bathroom down the short, paneled hallway. There were two bedrooms, both of them taking up one end of the house. Instead of a door, Kelly had a purple curtain for privacy. The sheet of notebook paper pinned to the material said NO ADULTS ALOWT.

Charlie knew better than to go into a murder suspect's room, but she used Lenore's phone to take a picture of the sign.

The Wilsons' bedroom was on the right, facing a steep hill behind the house. They slept in a large waterbed that took up most of the space. A tall chest of drawers kept the door from opening all the way. Charlie was glad she'd thought to put on the yellow glove as she opened the drawers, though to be honest, the Wilsons were neater than she was. She found some women's underwear, a few pairs of boxers, and a pair of jeans that looked like they came from the children's department. She grabbed two more T-shirts and shoved all of the clothes into the plastic grocery bag. Ken Coin was notorious for needlessly drawing out his searches. The Wilsons would be lucky if they were allowed back into their home by the weekend.

Charlie turned around, planning to go to the bathroom next, but something stopped her.

ALOWT.

How could Kelly Wilson reach the age of eighteen without knowing how to spell such a simple word?

Charlie hesitated once, then pulled back the curtain. She wouldn't enter the room. She would take pictures from the hall. Not as easy as it sounded. The bedroom was the size of a generous walk-in closet.

Or a prison cell.

Light slanted in from the narrow, horizontal window mounted high over the twin bed. The paneling on the walls had been painted a light lilac. The carpet was orange shag. The bedspread had Hello Kitty listening to a Walkman with large headphones over her ears.

This was not a Goth girl's room. There were no black walls and heavy metal posters. The closet door was open. Stacks of shirts were neatly folded on the floor. A few longer pieces hung from a sagging rod. Kelly's clothes were all lightly colored with ponies and rabbits and the sort of appliqués you would expect a ten-year-old girl to wear, not an eighteen-year-old almost woman.

Charlie photographed everything she could: the bedspread, the posters of kittens, the candy-pink lip gloss on top of the dresser. All the while, her focus was on the things that weren't there. Eighteen-year-olds had all kinds of makeup. They had pictures with their friends and notes from possible future boyfriends and secrets that they kept all to themselves.

Her heart jumped when she heard wheels spinning down the dirt track. She stood on the bed and looked out the window. A black van with SWAT on the side slowed to a stop in front of the yellow school bus. Two guys with rifles drawn jumped out of the van and entered the bus.

"How . . ." Charlie started to say, but then she realized it didn't matter how they'd managed to get here so quickly, because as soon as they cleared the bus, they would tear apart the house that she was standing in.

But Charlie wasn't exactly standing in the house. She was standing on Kelly Wilson's bed inside Kelly Wilson's bedroom.

"Fuck me," she whispered, because there was no other way to put it. She jumped off the bed. She used her rubber-gloved hand to swipe away the dirt from her tennis shoes. The deep purple fabric hid the grooves but a forensic tech with a sharp eye would know the size, brand, and model number before the sun went down.

Charlie needed to leave. She needed to take Ava outside, hands raised in the air. She needed to make it clear to the heavily armed SWAT team that they were cooperating.

"Fuck," Charlie repeated. How much time did she have? She stood on tiptoe and looked out the window. The two cops were searching the bus. The rest stayed inside the van. They either believed they had the element of surprise or they were looking for explosive devices.

Charlie saw movement closer by the house.

Lenore was standing by her car. Her eyes were wide as she stared at Charlie because any fool could tell that the slit of a window she was looking through was in one of the bedrooms.

Lenore jerked her head toward the front door. Her mouth mimed the words, "Get out."

Charlie jammed the plastic bag of clothes into her purse and made to leave.

The purple walls. The Hello Kitty. The kitten posters.

Thirty, maybe forty seconds. That's how long it would take them to clear the bus, get back in the van, and reach the front door.

She used her gloved hand to open the dresser drawers. Clothes. Underwear. Pens. No diary. No notebooks. She got on her knees and ran her hand between the mattress and boxspring, then looked underneath the bed. Nothing. She was checking between the stacked clothes on the closet floor when she heard the SWAT van doors *thunk* closed, the tires crunch against dirt as they drew closer to the house.

Teenagers' rooms were never this neat. Charlie rifled the contents of the tiny closet with one hand, dumping out two shoe boxes of toys, pulling clothes off hangers and tossing them onto the bed. She patted pockets, turned hats inside out. She stood on tiptoe and reached blindly onto the shelf.

The rubber glove skipped across something flat and hard.

A picture frame?

"Officers." Lenore's deep voice reached her ears through the thin walls. "There are two women in the house, both unarmed."

The cop wasn't interested. "Go back to your car! Now!"

Charlie's heart was going to blow up in her chest. She grabbed at the thing on the closet shelf. It was heavier than she thought. The sharp edge jabbed the top of her head.

A yearbook.

Pikeville Middle School class of 2012.

A deafening knock came at the front door. The walls rattled. "State police!" a man's voice boomed. "I am executing a search warrant. Open the door!"

"I'm coming!" Charlie jammed the yearbook into her purse. She had made it as far as the kitchen when the front door splintered open.

Ava screamed like she was on fire.

"Get down! Get down!" Lasers swept around the room. The house shook on its foundation. Windows were broken. Doors were kicked in. Men yelled orders. Ava kept screaming. Charlie was on her knees, hands in the air, eyes wide open so that she could see which man ended up shooting her.

No one shot her.

No one moved.

Ava's screaming stopped on a dime.

Six massive cops in full tactical gear took up every available inch of the room. Their arms were so tensed as they gripped their AR-15s that Charlie could make out the strands of muscle working to keep their fingers from moving to the triggers.

Slowly, Charlie looked down at her chest.

There was a red dot over her heart.

She looked at Ava.

Five more dots on her chest.

The woman was standing on the couch, knees bent. Her mouth was open, but fear had paralyzed her vocal cords. Inexplicably, she held a toothbrush in each of her raised hands.

The man closest to Ava lowered his rifle. "Toothbrushes."

Another rifle was lowered. "Looked like a God damn trigger switch."

"I know, right?"

More rifles were lowered. Someone chuckled.

The tension lightened incrementally.

From outside the house, a woman yelled, "Gentlemen?"

"Clear," the first guy called back. He grabbed Ava by the arm and pushed her out the door. He turned around to do the same to Charlie, but she escorted herself out, hands in the air.

She didn't lower her arms until she was out in the yard. She took a deep breath of fresh air and tried not to think about how she could've died if any one of those men hadn't taken the time to differentiate between a toothbrush and a detonator for a suicide vest.

In Pikeville.

"Jesus Christ," Charlie said, hoping it would pass for a prayer.

Lenore had stayed by the car. She looked furious to Charlie, which she had every right to be, but she only lifted her chin, asking the obvious question: *You okay?*

Charlie nodded back, but she didn't feel okay. She felt angry— that Rusty had sent her here, that she had taken such a stupid risk, that she had violated the law for reasons that were completely unknown to her, that she had risked getting shot in the heart with what was likely a fast-expanding hollow-point bullet.

All for a fucking yearbook.

Ava whispered, "What's happening?"

Charlie looked back at the house, which was still shaking from all the heavy men traipsing back and forth. "They're searching for things they can use in court against Kelly."

"Like what?"

Charlie listed off the things that she had been looking for. "A confession. An explanation. A diagram of the school. A list of people Kelly was mad at."

"She's never been mad at nobody."

"Ava Wilson?" A tall woman in bulky tactical gear walked toward them. She had her rifle slung to her side. A rolled-up piece of paper was in her fist. That was how they'd gotten here so quickly. The warrant had been faxed to the van. "Are you Ava Wilson, mother to Kelly Rene Wilson?"

Ava stiffened at the sound of authority. "Yes, sir. Ma'am."

"This is your house?"

"We rent it, yes, ma'am. Sir."

"Mrs. Wilson." The cop didn't seem concerned with pronouns. "I'm Captain Isaac with the state police. I have a warrant to search your house."

Charlie pointed out, "You're already searching it."

"We had reason to believe evidence might be tampered with." Isaac studied Charlie's bruised eye. "Were you accidentally injured during the breach, ma'am?"

"No. A different police officer hit me today."

Isaac glanced at Lenore, who was still apparently livid, then looked back at Charlie. "Are you two ladies together?"

"Yes," Charlie said. "Mrs. Wilson would like to see a copy of the warrant."

Isaac made a point of noticing the yellow glove on Charlie's hand.

"Dish-washing glove," Charlie said, which was technically true. "Mrs. Wilson would like to see a copy of the warrant."

"Are you Mrs. Wilson's lawyer?"

"I'm *a* lawyer," Charlie clarified. "I'm only here as a friend of the family."

Isaac told Ava, "Mrs. Wilson, per your friend's request, I am giving you a copy of the warrant."

Charlie had to lift Ava's arm so that the warrant could be placed in the woman's hand.

Isaac asked, "Mrs. Wilson, are there any weapons in the house?"

Ava shook her head. "No, sir."

"Any needles we should be worried about? Anything that's going to cut us?"

Again, Ava shook her head, though she seemed troubled by the question.

"Explosives?"

Ava's hand flew to her mouth. "Is there a gas leak?"

Isaac looked to Charlie for an explanation. Charlie shrugged. The mother's life was upside down. Logic was the last thing they should expect from her.

Isaac asked Ava, "Ma'am, do I have your consent to search your person?"

"Ye—"

"No," Charlie interrupted. "You don't have consent to search anything or anyone beyond the scope of the warrant."

Isaac glanced down at Charlie's purse, which had conformed roughly to the shape of a rectangular yearbook. "Do I need to search your bag?"

Charlie felt her heart flip. "Do you have cause?"

"If you've concealed evidence, or removed something from the house with the purposes of concealment, then—"

"That would be illegal," Charlie said. "Like searching a school bus when it's not specifically listed in your warrant and it's not part of the curtilage."

Isaac nodded once. "You would be correct, unless there was cause."

Charlie snapped off the yellow glove. "I did remove this from the house, but not intentionally."

"Thank you for being forthcoming." Isaac turned to Ava. She had a script to follow. "Ma'am, you can stay outside, or you can leave, but you cannot go back into the house until we've released it. Do you understand?"

Ava shook her head.

Charlie said, "She understands."

Isaac walked across the yard and joined the men inside the house.

Plastic containers were stacked by the door. Evidence logs. Zip ties. Plastic bags. Ava stared through the bay window. The television was still on. The screen was so large that Charlie could read the scroll along the bottom: PIKEVILLE PD SOURCE: SCHOOL SECURITY FOOTAGE WILL NOT BE RELEASED.

Security cameras. Charlie had not noticed them this morning, but now she recalled a camera at the end of every hallway.

The murder spree had been captured on video.

Ava asked, "What are we going to do?"

Charlie suppressed her first answer: *Watch your daughter get strapped to a gurney and executed.*

She told Ava, "My father will explain everything back at his office." She took the rolled-up warrant from the woman's sweaty hand. "There has to be an arraignment within forty-eight hours. Kelly will likely be held at the county jail, but then they'll transfer her somewhere else. There will be a lot of court appearances and plenty of opportunities to see her. None of this will happen quickly. Everything takes a long time." Charlie scanned the search warrant, which was basically a love letter from the judge allowing the cops to do whatever the hell they wanted. She asked Ava, "Is this your address?"

Ava looked at the warrant. "Yes, ma'am, that's the street number."

Through the open front door, Charlie saw Isaac start yanking out drawers in the kitchen. Silverware clattered. Carpet was being stripped from the floor. None of them were being gentle. They lifted their feet high as they stomped around, checking for hollow sounds under the floorboards, poking at the stained tile in the ceiling.

Ava grabbed Charlie's arm. "When will Kelly come home?"

"You'll need to talk about that with my father."

"I don't see how we can afford any of this," Ava said. "We ain't got no money, if that's why you're here."

Rusty had never been interested in money. "The state will pay for her defense. It won't be much, but I can promise you, my father will work his heart out for your daughter."

Ava blinked. She didn't seem to follow. "She's got chores to do."

Charlie looked into the woman's eyes. Her pupils were small, but that could be explained by the intense sunlight. "Are you on something?"

She looked down at her feet. "No, ma'am. There was a pebble but I kicked it away."

Charlie waited for an inappropriate smile, but the woman was being serious. "Did you take some medication? Or maybe you smoked a joint to take the edge off?"

"Oh, no, ma'am. I'm a bus driver. I can't take drugs. Children depend on me."

Charlie looked into her eyes again, this time for any sign of reason. "Did my father explain what's happening to Kelly?"

"He said he was working for her, but I don't know." She whispered, "My cousin says Rusty Quinn is a bad man, that he represents low-lifes and rapists and killers."

Charlie's mouth went dry. The woman did not seem to understand that Rusty Quinn was exactly the kind of man that her daughter needed.

"There's Kelly." Ava was looking at the television again.

Kelly Wilson's face filled the screen. Someone had obviously leaked a school photo. Instead of the heavy Goth makeup and black clothes, Kelly was wearing one of her rainbow pony T-shirts from the closet.

The photo disappeared and was replaced with live footage of Rusty leaving the Derrick County Hospital. He scowled at the reporter who shoved a microphone in his face, but he had left by the front doors for a reason. Rusty made a visible show of reluctantly stopping for the interview. Charlie could tell by the way his mouth was moving that he was offering a cavalcade of

Southern-y sound bites that would be played on a virtual loop by the national stations. This was how these high-profile cases worked. Rusty had to get out in front of the talking heads, to paint Kelly Wilson as a troubled teenager facing the ultimate punishment rather than as a monster who had murdered a child and her school principal.

Ava whispered, "Is a revolver a weapon?"

Charlie felt her stomach drop. She led Ava away from the house and stood with her in the middle of the track. "Do you have a revolver?"

Ava nodded. "Ely keeps it in the glove box of the car."

"The car he drove to work today?"

She nodded again.

"Does he own the gun legally?"

"We don't steal things, ma'am. We work for them."

"I'm sorry, what I mean is, is your husband a convicted felon?"

"No, ma'am. He's an honest man."

"Do you know how many bullets the gun holds?"

"Six." Ava sounded certain enough, but she added, "I think six. I seen it a million times, but I never paid attention to it. I'm sorry I can't remember."

"It's all right." Charlie had felt the same way when Delia Wofford was questioning her. *How many shots did you hear? What was the sequence? Was Mr. Huckabee with you? What happened to the revolver?*

Charlie had been right in the middle of it, but fear had dampened her recall.

She asked Ava, "When was the last time you saw the revolver?"

"I don't—oh." Ava's phone was ringing from the front pocket of her pajamas. She pulled out a cheap flip phone, the kind that let you pre-pay for minutes. "I don't know that number."

Charlie knew the number. It belonged to her iPhone, which

Huck apparently still had. "Get in the car," she told Ava, motioning for Lenore to help. "Let me answer this."

Ava gave Lenore a wary look. "I don't know if—"

"Get in the car." Charlie practically pushed the woman away. She answered the phone on the fifth ring. "Hello?"

"Mrs. Wilson, this is Mr. Huckabee, Kelly's teacher from middle school."

"How did you unlock my phone?"

Huck hesitated a good, long while. "You need a better password than 1-2-3-4."

Charlie had heard the same thing from Ben on numerous occasions. She walked up the track for more privacy. "Why are you calling Ava Wilson?"

He hesitated a second time. "I taught Kelly for two years. I tutored her a few months when she moved up to the high school."

"That doesn't answer the question."

"I spent four hours answering questions from two assholes with the GBI and another hour answering questions at the hospital."

"What assholes?"

"Atkins. Avery. Some ten-year-old with a cowlick and an older black chick kept tag-teaming me."

"Shit," Charlie mumbled. He probably meant Louis Avery, the FBI's North Georgia field agent. "Did he give you his card?"

"I threw it away," Huck said. "My arm's fine, by the way. Bullet went straight through."

"My nose is broken and I have a concussion," Charlie told him. "Why were you calling Ava?"

His sigh said he was humoring her. "Because I care about my students. I wanted to help. To make sure she had a lawyer. That she was being looked after by someone who wasn't going to exploit her or get her into more trouble." Huck abruptly dropped the bravado. "Kelly's not smart, Charlotte. She's not a murderer."

"You don't have to be smart to kill somebody. Actually, the

opposite is usually true." She turned back to look at the Wilson house. Captain Isaac was carrying out a plastic box full of Kelly's clothes.

Charlie told Huck, "If you really want to help Kelly, stay away from any and all reporters, don't go on camera, don't let them get a good photo of you, don't even talk to your friends about what happened, because they'll go on camera or they'll talk to reporters and you won't be able to control what comes out of their mouths."

"That's good advice." He let out a short breath and said, "Hey, I need to tell you that I'm sorry."

"For?"

"B2. Ben Bernard. Your husband called you this morning. I almost answered."

Charlie felt her cheeks flush.

He said, "I didn't know until one of the cops told me. This was after I had talked to him, told him what we'd been up to, why you were at the school."

Charlie put her head in her hand. She knew how certain types of men talked about women, especially the ones they screwed in their trucks outside of bars.

Huck said, "You could've warned me. It put us all in an even worse situation."

"You apologize, but really, it's my fault?" She couldn't believe this guy. "When would I have told you? Before Greg Brenner knocked me out? Or after you deleted the video? Or how about when you lied in your witness statement about how my nose got broken, which is a felony, by the way—the lying to cover a cop's ass, not the standing around with your thumb up your ass while a woman gets punched in the face. That's perfectly legal."

Huck pushed out another sigh. "You don't know what it's like running into something like that. People make mistakes."

"I don't know what it's like?" Charlie felt shaken by a sudden fury. "I think I was there, Huck. I think I got there before you did, so I know exactly what it's like to run into something like that, and not for nothing, but if you really grew up in Pikeville, then you know I've done it twice now, so fuck you with your 'You don't know what it's like.' "

"Okay, you're right. I'm sorry."

Charlie wasn't finished. "You lied about Kelly's age."

"Sixteen, seventeen." She could picture Huck shaking his head. "She's in the eleventh grade. What difference does it make?"

"She's eighteen, and the difference is the death penalty."

He gasped. There was no other word for it—the sudden, quick inhalation that came from absolute shock.

Charlie waited for him to speak. She checked the bars on the phone. "Hello?"

He cleared his throat. "I need a minute."

Charlie needed a minute, too. She was missing something big. Why had Huck been interviewed for four hours? The average interrogation lasted somewhere between half an hour and two hours. Charlie's had topped out at around forty-five minutes. The entirety of her and Huck's involvement with the crime had been less than ten minutes. Why had Delia Wofford brought in the FBI to play good cop/bad cop with Huck? He was hardly a hostile witness. He had been shot in the arm. But he'd said he was interrogated before he went to the hospital. Delia Wofford wasn't the kind of cop who didn't follow procedure. The FBI sure as shit didn't mess around.

So why had they kept their star witness at the police station for four hours? That wasn't how you treated a witness. That was how you treated a suspect who wasn't playing ball.

"Okay, I'm back," Huck said. "Kelly's—what are they calling it now? Remedial? Intellectually handicapped? She's in basic classes. She can't retain concepts."

"The law would call it diminished capacity, as in she's too incapable to form the mental state required for a crime, but that's a very hard argument to make," Charlie told him. "There are very different priorities between a government-run school system and a government-run murder prosecution. One is trying to help her and the other is trying to kill her."

He was so quiet that all she could hear was his breathing.

Charlie asked, "Did the two agents, Wofford and Avery, talk to you for four hours straight, or was there time in between?"

"What?" He seemed thrown by the question. "Yeah, one of them was always in the room. And your husband sometimes. And that guy, what's his name? He wears those shiny suits?"

"Ken Coin. He's the district attorney." Charlie shifted tactics. "Was Kelly bullied?"

"Not in my classroom." He added, "Off-campus, social media, we can't regulate that."

"So you're saying she was bullied?"

"I'm saying she was different, and that's never a good thing when you're a kid."

"You were Kelly's teacher. Why didn't you know that she was held back a grade?"

"I've got over a hundred twenty kids a year every year. I don't look back at their files unless they give me a reason."

"Being slow isn't a reason?"

"A lot of my kids are slow. She was a solid C student. She never got in trouble." Charlie could hear a tapping noise, a pen hitting the edge of a table. Huck said, "Look, Kelly's a good kid. Not smart, but sweet. She follows whatever is in front of her. She doesn't do things like today. That's not her."

"Were you intimate with her?"

"What the hell does—"

"Screwing. Fucking. You know what I mean."

"Of course not." He sounded disgusted. "She was one of my kids. Christ."

"Was anyone else having sex with her?"

"No. I would've reported it."

"Mr. Pinkman?"

"Don't even—"

"Another student at school?"

"How should I—"

"What happened to the revolver?"

If she hadn't been listening for it, she would've missed the slight catch in his breath.

And then he said, "What revolver?"

Charlie shook her head, silently berating herself for missing the obvious.

During her own interview with Delia Wofford, she had been too disoriented to put it together, but now Charlie could see that the woman had practically drawn her a picture. *You didn't see Mr. Huckabee hand the revolver to anyone? Did you see him put it anywhere on his person? On the ground?*

Charlie asked Huck, "What did you do with it?"

He paused again because that's what he did when he was lying. "I don't know what you're talking about."

"Is that how you answered the two agents?"

"I told them what I told you. I don't know. A lot was going on."

Charlie could only shake her head at his stupidity. "Did Kelly say something to you in the hall?"

"Not that I heard." He paused for the billionth time. "Like I said, a lot was happening."

The guy had been shot and barely grimaced. Fear had not dampened his recall.

She asked, "Whose side are you on?"

"There's no such thing as sides. There's just doing the right thing."

"I hate to blow apart your philosophy, Horatio, but if there's a right thing then there's a wrong thing, and as someone with a law degree, I can tell you that stealing the murder weapon from a double homicide, then lying about it to an FBI agent, can land you on the wrong side of a prison cell for a hell of a long time."

He kept up the silent act for two seconds, then said, "I don't know if we were in it, but there's a blind spot in the security cameras."

"Stop talking."

"But, if—"

"Shut up," Charlie warned him. "I'm a witness. I can't be your lawyer. What you tell me isn't privileged."

"Charlotte, I—"

She ended the call before he could dig the hole he was standing in any deeper.

CHAPTER FIVE

Predictably, Rusty's old Mercedes was not parked in the lot when Lenore pulled into her space behind the building. Charlie had watched her father leave the hospital on live television. He had been half an hour from the office, roughly the same distance away as the Wilson house, so he must have taken a detour.

Lenore told Ava, "Rusty's on his way," a lie she told multiple clients multiple times a day.

Ava didn't seem interested in Rusty's whereabouts. Her mouth gaped open as the security gate rolled closed behind them. The enclosed space, with its array of security lights and cameras, metal bars on the windows, and twelve-foot-high razor-wired perimeter fence, looked like the staging area inside a SuperMax prison.

Over the years, Rusty had continued to receive death threats because he continued to represent outlaw bikers, drug gangs, and child killers. Add to the list the union organizations, undocumented workers, and abortion clinics, and he had managed to piss off almost everyone in the state. Charlie's private theory was that most of the death threats came courtesy of the Culpeppers. Only a fraction came from the fine, upstanding citizens who believed Rusty Quinn served at the right hand of Satan.

There was no telling what they would do when word spread that Rusty was representing a school shooter.

Lenore parked her Mazda beside Charlie's Subaru. She turned around and looked at Ava Wilson. "I'll show you a place where you can freshen yourself."

"Do you got a TV?" Ava asked.

Charlie said, "Maybe it's best not to—"

"I wanna watch."

Charlie couldn't deny a grown woman TV privileges. She got out of the car and opened the door for Ava. The mother didn't move at first. She stared at the back of the seat in front of her, hands resting on her knees.

Ava said, "This is real, isn't it?"

"I'm sorry," Charlie said. "It is."

The woman turned slowly. Her legs looked like two twigs underneath the pajama pants. Her skin was so pale as to be almost transparent in the harsh daylight.

Lenore shut the driver's side door quietly, but the look on her face said she wanted to slam it off the car. She had been pissed off at Charlie from the moment she'd spotted her in the front bedroom of the Wilson house. But for Ava Wilson, she would've taken off Charlie's head and thrown it out the window on the drive back.

Lenore mumbled, "This isn't finished."

"Super!" Charlie smiled brightly, because why not pour more fuel onto the fire? There was nothing Lenore could say about Charlie's foolish actions that Charlie had not already said to herself. If there was one thing she excelled at, it was being her own inner mean girl.

She handed Ava Wilson the plastic bag of clothes so she could look for her keys.

"I've got it." Lenore unlocked the steel security screen and accordioned it back. The heavy metal door required a code and another key to engage the bar lock that went straight across the inside of the door and bolted into either side of the steel jamb. Lenore had to put some muscle into turning the latch. There was a deep *cha-chunk* before she could open the door.

Ava asked, "Y'all keep money in here or something?"

Charlie shivered at the question. She let Lenore and Ava enter first.

The familiar odor of cigarettes managed to make its way into Charlie's broken nose. She had banned Rusty from smoking in the building, but the order had come thirty years too late. He brought the stink in with him like Pig-Pen from the Peanuts comics. No matter how many times she cleaned or painted the walls or even replaced the carpet, the odor lingered.

"This way." Lenore gave Charlie another sharp look before escorting Ava to the reception area, a depressingly dark room with a metal roller shade that blocked the view to the street.

Charlie headed toward her office. Her first priority was to call her father and tell him to get his ass down here. Ava Wilson shouldn't be relegated to sitting on their lumpy couch, getting all of her information about her daughter from cable news.

Just in case, Charlie took the long way by Rusty's office to make sure he hadn't parked in the front. The white paint on his door had bled yellow from nicotine. Stains radiated into the Sheetrock and clouded the ceiling. Even the knob had a film around it. She pulled down the sleeve of her shirt to cover her hand and made sure the door was locked.

He wasn't there.

Charlie let out a long breath as she walked toward her office. She had purposefully staked her claim on the opposite side of the building, which in its previous life had housed the back offices of a chain of stationery supply stores. The architecture of the one-story structure was similar in higgledy-pigglediness to the farmhouse. She shared the reception area with her father, but her practice was completely separate from his. Other lawyers came and went, renting space by the month. UGA, Georgia State, Morehouse, and Emory sporadically sent interns who needed desks and phones. Rusty's investigator, Jimmy Jack Little, had set up shop in a former supply closet. As far as Charlie could tell,

Jimmy Jack used it to store his files, possibly hoping that the police would think twice before raiding an office inside a building filled with lawyers.

The carpet was thicker, the décor nicer on Charlie's side. Rusty had hung a sign over her door that read "Dewey, Pleadem & Howe," a joke on the fact that she kept most of her clients out of the courtroom. Charlie didn't mind arguing a case, but the majority of her clients were too poor to afford a trial, and too familiar with the Pikeville judges to waste their time fighting the system.

Rusty, on the other hand, would argue a parking ticket in front of the United States Supreme Court if they'd let him get that far.

Charlie searched her purse for her office keys. The bag slipped off her shoulder. Her mouth gaped open. Kelly Wilson's yearbook had a cartoon General Lee on the front because the school mascot was the Rebel.

Defense counsel who possesses a physical item under circumstances implicating a client in criminal conduct should disclose the location of or should deliver that item to law enforcement authorities.

It wasn't lost on Charlie that she had lectured Huck about concealing evidence while she had Kelly Wilson's yearbook tucked under her arm.

Though, arguably, Charlie was caught in the legal equivalent of Schrödinger's Cat. She wouldn't know if there was evidence inside the yearbook until she opened the yearbook. She looked for her keys again. The easiest thing to do would be to dump the book onto Rusty's desk and let him deal with it.

"Let's go." Lenore was back, and clearly ready to say her piece.

Charlie indicated the bathroom across the hall. She couldn't do this on a full bladder.

Lenore followed her inside and shut the door. "Half of me wonders if it's even worth laying into you, because you're too dumb to know how stupid you are."

"Please listen to that half."

Lenore jabbed her finger at Charlie. "Don't give me your smart mouth."

A cornucopia of smartass responses filled her head, but Charlie held back. She unbuttoned her jeans and sat on the toilet. Lenore had bathed Charlie when she was too grief-stricken to take care of herself. She could watch her pee.

"You never think, Charlotte. You just *do*." Lenore paced the tight room.

"You're right," Charlie said. "And I know you're right, just like I know you can't make me feel any worse than I already do."

"You're not getting out of it that easy."

"Does this look easy?" Charlie held her arms out wide to show off the damage. "I got caught up in a war zone this morning. I antagonized a cop into making this happen." She indicated her face. "I humiliated my husband. Again. I fucked a guy who is either a martyr, a pedophile, or a psychopath. I broke down in front of you. And you don't even want to know what I was doing when the SWAT team came in. I mean, seriously, you do *not* want to know because you need plausible deniability."

Lenore's nostrils flared. "I saw their guns pointed at your chest, Charlotte. Six men, all with their rifles up, all a trigger's width from murdering you while I stood outside wringing my hands like a helpless old woman."

Charlie realized that Lenore wasn't angry. She was frightened.

"What on earth were you thinking?" Lenore demanded. "Why would you risk your life like that? What was so important?"

"Nothing was that important." Charlie's shame was amplified by the sight of the tears rolling down Lenore's face. "I'm sorry. You're right. I shouldn't have done that. Any of it. I'm an idiot and a fool."

"You sure as hell are." Lenore grabbed the toilet paper and rolled out enough to blow her nose.

"Please yell at me," Charlie begged. "I can't take it when you're upset."

Lenore looked away, and Charlie wanted to disappear into a pool of self-hate. How many times had she had this same discussion with Ben? The time at the grocery store that Charlie had shoved a man who'd slapped his wife. The time she'd almost got clipped by a car trying to help a stranded motorist. Antagonizing the Culpeppers when she saw them downtown. Going to the Holler during the middle of the night. Spending her days defending sleazy meth heads and violent felons. Ben claimed that Charlie would sprint headfirst into a buzz saw if given the right set of circumstances.

Lenore said, "We can't both cry."

"I'm not crying," Charlie lied.

Lenore handed her the toilet-paper roll. "Why do you think the guy's a psychopath?"

"I can't tell you." Charlie buttoned her jeans, then went to the sink to wash her hands.

"Do I need to worry about you going back to before?"

Charlie didn't want to think about before. "There's a blind spot in the security cameras."

"Did Ben tell you that?"

"You know Ben and I don't talk about cases." Charlie cleaned under her arms with a wet paper towel. "The psychopath has my phone. I need to get it turned off and replaced with a new one. I missed two hearings today."

"The courthouse locked down the minute news broke about the shooting."

Charlie remembered this was procedure. There had been a false alarm once before. Like Ava Wilson, she was having a hard time believing that any of this was real.

Lenore said, "There's two sandwiches in a Tupperware bowl on your desk. I'll go to the phone store for you if you eat them."

"Deal," Charlie agreed. "Listen, I'm sorry about today. I'll try to be better."

Lenore rolled her eyes. "Whatever."

Charlie waited until the door was closed to finish her whore's bath. She studied her face in the mirror as she cleaned herself. She was looking worse by the hour. There were two bruises, one under each eye, that made her look like a domestic violence victim. The bridge of her nose was dark red and had a bump on top of the other bump from the last time her nose had been broken.

She told her reflection, "You're going to stop being an idiot."

Her reflection looked as dubious as Lenore.

Charlie went back to her office. She dumped her purse on the floor to find her keys. Then she had to figure out how to shove everything back in. Then she realized that Lenore had already unlocked the door because Lenore was always two steps ahead of her. Charlie dropped her purse on the couch beside the door. She turned on the lights. Her desk. Her computer. Her chair. It felt good to be among familiar things. The office wasn't her home, but she spent more time here, especially since Ben had moved out, so it was the next best thing.

She crammed down one of the peanut butter and jelly sandwiches Lenore had left on the desk. She skimmed her inbox on the computer and answered the emails asking if she was okay. Charlie should've listened to her voicemail, called her clients, and checked with the court to see when her hearings would be rescheduled, but she was too jittery to concentrate.

Huck had all but admitted to taking the murder weapon from the scene.

Why?

Actually, the better question was *how*?

A revolver was not a small thing, and considering it was the murder weapon, the police would have been searching for it almost immediately. How did Huck sneak it out of the building? In his pants? Did he slip it into an unwitting paramedic's bag? Charlie supposed the Pikeville police had given Huck a wide berth. You didn't frisk an innocent civilian you'd accidentally shot. Huck had also erased the video that Charlie had taken, proving he was firmly on their side—inasmuch as Mr. Huckleberry believed in sides.

But agents Delia Wofford and Louis Avery had no such loyalty to Mr. Huckabee. No wonder they had drilled him for four hours while the bullet wound in his arm slowly seeped. They probably suspected he'd taken the weapon, just like they suspected the local cops were idiots for letting him walk out the door without doing a thorough search.

Lying to an FBI agent carried up to five years in federal prison and a $250,000 fine. Add on top of that the destruction of evidence, lying to hinder an investigation, and the possibility of Huck being charged as an accomplice after the fact to double homicide, and he would never work in a school, or probably anywhere else, ever again.

All of which made things tricky for Charlie. Unless she wanted to destroy the man's life, she would need to find a way to tell her father about the gun without implicating Huck. She knew what Rusty would do if he smelled blood. Huck was the kind of handsome, clean-cut do-gooder that juries ate up with a spoon. His war record, his benevolent choice of profession, wouldn't matter if he testified from the stand in an orange prison jumpsuit.

She looked at the clock over the couch: 2:16 PM.

This day was like a fucking never-ending sphere.

Charlie opened a new Word document on her computer. She should type out everything she remembered and give it to Rusty. He had likely heard Kelly Wilson's story by now. Charlie could at least tell him what the prosecution had heard.

Her hands hovered over the keyboard, but she didn't type. She watched the blinking cursor. She didn't know where to start. Obviously, from the beginning, but the beginning was the hard part.

Charlie's daily routine was normally set in granite. She got up at five. She fed the various animals. She went for a run. She showered. She ate breakfast. She went to work. She went home. With Ben gone, her nights were filled with reading case files, watching mindless TV, and clock-watching for a non-demeaning time to go to bed.

Today hadn't been like that, and Rusty would need to know the reason why.

The least Charlie could do was find out Huck's first name.

She opened the browser on her computer. She searched for "Pikeville Middle School faculty."

The little rainbow wheel started spinning. Eventually, the screen showed the message: *WEBSITE NOT RESPONDING.*

She tried to get around the landing page, typing in different departments, teachers' names, even the school newspaper. They all brought back the same message. The Pikeville Department of Education servers didn't have the capacity to handle hundreds of thousands of curiosity seekers trying to access their website.

She clicked open a fresh search page. She typed "Huckabee Pikeville."

"Crap," Charlie mumbled. Google had asked, *Do you mean huckleberry?*

The first site listed was a wiki entry saying that the huckleberry was the state fruit of Idaho. Then there were several stories about school boards trying to ban *Huckleberry Finn*. At the bottom of the page was an Urban Dictionary entry that claimed "I'm your huckleberry" was nineteenth-century slang for "I'm your man."

Charlie tapped her finger on the mouse. She should look at CNN or MSNBC or even Fox, but she couldn't bring herself to type in the news sites. An entire hour had passed without the slideshow coming back into her head. She didn't want to invite the flood of bad memories.

Besides, this was Rusty's case. Charlie was likely going to be called as a witness for the prosecution. She would corroborate Huck's story, but that would only give the jury a small piece of the puzzle.

If anyone knew more, it was Mrs. Pinkman. Her room was directly across from where Kelly had most likely stood when she began shooting. Judith Pinkman would've been first on the scene. She would have found her husband dead. Lucy dying.

"Please, help us!"

Charlie could still hear the woman's screams echoing in her ears. The four shots had already been fired. Huck had dragged Charlie behind the filing cabinet. He was calling the police when she heard two more shots.

Charlie was astonished by the sudden vividness of the memory.

Six gunshots. Six bullets in the revolver.

Otherwise Judith Pinkman would've been shot in the face when she opened the door to her classroom.

Charlie looked up at the ceiling. The thought had teased out an old image that she did not want to see.

She had to get out of this office.

She picked up the plastic bowl with the second PB&J and went to find Ava Wilson. Charlie knew that Lenore had already offered Ava food—she had that typically Southern impulse to feed everyone she met—just as Charlie was sure Ava was too stressed out to eat, but she didn't want the woman to be alone for too long.

In the reception area, Charlie found a familiar scene: Ava Wilson on the couch in front of the television, the sound up too loud.

She asked Ava, "Would you like my other sandwich?"

Ava did not answer. Charlie was about to repeat the question when she realized that Ava's eyes were closed. Her lips were slightly parted, a soft whistle passing between a gap where one of her teeth was missing.

Charlie didn't wake her. Stress had a way of shutting down your body when it couldn't take any more. If Ava Wilson had a moment's peace today, this would be it.

The remote control was on the coffee table. Charlie never asked why it was always sticky. Most of the buttons didn't work. The others got stuck. The power button was unresponsive. The mute had evaporated—there was an open rectangle where the button had been. She went to the set to see if there was another way to turn it off.

On screen, the news was in that lull period where there was no real information to report, so they'd brought on a panel of pundits and psychiatrists to speculate what *might* have happened, what Kelly *possibly* had been thinking, why she *could* have done the things that she did.

"And there *is* precedent," a pretty blonde said. "If you remember the Boomtown Rats song from—"

Charlie was about to yank the cord out of the wall when the main anchor interrupted the shrink. "We've got breaking news. I'll send you live to a press conference going on now in Pikeville, Georgia."

The image changed again, this time to a podium set up in a familiar-looking space. The lunchroom at the police station. They had cleared the tables away and stuck a blue flag with a City of Pikeville logo on the wall.

A chubby man wearing pleated tan Dockers and a white button-down shirt stood behind the podium. He looked to his left, and the camera panned to Ken Coin, who seemed irritated when he waved for the man to go ahead.

Coin had clearly wanted to take the stage first.

The man moved the microphone down, then up, then down again. He leaned over, his lips too close, and said, "I'm Rick Fahey. I'm Lucy Alex—" his voice caught. "Lucy Alexander's uncle." He used the back of his hand to wipe away tears. His face was red. His lips were too pink. "The family has asked me—oh." Fahey took a folded piece of notebook paper out of his back pocket. His hands were shaking so hard that the paper fluttered as if from a sudden wind. Finally, Fahey flattened the page down on the podium and said, "The family asked me to read this statement."

Charlie looked back at Ava. She continued to sleep.

Fahey read, " 'Lucy was a beautiful child. She was creative. She loved to sing and play with her dog, Shaggy. She was in Ms. Dillard's Bible class at Mountain Baptist, where she loved reading the Gospels. She spent summers at her grandparents' farm down in Ellijay, where she helped them pick a-apples . . .' " He took a handkerchief out of his back pocket and patted the sweat and tears from his round face. " 'The family has put its trust in God to help us through this trying time. We ask for the thoughts and prayers of the community. Also, we would like to express our support for the Pikeville Police Department and the Dickerson County district attorney's office—Mr. Ken Coin—to do everything they can to quickly bring justice to Lucy's murd—' " His voice caught again. " 'Murderer.' " He looked up at the reporters. "That's what Kelly Wilson is. A cold-blooded murderer."

Fahey turned to Ken Coin. The two exchanged a solemn nod of a promise that had likely been made.

Fahey continued, " 'The family would like to ask in the meantime that the media and others respect our privacy. No funeral arrangements have been made yet.' " His focus moved off into the distance, past the throng of microphones, past the cameras. Was he thinking about Lucy's funeral, how her parents would have to choose a child-size casket to bury their daughter in?

She had been so small. Charlie could remember how delicate the girl's hand had felt when she gripped it inside her own.

"Mr. Fahey?" one of the reporters asked. "Could you tell us—"

"Thank you." Fahey left the podium. Ken Coin gave him a firm pat on the arm as they passed each other.

Charlie watched her husband's boss grip the sides of the podium like he was about to sodomize it. "I'm Ken Coin, the district attorney for the county," he told the crowd. "I'm here to answer your questions about the prosecution of this vile murder. Make no mistake, ladies and gentlemen. We will claim an eye for an eye in this egregious—"

Charlie unplugged the television. She turned to make sure that

Ava hadn't woken up. The woman was in the same position, still wearing her pajamas. The bag of clothes was on the floor at her feet. Charlie was trying to remember if they had a blanket somewhere when the back door banged open and slammed closed.

Only Rusty entered the building making that much racket.

Fortunately, the sounds had not awakened Ava. She only shifted on the couch, her head lolling to the side.

Charlie left the sandwich on the coffee table before she went back to find her father.

"Charlotte?" Rusty boomed. She heard his office door pop open. The knob had already dug a hole in the wall. He never passed up an opportunity to make noise. "Charlotte?"

"I'm here, Daddy." She stopped outside the doorway. His office was so cluttered there was nowhere inside to stand. "Ava Wilson's in reception."

"Good girl." He didn't look up from the papers in his hands. Rusty was a jittery half-tasker, never fully concentrating on one thing at a time. Even now, he was tapping his foot, reading, spontaneously humming, and carrying on something like a conversation. "How's she doing?"

"Not great. She dozed off a little while ago." Charlie talked to the top of his head. He was seventy-four years old and his hair was still a thick salt and pepper that he kept too long on the sides. "You need to go slow with her. I'm not sure how much she's following."

"Noted." He made a note on the papers. Rusty's bony fingers held a pen the same way he held a cigarette. Anyone who talked to him on the phone expected him to look like a cross between Colonel Sanders and Foghorn Leghorn. He was not. Rusty Quinn was a tall, rangy beanpole of a man, but not in the same way as Ben, because Charlie would've thrown herself off the mountain before she married someone like her father.

Other than their height and an inability to throw out old underwear, the two men in her life were nothing alike. Ben was a dependable but sporty minivan. Rusty was an industrial-size bull-dozer. Despite two heart attacks and a double bypass, he gladly continued to indulge his vices: Bourbon. Fried chicken. Unfiltered Camels. Screaming arguments. Ben was drawn to thoughtful discussions, IPA, and artisanal cheeses.

Actually, Charlie realized that there was a new similarity between the two: today, both men were having a hard time looking at Charlie.

She asked, "What's she like?"

"The girl?" Rusty dashed off another note, humming as if the pen had some sort of rhythm. "Slip of a thing. Coin must be shittin' his pants. Jury's gonna fall in love with her."

"Lucy Alexander's family might have something to say about that."

"I am girded for battle."

Charlie stubbed her toe on the carpet. There was nothing he couldn't turn into a contest. "You could try to do a deal with Ken, take the death penalty off the table."

"Bah," he answered, because they both knew Ken wouldn't deal. "I think we got a unicorn here."

Charlie's head snapped up. A unicorn was their word for an innocent client; a rare, mythical creature few had ever seen. She said, "You can't be serious."

"'Course I'm serious. Why wouldn't I be serious?"

"I was there, Daddy." She wanted to shake him. "I was right in the middle of it."

"Ben caught me up to speed on what happened." He coughed into the crook of his arm. "Sounds like you had a real rough time of it."

"That is a magnificent understatement."

"I am renowned for my subtlety." Charlie watched him shuffle the papers. The humming resumed. She counted to thirty before he finally looked at her over his reading glasses. He was blissfully silent for almost another ten seconds, then a smile cracked open his mouth. "Those are some real shiners, tough girl. You look like a bandito."

"I was elbowed in the face."

"I already told Coin to get his checkbook at the ready."

"I didn't file a complaint."

He kept smiling. "Good idea, baby. Hold your fire till this settles down. Never kick a fresh turd on a hot day."

Charlie put her hand to her eyes. She was too tired for the merry-go-round. "Dad, I need to tell you something."

Her words went unanswered. She dropped her hand.

Rusty said, "This about why you were at the school this morning?" He had no problem looking at Charlie now. Their eyes locked for a very brief but uncomfortable moment before she looked away.

He said, "So now you know I know."

"Did Ben tell you?"

He shook his head. "Ol' Kenny Coin had the pleasure."

Charlie wasn't going to apologize to her father. "I'll write down everything I can remember from today, what I told the GBI agent who took my statement. She's a SAC, Delia Wofford. I've got her card. She interviewed the other witness along with an agent named Avery or Atkins. Ben was in the room with me. I think Coin was behind the mirror or in the other room most of the time."

Rusty made sure she was finished before saying, "Charlotte, I am assuming if you were not okay, you would tell me."

"Russell, I am assuming that you are smart enough to extrapolate that information from the raw data."

"Hello, familiar impasse." He dropped the papers on his desk. "The last time I tried to guess your mood, a first-class stamp was twenty-nine cents and you stopped talking to me for sixteen and three-quarter days."

Charlie had long lost the will to negotiate his sympathy. "I heard there's a hole in the school's security footage."

"Where'd you get that?"

"The gettin' place."

"Pick up anything else while you were there?"

"They're worried about the murder weapon. Like, maybe they don't know exactly where it ended up."

His eyebrows jumped. "That's a pickle."

"That's a guess," Charlie said, not wanting to throw scent onto Huck. "The GBI agent was asking me a lot of questions about where it was, when did I see it last, who had it when/what/where. Revolver. I'm not one hundred percent, but I think it was a six-shot."

Rusty's eyes narrowed. "There's something else, right? If I am allowed the extrapolation?"

Charlie turned around, knowing he would follow. She was halfway across the building when she heard his heavy footsteps behind her. He had a long, quick stride because he thought walking fast passed for cardio. She heard his fingers tap the wall. He hummed what sounded like "Happy Birthday." The only time Charlie ever saw her father completely still was inside a courtroom.

Charlie found her bag on the couch in her office. She pulled out the yearbook.

Rusty came to a breathless standstill. "What's that?"

"It's a yearbook. Sometimes it's called an annual."

He crossed his arms over his chest. "You need to be more specific with your old pappy."

"You buy it at school at the end of the year. It has class pictures and club photos and people write things in the pages, like 'I'll never forget you' or 'Thanks for helping me in biology.'" She shrugged. "It's a stupid thing. The more signatures you get, the more popular you are."

"That explains why you never brought one home."

"Ha ha."

He asked, "So, was our gal popular? Not popular?"

"I didn't open it." Charlie waved the book in Rusty's face, indicating he should take it.

He kept his arms crossed, but she saw that switch flick inside him, the same one that came on inside the courtroom.

He asked, "Where was this found?"

"In Kelly Wilson's closet in her home."

"Before the execution of the search warrant?"

"Yes."

"Did anyone from law enforcement tell you there was going to be a search warrant filed?"

"No."

"Did the mother—"

"Ava Wilson."

"Did Ava Wilson give this to you to hold on to?"

"No."

"Is she your client?"

"No, and thanks for trying to help me lose my license."

"You'd have the best attorney in the country making sure you kept it." Rusty nodded toward the yearbook. "Open it for me."

"Take it or I'll drop it on the floor."

"God damn, you make me miss your mama." Rusty's voice had a funny quiver. He rarely mentioned Gamma, and if he did, it was only to make a not-always-favorable comparison to Charlie. He took the yearbook and gave her a salute. "Many thanks."

She watched his exaggerated march up the hallway.

Charlie called, "Hey, asshole."

Rusty turned around, grinning as he marched back the same way he'd left. He opened the yearbook with a flourish. The inside flap was filled with written messages, some in black ink, some in blue, a few in pink. Different handwriting. Different signatures. Rusty turned the page. More ink colors. More hastily scratched missives.

If Kelly Wilson was a loner, she was the most popular loner at school.

Rusty said, "Excuse me, miss. I'm not stepping on your scruples here if I ask you to read me some of this?" He tapped his temple. "Don't have my spectacles."

Charlie indicated that he should turn the book around. She read the first line that jumped out at her, a blocky print that looked like it belonged to a boy. " 'Hey girl thanks for the awesome head. You suck.' " She looked up at her father. "Whoa."

"Whoa, indeed." Rusty was unshockable. Charlie had given up trying years ago. "Continue."

" 'Gonna rape you bitch.' No signature." She skimmed around. "Another rape threat, 'Gonna do some sodomy on your ass bitch,' sodomy spelled with an *i*."

"At the end or in the middle?"

"End." She searched for some pink cursive, hoping the girls proved to be a lesser evil. " 'You are a fucking whore and I hate you and I want you to die—six exclamation points. K-I-T, Mindy Zowada.' "

"K-I-T?" Rusty asked.

"Keep in touch."

"Heartfelt."

Charlie scanned the other notes, which were equally as lewd as the first few. "They're all like that, Dad. Either calling her a whore or referring to sex or asking for sex or saying they're going to rape her."

He turned to the next page, which had been left blank so that classmates could write more notes. There were no notes. A giant cock and balls took up most of the space. At the top was a drawing of a girl with stringy hair and wide eyes. Her mouth was open. There was an arrow pointed at her head with the word KELLY.

Rusty said, "A picture slowly starts to emerge."

"Keep going."

He turned more pages. More drawings. More lewd messages. Some rape threats. Kelly's class picture had been defiled; this time the cock and balls pointing at her mouth was ejaculating. Charlie said, "They must have passed this around the school. Hundreds of kids were in on it."

"She was how old do you think when this was done?"

"Twelve or thirteen?"

"And she kept it a-a-a-all this time." He drew out the word as if he was testing how it would sound in front of a jury. Charlie couldn't fault him the performance. He was holding in his hands a textbook example of a mitigating factor.

Kelly Wilson had not only been bullied at school. The sexual aggression in the messages from her classmates pointed to something even darker.

Rusty asked, "Did the mother say the girl was sexually assaulted?"

"The mother thinks the girl is a snowflake."

"All right," Rusty said. "So, if something happened, then it might be in her school records or there might be somebody you could ask at the DA's office who—"

"No." Charlie knew to shut him down quickly. "You can ask Ava to request a copy of her school records and you can do a juvenile court query on a possible file."

"I will do exactly that."

Charlie said, "You need a really good computer guy, someone who can do forensic searches into social media accounts. If enough kids were involved in this yearbook project, there might even be a separate Facebook page for it."

"I don't need a guy. I've got CNN." He was right. The media would already have experts scouring the web. Their reporters would be talking to Kelly's classmates, her teachers, looking for friends or people who claimed to be friends who were willing to go on camera and say anything, true or not, about Kelly Wilson.

Charlie asked, "Did you get a chance to check on Mrs. Pinkman?"

"I tried to pay a social visit, but she was heavily sedated." He exhaled a raspy breath. "Bad enough to lose a partner, but to lose 'em like that is the very definition of anguish."

Charlie studied him, trying to figure out his tone. Twice now he had mentioned Gamma. She supposed that was her fault, considering her involvement this morning at the school. Another arrow she had slung her father's way. "Where did you go today after the hospital?"

"Took a little side trip down to Kennesaw to do a satellite interview. You'll be treated to your daddy's handsome visage all over your TV tonight."

Charlie wasn't going to be near a TV if she could help it. "You're going to have to be careful with Ava, Daddy. She doesn't understand a lot. I don't think it's just shock. She doesn't track."

"Daughter has the same problem. I'd put her IQ in the low seventies." He tapped the yearbook. "Thanks for the help, my dear. Did Ben get in touch with you this morning?"

Her heart flipped the same way it had when she'd first heard that Ben had called. "No, do you know why he was calling me?"

"I do."

Her desk phone rang. Rusty started to leave.

"Dad?"

"You will need your umbrella tomorrow. Sixty-three percent chance of rain in the AM." He hummed a passable "Happy Birthday," giving her a salute as he backed down the hall, knees high like a marching-band leader.

She said, "You're going to give yourself another heart attack."

"You wish!"

Charlie rolled her eyes. He always had to make a fucking exit. She picked up the phone. "Charlie Quinn."

"I'm not supposed to be talking to you," Terri, the youngest of Ben's older sisters, said. "But I wanted to make sure you were all right."

"I'm good." Charlie could hear Terri's twins screaming in the background. Ben called them "Denise" and "Denephew." She told Terri, "Ben said he called you guys this morning."

"He was pretty upset."

"Upset *at* me or *about* me?"

"Well, you know that's been a damn nine-month-long mystery."

It wasn't, actually, but Charlie knew anything she told Terri would be passed on to Carla and Peggy, who would tell Ben's mother, so she kept her mouth firmly shut.

Terri asked, "You there?"

"Sorry, I'm at work."

Terri didn't take the hint. "I was thinking when Ben called about how funny he is about talking about things. You have to poke and poke and poke and then maybe, eventually, he'll tell you back in 1998 you stole a French fry off his plate and it really hurt his feelings."

She said more, but Charlie tuned her out, listening instead to Terri's children try to kill each other. Charlie had been sucked in by Ben's bitchy sisters once before, taking them at face value when she should have realized there was a reason Ben only saw them at Thanksgiving. They were bossy, unthinking women who tried to rule Ben with an iron fist. He was in college before he realized that men were allowed to pee standing up.

Terri said, "And then I was talking to Carla about this thing going on with you two. Doesn't make any sense at all. You know he loves you. But he's got something up his butt and he won't say anything." She stopped a moment to yell at her children, then picked up the conversation where she'd left off. "Has Benny said anything to you yet? Given you any kind of reason?"

"No," Charlie lied, thinking if they knew Ben at all, they would know that he would never walk out without a reason.

"Keep poking at him. I bet it's nothing."

It wasn't nothing.

"He's too sensitive for his own good. Did I ever tell you about the time at Disneyland when—"

"All we can do is work on it."

"Y'all need to work harder," she said. "Nine months is too long,

Charlie. Peggy was saying the other day how she grew a whole baby in nine months so why can't y'all figure out—shit."

Charlie felt her hand tighten around the phone.

"Shit," Terri repeated. "You know I don't think before I speak. That's just how I am."

"It's fine, really. Don't worry about it. But, look, I've got a client calling on the other line." Charlie spoke too fast to let her get a word in. "Thanks so much for calling. Please send my best to the others and I'll talk to you later."

Charlie slammed down the phone.

She put her head in her hands. The worst part about that phone call was that she wasn't going to be able to climb into bed with Ben tonight, put her head on his chest and tell him what an awful fucking bitch his sister was.

Charlie slumped back in her chair. She saw that Lenore had kept her part of the bargain. A brand new iPhone was plugged into the back of her computer. Charlie pressed the home button. She tried 1-2-3-4 for the password, but it didn't take. She put in her birthday, and the phone unlocked.

The first thing she pulled up was her list of voicemails. One message from Rusty this morning. Several messages from friends after the shooting.

Nothing from Ben.

The distinct rumble of Rusty's voice echoed through the building. He was leading Ava Wilson back to his office. Charlie could guess what he was saying by the cadence of his voice. He was giving his usual speech: "You don't have to tell me the *whole* truth, but you do have to tell me the truth."

Charlie wondered if Ava was capable of grasping the subtlety. And she prayed that Rusty wouldn't float his unicorn theory past the woman. Ava was already drowning in her own version of false hope. She didn't need Rusty to weigh her down with more.

Charlie tapped her computer awake. The browser was still open on huckleberries. She did a new search: "Mindy Zowada Pike-ville."

The girl who had called Kelly Wilson a fucking whore in her yearbook had a Facebook page. Mindy's setting was private, but Charlie could see her banner, which was heavy on the Justin Bie-ber. The account photo of Mindy showed her dressed as a Rebel cheerleader. She looked exactly the way Charlie thought she'd look: pretty and nasty and smug.

Charlie skimmed Mindy's list of likes and dislikes, annoyed that she was too old to understand half of what the teenager was into.

She tapped her finger on the mouse again.

Charlie had two Facebook accounts: one in her own name, and another in a fake name. She had created the second account as a joke. Or at least she'd initially let herself believe it was a joke. After creating an email address for the account and a profile picture of a pig wearing a bow tie, she had finally accepted that she was going to use it to spy on the Culpepper girls who had tormented her in high school. That they had all accepted a friend request from Iona Trayler proved correct a lot of stereotypes that Charlie had about their intelligence. Weirdly, she had also been friended by an ex-tended family of Traylers who sent her greetings on her made-up birthday and were always asking her to pray for ailing aunts and distant cousins.

Charlie logged in to the Trayler account and sent out a friend request to Mindy Zowada. It was a shot in the dark, but she wanted to know what the girl who'd been so vile to Kelly Wilson was say-ing about her now. That Charlie had extended her catfishing from the Culpeppers to another girl's tormentors would be a neurosis to analyze at a later date.

Charlie collapsed the browser. The blank Word document was on her desktop. There was nothing else she could do to procras-tinate, so she started typing up her statement for Rusty. She re-layed the events in as dry a manner as possible, thinking about the morning the way she might think about a story she had read in the newspaper. This happened, then this happened, then this happened.

Horrible things were a hell of a lot easier to digest when you took away the emotion.

The school part of the story did not deviate from what she'd told Delia Wofford. The Word document could be subpoenaed, and there was nothing to Charlie's recollection that was much different than what she had told the agent. What had changed was her certainty. Four shots before Mrs. Pinkman screamed. Two shots after.

Charlie stopped typing. She stared at the screen until the words blurred. Had Mrs. Pinkman opened the door when she heard the four initial gunshots? Had she screamed when she saw her husband and a child on the ground? Had Kelly Wilson emptied the remaining bullets in the revolver in an attempt to shut her up?

Unless Kelly opened up to Rusty, they might not know the truth about the sequence for weeks, possibly months, until Rusty held the forensic reports and witness statements in his hands.

Charlie blinked her eyes to clear them. She hit the return key for a new paragraph, skipping over her conversation with Ben at the police station and jumping right into the interview she had granted Delia Wofford. For all of Charlie's sphere bullshit, she was right about the passage of time sharpening perspective. Again, it was the certainty that had changed. She would have to amend parts of the statement she had made to the GBI before signing off on it.

An alert chirped on her computer.

TraylerLvr483@gmail.com: Mindy Zowada has accepted your friend request!

Charlie expanded the girl's Facebook page. Mindy's banner had been changed to a single burning candle fluttering in the wind.

"Oh for fucksakes," Charlie mumbled, scrolling down to the posts.

Six minutes ago, Mindy Zowada had written:

idk what to do i am so sad about this thot kelly was a good person i guess all we can do is pray?

Funny, considering what the girl thought about Kelly Wilson five years ago.

Charlie scrolled through the replies. The first three concurred with Mindy's assessment that they were all shocked—shocked!—that the girl they bullied on a school-wide scale had snapped. The fourth reply was the asshole in the bunch, because the point of Facebook was that there was always an asshole who would shit on everything, from an innocent photo of a cat to a video of your kid's birthday party.

Nate Marcus wrote:

i know what was wrong with her she was a fucking slut that fucked the whole football team so maybe thats why she did it because she has aids

Chase Lovette responded:

aw man they gone hang that bitch she sucked my cock clean off maybe my wikked cum made her do it

Then Alicia Todd supplied:

bitch gonna burn in hell kelly wilson so sorry uuuu!

Charlie had to read the sentence aloud before she guessed that the four "u"s meant "for you."

She wrote down all the names, thinking Rusty would want to

have a word with them. If they had been in Kelly's class in middle school, at least some of the posters would now be over the age of eighteen, which meant that Rusty would not need their parents' permission to speak with them.

"Lenore took Ava Wilson to meet her husband."

The sound of Rusty's voice made her jump. The noisiest man alive had managed to sneak up on her.

"They wanna be alone for a while, talk this through." Rusty plopped down on the couch across from her desk. He tapped his hands against his legs. "Don't know that they can afford a hotel. Guess they'll sleep in their car. Revolver's not in the glove box, by the by."

Charlie looked at the time: 6:38 PM. Time had crawled and then it had sprinted.

She asked, "You didn't talk to her about innocence?"

"Nope." He leaned back on the couch, one hand on the cushions, the other still tapping his leg. "Didn't talk to her about much, to be honest. I wrote down some things for her to show her husband—what to expect in the coming weeks. She thinks the girl's gonna come home."

"Like a good little unicorn?"

"Well, Charlie Bear, there's innocent and there's not guilty, and there's not a lot of rhyme or reason in between." He gave her a wink. "Why don't you drive your old daddy home?"

Charlotte hated going to the farmhouse, even to drop him off. She hadn't been inside the HP in years. "Where's your car?"

"Had to drop it off for service." He tapped his knee harder. There was a rhythm to the beats now. "Did you figure out why Ben called you this morning?"

Charlie shook her head. "Do you know?"

He opened his mouth to answer, but then grinned instead.

She said, "I can't deal with your motherfuckery right now, Rusty. Just tell me the truth."

He groaned as he got up from the couch. "'Seldom does complete truth belong to any human disclosure.'"

He left before Charlie could find something to throw at him.

She didn't hurry to meet him at the car because, despite his harried rushing around, Rusty was always late. She printed out a copy of her statement. She emailed a copy to herself in case she wanted to look at it at home. She grabbed a stack of files she needed to work on. She checked the Facebook page again for new posts. Finally, she gathered up her things, locked up her office, and found her father standing outside the back door smoking a cigarette.

"Such a scowl on your pretty face," he said, grinding the cigarette on the heel of his shoe and dropping the butt into his coat pocket. "You're gonna get those same lines around your mouth that your grandmama had."

Charlie tossed her bag into the back seat of her car and got in. She waited for Rusty to lock up the building. He brought the trace of cigarette smoke with him. By the time she pulled onto the road, she might as well have been inside a Camel factory.

She rolled down the window, already annoyed that she had to go to the farmhouse. "I'm not saying anything about how stupid it is to smoke after having two heart attacks and open-heart surgery."

"That is called paralipsis, or, from the Greek, apophasis," Rusty informed her. "A rhetorical device by which you add emphasis to a subject by professing to say little or nothing about it." He was tapping his foot with glee. "Also, a rhetorical relative of irony, whom I believe you went to school with."

Charlie reached into the back seat and found the printout of her statement. "Read this. Silent car until the HP."

"Yes, ma'am." Rusty found his reading glasses in his pocket. He turned on the dome light. His foot tapped as he read the first paragraph. And then his foot stopped tapping.

She could tell from the heat on the side of her face that he was staring at her.

Charlie said, "All right. I'll own it. I don't know the guy's first name."

The pages fluttered as Rusty's hand dropped to his lap.

She looked at him. He had taken off his reading glasses. Nothing was tapping or clapping or jumping. He was staring out the window, silent, his gaze fixed on the distance.

She asked, "What's wrong?"

"Headache."

Her father never complained about real ailments. "Is it about the guy?" Rusty said nothing, so she asked, "Are you mad at me about the guy?"

"Of course not."

Charlie felt anxious. For all of her bluster, she could not abide disappointing her father. "I'll get his name tomorrow."

"Not your job." Rusty tucked his glasses into his shirt pocket. "Unless you plan to keep seeing him?"

Charlie sensed an odd weight behind his question. "Would it matter?"

Rusty didn't answer. He was staring out the window again.

She said, "You need to start humming or making stupid jokes or I'm going to take you to the hospital so they can make sure nothing's wrong with your heart."

"It's not *my* heart I'm worried about." The statement came across as hokey, absent his usual flourishes. He asked, "What happened between you and Ben?"

Charlie's foot almost slipped off the gas.

In nine months, Rusty had not asked her this question. She had waited five days to tell him that Ben had left. Charlie was standing in his office doorway. She had planned to relay to her father the fact of Ben leaving, nothing more, which was exactly what she'd done. But then Rusty had nodded curtly, like she was reminding him to get a haircut, and his ensuing silence had brought out a sort of verbal diarrhea that Charlie hadn't experienced since the ninth grade. Her mouth would not stop moving. She'd told Rusty that she hoped Ben would be home by the weekend. That she hoped he would return her calls, her texts, her voicemails, the note she had left on the windshield of his car.

Finally, probably to shut her up, Rusty had quoted the first stanza from Emily Dickinson's " 'Hope' is the thing with feathers."

"Dad," Charlie said, but she couldn't think of anything more to say. An oncoming car's headlights flashed into her eyes. Charlotte looked in her rearview mirror, watching the red taillights recede. She didn't want to, but she told Rusty, "It wasn't one thing. It was a lot of things."

He said, "Maybe the question is, how are you going to fix it?"

She could see now that talking about this was a mistake. "Why do you assume I'm the only one who can fix it?"

"Because Ben would never cheat on you or do anything to purposefully hurt you, so it must be something that you did or are not doing."

Charlie bit her lip too hard.

"This man you're seeing—"

"There's no seeing," she snapped. "It happened once, and it was the first and only time, and I don't appreciate—"

"Is it because of the miscarriage?"

Charlie's breath caught in her chest. "That was three years ago." And six. And thirteen. "Besides, Ben would never be that cruel."

"That's true, Ben would not be cruel."

She wondered at his comment. Was he implying that Charlie would be?

Rusty sighed. He curled the stack of papers in his hand. His foot tapped the floorboard twice. He said, "You know, I've had a long, long time to think about this, and I think what I loved most about your mother was that she was a hard woman to love."

Charlie felt the sting of the implied comparison.

"Her problem, her only problem, if you ask the man who worshipped her, was that she was too damn smart." He tapped his foot along with the last three words to add emphasis. "Gamma knew everything, and she could tell you without having to give it a moment's worth of thinking. Like the square root of three. Just off the top of her head, she'd say . . . well, hell, I don't know the answer, but she'd say—"

"One point seven-three."

"Right, right," he said. "Or someone would ask, say, what's the most common bird on earth?"

Charlie sighed. "The chicken."

"The deadliest thing on earth?"

"Mosquito."

"Australia's number one export?"

"Uh . . . iron ore?" She furrowed her brow. "Dad, where is this going?"

"Let me ask you this: What were my contributions to that little exchange we just had?"

Charlie couldn't follow. "Dad, I'm too tired for riddles."

"A visual aid—" He played at the window button, rolling it down a fraction, then up a fraction, then down, then up.

She said, "Okay, your contributions are to annoy me and break my car."

"Charlotte, let me give you the answer."

"Okay."

"No, darling. Listen to what I'm saying. Sometimes, even if you know the answer, you've got to let the other person take a shot. If they feel wrong all the time, they never get the chance to feel right."

She chewed her lip again.

"We return to our visual aid." Rusty pressed the window button again, but held it this time. The glass slid all the way down. Then he pressed in the other direction and the window rolled back up. "Nice and easy. Back and forth. Like you'd volley a ball on the tennis court, except this way I don't have to run around a tennis court to show you."

Charlie heard him tap his foot along with the car blinker as she took a right onto the farmhouse driveway. "You really should've been a marriage counselor."

"I tried, but for some reason, none of the women would get into the car with me."

He nudged her with his elbow, until she reluctantly smiled.

He said, "I remember one time your mama said to me—she said, 'Russell, I've got to figure out before I die whether I want to be happy or I want to be right.'"

Charlie felt a weird pang in her heart, because that sounded exactly like the kind of announcement Gamma would make. "Was she happy?"

"I think she was getting there." He blew out a wheezy breath. "She was inscrutable. She was beautiful. She was—"

"Goat fucker?" The Subaru's lights showed the broad side of the farmhouse. Someone had spray-painted GOAT FUCKER across the white clapboard in giant letters.

"Funny thing about that," Rusty said. "Now, the goat, that's been there a week or two. The fucker just showed up today." He slapped his knee. "Damn efficient of 'em, don't you think? I mean, the goat's already there. No need to pull out the Shakespeare."

"You need to call the police."

"Hell, honey, the police probably did it."

Charlie pulled the car close to the kitchen door. The floodlights came on. They were so bright that she could see the individual weeds in the overgrown yard.

She didn't want to, but she offered: "I should go with you to make sure there's no one inside."

"Nope." He threw open the door and jumped out. "Be sure to bring your umbrella tomorrow. I am extremely certain about the rain."

She watched his jaunty walk to the house. He stood on the porch where all those years ago Charlie and Sam had left their socks and sneakers. Rusty unlocked the two locks and threw open the door. Instead of going inside, he turned to salute her, well aware that he was standing between the GOAT and the FUCKER.

He shouted, " 'What's done cannot be undone! And now, to bed, to bed, to—' "

Charlie threw the car into reverse.

There was no need to pull out the Shakespeare.

CHAPTER SIX

Charlie sat in the garage, hands wrapped around the steering wheel.

She hated everything about going into her empty house.

Their empty house.

She hated hanging her keys on the hook by the door because Ben's hook was always empty. She hated sitting on the couch because Ben wasn't on the other side with his spidery toes hooked onto the coffee table. She couldn't even sit at the kitchen counter because Ben's empty bar stool made her too sad. Most nights, she ended up eating a bowl of cereal over the sink while she stared into the darkness outside the window.

This was no way for a woman to feel about her husband after almost two decades of marriage, but absent her actual husband, Charlie had been rocked by a kind of lovesickness that she hadn't experienced since high school.

She hadn't washed Ben's pillowcase. His favorite beer still took up door space in the refrigerator. She had left his dirty socks by the bed because she knew if she picked them up, he would not be back to leave another pair.

During the first year of their marriage, one of their biggest arguments had been over Ben's habit of taking off his socks every night and dropping them on the floor of the bedroom. Charlie had started kicking them under the bed when he wasn't looking, and one day Ben had realized that he didn't have any socks left and Charlie had laughed and he had yelled at her and she had yelled back at him and because they were both twenty-five, they had ended up fucking each other on the floor. Magically, the fury she'd once felt every time she saw the socks had been dialed back to a mild irritation, like the tail end of a yeast infection.

The first month without Ben, when it had finally dawned on Charlie that his leaving wasn't a blip, that he might not ever come back, she had sat on the floor by the socks and sobbed like a baby.

That had been the last and only time she had allowed herself to give in to her sorrow. After that long night of tears, Charlie had forced herself to stop sleeping late and to brush her teeth at least twice a day and bathe regularly and to do all those other things that showed the world that she was a functioning human being. She knew this from before: the moment she let her guard down, the world would spiral into a distant but familiar abyss.

Her first four years of college had been a headlong plunge into a bacchanalia she had only glimpsed in high school. With Lenore not there to slap some sense into her, Charlie had let loose. Too much alcohol. Too many boys. A blurring of the lines that only mattered the next morning when she didn't recognize the boy in her bed, or whose bed she was in, and couldn't recall if she had said yes or no or blacked out from the copious amounts of beer she had poured down her throat.

By some miracle, she had managed to clean up her act long enough to ace the LSAT. Duke was the only law school she applied to. Charlie had wanted to start over. New university. New city. The gamble had worked out after a long stretch of nothing working out. She had met Ben in *Intro to Writing or Elements of the Law.* On their third date, they had both agreed they were going to get married eventually, so they might as well go ahead and get married now.

A loud scraping noise pulled her out of her thoughts. Their neighbor was dragging his garbage can to the curb. Ben used to be in charge of that chore. Since he left, Charlie had accumulated so little garbage that most weeks she left a single bag at the end of the driveway.

She looked at herself in the rearview mirror. The bruises underneath her eyes were solidly black now, like a football player's. She felt achy. Her nose throbbed. She wanted soup and crackers and some hot tea, but there was no one to make it for her.

She shook her head. "You are so fucking sad," she told herself, hoping the verbal humiliation would snap her out of it.

It did not.

Charlie dragged herself out of the car before she was tempted to close the garage door and turn on the engine.

She ignored the empty space where Ben's truck was not parked. The storage shelves that held neatly labeled boxes and sporting goods that he hadn't yet claimed. She found a bag of cat food in the metal cabinet Ben had put together last summer.

They used to secretly laugh at other people whose garages were so filled with clutter that they couldn't park inside. Tidiness was one of the things they were both really good at. They cleaned the house together every Saturday. Charlie washed clothes. Ben folded. Charlie did the kitchen. Ben vacuumed the rugs and dusted the furniture. They read the same books at the same time so that they could talk about them. They binge-watched Netflix and Hulu together. They snuggled on the couch and talked about their work days and their families and what they were going to do over the weekend.

She blushed when she recalled how smug they had been about their fantastic marriage. There were so many things that they agreed on: which way the toilet-paper roll should go, the number of cats a person should keep, the appropriate number of years to mourn if a spouse was lost at sea. When their friends would argue loudly in public, or make cutting remarks about each other at a dinner party, Charlie would always look at Ben, or Ben would look at Charlie, and they would smile because their relationship was so fucking solid.

She had belittled him.

That's what Ben's leaving was about.

Charlie's shift from supportive spouse to raging harpy had not been gradual. Seemingly overnight, she was no longer capable of compromise. She was no longer able to let things go. Everything Ben did irritated her. This wasn't like the socks. There was no chance of fucking their way past it. Charlie was aware of her nagging behavior, but she couldn't stop it. Didn't *want* to stop it. She felt the most angry when she mordantly feigned interest in things that had genuinely interested her before: the politics at Ben's job, or the personality quirks of their various pets, or that weird bump one of Ben's coworkers had on the back of his neck.

She had gone to a doctor. There was nothing wrong with her hormones. Her thyroid was fine. The problem was not medical. Charlie was just a bitchy, domineering wife.

Ben's sisters had been ecstatic. She could remember them blinking their eyes that first time Charlie had laid into Ben at Thanksgiving like they had just come out of the wilderness.

Now she's one of us.

Invariably, one or two of them had started calling her almost every day, and Charlie had vented like a steam engine. The slouching. The loping walk. The chewing on the tip of his tongue. The humming when he brushed his teeth. Why did he bring home skim milk instead of two percent? Why did he leave the trash bag by the back door instead of taking it to the garbage can when he knew that the raccoons would get it?

Then she had started telling the sisters about personal things. That time Ben had tried to contact his long-absent father. Why he had stopped talking to Peggy for six months when she went to college. What had happened with that girl they all liked—but not better than Charlie—whom he insisted he'd broken up with but they all suspected had broken his heart.

She argued with him in public. She cut him down at dinner parties.

This wasn't just belittling. After almost two full years of constant abrasion, Charlie had worn Ben down to a nub. The resentment in his eyes, the persistent requests that she let something— anything—go, fell on deaf ears. The two times that he had managed to drag her into couples therapy, Charlie had been so nasty to him that the therapist had suggested that she see them separately.

It was a wonder Ben had the strength left to pack his bags and walk out the door.

"Fu-u-uck," Charlie drew out the word. She had spilled cat food all over the back deck. Ben had been right about the appropriate number of cats. Charlie had started feeding strays, and the strays had multiplied and now there were squirrels and chipmunks and, to her horror, a possum the size of a small dog that shuffled onto the back deck every night, staring at her through the glass door, his beady red eyes flashing in the light from the television.

Charlie used her hands to scrape up the food. She cursed Ben for having the dog this week because Barkzilla, their greedy Jack Russell terrier, would've hoovered all of the kibble in seconds. Since she had skipped her chores this morning, there was more to do tonight. She added food and water to the appropriate bowls, used the pitchfork to shift the hay they'd laid down for bedding. She topped off the bird feeders. She washed down the deck. She used the outside broom to knock down some spiderwebs. She did everything she could to keep from going inside until, finally, it was too dark and too cold not to.

Ben's empty key hook greeted her by the door. The empty bar stool. The empty couch. The emptiness followed her upstairs into the bedroom, into the shower. Ben's hair was not stuck to the soap, his toothbrush wasn't by the sink, his razor wasn't on her side of the counter.

Charlie's toxic level of patheticness was so pronounced that by the time she slouched downstairs in her pajamas, even pouring a bowl of cereal felt like too much work.

She fell onto the couch. She didn't want to read. She didn't want to stare at the ceiling and moan. She did what she had avoided doing all day and turned on the television.

The channel was already tuned to CNN. A pretty blonde teenager was standing in front of the Pikeville Middle School. She held a candle in her hand because there was some kind of vigil going on. The banner underneath her face identified her as CANDICE BELMONT, NORTH GEORGIA.

The girl said, "Mrs. Alexander talked about her daughter all the time in class. Called her 'the Baby' because she was so sweet, like a little baby. You could really tell that she loved her."

Charlie muted the sound. The media were milking the tragedy the same way she was milking her self-pity over Ben. As someone who had been on the inside of violence, who had lived with its aftermath, she felt sick whenever she saw these kinds of stories covered. The sharp graphics. The haunting music. The montages of grieving people. The stations were desperate to keep viewers watching, and the easiest way they'd found to achieve that goal was to report everything they heard and sort out the truth later.

The camera cut away from the blonde at the vigil to the handsome field reporter, his shirtsleeves rolled up three-quarters, the candlelight glowing softly in the background. Charlie studied his pantomimed grief as he tossed the story back to the studio. The news anchor behind the desk had the same solemn expression on his face as he continued reporting what was not the news. Charlie read the chyron crawling at the bottom of the screen, a quote from the Alexander family: UNCLE: KELLY RENE WILSON "A COLD-BLOODED MURDERER."

Kelly had been promoted to three names now. Charlie supposed some producer in New York had decided that it sounded more menacing.

The scroll stopped. The anchor disappeared. Both were replaced by an illustration of a locker-lined hallway. The drawing was three-dimensional, but had an odd flatness, Charlie supposed to make it very clear that this was not real. A lawyer had apparently not been satisfied by the crudeness. The word "RE-ENACTMENT" flashed red in the upper-right corner of the screen.

The drawing became animated. A figure entered the hallway, moving stiffly, drawn in a blocky style. The figure's long hair and dark clothing all pointed to Kelly Wilson.

Charlie unmuted the sound.

". . . approximately six fifty-five, the alleged shooter, Kelly Rene Wilson, walked into the hallway." The animated Kelly stopped in the middle of the screen. There was a gun in her hand, more like a nine-millimeter than a revolver. "Wilson was said to be standing in this location when Judith Pinkman opened the door to her classroom."

Charlie moved to the edge of the couch.

A squared-off Mrs. Pinkman opened her door. For some reason, the animator had made her white-ish blonde hair silvery gray, styled it in a bun instead of down around her shoulders.

"Wilson saw Pinkman and fired two shots," the anchor continued. The gun in Kelly's hands showed two puffs of smoke. The bullets were indicated by straight lines, more like arrows. "Both shots missed, but principal Douglas Pinkman, Judith Pinkman's husband of twenty-five years, ran from his office when he heard the gunfire."

The virtual Mr. Pinkman floated out of his office, his legs not moving at the same pace as his forward movement.

"Wilson saw her former principal and fired two more shots." The gun puffed again. The arrow-bullets traced to Mr. Pinkman's chest. "Douglas Pinkman was instantly killed."

Charlie watched the virtual Mr. Pinkman fall flat to his side, his hand to his chest. Two squid-like red blotches appeared in the middle of his blue, short-sleeved shirt.

Which was wrong, too, because Mr. Pinkman's shirt had been long-sleeved and white. And he hadn't worn his hair in a buzz cut.

It was as if the animator had decided that a middle-school principal looked like a 1970s G-man and an English teacher was an old biddy with a bun on her head.

"Next," the anchor narrated, "Lucy Alexander entered the hallway."

Charlie squeezed her eyes shut.

The anchor said, "Lucy had forgotten to get lunch money from her mother, a biology teacher who was at a department meeting across the street when the shootings occurred." There was a moment of silence, and Charlie saw an image in her head of Lucy Alexander—not the squared-off drawing that the animators would have gotten wrong, but the actual little girl—swinging her arms, smiling as she rounded the corner. "Two more shots were fired at the eight-year-old girl. The first one went into her upper torso. The second bullet went through the office window behind her."

There were three loud knocks.

Charlie opened her eyes. She muted the TV.

Another two knocks.

Panic shot through her heart. She always felt a flicker of fear every time an unknown person knocked at her door.

Charlie stood from the couch. She thought about the gun in her bedside table as she looked out the front window.

She smiled as she went to open the door.

All day, Charlie had been so busy wondering how things could get worse that she had never thought how things could get better.

"Hey." Ben stood on the porch, hands in his pockets. "Sorry I'm bothering you so late. I need to get a file out of the closet."

"Oh," was all that she could say, because the rush of wanting him was too overwhelming to say more. Not that he'd made an effort. Ben had changed into sweatpants and a T-shirt she didn't recognize, which made her wonder if Kaylee Collins, the twenty-six-year-old at his office, had bought him the shirt. What else had the girl changed? Charlie wanted to smell his hair to see if he was using their shampoo. To check his underwear to see if it was the same brand.

Ben asked, "May I come in?"

"It's still your house." Charlie realized she would have to actually move so he could come in. She stepped back, holding open the door.

Ben stopped in front of the television. The animation had come to an end. The anchor was back on screen. Ben said, "Someone's leaking details, but they don't have the right details."

"I know," Charlie said. They weren't just wrong about what had happened when, they were wrong about how the people looked, where they stood, how they moved. Whoever was leaking information to the media was likely not on the inside, but they were close enough to get a payday for whatever specious information they could provide.

"So." Ben scratched his arm. He looked down at the floor. He looked back up at Charlie. "Terri called me."

She nodded, because of course his sister had called him. What was the point of saying something awful to Charlie if Ben didn't know about it?

Ben said, "I'm sorry she brought it up."

She lifted up one shoulder. "Doesn't matter."

Nine months ago, he would've said it mattered, but now, he simply shrugged back. "So, I'll go upstairs, if that's okay?"

Charlie gestured toward the stairs like a maître d'.

She listened to his light footsteps as he sprinted up the stairs, wondering how she had forgotten what that sounded like. His hand squeaked on the banister as he rounded the landing. The polish was worn from the wood where he did this every time.

How was that detail not in her wallowing book?

Charlie stood where he had left her. She stared blankly at the flat-screen TV. It was massive, bigger than anything in the Holler. Ben had worked all day to get the components tied in. Around midnight, he'd asked, "Wanna watch the news?"

When Charlie had agreed, he'd pressed some keys on his computer and suddenly, Charlie was watching a video of a bunch of gnus.

Upstairs, she heard a door open. Charlie crossed her arms low over her stomach. What was the proper thing for a wife to do when her estranged husband, who hadn't been inside their house in nine months, was inside the house?

She found Ben in the guest room, which was more of a catchall for extra books, some filing cabinets, and the custom shelves that used to hold Ben's *Star Trek* collectibles.

It was when Charlie had realized the *Star Trek* stuff was gone that she had known Ben was serious.

"Hey," she said.

He was inside the walk-in closet, rummaging through file boxes.

"Need help?" she asked.

"No."

Charlie bumped her leg against the bed. Should she leave? She should leave.

"My plea bargain from today," Ben said, so she guessed he was looking for old notes relating to the case. "Guy lied about his accomplice."

"I'm sorry." Charlie sat on the bed. "You should take Barkzilla's squeaky. I found it by the——"

"I got him a new one."

Charlie looked down at the floor. She tried not to think about Ben at the pet store looking for a toy for their dog without her. Or with someone else. "I wonder if the person who leaked the bad timeline to the news did it for the attention or did it to throw off the press."

"Dickerson County is looking at the security footage from the hospital."

Charlie couldn't see the connection. "Great."

"Whoever slashed your dad's tires was probably some idiot acting out, but they're taking it seriously."

"Asshole," Charlie muttered, because Rusty had lied about why he needed a lift.

Ben poked his head out of the closet. "What?"

"Nothing," she said. "Someone spray-painted his house, too. They wrote 'goat fucker.' Or just 'fucker' because the 'goat' was already there."

"I saw the 'goat' last weekend."

"What were you doing at the HP last weekend?"

He stepped out of the closet with a file box in his hands. "I see your dad the last Sunday of every month. You know that."

Rusty and Ben had always had a weird kind of friendship. They treated each other like contemporaries despite the age difference. "I didn't realize you were still doing that."

"Yeah, well." He put the box on the bed. The mattress sagged from the weight. "I'll update Keith about the 'fucker.'" He meant Keith Coin, the chief of police and Ken Coin's older brother. "He said he'd send someone around about the goat, but with what happened today . . . ." His voice trailed off as he took the top off the box.

"Ben." Charlie watched him search the files. "Do you feel like I never let you answer questions?"

"Aren't you letting me answer one right now?"

She smiled. "I mean, because Dad did this convoluted thing with the car window, and—that part doesn't matter. He basically said that you have to choose between being right and being happy. He said that was something Gamma told him she needed to decide before she died, whether she wanted to be right or happy."

He looked up from the box. "I don't understand why you can't be both."

"I guess if you're right too many times, like you know too much, or you're too smart and you let people know it . . ." She wasn't sure how to explain. "Gamma knew the answer to a lot of things. To everything, actually."

"So your dad said she would've been happier if she pretended she wasn't as smart as she was?"

Charlie instinctively defended her father. "Gamma said it, not Dad."

"That sounds like a problem with their marriage, not ours." He rested his hand on the box. "Charlie, if you're worried that you're like your mom, that's not a bad thing. From everything I've heard, she was an amazing person."

He was so fucking decent it took her breath away. "You're an amazing person."

He gave a sharp, sarcastic laugh. She had tried this before, overcorrecting her bitchiness, treating him like a toddler in need of a participation trophy.

She said, "I'm serious, Ben. You're smart and funny and—" His surprised look cut off her praise. "What?"

"Are you crying?"

"Shit." Charlie tried not to cry in front of anybody but Lenore. "I'm sorry. I've been doing this since I woke up."

He was utterly still. "You mean since the school?"

Charlie smoothed together her lips. "Before that."

"Do you even know who that guy is?"

She was sick of the question. "The whole point of being with a stranger is that they're a stranger, and in a perfect world, you never have to see them again."

"Good to know." He pulled out a file and paged through it.

Charlie pushed herself up on her knees so she could look him in the eye. "It's never happened before. Not once. Not even close."

Ben shook his head.

"I never looked at another man when I was with you."

He put the file back into the box and pulled out another one. "Did you come with him?"

"No," she said, but that was a lie. "Yes, but I had to use my hand, and it was nothing. Like a sneeze."

"A sneeze," he repeated. "Great, now every time I sneeze, I'm going to think of you coming with fucking Batman."

"I was lonely."

"Lonely," he echoed.

"What do you want me to say, Ben? I want *you* to make me come. I want to be with *you*." She tried to touch his hand but he moved it away. "I'll do whatever it takes to make this better. Just tell me."

"You know what I want."

The marriage counselor again. "We don't need some frumpy licensed social worker with a bad haircut to tell me I'm the problem. I know I'm the problem. I'm trying to fix it."

"You asked what I wanted and I told you."

"What's the point of picking apart something that happened thirty years ago?" Charlie sighed, exasperated. "I know I'm angry about it, Ben. I'm fucking furious. I don't try to hide it. I don't pretend it didn't happen. If I was obsessed with it and wouldn't shut up about it, she would say something was wrong with that, too."

"You know that's not what she said."

"God, Ben, what's the point of this? Do you still even want me?"

"Of course I do." He looked anxious, like he wanted to take back his answer. "Why can't you understand that part doesn't matter?"

"It matters." She moved closer to him. "I miss you, babe. Don't you miss me?"

He shook his head again. "Charlie, that's not going to fix things."

"It might fix them a little." She stroked back his hair. "I want you, Ben."

He kept shaking his head, but he didn't push her away.

"I'll do whatever you want." Charlie moved closer. Throwing herself at him was the only thing she hadn't tried. "Tell me and I'll do it."

"Stop," he said, but didn't stop her.

"I want you." She kissed his neck. The way his skin reacted to her mouth made Charlie want to cry. She kissed along his jaw, up to his ear. "I want to feel you inside of me."

Ben let out a low groan as her hands moved down his chest.

She kept kissing him, licking him. "Let me go down on you."

He inhaled a shaky breath.

"You can have whatever you want, babe. My mouth. My hands. My ass."

"Chuck." His voice was hoarse. "We can't—"

She kissed him on the lips, and kept kissing him until he finally kissed her back. His mouth was like silk. The feel of his tongue sent a rush between her legs. Every nerve in her body was on fire. His hand went to her breast. He was getting hard, but Charlie reached down to make him harder.

Ben covered his hand over hers. At first, she thought he was helping her but then she realized he was stopping her.

"Oh God." She backed away quickly, jumping off the bed, standing with her back to the wall, embarrassed, humiliated, frantic. "I'm sorry. I'm so sorry."

"Charlie—"

"No!" She held up her hands like a traffic cop. "If you say something now, then it'll be the end, and it can't be the end of things, Ben. That can't happen. It's too much after—"

Charlie cut herself off, but her own words rang in her ears like a warning.

Ben stared at her. His throat moved as he swallowed. "After what?"

Charlie listened to the blood pounding in her ears. She felt jittery, like her toes were dangling over the edge of a bottomless chasm.

Ben's phone played the opening bars of the *COPS* theme, the ringtone he'd set for the Pikeville Police Department.

Bad boys, bad boys, whatchu gonna do . . .

She said, "It's work. You have to answer."

"No, I don't." He tilted up his chin, waiting.

Bad boys, bad boys . . .

He said, "Tell me what happened today."

"You were there when I gave my statement."

"You ran toward the gunshots. Why? What were you thinking?"

"I didn't run toward gunshots. I ran toward Mrs. Pinkman screaming for help."

"You mean Heller?"

"That's exactly the kind of Oprah bullshit a therapist would say." She had to yell to be heard over his stupid phone. "That I put myself in danger because thirty years ago, when someone really needed me, I ran away."

"And look what happened!" Ben's sudden flash of anger reverberated through the quiet.

The ringtone had stopped.

The silence rumbled like thunder.

She said, "What the *fuck* does that mean?"

Ben's jaw was clenched so tight she could practically hear his teeth grinding. He grabbed the box off the bed and threw it back into the closet.

"What are you talking about, Ben?" Charlie felt shaky, like something irreparable had torn apart. "Do you mean, look at what happened then, or look at what happened today?"

He shoved boxes around on the shelves.

She stood in the closet doorway, trapping him. "You don't get to throw shit around and then turn your back on me."

He said nothing.

Charlie heard the distant ring of her cell phone buried deep in her purse downstairs. She counted out five long rings, holding her breath through the pauses until voicemail picked up.

Ben kept moving boxes around.

The silence began to fester. She was going to start crying again because crying was all that she could do today.

"Ben?" She finally broke, begging, "Please tell me what you meant."

He took the lid off one of the boxes. He traced his finger along the labeled files. She thought he was going to keep ignoring her, but he said, "Today is the third."

Charlie looked away. That's why Ben had called her this morning. It's why Rusty had hummed "Happy Birthday" while she had stood by like an imbecile asking him again and again to tell her what he knew.

She said, "I saw last week on the calendar, what day it was, but—"

Ben's phone started ringing again. Not the police this time, but a normal ring. Once. Twice. He answered on the third ring. She heard his curt responses, "When?" then, "How bad is it?" then, his tone deeper, "Did the doctor say . . ."

Charlie leaned her shoulder against the doorjamb. She had heard variations on this call multiple times before. Someone in the Holler had punched his wife too hard or grabbed a knife to end a fight and someone else had grabbed a gun, and now the assistant district attorney had to go to the station and offer a deal to the first person who talked.

"Will he make it?" Ben asked. He started nodding again. "Yeah. I'll handle it. Thanks."

Charlie watched him end the call, slip his phone back into his pocket. She said, "Let me guess, a Culpepper got arrested?"

He didn't turn around. He gripped the edges of the shelf like he needed something to hold on to.

"Ben?" she asked. "What is it?"

Ben sniffed. He wasn't a complete stoic, but Charlie could count on one hand the times she had seen her husband cry. Except he wasn't just crying now. His shoulders were shaking. He seemed racked by grief.

Charlie started crying, too. His sisters? His mother? His selfish father who had run off when Ben was six?

She put her hand on his shoulder. He was still shaking. "Babe, what is it? You're scaring me."

He wiped his nose. He turned around. Tears streamed from his eyes. "I'm sorry."

"What?" Her voice was almost a whisper. "Ben, what?"

"It's your dad." He swallowed back his grief. "They had to life-flight him to the hospital. He——"

Charlie's knees began to buckle. Ben caught her before she hit the floor.

Will he make it?

"Your neighbor found him," Ben said. "He was at the end of the driveway."

Charlie pictured Rusty walking to the mailbox—humming, marching, snapping his fingers—then clutching his heart and falling to the ground.

She said, "He's so . . ." *Stupid. Willful. Self-destructive.* "We were in my office today, and I told him he was going to have another heart attack, and now——"

"It wasn't his heart."

"But——"

"Your dad didn't have a heart attack. Somebody stabbed him."

Charlie's mouth moved soundlessly before she could get out the word, "stabbed?" She had to repeat it, because it didn't make sense. "Stabbed?"

"Chuck, you need to call your sister."

WHAT HAPPENED TO CHARLOTTE

Charlotte turned to her sister and shouted, "Last word!"

She ran toward the HP before Samantha could think of a good

comeback. Red clay swirled up from Charlotte's feet and gummed onto her sweaty legs. She jumped up the porch steps, kicked off her shoes, peeled off her socks, and pushed open the door in time to hear Gamma say, *"Fuck!"*

Her mother was bent at the waist, one hand braced on the counter, the other at her mouth like she had been coughing.

Charlotte said, "Mom, that's a bad word."

Gamma stood up. She used a tissue from her pocket to wipe her mouth. "I said 'fudge,' Charlie. What did you think I said?"

"You said—" Charlotte saw the trap. "If I say the bad word, then you'll know that I know the bad word."

"Don't show your work, sweetheart." She tucked the tissue back into her pocket and headed toward the hall. "Have the table set before I get back."

"Where are you going?"

"Undetermined."

"How will I know how fast to set the table if I don't know when you're going to get back?" She listened for an answer.

Gamma's sharp coughs echoed back.

Charlotte grabbed the paper plates. She dumped the box of plastic forks onto the table. Gamma had bought real silverware and plates at the thrift store, but no one could find the box. Charlotte knew it was in Rusty's study. They were supposed to unpack the room tomorrow, which meant that somebody would have to wash dishes at the sink tomorrow night.

Samantha slammed the kitchen door closed so hard that the wall shook.

Charlotte didn't take the bait. She tossed out the paper plates onto the table.

Suddenly, without warning, Samantha threw a fork at her face.

Charlotte was opening her mouth to scream for Gamma when she felt the tines of the fork stab her bottom lip. She instinctively closed her mouth.

The fork stayed, a quivering arrow in a bull's-eye.

Charlotte said, "Holy crap, that was amazing!"

Samantha shrugged, like the hard part wasn't catching a somersaulting fork between your lips.

Charlotte said, "I'll wash the dishes if you can do that twice in a row."

"You toss it into my mouth once, and I'll wash dishes for a week."

"Deal." Charlotte took aim, weighing her options: bean Samantha in the face on purpose or really try to get it into her mouth?

Gamma was back. "Charlie, don't throw utensils at your sister. Sam, help me look for that frying pan I bought the other day."

The table was already set, but Charlotte didn't want to be enlisted into the search. The boxes smelled like mothballs and cheesy dog feet. She straightened the plates. She re-lined up the forks. They were going to have spaghetti tonight, so they would need knives because Gamma always undercooked the noodles and they clumped together like strands of tendons.

"Sam." Gamma had started coughing again. She pointed toward the air conditioner. "Turn that thing on so we can get some air moving in here."

Samantha looked at the giant box in the window like she'd never seen an air conditioner before. She had been moping since the red-brick house had burned down. Charlotte had been moping, too, but on the inside, because Rusty already felt bad enough without them rubbing it in.

Charlotte picked up an extra paper plate. She tried to fold it into an airplane so that she could give it to her father.

Samantha asked, "What time are we supposed to pick up Daddy from work?"

Gamma said, "He'll get a ride from somebody at the courthouse."

Charlotte hoped Lenore would give him a ride. Rusty's secretary had loaned her a book called *Lace*, which was about four friends, and one of them was raped by a sheikh, only you don't know which one, and she got pregnant and no one told the daughter what happened until she was an adult and she got really rich and she asked them, *"Which one of you bitches is my mother?"*

"Well, shit." Gamma stood up. "I hope you girls don't mind being vegetarian tonight."

"Mom." Charlotte dropped down into the chair. She put her head in her hands, feigning sickness in hope of soliciting a can of soup for dinner instead. "My stomach hurts."

Gamma asked, "Don't you have homework?"

"Chemistry." Charlotte looked up. "Can you help me?"

"It's not rocket science."

Charlotte asked, "Do you mean, it's not rocket science, so I should be able to figure it out on my own, or do you mean, it's not rocket science, and that is the only science that you know how to perform, and so therefore you cannot help me?"

"There were too many conjunctions in that sentence," Gamma said. "Go wash your hands."

"I believe I had a valid question."

"Now."

Charlotte ran into the hall. It was so long that you could stand in the kitchen and treat it as a bowling alley. At least that was what Gamma said, and that was exactly what Charlotte was going to do as soon as she could get a ball.

She opened one of the five doors and found the stairs to the yucky basement. She tried another and found the hallway to the bachelor farmer's scary bedroom.

"Fudge!" Charlotte bellowed, but only for Gamma's sake.

She opened another door. The chifforobe. Charlotte grinned, because she was playing a joke on Samantha, or maybe not a joke—whatever it was called when you wanted to scare the crap out of somebody.

She was trying to convince her sister that the HP was haunted.

Yesterday, Charlotte had found a weird black-and-white photograph in one of the thrift store boxes. At first, she had started to color it, but she only got as far as yellowing the teeth when she had the idea to stick the picture in the bottom drawer of the chifforobe for Samantha to find.

Her sister had been appropriately freaked out, probably because the night before, Charlotte creaked the boards outside of her room so that Samantha would follow her down to the scary bedroom where the bachelor farmer had died, where she planted the idea that the old geezer had left the house in body, but not spirit. As in, he was a ghost.

Charlotte tried another door. "Found it!"

She yanked the cord for the light. She pulled down her shorts, but froze when she noticed a sprinkling of blood on the toilet seat.

This wasn't the blood like Samantha sometimes left when she was having her period. This was a sprinkle, the kind that came out of your mouth when you coughed too hard.

Gamma was coughing too hard a lot.

Charlotte pulled up her shorts. She turned on the faucet and cupped her hands under the water. She splashed the toilet seat to wash away the red spots. Then she saw that there were more red dots on the floor. She threw some water on those, then on the mirror because there was some there, too. Even the moldy edge of the corner shower had been sprayed.

The phone rang in the kitchen. Charlotte waited through two more rings, wondering if they were going to answer it. Gamma wouldn't let them pick up sometimes because it might be Rusty. She was still upset about the fire, but she wasn't moping like Samantha. She was screaming, mostly. And she cried, too, but only Charlotte knew about that.

The handle of the ball-peen hammer was soaked by the time Charlotte banged off the faucet. Her butt got wet when she sat down on the toilet seat. Charlotte could see that she had made a mess. Some of the water had turned pink. She pulled up her shorts. She dotted at the water with a wad of toilet paper. The paper began to disintegrate, so she used more. And then she used even more.

Paper was supposed to absorb stuff, but all she was doing was creating a giant wad of wet paper that would clog the toilet if she tried to flush it.

Charlotte stood up. She looked around the bathroom. The pink was gone, but there was still a lot of water. The room was kind of damp anyway. The shower mold was something out of a movie with a lagoon where a swamp monster comes out.

In the hall, a box jangled. Sam let out a strangled noise, like she'd stubbed her toe.

"Fudge," Charlotte said, for real this time. The wad of toilet paper was pink with blood. She shoved it into the front pocket of her shorts. There wasn't time to pee. She shut the bathroom door behind her. Samantha was ten feet away. Charlotte punched her sister in her arm to distract her from the wet lump in her shorts. Then she galloped the rest of the way up the hall because horses were faster.

"Dinner!" Gamma called. She was standing by the stove when Charlotte cantered into the kitchen.

Charlotte said, "I'm right here."

"Your sister isn't."

Charlotte saw the thick noodles Gamma dug out of the pot with a pair of tongs. "Mom, please don't make us eat that."

"I'm not going to let you starve."

"I could eat a bowl of ice cream."

"Do you want explosive diarrhea?"

Charlotte got sick from anything that had milk in it, but she was pretty sure the ropey spaghetti would have the same effect. "Mama, what would happen if I ate two bowls of ice cream? Really big ones."

"Your intestines would burst and you would die."

Charlotte studied her mother's back. Sometimes, she couldn't tell when Gamma was being serious.

The phone gave the trill of a ring. Charlotte grabbed the receiver before Gamma could tell her not to.

"Hello?" she said.

"Hey there, Charlie Bear." Rusty chuckled, like he hadn't said the same words to her a million times before. "I was hoping to speak with my dear Gamma?"

Gamma could hear Rusty's question from across the room because he always talked too loud on the phone. She shook her head at Charlotte, and mouthed the word "no" to make it clear.

"She's brushing her teeth," Charlotte said. "Or maybe she's flossing by now? I heard squeaking, but I thought it was a mouse, only—"

Gamma grabbed the phone. She told Rusty, " 'Hope' is the thing with feathers / That perches in the soul / And sings the tune without the words / And never stops—at all.' "

She put the phone back on the hook. She asked Charlotte, "Did you know that the chicken is the most common bird on earth?"

Charlotte shook her head. She did not know that.

"I'll help you with your chemistry after supper, which will not be ice cream."

"The chemistry won't be ice cream, or the supper?"

"Clever girl." She held Charlotte's face in one hand. "You're going to find a man one day who is going to fall head over heels in love with that brain of yours."

Charlotte pictured a man tripping and flipping through the air like the plastic fork. "What if he breaks his neck when he falls?"

Gamma kissed the top of Charlotte's head before leaving the kitchen.

Charlotte sunk into the chair. She leaned back and saw that her mother was heading toward the pantry. Or the basement stairs. Or the chifforobe. Or the bedroom. Or the bathroom.

She dropped the chair back to the floor. She leaned her elbows on the table.

Charlotte wasn't sure she wanted a man to fall in love with her. There was a boy at school who was in love with Samantha. Peter Alexander. He played jazz guitar and wanted to move to Atlanta and join a band when he got out of high school. At least, that's what he wrote about in the long, boring letters that Samantha used to keep hidden between her mattress and boxspring.

Peter was the thing that Samantha moped about losing the most. Charlotte had seen Samantha let him touch her under her shirt, which meant that she really liked him, because you weren't supposed to do that otherwise. He had a cool leather jacket that he'd let her borrow and it had been burned up in the fire. He'd gotten into a lot of trouble with his parents for losing it. He wasn't talking to Samantha anymore.

Charlotte had a lot of friends who weren't talking to her, too, but Rusty said that was because their parents were imbeciles who didn't think it was a bad thing for a black man to be executed on death row even though he was innocent.

She whistled between her teeth as she folded down the sides of the paper plate and tried again to turn it into an airplane. Rusty had also told Charlotte that the fire had switched things around for a little while. Gamma and Samantha, who were usually the logical ones, had changed places with Rusty and Charlotte, who were usually the emotional ones. It was like *Freaky Friday*, except they couldn't get a basset hound because Samantha was allergic.

Charlotte licked the creases of the plane, hoping her spit would help it retain the shape. She hadn't told Rusty that her logical switch hadn't really flipped. She was pretending like everything was okay when it wasn't okay. Charlotte had lost stuff, too, like all of her Nancy Drews, her goldfish—which was *an actual living thing*—her Brownie badges, and six dead insects she had been saving for next year because she knew that in honors biology, the first assignment was that you had to pin insects to a board and identify them for the teacher.

Several times, Charlotte had tried to talk about her sadness with Samantha, but all Samantha would do was start listing all the things she had lost, like it was a contest. So then Charlotte had tried to talk about other things, like school and TV shows and the book she had checked out from the library, but Samantha would stare at her until Charlotte got the message and went away.

The only time her sister treated her like a normal human being was at night when they washed their shirts and shorts and sports bras out at the bathroom sink. Their track clothes and sneakers were the only things they had left after the fire, but Samantha didn't talk about them. She would walk Charlotte slowly, patiently, through the blind pass, like it was the only thing left in their lives that mattered. *Bend your front leg, hold your hand straight behind you, lean forward, into the track, but don't push off until I'm at my mark. Once you feel the baton snap into your hand—go.*

"Don't look back," Samantha would say. "You have to trust me to be there. Just keep your head down and run."

Samantha had always loved running. She wanted to get a track scholarship so she could run all the way to college and never come back to Pikeville, which meant she could be gone in a year because Gamma was going to let her skip another grade if she scored a perfect 1600 on the SAT.

Charlotte gave up on the airplane, defeated. The plate wouldn't hold its new shape. It wanted to stay a plate. She should get some notebook paper and do it the right way. Charlotte wanted to throw the airplane off the old weather tower. Rusty had promised to take her there because he was working on a surprise for Gamma.

The bachelor farmer had been a Citizen Scientist with the National Weather Service Cooperative Observers Program. Rusty had found boxes full of Weather Journal Data forms in the barn where the farmer had recorded the temperature, barometric pressure, precipitation, wind and humidity almost every day since 1948.

There were thousands of volunteers around the country just like him who sent their readings to the National Oceanic and Atmospheric Administration to help scientists predict when storms and tornadoes were going to form. Basically, you had to do a lot of math, and if there was one thing that could make Gamma happy, it was doing math every day.

The weather tower was going to be the biggest surprise of her life.

Charlotte heard a car in the driveway. She grabbed the failed airplane and tore it to pieces so that Rusty wouldn't guess what she was up to, because he'd already told her she couldn't climb to the top of the metal tower and throw a paper airplane off it. At the trash can, she dug into her shorts and pulled out the gross clumps of wet toilet paper. She wiped her hands on her shirt. She ran to the door to see her father.

"Mama!" Charlotte yelled, but she didn't tell her that Rusty was here.

She pulled open the door, smiling, and then she stopped smiling because two men were on the front porch.

One of them stepped back onto the stairs. Charlotte saw his eyes go wide, like he wasn't expecting the door to open, and then she saw that he was wearing a black ski mask, and a black shirt and leather gloves, and then she saw the barrel of a shotgun stuck in her face.

"Mom!" Charlotte screamed.

"Shut up," Black Shirt hissed, pushing Charlotte back into the kitchen. His heavy boots tracked in red clay from the yard. Charlotte should've been terrified, she should've been screaming, but all she could think about was how mad Gamma was going to be about having to clean the floor again.

"Charlie Quinn," Gamma called from the bathroom. "Do not shriek at me like a street urchin."

Black Shirt said, "Where's your daddy?"

"P-please," Charlotte stuttered. She was talking to the second guy. He was in a mask and gloves, too, but he had on a white Bon Jovi T-shirt, which made him feel less threatening, even though he had a gun. "Please don't hurt us."

Bon Jovi was looking past Charlotte, down the hallway. She

could hear her mother's slow footsteps. Gamma must have seen him when she came out of the bathroom. She knew something was wrong, that Charlotte wasn't in the kitchen on her own.

"Hey." Black Shirt snapped his fingers for Charlotte's attention. "Where's your fucking daddy?"

Charlotte shook her head. Why would they want Rusty?

Black Shirt asked, "Who else is in the house?"

She said, "My sister's in—"

Suddenly, Gamma's hand was wrapped around Charlotte's mouth. Her fingers dug into her shoulder. She told the men, "There's fifty dollars in my purse and another two hundred in a Mason jar in the barn."

"Fuck that," Black Shirt said. "Call your other daughter in here. Don't try any shit."

"No." Bon Jovi seemed nervous. "They were supposed to be at track practice, man. Let's just—"

Charlotte was violently jerked out of Gamma's arms. Black Shirt's hand gripped her neck, his fingers like clamps. The back of her head was pinned to his chest. She felt his fingers cinching around her esophagus, pulling it like a handle.

He told Gamma, "Call her, bitch."

"Sa—" Gamma was so scared that she could hardly raise her voice. "Samantha?"

They listened. They waited.

Bon Jovi said, "Forget it, man. He's not here. Let's do like she said and take the money and go."

"Grow some balls, you fucking pussy." Black Shirt tightened his grip on Charlotte's throat. The pain burned like fire. She couldn't breathe. She went up on her toes. Her fingers wrapped around his wrist, but he was too strong.

He told Gamma, "Get her in here before I—"

"Samantha!" Gamma's tone was sharp. "Please ensure the faucet valve is closed and quickly make your way into the kitchen."

Bon Jovi stepped away from the mouth of the hallway so that

Samantha couldn't see him. He told Black Shirt, "Come on, man. She did what you said. Let her go."

Slowly, Black Shirt loosened his grip on Charlotte's neck. She gagged on the rush of air. She tried to go to her mother, but his hand flattened to her chest. He pinned Charlotte tight against his body.

Gamma said, "You don't have to do this." She was talking to Bon Jovi. "We don't know who you are. We don't know your names. You can leave now and we won't tell anyone."

"Shut the fuck up." Black Shirt shifted back and forth. "I'm not stupid enough to believe a God damn thing any of you say."

"You can't—" Gamma coughed into her hand. "Please. Let my daughters go and I'll—" She coughed again. "You can take me to the bank. Keep the car. I'll give you every penny we have."

"I'm'a take whatever I want." Black Shirt's hand slid down Charlotte's chest. He pressed hard against her sternum, rubbed into her back. His private parts poked her. She felt a sudden sickness. Her bladder wanted to release. Her face turned hot.

"Stop it." Bon Jovi grabbed Charlotte's arm. He pulled, then pulled harder, and finally, he managed to wrench her away.

"Baby." Gamma enveloped Charlotte, throwing her arms tight around her shoulders, kissing her head, then her ear. She whispered, "Run if you—"

Without warning, Gamma let go, almost pushing Charlotte away. She took two steps back until she was against the kitchen counter. Her hands were in the air.

Black Shirt had the shotgun pointed at her chest.

"Please." Gamma's lips trembled. "Please. I beg you," her voice was low, like it was just her and Black Shirt in the room. "You can do anything you want to me, but don't hurt my baby."

"Don't worry." Black Shirt whispered, too. "It only hurts the first couple'a dozen times."

Charlotte started to shake.

She knew what he meant. The dark look in his eyes. His tongue darting out between his wet lips. The way his *thing* had pressed into her back.

Her knees stopped working.

She stumbled back into the chair. Sweat covered her face. More sweat poured down her back. She looked at her hands, but they weren't like her normal hands. The bones were vibrating inside as if a tuning fork had been struck against her chest.

Gamma said, "It's okay."

Black Shirt said, "No it ain't."

They weren't talking to each other anymore. Samantha was standing in the doorway, frozen like a frightened rabbit.

Black Shirt asked, "Who else is in the house?"

Gamma shook her head. "Nobody."

"Don't lie to me, bitch."

Charlotte's hearing became muffled. She heard her father's name, saw the angry look in Gamma's eyes.

Rusty. They were looking for Rusty.

Charlotte began to rock, unable to stop the back and forth movement as she instinctively tried to calm herself. This wasn't a movie. There were two men inside the house. They had guns. They didn't want money. They had come for Rusty, but now that they knew Rusty wasn't here, Black Shirt had decided he wanted something else. Charlotte knew what that something else was. She had read about it in Lenore's book. And Gamma was only here because Charlotte had called her and Samantha was only here because Charlotte had told the men that her sister was in the house.

"I'm sorry," Charlotte whispered. She couldn't hold her bladder anymore. She felt the warm liquid slide down her leg. She closed her eyes. She rocked back and forth. "I'm-sorry-I'm-sorry-I'm-sorry."

Samantha squeezed Charlotte's hand so hard she could feel the bones move.

Charlotte was going to throw up. Her stomach kept clenching, rolling like she was trapped on a boat in the pitching sea. She squeezed her eyes closed. She thought about running. The soles of her shoes slapping the ground. Her legs burning. Her chest aching for air. Samantha was beside her, ponytail flapping in the wind, smiling, telling Charlotte what to do.

Breathe through it. Slow and steady. Wait for the pain to pass.

"I said shut the fuck up!" Black Shirt screamed.

Charlotte lifted her head, but it was like she was moving through a thick oil.

There was an explosion, then a blast of hot liquid slashed at her face and neck so hard that she fell against Samantha at the table.

Charlotte started screaming before she knew why.

Blood was everywhere, like a hose had been turned on. It was warm and viscous and it covered her face, her hands, her entire body.

"Shut up!" Black Shirt slapped Charlotte across the face.

Samantha grabbed her. She was sobbing, shaking, screaming.

"Gamma," Samantha whispered.

Charlie clung to her sister. She turned her head. She made herself look at her mother, because she wanted to make sure she never forgot what these fuckers had done.

Bright white bone. Pieces of heart and lung. Cords of tendon and arteries and veins and life spilled out of her gaping wounds.

Bon Jovi yelled, "Jesus Christ, Zach!"

Charlie kept herself still, unresponsive. She was never going to give herself away ever again.

Zachariah Culpepper.

She had read his case files. Rusty had represented him at least four times. Gamma had said just last night that if Zach Culpepper paid his bills, the family wouldn't have to live at the farmhouse.

"Fuck!" Zach was staring at Samantha. She had read the files, too. "Fuck!"

"Mama . . ." Charlie said, trying to distract them, to convince Zach that she didn't know. "Mama, Mama, Mama . . ."

"It's all right." Samantha tried to soothe.

"It ain't all right." Zach threw his mask on the floor. He had raccoon eyes from Gamma's blood. He looked like his mugshot, but uglier. "God dammit! What'd you have to use my name for, boy?"

"I d-didn't—" Bon Jovi stammered. "I'm sorry."

"We won't tell." Samantha was looking down at the floor like it wasn't too late. "We won't say anything. I promise."

"Girl, I just blew your mama to bits. You really think you're walking out of here alive?"

"No," Bon Jovi said. "That's not what we came for."

"I came here to erase some bills, boy," Zach said. "Now I'm thinking it's me that Rusty Quinn's gotta pay."

"No," Bon Jovi repeated. "I told you—"

Zach shut him up by jamming the shotgun into his face. "You ain't seein' the big picture here. We gotta get outta town, and that takes a hell of a lot of money. Everybody knows Rusty Quinn keeps cash in his house."

"The house burned down," Samantha said. "Everything burned down."

"Fuck!" Zach screamed. "Fuck!" He pushed Bon Jovi into the hallway. He kept the shotgun pointed at Samantha's head, his finger on the trigger.

"No!" Charlie pulled her sister down to the floor, away from the shotgun. She felt grit on her knees. Shattered bone riddled the floor. She looked at Gamma. She took her waxy, white hand. The heat had already left her body. She whispered, "Don't be dead, Mama. Please. I love you. I love you so much."

She heard Zach say, "Why you actin' like you don't know how this is gonna end?"

Sam tugged at Charlie's arm. "Charlie, get up."

Zach said, "We ain't leaving this place without you getting some blood on your hands, too."

Sam repeated, "Charlie, get up."

"I can't." She was trying to hear what Bon Jovi was saying. "I can't let—"

Samantha practically picked her up and put her back in the chair. "Run when you can," she whispered to Charlie, the same thing Gamma had tried to tell her. "Don't look back. Just run."

"What're you two saying?" Zach walked back to the table. His boots crunched something on the floor. He pressed the shotgun to Sam's forehead. Charlie could see pieces of Gamma stuck to the barrel.

He asked Sam, "What did you tell her to do? Make a run for it? Try to get away?"

Charlie made a noise in her throat, trying to divert his attention.

Zach kept the shotgun on Sam, but he smiled at Charlie, showing a row of crooked, stained teeth. "What'd she tell you to do, baby doll?"

Charlie tried not to think about the way his voice changed when he talked to her.

"Come on, honey." Zach stared at her chest. He licked his lips again. "Ain't we gonna be friends?"

"S-stop," Sam said. The shotgun was pressed so hard into her forehead that a trickle of blood seeped out. "Leave her alone."

"Was I talking to you, bitch?" Zach leaned into the shotgun. Sam's head tilted back from the pressure. "Was I?"

Sam's jaw tightened. Her fists clenched. It was like watching a pot finally come to boil, except it was rage bubbling up inside of her. She shouted, "You leave us alone, Zachariah Culpepper."

Zach shifted his weight back on his heels, startled by her defiance.

Sam said, "I know exactly who you are, you fucking pervert."

He gripped the shotgun in his hands. His lip curled. "I'm gonna peel off your eyelids so you can watch me slice out your sister's cherry with my knife."

They glared at each other. Sam wasn't going to back down. Charlie had seen her like this before, that look she got in her eyes when she wasn't going to listen to anybody. Except this wasn't

Rusty, or the mean girls at school. This was a man with a shotgun, with a temper, who had almost beaten another man to death last year.

Charlie had seen the photos in Rusty's files. She had read the police report. Zachariah had fractured the guy's skull with his bare hands.

A whimper came out of Charlie's mouth.

"Zach," Bon Jovi said. "Come on, man."

Charlie waited for Sam to look away, but she didn't. Wouldn't. Couldn't.

Bon Jovi said, "We had a deal, all right?"

Zach didn't move. None of them moved.

"We had a deal," Bon Jovi repeated.

"Sure." Zach tossed the shotgun to Bon Jovi. "A man's only as good as his word."

He acted like he was going to walk away, but his hand moved fast, like a rattlesnake striking. He grabbed Sam's face and pushed her so hard back into the sink that her head clanged against the cast iron.

"No!" Charlie screamed.

"You think I'm a pervert now?" Zach was so close to Sam that his spit globbed onto her face. "You got something else to say about me?"

Sam's mouth opened, but she couldn't scream. She grabbed at his arm with her hands, scratching, clawing, but Zach's fingernails were digging into her eyeballs. Blood cried down like tears. Sam's feet kicked out. She gasped for air.

"Stop it!" Charlie jumped on Zach's back, punching him with her fists. "Stop!"

He threw her across the room. Charlie's head smacked into the wall like a clattering bell. Her vision doubled, but then it sharpened on Sam. Zach had left her on the floor. Blood streamed down her cheeks, pooled into the collar of her shirt.

"Sammy!" Charlie cried. She tried to look at Sam's eyes, to see the damage he had done. "Sam? Look at me. Can you see? Look at me, please!"

Carefully, Sam tried to open her eyelids. They were torn like pieces of wet paper.

Zach said, "What the fuck is this?"

The bathroom faucet hammer. He picked it up off the floor. He winked at Charlie. "Wonder what I can do with this?"

"Enough!" Bon Jovi snatched away the hammer and threw it down the hallway.

Zach shrugged. "Just having a little fun, brother."

"Both of you stand up," Bon Jovi said. "Let's get this over with."

Charlie didn't move. Sam blinked away blood.

"Help her up," Bon Jovi told Zach. "You promised, man. Don't make this worse than it has to be."

Zach yanked Sam up so hard that her shoulder made a popping sound. She bumped against the table. Zach pushed her toward the door. She bumped into a chair. Charlie grabbed her hand to keep her from falling.

Bon Jovi opened the door. "Go."

Charlie went first, shuffling sideways to help Sam down the stairs. Sam had her other hand out in front of her like she was blind. Charlie saw their shoes and socks. If they could put them on, they could run. But only if Sam could see where to go.

"Can you see?" Charlie asked her. "Sam, can you see?"

"Yes," Sam said, but that had to be a lie. She couldn't even open her eyelids all the way.

"This way," Bon Jovi indicated the field behind the HP. The soil was freshly planted. They weren't supposed to walk on it, but Charlie walked where she was told, guiding Sam behind her, helping her navigate the deep furrows.

Charlie asked Bon Jovi, "Where are we going?"

Zach dug the shotgun into Sam's back. "Keep walking."

"I don't understand," Charlie said to Bon Jovi. "Why are you doing this?"

He shook his head.

Charlie asked, "What did we do to you, mister? We're just kids. We don't deserve this."

"Shut up," Zach warned. "Both of you shut the fuck up."

Sam squeezed Charlie's hand even tighter than before. She had her head up, like she was a dog trying to get a scent. Instinctively, Charlie knew what her sister was doing. Two days ago, Gamma had shown them a topographical map of the area. Sam was trying to remember the landmarks, to get her bearings.

Charlie tried to, too.

The neighbor's acreage went past the horizon, but the ground was completely flat that way. Even if Charlie managed to zigzag as she ran, Sam would end up tripping and falling. Trees bordered the far right side of the property. If she could lead Sam that way, they might be able to find a place to hide. There was a creek on the other side of the forest that went underneath the weather tower. Beyond that was a paved road, but people didn't use it. There was an abandoned barn half a mile north. A second farm was two miles east. That would be the best bet. If she could get Sam to the second farm, they could call Rusty and he would save them.

Zach said, "What's that?"

Charlie looked back at the farmhouse. She saw headlights, two floating dots in the distance. Not Lenore's van. "It's a car."

"Shit, they're gonna make my truck in two seconds." Zach jammed the shotgun into Samantha's back, using it like a rudder to steer her. "Y'all keep moving or I'll shoot you right here."

Right here.

Charlie stiffened at the words. She prayed that Sam hadn't heard them, that she didn't get their meaning.

"There's another way out of this." Sam's head was turned toward Bon Jovi, even though she couldn't see him.

Zach snorted.

Sam said, "I'll do whatever you want." She cleared her throat. "Anything."

"Shit," Zach said. "You don't think I'm gonna take what I want anyways, you stupid bitch?"

Charlie swallowed back the taste of bile. She saw a clearing up ahead. She could run with Sam there, find a place to hide.

Sam said, "We won't tell them it was you. We'll say you had your masks on the entire time and——"

"With my truck in the driveway and your mama dead in the house?" Zach snorted again. "Y'all Quinns think you're so fucking smart, can talk your way outta anything."

Charlie didn't know any places to hide in the woods. She'd been stuck unpacking boxes since they moved, no time for exploring. Charlie and Sam's best bet was to run back to the HP where the policeman was. Charlie could lead Sam across the field. Her sister would have to trust her, the same way she kept saying Charlie should trust her with the blind pass. Sam was a fast runner, faster than Charlie. As long as she didn't stumble——

"Listen to me," Sam said. "You've got to leave town anyway. There's no reason to kill us, too." She turned toward Bon Jovi. "Please, just think about it. All you have to do is tie us up. Leave us somewhere they won't find us. You're going to have to leave town either way. You don't want more blood on your hands."

Bon Jovi was already shaking his head. "I'm sorry."

Charlie felt a finger slide up her back. She shivered, and Zach laughed.

"Let my sister go," Sam said. "She's thirteen. Just a kid."

"Don't look like no kid to me." Zach made pinching motions at Charlie's chest. "Got them nice high titties."

"Shut up," Bon Jovi warned. "I mean it."

"She won't tell anyone," Sam tried. "She'll say it was strangers. Won't you, Charlie?"

"Black fella?" Zach asked. "Like the one your daddy got off for murder?"

Charlie felt his fingers brush across her breast. She turned on him, screaming, "You mean like he got you off for showing your wiener to a bunch of little girls?"

"Charlie," Sam begged. "Please, be quiet."

"Let her speak," Zach said. "I like it when they got a little fight in 'em."

Charlie glared at him. She marched through the woods, pulling Sam behind her, trying not to go too fast, anxious to go fast enough so that Zach didn't walk alongside her.

"No," Charlie whispered. Why was she going fast? She needed to go slow. The farther they got away from the HP, the more dangerous it would be to break off and run back. Charlie stopped. She turned around. She could barely see the lights in the kitchen.

Zach had the shotgun in Sam's back again. "Move."

Pine needles cut into Charlie's bare feet as she trudged deeper into the woods. The air got cooler. Her shorts were stiff with dried urine. She could feel the inside of her thighs starting to chafe. Every step felt like it was wearing away a fresh layer of skin.

She glanced back at Sam. Her eyes were closed, hand out in front of her. Leaves rustled under their feet. Charlie stopped to help Sam over a fallen tree. They walked through the stream, the water like ice on her feet. The clouds shifted, letting in a sliver more of moonlight. In the distance, Charlie could see the outline of the weather tower, the rusted steel structure like a skeleton against the dark sky.

Charlie felt her sense of direction click into place. If the tower was on her left, then they were walking east. The second farm was about two miles north on her right.

Two miles.

Charlie's best mile was 7.01. Sam could do 5.52 on a flat surface. The forest wasn't flat. The moonlight was unpredictable.

Sam could not see. They could do an eight-minute mile, maybe, if Charlie paid attention, if she looked straight in front of her instead of looking back.

She scanned ahead, searching for the best path, the clearest route.

It was too late.

"Sam." Charlie stumbled to a stop. A trickle of urine rolled down her leg again. She gripped her sister around the waist. "There's a shovel. A shovel."

Sam's fingers felt along her face, pushed up her eyelids. She sucked in a quick rush of air when she saw what was in front of them.

Six feet away, dark, wet earth opened up like a wound in the ground.

Charlie's teeth were chattering again. She could hear the clicking. Zach and Bon Jovi had dug a grave for Rusty, and now they were going to use it for Sam and Charlie.

They had to run.

Charlie knew that now, felt it to the core of her being. Sam could see, at least enough to see the grave. Which meant she might be able to see enough to run. There was no choice. They couldn't stand here politely waiting for their own murders.

And whatever else Zachariah Culpepper had in mind.

Charlie squeezed Sam's hand. Sam squeezed back that she was ready. All they had to do was wait for the right moment.

"All right, big boy. Time for you to do your part." Zach leaned the shotgun butt on his hip. He slapped open a switchblade with his other hand. "The guns'll be too loud. Take this. Right across the throat like you do with a pig."

Bon Jovi stood there, unmoving.

Zach said, "Come on, like we agreed. You do her. I'll take care of the little one."

Bon Jovi said, "She's right. We don't have to do this. The plan wasn't ever to hurt the women. They weren't even supposed to be here."

"Say what now?"

Sam squeezed Charlie's hand even harder. They both watched, waited.

Bon Jovi said, "What's done is done. We don't have to make it worse by killing more people. Innocent people."

"Jesus Christ." Zach worked the knife closed then shoved it back into his pocket. "We went over this back in the kitchen, man. Ain't like we gotta choice."

"We can turn ourselves in."

"Bull. Shit."

Sam leaned into Charlie, pushing her a few steps to the right, getting her ready to go.

Bon Jovi said, "I'll turn myself in. I'll take the blame for everything."

"The hell you will." Zach shoved Bon Jovi in the chest. "You think I'm gonna go down on a murder charge 'cause you grew a fucking conscience?"

Sam let go of Charlie's hand.

Charlie felt her heart drop into her stomach.

Sam whispered, "Charlie, run."

"I won't tell," Bon Jovi said. "I'll say it was me."

Charlie tried to grab Sam's hand back. They had to stay close so that she could show Sam the way.

"In my got-damn truck?"

Sam waved her away, whispering, "Go."

Charlie shook her head. What did she mean? She couldn't go without Sam. She couldn't leave her sister here.

"Motherfucker." Zach had the shotgun pointed at Bon Jovi's chest. "This is what's gonna happen, son. You're gonna take my knife and you're gonna slice open that bitch's throat, or I will blow a hole in your chest the size of Texas." He stamped his foot. "Right now."

Bon Jovi pointed his gun at Zach's head. "We're gonna turn ourselves in."

"Get that fucking gun outta my face, you pansy-ass piece of shit."

Sam nudged Charlie, telling her to move. "Go."

Charlie didn't move. She wasn't going to leave her sister.

Bon Jovi said, "I'll kill you before I kill them."

"You ain't got the balls to pull that trigger."

"I'll do it."

Charlie heard her teeth chattering again. Should she go? Would Sam follow her? Is that what she meant?

"Run," Sam begged. "You have to run."

Don't look back. You have to trust me to be there.

"Piece of shit." Zach's free hand snaked out.

Bon Jovi backhanded the shotgun.

"Run!" Sam shoved her hard. *"Charlie, go!"*

Charlie fell back onto her ass, slamming into the ground. She saw the bright flash of the gun firing, heard the sudden explosion of the bullet leaving the barrel, and then a mist puffed from the side of Sam's head.

Sam spun through the air, almost somersaulting like the fork had, into the gaping mouth of the grave.

Thunk.

Charlie stared at the open earth, waiting, begging, praying, for Sam to sit up, to look around, to say something, anything, that indicated that she was alive.

"Shit," Bon Jovi said. "Christ. Jesus Christ." He dropped the gun like it was poison.

Charlie saw the glint of metal from the weapon as it hit the ground. The flash of shock on Bon Jovi's face. The sudden white of Zach's teeth when he grinned.

At Charlie.

He was grinning at Charlie.

She scrambled away, crab-like, on her hands and heels.

Zach started toward her, but Bon Jovi grabbed his shirt. "What the fuck are we going to do?"

Charlie's back hit a tree. She pushed herself up. Her knees shook. Her hands shook. Her whole body was shaking. She looked at the grave. Her sister was in a grave. Sam had been shot in the head. Charlie couldn't see her, didn't know if she was alive or dead or needed help or—

"It's okay, sweetpea," Zach told Charlie. "Stay right there for me."

"I j-just—" Bon Jovi stuttered. "I just killed . . . I just . . ."

Killed.

He couldn't have killed Sam. The bullet from the gun was small, not like the shotgun. Maybe it hadn't really hurt her. Maybe Sam was okay, hiding in the grave, ready to spring up and run.

But she wasn't springing up. She wasn't moving, or talking, or shouting, or bossing everybody around.

Charlie needed her sister to speak, to tell her what to do. What would Sam say right now? What would she tell Charlie to do?

Zach said, "You cover this bitch up. Lemme take the little one off for a minute."

"Christ."

Sam wouldn't be talking right now, she would be yelling, furious at Charlie for just standing there, for blowing this chance, for not doing what Sam had coached her to do.

Don't look back . . . trust me to be there . . . keep your head down and—

Charlie ran.

Her arms flailed. Her feet struggled for purchase. Tree limbs slashed at her face. She couldn't breathe. Her lungs felt like needles were stabbing into her chest.

Breathe through it. Slow and steady. Wait for the pain to pass.

They used to be best friends. They used to do everything together. And then Sam had gone to high school and Charlie had been left behind, and the only way she could get her sister's attention was to ask Sam to teach her how to run.

Don't hold the tension. Breathe in for two strides. Breathe out for one.

Charlie hated every part of running because it was stupid and it hurt and it made you sore, but she had wanted to spend time with Sam, to do something that her sister was doing, to maybe be better at it one day than Sam was, so Charlie went to the track with her sister, she joined the team at school, and she timed herself every day because every day, she was getting faster.

"Get back here!" Zach yelled.

Two miles to the second farmhouse. Twelve, maybe thirteen minutes. Charlie couldn't run faster than a boy, but she could run for longer. She had the stamina, the training. She knew how to ignore the pain in her body. To breathe into the shock in her lungs when the air sliced like a razor.

What she had never trained for was the panic from hearing the heavy tread of boots pounding dirt behind her, the way the *thud-thud-thud* vibrated inside of her chest.

Zachariah Culpepper was coming after her.

Charlie ran faster. She tucked her arms into her sides. She forced out the tension in her shoulders. She imagined her legs were pistons in a fast-working machine. She tuned out the pinecones and sharp rocks gouging open her bare feet. She thought about the muscles that were helping her move—

Calves, quads, hamstrings, tighten your core, protect your back.

Zachariah was getting closer. She could hear him like a steam engine bearing down.

Charlie vaulted over a fallen tree. She scanned left, then right, knowing she shouldn't run in a straight line. She needed to locate the weather tower, to make sure she was heading in the correct direction, but she knew if she looked back she would see Zachariah Culpepper, and that seeing him would make her panic even more, and if she panicked even more, she would stumble, and if she stumbled, she would fall.

And then he would rape her.

Charlie veered right, her toes gripping the dirt as she altered direction. At the last minute, she saw another fallen tree. She flung herself over it, landing awkwardly. Her foot twisted. She felt her anklebone touch earth. Pain sliced up her leg.

She kept going.

And going.

And going.

Her feet were sticky with blood. Sweat dripped down her body. Her lungs burned in her chest, but not as much as it would burn if Zachariah pinched her breast again. Her guts cramped, her bowels had turned to liquid, but that was nothing compared to how she would feel if Zachariah shoved his thing inside of her.

Charlie scanned ahead for light, any indication of civilization.

How much time had passed?

How much longer could he keep running?

Picture the finish line in your head. You have to want it more than the person behind you.

Zachariah wanted something. Charlie wanted something more—to get away, to get help for her sister, to find Rusty so he could figure out a way to make it all better.

Suddenly, Charlie's head jerked back with such violence that she felt like she was being decapitated.

Her feet flew out into the air in front of her.

Her back slammed against the ground.

She saw her breath *huff* out of her mouth like it was a real thing.

Zachariah was on top of her. His hands were everywhere. Grabbing her breasts. Pulling her shorts. His teeth clashed against her closed mouth. She scratched at his eyes. She tried to bring up her knee into his crotch but she couldn't bend her leg.

Zachariah sat up, straddling her.

Charlie kept slapping at him, tried in vain to buck off the tremendous weight of his body.

He worked his belt back through the buckle.

Her mouth opened. She had no breath left to scream. She was dizzy. Vomit burned up her throat. She closed her eyes and saw Sam twisting through the air. She could hear the *thump* of her sister's body hitting the grave like it was happening all over again. And then she saw Gamma. On the kitchen floor. Back to the cabinet.

Bright white bone. Pieces of heart and lung. Cords of tendon and arteries and veins and life spilling out of her gaping wounds.

"No!" Charlie screamed, her hands turning into fists. She pounded into Zachariah's chest, swung so hard at his jaw that his head whipped around. Blood sprayed out of his mouth—big globs of it, not like the tiny dots from Gamma.

"Fucking bitch." He reared back his hand to punch her.

Charlie saw a blur out of the corner of her eye.

"Get off her!"

Bon Jovi flew through the air, tackling Zachariah to the ground. His fists swung back and forth. He straddled Zachariah the same way Zachariah had straddled Charlie. Bon Jovi's arms windmilled as he beat the other man into the ground.

"Motherfucker!" he yelled. "I'll fucking kill you!"

Charlie backed away from the men. Her hands pressed deep into the earth as she forced herself to stand. She stumbled. She wiped her eyes. Sweat had turned the dried blood on her face and neck back to liquid. She spun around in a circle, blind as Sam. She couldn't get her bearings. She didn't know which way to run, but she knew that she had to keep moving.

Her ankle screamed as she ran back into the woods. She didn't look for the weather tower. She didn't listen for the stream, or try to find Sam, or head toward the HP. She kept running, then walking, then she felt so exhausted that she wanted to crawl.

Finally, she gave into it, collapsing to her hands and knees.

She listened for footsteps behind her, but all she could hear was her own heavy breaths panting out of her mouth.

She threw up. Bile hit the ground and splattered back into her face. She wanted to lie down, to close her eyes, to go to sleep and wake up in a week when this was all over.

Sam.

In the grave.

Bullet in her head.

Gamma.

In the kitchen.

Bright white bone.

Pieces of heart and lung.

Cords of tendon and arteries and veins and her life gone in the flash of a shotgun because of Zachariah Culpepper.

Charlie knew his name. She knew Bon Jovi's build, his voice, the way he'd stood silently by while Gamma was murdered, the way his hand had arced through the air when he'd shot Sam in the head, the way Zachariah had called him brother.

Brother.

She would see them both dead. She would watch the executioner strap them to the wooden chair and put the metal hat on their heads with the sponge underneath so that they wouldn't catch on fire and she would look between Zachariah Culpepper's legs to watch the urine come out when he realized that he was going to be electrocuted to death.

Charlie got up.

She stumbled, then she walked, then she jogged and eventually, finally, she saw the light on the porch outside the second farmhouse.

CHAPTER SEVEN

am Quinn alternated her arms, left, then right, then left again, as she cut a narrow channel through the cool waters of the swimming pool. She turned her head every third stroke and drew in a long breath. Her feet fluttered. She waited for the next breath.

Left-right-left-breathe.

She had always loved the calmness, the simplicity, of the free-style stroke; that she had to concentrate just enough on swimming so that all extraneous thoughts cleared her mind. No telephones rang under the water. No laptops pinged with urgent meetings. There was no reading emails in the pool.

She saw the two-meter line, the indication that the lane was about to end, and coasted until her fingers touched the wall.

Sam kneeled on the floor of the pool, breathing heavily, checking her swimmer's watch: 2.4 kilometers at 150 seconds per 100 meters, so 37.5 seconds per 25-meter length.

She felt a pang of disappointment when she saw the numbers, which were within seconds of yesterday's, because her competitive streak glowed in white-hot opposition to her physical capabilities. Sam glanced down the length of the pool, wondering if she had another short burst inside of her.

No.

Today was Sam's birthday. She was not going to tire herself out so much that she had to use her cane to walk to the office.

She pushed herself up onto the edge of the pool. She quickly showered off the salt water. The tips of her fingers were furrowed and rough against the Egyptian cotton towel. Somewhere in the back of Sam's mind, her mother's voice told her that the body's response to being submerged so long was to wrinkle the pads of the fingers and toes in order to improve grip.

Gamma had been forty-four when she'd died, the same age that Sam was now.

Or at least would be in another three and a half hours.

Sam kept on her prescription goggles while she rode the elevator up to her apartment. The chrome on the back of the doors showed her wavy reflection. Slim build. Black one-piece suit. Sam ran her fingers through her hair to help it dry. Twenty-eight years ago, she had walked into the woods behind the farmhouse with hair the color of a raven's feather. Almost a month later, she'd awakened in the hospital to find a shock of white stubble growing from her shaved head.

Sam had gotten used to the double-takes, the surprised looks when strangers realized that the gray-haired old woman in the back of the classroom, buying wine at the supermarket, walking through the park, was actually a young girl.

Though admittedly, that wasn't happening nearly as much lately. Sam's husband had warned her that one day, her face would finally catch up to her hair.

The elevator doors slid open.

The sun was winking through the floor-to-ceiling windows that lined her apartment. Down below, the Financial District was wide awake, car horns and cranes and the usual din of activity muffled behind the triple-paned glazing.

Sam walked to the kitchen, turning off lights as she went. She exchanged her goggles for her glasses. She put out food for the cat. She filled the kettle. She prepared her tea infuser, mug, and spoon, but before boiling the water, she went to the yoga mat in her living room.

She took off her glasses. She ran through a series of stretches to keep her muscles limber. She ended up on the mat, legs crossed.

She rested the backs of her hands on her knees. She touched her middle fingers to her thumbs in a light pinch. She closed her eyes, breathed deeply, and considered her brain.

Several years after she had been shot, a psychiatrist had shown Sam a cortical homunculus of the motor areas of her brain. The man had wanted her to see the path the bullet had traveled so that Sam could understand the structures that had been damaged. He wanted her to think about those structures at least once a day, to spend as much time as she could muster in contemplating the individual folds and crevices, and to visualize her brain and body working in perfect tandem as they had before.

Sam had resisted. The exercise seemed some part wishful thinking, most part voodoo.

Now, it was the only thing that kept her headaches at bay, her equilibrium in check.

Sam had consequently done more in-depth research of the brain, seen MRIs, and studied dense neurological tomes, but that first drawing had never been replaced as a guide through her meditation. In her mind's eye, the cross-sections of the left motor and sensory cortices were forever highlighted in bright yellow and green. Each section was labeled with the correspondingly influenced anatomy. Toes. Ankle. Knee. Hip. Trunk. Arm. Wrist. Fingers.

Sam felt an analogous tingle in the different areas of her body as she silently examined the factions that made up the whole.

The bullet had entered her skull on the left, just above her ear. The left side of the brain controls the right, the right side the left. In medical terms, the injury was considered to have taken place in a more superficial portion of the brain. Sam had always found the word *superficial* misleading. True, the projectile had not crossed the midbrain or lodged deep into the limbic system, but Broca's Area, where speech takes place, Wernicke's Area, where speech is understood, and the various regions that controlled movement on the right side of her body, had been inexorably altered.

Superficial— [soo-per-fish-*uh*-l] *of or relating to the surface, frivolous, cursory, apparent rather than real.*

There was a metal plate in her head. The scar over her ear was the size and width of her index finger.

Sam's memory of that day remained fragmented. She was certain of only a few things. She remembered the mess that Charlie had made in the bathroom. She remembered the Culpepper brothers, the smell of them, the almost tangible taste of their menace. She did not remember witnessing Gamma's death. She did not remember what steps she took to crawl out of the grave. She remembered Charlie urinating on herself. She remembered yelling at Zachariah Culpepper. She remembered her raw, aching need that Charlie should run, that she should be safe, that she should live no matter the cost to Sam.

Physical therapy. Occupational therapy. Speech therapy. Cognitive therapy. Talk therapy. Aqua therapy. Sam had to learn how to talk again. To think again. To make connections again. To converse. To write. To read. To comprehend. To dress herself. To accept what had happened to her. To acknowledge that things were different. To learn how to study again. To return to school again. To articulate her thought processes again. To understand rhetoric and logic and motion, function and form.

Sam often compared her first year of recovery to a record on an old turntable. She awoke at the hospital with everything playing at the wrong speed. Her words slurred. Her thoughts moved as if through cake batter. Working her way back to 33⅓ rpm seemed impossible. No one believed she could do it. Her age, they all felt, could be the magic component. As one of her surgeons had told her, if you were going to be shot in the head, it was good to have it happen when you were fifteen years old.

Sam felt a nudge at her arm. Count Fosco, the cat, was finished with breakfast and wanted attention. She scratched his ears, listening to his soothing purr, and wondered if she was better off forgoing the meditation and simply adopting more cats.

She put on her glasses. She went back to the kitchen and turned on the kettle. The sun was tilting across the lower end of Manhattan. She closed her eyes and let the warmth bathe her. When she opened her eyes again, she saw that Fosco was doing the same. He seemed to love the radiant heat under the kitchen floor. Sam couldn't get used to the sudden feeling of warmth on her bare feet when she woke in the morning. The new apartment had modern bells and whistles that her last apartment had not.

Which was the reason for the new apartment—that nothing about it reminded her of the old.

The kettle whistled. She poured her mug of tea. She set the egg timer to three and a half minutes in order for the leaves to steep. She got yogurt from the fridge and mixed in granola with a spoon from the drawer. She took off her regular glasses and put on her reading glasses; her eyes had never been able to adjust to multifocal lenses.

Sam turned on her phone.

There were several work emails, a few birthday greetings from friends, but Sam scrolled down until she found the expected birthday missive from Ben Bernard, her sister's husband. They had met once a very long time ago. The two would probably not recognize each other in the street, but Ben had an endearing sense of responsibility toward Charlie, that he would do for his wife what she could not do herself.

Sam smiled at Ben's message, a photo of Mr. Spock giving a Vulcan salute, with the words: *Logic dictates that I should wish you a happy birthday.*

Sam had only once returned an email from Ben, on 9/11, to let him know that she was safe.

The egg timer buzzed. She poured some milk into her hot tea, then sat back at the counter.

Sam pulled a notepad and pen from her briefcase. She tackled the work emails, answering some, forwarding others, making follow-up notes, and worked until her tea was cold and the yogurt and granola were gone.

Fosco jumped onto the counter to inspect the bowl.

Sam looked at the time. She should take her shower and go into the office.

She looked down at her phone. She tapped her fingers on the counter.

She swiped over to the screen for voicemails.

Another anticipated birthday missive.

Sam had not seen her father face-to-face in over twenty years. They had stopped talking when Sam was in law school. There had been no argument or official break between them, but one day, Sam was the good daughter who called her father once or twice a month, and the next day, she was not.

Initially, Rusty had tried to reach out to her, and when Sam did not reach back, he had started calling during her class hours to leave phone messages at her dorm. He wasn't overly intrusive. If Sam happened to be in, he did not ask to speak with her. He never asked her to call him back. The relayed messages said that he was there if she needed him, or that he had been thinking about her, or he had thought to check in. During the ensuing years, he had called reliably on the second Friday of every month and on her birthday.

When Sam had moved to Portland to work in the district attorney's office, he had left messages at her office on the second Friday of every month and on her birthday.

When she had moved to New York to start her career in patent law, he had left messages at her office on the second Friday of every month and on her birthday.

Then there was suddenly such a thing as mobile phones, and on the second Friday of every month and on her birthday, Rusty had left voicemails on Sam's flip phone, then her Razr, then her Nokia, then her BlackBerry, and now it was her iPhone that told Sam that her father had called at 5:32 this morning, on her birthday.

Sam could predict the pattern of his calls if not the exact content. Rusty had developed a peculiar formula over the years. He would start with the usual ebullient greeting, render a weather report because, for unknowable reasons, he felt the weather in Pikeville mattered, then he would add a strange detail about the occasion of his call—the day of her birth, that particular second Friday on which he was reaching out—and then a non sequitur in lieu of a farewell.

There had been a time when Sam scowled at Rusty's name on a pink *while-you-were-away* message, deleted his voicemails without a second thought, or delayed listening to them for so long that they rolled off the system.

Now, she played the message.

"Good morning, Sammy-Sam!" her father bellowed. "This is Russell T. Quinn, at your service. It is currently forty-three degrees, with winds coming out of the southwest at two miles per hour. Humidity is at thirty-nine percent. Barometric pressure is holding at thirty." Sam shook her head in bewilderment. "I am calling you today, the very same day that, in 1536, Anne Boleyn was arrested and taken to the Tower of London, to remind you, my dear Samantha, to not lose your head on your forty-fourth birthday." He laughed, because he always laughed at his own cleverness. Sam waited for the sign-off. " 'Exit, pursued by a bear.' "

Sam smiled. She was about to delete the voicemail when, uncharacteristically, Rusty added something new.

"Your sister sends her love."

Sam felt her brow furrow. She scrubbed back the voicemail to listen to the last part again.

". . . a bear," Rusty said, then after a short pause, "Your sister sends her love."

Sam doubted very seriously that Charlie had sent any such thing.

The last time she'd talked to Charlie—the last time she had even been in the same room with her—there had been a definite and immediate ending to their relationship, an understanding that there was neither the need nor the desire for either of them to talk to each other ever again.

Charlie had been in her last year at Duke. She had flown to New York to visit Sam and to interview at several white shoe firms. Sam realized at the time that her sister was not visiting her so much as treating Sam's apartment as a free place to stay in one of the most expensive cities on earth, but almost a decade had passed since she'd seen her little sister, and Sam had been looking forward to the two of them reacquainting as adults.

The first shock of the trip was not that Charlie had brought a strange man with her, but that the strange man was her husband. Charlie had dated Ben Bernard for less than a month before legally binding herself to someone about whom she knew absolutely nothing. The decision was irresponsible and dangerous, and but for the fact that Ben was one of the most kind, most decent human beings on the planet—not to mention that he was clearly head over heels in love with Charlie—Sam would have been livid with her sister for such a stupid, impetuous act.

The second shock was that Charlie had canceled all of her interviews. She had taken the money Sam had sent to buy proper business attire and instead used it to purchase tickets to see Prince at Madison Square Garden.

This brought about the third, most fatal shock.

Charlie was planning to work with Rusty.

She had insisted that she would only be in the same building with their father, not involved in Rusty's actual practice, but to Sam, the distinction held no difference.

Rusty took risks at work that followed him home. The people who were in his office, in the office that Charlie would soon share, were the kinds of people who burned down your house, who went to your home looking for you, and when they found out you weren't there, murdered your mother and shot your sister and chased you through the woods with a shotgun because they wanted to rape you.

The final altercation between Sam and Charlie had not taken place immediately. They had argued in fits and starts for three long days in Charlie's planned five-day visit.

Then on the fourth day, Sam had finally exploded.

She had always had a slow-boiling temper. It's what had made her lash out at Zachariah Culpepper in the kitchen while her mother was lying dead a few feet away, her sister was covered in urine, and a blood-smeared shotgun was pointed directly at her face.

Subsequent to her brain injury, Sam's temper had become almost unmanageable. There were countless studies that showed how certain types of damage to the frontal and temporal lobes could lead to impulsive, even violent, anger, but the ferocity of Sam's rage beggared scientific explanation.

She had never hit anyone, which was a piteous victory, but she threw things, broke things, attacked even cherished objects as if she were ruled by insanity. The physical acts of destruction paled in comparison to the damage rendered by her sharp tongue. The fury would take hold, Sam's mouth would open, and hate would spew like acid.

Now, the meditation helped smooth out her emotions.

The laps in the pool helped redirect her anxiety into something positive.

Back then, nothing had been able to stop Sam's venomous rage.

Charlie was spoiled. She was selfish. She was a child. She was a whore. She wanted to please her father too much. She had never loved Gamma. She had never loved Sam. She was the reason they had all been in the kitchen. She was the reason Gamma had been murdered. She had left Sam to die. She had run away then, just like she was going to run away now.

That last part, at least, had proven to be true.

Charlie and Ben had returned to Durham in the middle of the night. They had not even stopped to pack their few belongings.

Sam had apologized. Of course she had apologized. Students didn't have voicemail or email back then, so Sam had sent a certified letter to Charlie's off-campus apartment along with the carefully packed box of things they had left in New York.

Writing the letter was without question the hardest thing that Sam had ever done in her life. She had told her sister that she loved her, had always loved her, that she was special, that their relationship meant something. That Gamma had adored her, had cherished her. That Sam understood that Rusty needed Charlie. That Charlie needed to be needed by their father. That Charlie deserved to be happy, to enjoy her marriage, to have children—lots of children. That she was old enough to make her own decisions. That everyone was so proud of her, happy for her. That Sam would do anything if Charlie would forgive her.

"Please," Sam had written at the end of the letter. "You have to believe me. The only thing that got me through months of agony, years of recovery, a lifetime of chronic pain, is the fact that my sacrifice, and even Gamma's sacrifice, gave you the chance to run to safety."

Six weeks had passed before Sam had received a letter in return.

Charlie's response had been a single, honest, compound complex sentence. "I love you, I know that you love me, but every time we see each other, we see what happened, and neither one of us will ever move forward if we are always looking back."

Her little sister was a lot smarter than Sam had ever given her credit for.

Sam took off her glasses. She gently rubbed her eyes. The scars on her eyelids felt like Braille beneath her fingertips. For all of her complaints about *superficial*, she worked very hard to mask her injuries. Not because she was embarrassed, but because other people were curious. There was no more effective conversation stopper than the words, "I was shot in the head."

Makeup covered the pink ridges where her eyelids had been torn. A three-hundred-dollar haircut covered the scar on the side of her head. She tended to dress in flowy black pants and shirts to help camouflage any hesitation in her gait. When she spoke, she spoke clearly, and when exhaustion threatened to loosen her hold on language, she kept her own counsel. There were days that Sam needed a cane to walk, but over the years, she had learned that the only reward for physical hard work was more physical hard work. If she was late at the office and she wanted a car to take her the six blocks home, she took the car.

Today, she walked the six blocks to work with relative ease. In honor of her birthday, she'd worn a colorful scarf to brighten up her usual black. As she took a left onto Wall Street, a strong gust of wind barreled off the East River. The scarf flew behind her like a cape. Sam laughed as she tangled with the silk scarf. She wrapped it around her neck and held loosely on to the ends as she walked through her new neighborhood.

Sam had not been a resident of the area for long, but she had always loved the history, that Wall Street had been, in fact, an earthen wall meant to secure the northern boundary of New Amsterdam; that Pearl Street and Beaver Street and Stone Street were named after the wares that Dutch traders sold along the muddy lanes that spoked out from where tall, wooden sailing boats had once docked.

Seventeen years ago, when Sam had first moved to New York, she'd had her choice of law firms. In the world of patent law, her Stanford master's in mechanical engineering carried significantly more weight than her master's from Northwestern Law. Sam had passed both the New York bar and the patent bar on her first attempts. She was a woman in a male-dominated field that desperately needed diversity. The firms' proffers had practically been extended on bended knee.

She had joined the first firm whose signing bonus was enough to cover the down payment on a condo in a building with an elevator and a heated pool.

The building was in Chelsea, a lovely prewar mid-rise with high ceilings and a swimming pool in the basement that looked like a Victorian-era natatorium. Despite the rapid improvement of Sam's finances over the years, she had happily lived in the cramped, two-bedroom apartment until her husband had died.

"Happy birthday." Eldrin, her assistant, was waiting outside the elevator when the doors opened. Sam's routine was so fixed that he could predict her movements down to the second.

"Thank you." She let him take her briefcase, but not her purse.

He walked with her through the offices, doling out her schedule as he always did. "Your UXH meeting is at ten thirty in conference room six. You've got a phone call with Atlanta at three, but I told Laurens you have a hard out at five for a very important meeting."

Sam smiled. She had birthday drinks scheduled with a friend.

He said, "There's a bit of an urgent detail about the partner meeting next week. You need to nail down a point for them. I left the packet on your desk."

"Thank you." Sam stopped at the office kitchen. She didn't expect Eldrin to fetch her tea every morning, but because of their routine, he'd been relegated to watching Sam prepare it.

She said, "I had an email from Curtis this morning." She pulled a tea sachet from the tin on the counter. "I want to be in Atlanta next week for the Coca-Cola deposition." Among other locales, Stehlik, Elton, Mallory and Sanders had satellite offices in Atlanta. Sam made monthly trips to the city, staying at the Four Seasons, walking the two blocks to the Peachtree Street offices, and ignoring the fact that Pikeville was a two-hour drive up the interstate.

"I'll let travel know." Eldrin retrieved a carton of milk from the refrigerator. "I can also ask if Grainger has—oh no." He was looking at the muted television in the corner. A graphic spun ominously onto the screen. SCHOOL SHOOTING.

As a victim of gun violence, Sam had always felt a particular horror when she learned of a mass shooting, but like most Americans, she had become somewhat acclimated to their almost monthly occurrence.

The screen showed a little girl's photograph, obviously from a school yearbook. The name underneath read LUCY ALEX-ANDER.

Sam added milk to the tea. "I dated a boy in school named Peter Alexander."

Eldrin raised his eyebrows as he followed her out of the kitchen. She wasn't usually easy with details about her personal life.

Sam continued toward her office. Eldrin continued the rundown of the day's itinerary, but she only listened with half an ear. She hadn't thought about Peter Alexander in a long while. He had been a moody boy, given to long, tedious speeches about the torture inherent in being an artist. Sam had let him touch her breasts, but only because she had wanted to know what it felt like.

It felt sweaty, frankly, because Peter had no idea what he was doing.

Sam dropped her purse by her desk, a glass and steel chunk that anchored her sun-filled corner office. Her view, like most views in the Financial District, was of the building directly across the way. There had been no rules regarding setbacks when the Canyons of Wall Street had been erected. Twenty feet of sidewalk was all that separated most buildings from the street.

Eldrin finished his spiel as she placed her tea on a coaster beside her computer.

Sam waited for him to leave. She sat down in her chair. She found her reading glasses in her briefcase. She began the review of her notes for the ten thirty meeting.

Sam had understood when she decided on patent law as a career that the job was basically one of trying to sway the transfer of large sums of money: one incredibly wealthy corporation sued another incredibly wealthy corporation for using a similar set of stripes on their new athletic shoes, or co-opting a particular color from their brand, and very expensive lawyers had to argue in front of very bored judges about the percentages of cyan in a certain Pantone.

Long gone were the days of Newton and Leibniz battling for the right to be identified as the inventor of calculus. Most of Sam's time was spent combing through the minutiae of design schematics and referencing patent applications that sometimes reached back to the early days of the industrial revolution.

She loved every single second of it.

She loved the melding of science and law, delighted in the fact that she had somehow managed to distill the single best parts of her mother and father into a rewarding life.

Eldrin knocked on her glass door. "I wanted to update you. Looks like that school shooting took place in North Georgia."

Sam nodded. "North Georgia" was a nebulous catchall for any area outside of Atlanta. "Do they know how many victims?"

"Only two."

"Thanks." Sam tried not to dwell on the "only," because Eldrin was correct that two was a low body count. The story would probably roll off the news by tomorrow.

She turned to her computer. She pulled up a rough draft of a brief that she wanted to be conversant with for her ten thirty meeting. A second-year associate had taken a stab at a response to a summary motion made in the case of *SaniLady, a division of UXH Financial Holdings, Ltd. v. LadyMate Corp., a division of Nippon Development Resources, Inc.*

After six years of back and forth, two failed mediations and a screaming match that took place mostly in Japanese, the case was going to trial.

At issue was the design of a hinge that controlled the movement of the self-closing lid on a partition-mounted public restroom sanitary napkin and tampon disposal bin. The LadyMate Corporation produced several iterations of the ubiquitous container, from the *FemyGeni* to the original *LadyMate* to the strangely named *Tough Guy*.

Sam was the only person involved in the entire case who had actually used one of these bins. If she had been consulted during their design, she would've gone for truth in advertising and called them all the *Motherfucker*, because that was usually the first thing that came into a woman's mind when she had to use one.

Sam also would have designed the spring-loaded piano hinge as two components for the extra .03 cent manufacturing cost rather than risk a single, integrated hinge that invited a patent infringement lawsuit that would result in millions of dollars in legal fees, not to mention the damages if Nippon lost the case.

If the brief on her computer had anything to do with it, UXH would not be seeing those damages. Patent law wasn't the most baroque area of litigation, but the second-year associate who had drafted the brief wrote with the adroitness of a piece of sandpaper.

This was why Sam had taken a three-year detour into the Portland district attorney's office. She had wanted to be able to speak the language of a courtroom.

Sam scrolled through the document, making notes, rewriting a long passage in an approximation of simple English, adding a modicum of flourish to the end because she knew that it would perturb her opposing counsel, a man who had, upon his first meeting with Sam, told her to fetch him a coffee, two sugars, and tell her boss that he did not like to wait.

Gamma had been right about so many things. Sam Quinn was given far more respect than Samantha Quinn could have ever hoped for.

At exactly ten thirty-four, Sam was the last person to enter the conference room. The tardiness was by design. She did not relish chastising stragglers.

She took her seat at the head of the table. She looked out at the sea of young, white men whose degrees from Michigan and Harvard and MIT gave them a bloated sense of their own self-importance. Or perhaps the bloat was warranted. They were sitting in the gleaming, glass-lined offices of one of the most important patent firms in the world. If they thought that they were captains of industry, it was likely because they soon would be.

But for now, they had to prove themselves to Sam. She listened to their updates, commented on their proposed strategies, and generally let them toss ideas back and forth until she felt that they were biting their own tails. Sam was notorious for running lean meetings. She asked for case law to be researched, a rewriting of briefs to be completed by tomorrow, the incorporation of a certain patent application from the 1960s to be integrated more deeply into their work product.

She stood from her chair, so everyone else did. She made an anodyne comment about looking forward to their results as she left the conference room.

They followed her, keeping their distance, because they all worked on the same side of the building. Sam often felt like the long walk back to her office was akin to being stalked by a pack of geese. Invariably, one would push ahead, hoping to make his name known, or to prove to the others that he wasn't afraid of her. A few peeled off for other meetings, wishing her happy birthday. Someone asked if she had enjoyed her recent trip to Europe. Another young man, a bit overeager since word had spread that Sam would soon become a named partner, followed her all the way to her office door, relaying a long story that ended with the detail that his grandmother had been born in Denmark.

Sam's husband had been born in Denmark.

Anton Mikkelsen was twenty-one years Sam's senior, a professor at Stanford from whom she had taken a Technology in Society course entitled *Engineering the Roman Empire Design*. Anton's passion for the subject had captivated Sam. She had always been drawn to people who were delighted by the world, who looked out rather than in.

For his part, Anton had been completely hands-off while Sam was his student, aloof even, so that she was convinced she had done something wrong. It wasn't until after she had graduated, when she was in her second year at Northwestern, that Anton had reached out.

At Stanford, Sam had been one of only a handful of women

studying in a male-dominated field. She had infrequently received emails from some of her professors. The subject lines tended to show a combination of desperation and a loose understanding of ellipsis: *"I can't get you out of my mind . . ."* or, *". . . You have to . . . help me . . ."* As if they were being driven mad by their desire and only Sam could alleviate the pain. Their collective insecurities had been one of the reasons she had applied to law school rather than pursue her Ph.D. The thought of any one of these pathetic, middle-aged lotharios being in charge of her thesis was untenable.

Anton had been well aware of his colleagues' reputations when he first emailed Sam.

"I apologize if you find this contact unwanted," he had written. "I waited three years to ensure that my professional authority has no overlap with, nor impact upon, your chosen field."

He had retired early from Stanford. He had taken a job as a consultant for an overseas engineering firm. He had established his home base in New York so that he could be closer to her. They had married four years after Sam was named an associate at the firm.

Anton had opened up her life in ways that Sam had never fathomed.

Their first trip abroad was magical. Except for an ill-considered freshman jaunt to Tijuana, Sam had never before been outside of the United States. Anton had taken her to Ireland, where as a boy he had summered with his mother's people. To Denmark, where he had learned to love design. To Rome to show her the ruins, to Florence to show her the Duomo, to Venice to show her love.

They had traveled extensively throughout their marriage, Anton taking jobs or Sam attending a conference with the sole purpose of being somewhere new. Dubai. Australia. Brazil. Singapore. Bora Bora. Every new country, every new foreign city that Sam set foot in, she thought of Gamma, the way her mother had urged Sam to leave, to see the world, to live anywhere but Pikeville.

That Sam had done this with a man whom she adored made each journey that much more rewarding.

Sam's office phone rang.

She sat back in her chair. She glanced at the time. Her three o'clock call from Atlanta. She had lost herself in work again, skipping lunch, inexorably lost in a patent design for a narrow plated pintle hinge.

Laurens Van Loon was Dutch, living in Atlanta, and their in-house specialist on international patent law. He was calling about the UXH case, but like Sam, he was an enthusiastic traveler. Before they talked shop, he wanted to know all about the trip she had taken a few weeks ago, a ten-day tour through Italy and Ireland.

There had been a time in Sam's life when she talked about foreign cities in terms of their culture, the architecture, the people, but money and the passage of time had made her more likely to talk about the hotels.

She told Laurens about her stay at the Merrion in Dublin, how the garden suite did not overlook a garden, but a rear alley. That the Aman on the Grand Canal was breathtaking, the service impeccable, the little courtyard where she drank her tea every morning one of the most tranquil spots in the city. In Florence there was the Westin Excelsior, which had a magnificent view of the Arno, but the noise from the rooftop bar had occasionally echoed down into her suite. In Rome, she told Laurens, she had stayed at the Cavalieri, for its baths and beautiful pools.

This last part was a lie.

Sam had booked a room at the Raffaello, because the budget hotel was the only place that she and Anton could afford during that first magical trip to Rome.

For Laurens's benefit, Sam continued to prevaricate, recommending restaurants and museums from past journeys. She did not tell him that in Dublin, she had stood in the Long Room of the Old Library at Trinity College, looking up at the beautiful barrel-vaulted ceiling with tears in her eyes. Nor did Sam relay that in Florence, she had sat on one of the many benches inside the Galleria dell'Accademia, where Michelangelo's *David* was displayed, and sobbed.

Rome had been filled with equal parts nostalgia and grief. The Trevi Fountain, the Spanish Steps, the Pantheon, the Colosseum, the Piazza Navona where Anton had proposed to her while they drank wine under the moonlight.

Sam had first seen all of these wonderful sites with her husband, and now that Anton was dead, she would never see them with the same pleasure again.

"Your trip sounds amazing," Laurens said. "Ireland and Italy. So, that's the 'I' countries, though I suppose you technically should have included India."

"Iceland, Indonesia, Israel . . ." Sam smiled at his laughter. "I think we should probably stop discussing hotels and move on to the exciting world of sanitary napkin disposal."

"Yes, of course," Laurens said. "But may I ask you—I hope this is not intrusive?"

Sam braced herself for a question about Anton, because even a year later, people asked.

"This school shooting," Laurens said.

Sam felt ashamed that she had forgotten about it. "Is this a bad time to speak?"

"No, no. Of course it's terrible. But I saw this man on television. Russell Quinn, the attorney who is representing the suspect."

Sam gripped the receiver so tightly that a tremor developed in her thumb. She had not connected the dots, but Rusty volunteering to defend someone who had shot and killed two people inside of a school should not have come as a surprise.

Laurens said, "I know that you're from Georgia, so I wondered if there was a relation." He added, "It seems this man is quite the liberal champion."

Sam was at a loss for words. She finally managed, "It's a common name."

"It is?" Laurens was always eager to learn more about his adopted city.

"Yes. From before the Civil War." Sam shook her head, because she could have come up with a better lie. All that she could do now was move on. "So, I heard from UXH's in-house people that Nippon is about to have a shake-up in their corner suites."

Laurens hesitated slightly before changing the conversation to work. Sam listened to him run down the rumors he had heard, but her attention strayed to her computer.

She opened the *New York Times* website. Lucy Alexander. The shooting had taken place at Pikeville Middle School.

Sam's middle school.

She studied the child's face, looking for a familiar shape of the eye, a curve of the lip, that might remind her of Peter Alexander, but she found nothing. Still, Pikeville was a very small town. The odds were strong that the girl was somehow related to Sam's former beau.

She scanned down the article for details about the shooting. An eighteen-year-old girl had brought a weapon to school. She had started shooting right before the first bell. The gun was wrested away by an unnamed teacher, a highly decorated former Marine who now taught history to teenagers.

Sam scrolled down to another photo, this one of the second victim.

Douglas Pinkman.

The phone slipped from Sam's hand. She had to retrieve it from the floor. "I'm sorry," she told Laurens, her voice somewhat unsteady. "Could we follow up on this tomorrow?"

Sam barely registered his consent. She could only stare at the photograph.

During her tenure at the school, Douglas Pinkman had coached both the football and track team. He had been Sam's earliest champion, a man who believed that if she trained hard enough, pushed herself enough, she could win a scholarship to the college of her choice. Sam had known that her intellect could get her that and more, but she had been intrigued by the prospect of her body working at the same efficient levels as her mind. Running, too, was something that she really enjoyed. The open air. The sweat. The release of endorphins. The solitude.

And now, Sam was forced to use a cane on her bad days and Mr. Pinkman had been murdered outside his school office.

She scrolled down, searching for more details. Shot twice in the chest with hollow-point bullets. Pinkman's death, anonymous sources reported, was instantaneous.

Sam clicked open the *Huffington Post*, knowing they would give more attention to the story than the *Times*. The entire front page was dedicated to the shooting. The banner read TRAGEDY IN NORTH GEORGIA. Photos of Lucy Alexander and Douglas Pinkman were placed side by side.

Sam skimmed the hyperlinks:

HERO MARINE PREFERS TO REMAIN ANONYMOUS

ATTORNEY FOR SUSPECT RELEASES STATEMENT

WHAT HAPPENED WHEN: A TIMELINE OF THE SHOOTING

PINKMAN WIFE WATCHED HUSBAND DIE

Sam did not want to see the attorney for the suspect. She clicked on the last link.

Her lips parted in surprise.

Mr. Pinkman had married Judith Heller.

What a strange world.

Sam had never met Miss Heller in person, but of course she knew the woman's name. After Daniel Culpepper had shot Sam, after Zachariah had tried and failed to rape Charlie, Charlie had run to the Heller farm for help. While Miss Heller took care of her, the woman's elderly father had sat on the front porch, armed to the teeth, in case one of the Culpeppers showed up before the police did.

For obvious reasons, Sam had only learned these details much later. Even during the first month of her recovery, she could not retain the sequence of events. She had vague memories of Charlie sitting on her hospital bed repeating the story of their survival over and over again because Sam's short-term memory was a sieve. Her eyes were still bandaged. She was blind, helpless. She would reach out for Charlie's hand, slowly identify her voice, and continually ask the same questions.

Where am I? What happened? Why isn't Gamma here?

Each time, dozens, perhaps over one hundred times, Charlie had answered.

You are in the hospital. You were shot in the head. Gamma was murdered.

Then Sam would fall asleep, or a certain number of minutes would pass, and she would reach out for Charlie, asking her again—

Where am I? What happened? Why isn't Gamma here?

Gamma is dead. You are alive. Everything is going to be okay.

Sam had not considered for many years the emotional consequences of her thirteen-year-old sister having to tell and retell their story. She did know that after a while, Charlie's tears had stopped. The emotion had abated, or at least managed to conceal itself. While Charlie exhibited no reluctance to talk about the events, she had begun to relay them at a remove. Not exactly as if everything had happened to someone else, but as if she wanted to make it clear that the tragedy had lost its grip on her.

The affect came across most clearly in the trial transcripts. At various times in Sam's life, she had read the twelve-hundred-fifty-eight-page document as an exercise in memory. *This* happened to me, then *this* happened to me, then *this* is how I managed to live.

Charlie's testimony during the prosecutor's examination was dry, more like a reporter narrating a story. *This* happened to Gamma. *This* happened to Sam. *This* is what Zachariah Culpepper tried to do. *This* is what Miss Heller said when she opened her back door.

Fortunately, Judith Heller's testimony served to color between some of Charlie's stark lines. On the stand, the woman had described her shock when she'd found a blood-covered, terrified little girl standing on her porch. Charlie had been shaking so hard that at first she could not speak. When she was finally inside, finally able to form words with her mouth, inexplicably, she had asked for a bowl of ice cream.

Miss Heller had not known what to do but comply while her father called the police. Nor did she know that the ice cream would make Charlie sick. She had served two bowls before Charlie ran to the toilet. It was only through the closed bathroom door that Charlie had told Miss Heller that she thought that her mother and sister were dead.

A loud squawking distracted Sam from her thoughts.

Laurens had hung up minutes ago, but Sam was still holding the phone. She put down the receiver. Her hand lingered.

Consider the etymology of the phrase "hang up the phone."

The *Huffington Post* page automatically reloaded. The Alexander family was giving a live news conference.

Sam turned the sound down low. She watched the video. A man named Rick Fahey spoke on behalf of the family. She listened to his pleas for privacy, knowing they would fall on deaf ears. Sam supposed the one silver lining of being in a coma was that after being shot, she did not have to listen to endless speculation about her case on the news.

On the video, Fahey stared directly at the camera. He said, "That's what Kelly Wilson is. A cold-blooded murderer."

Fahey's head turned. He exchanged a look with a man who could only be Ken Coin. Instead of his ill-fitting police uniform,

Coin was wearing a shiny, navy blue suit. Sam knew that he was the current district attorney for Pikeville, but she wasn't sure where she had obtained that information.

Regardless, the look between the two men confirmed the obvious, that this was going to be a death penalty case. That explained Rusty's involvement. He had long been a vocal opponent of the death penalty. As a defense attorney, as someone who had been instrumental in the exonerations of convicted men, he believed that the chance for mistake was too high.

From the Culpepper trial transcripts, Sam knew that her father had spoken from the stand for almost a full hour, delivering a moving, impassioned plea to spare Zachariah Culpepper on the grounds that the state had no moral authority to take a life.

Charlie had argued just as forcefully for death.

Sam had fallen somewhere in the middle. She was at that point unable to clearly verbalize her thoughts. Her letter to the court had requested life in prison for Zachariah Culpepper. This was not a show of compassion. At the time, Sam was a resident of the Shepherd Spinal Center in Atlanta. The people who assisted her through the arduous months of recovery were professional and compassionate, but Sam had felt like a rabbit trapped in a snare.

She could not get in or out of bed without assistance.

She could not use the toilet without assistance.

She could not leave her room without assistance.

She could not eat when she wanted to eat, or consume what she wanted to eat.

Because her fingers could not navigate a button or zip, she could not wear the clothes that she wanted to wear.

Because she could not lace her sneakers, she was forced to wear ugly, Velcroed orthopedic shoes.

Washing herself, brushing her teeth, combing her hair, taking a walk, going outside into the sunlight or the rain, were all done at someone else's pleasure.

Rusty, citing his high moral principles, had wanted the judge to give Zachariah Culpepper life in prison. Charlie, burning with a need for revenge, had wanted a sentence of death. Sam had asked that Zachariah Culpepper be sentenced to a long, wretched existence, deprived of any sense of self-determination, because she had learned firsthand exactly what it felt like to be a prisoner.

Maybe they had all gotten their wish. Because of appeals and temporary reprieves and legal maneuverings, Zachariah Culpepper was currently one of the longest-serving inmates on Georgia's death row.

He continued to profess his innocence to anyone who would listen. He continued to claim that Charlie and Sam had colluded to frame him and his brother because he owed Rusty several thousand dollars in legal bills.

In retrospect, Sam should have argued for death.

She closed the browser on her computer.

She opened a blank email and sent apologies to her friend, begging off their birthday drinks tonight. She told Eldrin to hold her calls. She put on her reading glasses.

She returned her attention to the narrow plated pintle hinge.

When Sam looked up from her computer, darkness had turned her windows black. Eldrin was gone. The office was quiet. Not for the first time, she was alone on the floor.

She had also sat too long without moving. She performed some seated stretches. Her body was stiff, but eventually, determinedly, she was able to stand. She unfolded the collapsible cane she kept in her bottom desk drawer. She wrapped her scarf around her neck. She considered calling a car, but by the time one showed up, she could walk the six blocks home.

She regretted the decision the moment she stepped outside.

The wind off the river was cutting. Sam gripped the scarf in one hand. Her other hand held tight to the cane. Her briefcase and purse weighed down the crook of her arm. She should have waited for the car. She should have had drinks with her friend. She should have done a lot of things differently today.

The night doorman wished Sam happy birthday as she entered her building. She stopped to thank him, to ask after his children, but her leg ached too much to stand.

She rode up in the elevator alone.

She stared at her reflection in the back of the doors.

A solitary, white-haired figure stared back.

The doors slid open. Fosco rolled and stretched on the floor as Sam walked into the kitchen. She made herself eat some leftover Thai from Saturday night's birthday dinner party. The bar stool was uncomfortable. She sat on the edge, both feet on the floor. Pain spread up the side of her leg like a hot blade was splaying open the muscle.

She looked at the clock. Too early to go to bed. Too tired to concentrate on work. Too exhausted to read the new book she had received as a birthday present.

At her old apartment in Chelsea, she and Anton had eschewed television-watching. Sam stared at screens all day. There was only so much blue light that her eyes could take before a headache began to gnaw behind her eyes.

The new apartment had come with a large television already installed in the den. Sam had often found herself drawn to the dark room, one of those windowless boxes that builders called *bonus spaces* because they could not legally call them bedrooms.

Sam sat down on the couch. She placed an empty wineglass on the coffee table. Beside this, she put a bottle of 2011 Tenuta Poggio San Nicolò.

Anton's favorite wine.

Fosco jumped into her lap. Sam absently scratched between his ears. She studied the elegant label on the wine bottle, the delicate scrollwork around the border, the simple red wax seal at the center.

The liquid inside might as well be poison.

Sam believed that it was wines like the San Nicolò that had killed her husband.

As Anton's consultancy business had expanded, as Sam's practice had grown, they were able to afford better things. Five-star hotels. First-class flights. Suites. Private tours. Fine dining. One of Anton's lifelong passions was wine. He loved enjoying a glass at lunch, another glass, perhaps two, with dinner. The dry reds were his particular favorite. Occasionally, when Sam wasn't around, he would accompany the drink with a cigar.

Anton's doctors pointed to fate and perhaps the cigars, but Sam thought the high levels of tannin in the wines had killed him.

Esophageal cancer.

Less than two percent of all cancers were of this kind.

Tannin, a naturally occurring astringent, lends certain plants a defense against insects and predators. The chemical compound can be found in many fruits, berries, and legumes. There are several real-world applications for tannoids. Vegetable and synthetic tannins are employed in leather-making. The pharmaceutical world frequently uses tannate salts in the production of antihistamines and antitussive medications.

In red wine, tannin acts as a structural component, a reaction from the skin of the grape making contact with the pips. Wines with higher levels of tannins age better than ones with lower levels, thus the more mature, the more expensive the bottle, the higher the concentration of tannins.

Tannin also occurs naturally in tea, but the coagulating power can be neutralized by the proteins found in milk.

To Sam's thinking, proteins and tannins were at the crux of Anton's illness; particularly histatins, which are salivary proteins secreted by glands in the back of the tongue. The fluid contains antimicrobial and antifungal properties, but also plays a key role in wound closure.

This last function is perhaps the most vital. Cancer, after all, is the result of abnormal cell growth. If histatins don't protect and repair the tissues lining the esophagus, then the DNA of the cells can become altered, and abnormal growth can begin.

Tannins are known to suppress the production of histatins in the mouth.

Every toast Anton made, every *salut*, had contributed to the malignancy growing inside the tissues lining his esophagus, spreading to his lymph nodes and finally into his organs.

At least that was Sam's theory. As she had watched her beautiful, vibrant husband wither away over the course of two long years, she had clung to what appeared to be a tangible explanation—an x that had caused y. Anton had tested negative for oral HPV, a viral infection linked to roughly seventy percent of cancers of the head and neck. He was only an occasional smoker. He was not an alcoholic. There was no history of cancer in his immediate family.

Ergo, tannins.

To accept that fate had played any role in his sickness, that lightning had struck Sam not twice but three times, was beyond her intellectual and emotional capacity.

Fosco pressed his head into Sam's arm. He had been Anton's cat. There was likely some sort of Pavlovian reaction to the scent of the wine.

Sam gently set him aside as she moved to the edge of the couch. She poured a glass of wine that she would not drink for her husband that she could not see.

Then, she did what she had been avoiding since three this afternoon.

She turned on the television.

The woman who Sam would always think of as Miss Heller was standing outside the front entrance to the Dickerson County Hospital. Understandably, she looked devastated. Her long blondish gray hair was untamed, tendrils blowing wild in the wind. Her eyes were bloodshot. The thin line of her lips was almost the same color as her skin.

She said, "The tragedy of today cannot be erased by the death of another young woman." She stopped. Her lips pressed together. Sam heard cameras clicking, reporters clearing their throats. Mrs. Pinkman's voice remained strong. "I pray for the Alexander family. I pray for my husband's soul. For my own salvation." Again, she pressed together her lips. Tears glistened in her eyes. "But I also pray for the Wilson family. Because they have suffered today as much as any of us have suffered." She looked directly into the camera, shoulders squared. "I forgive Kelly Wilson. I absolve her of this horrible tragedy. As Matthew says, 'for if you forgive other people who have sinned against you, your heavenly Father will also forgive you your sins.'"

The woman turned and walked back into the hospital. Guards blocked the doors to keep reporters from following her.

Sam let out a breath that had been held deep inside her chest.

The anchor came back onscreen. He was sitting at a desk with a panel of self-styled experts. Their words floated over Sam's head as she pulled Fosco into her lap.

A British friend of Sam's had claimed that England had lost its stiff upper lip the day that Princess Diana had died. Overnight, a culture given to wry comments in lieu of emotion had turned into a weepy mess. The friend called this phenomenon yet another unwelcome Americanization—the Brits were constantly complaining about America, even as they greedily consumed American products and culture—and said that the public outpouring of grief over Diana's death had forever altered the way that his people could acceptably respond to tragedy.

There was probably some truth to his theory, even the part about blaming America, but Sam believed the worst result of these seemingly unrelenting national tragedies was that a formula for recovery had emerged. The Boston Marathon attacks. San Bernardino. The Pulse Nightclub.

People were outraged. They were glued to their televisions, to their web pages, to their Facebook feeds. They vocally expressed sorrow, horror, fury, pain. They cried for change. They raised money. They demanded action.

And then they went back to their lives until the next one happened again.

Sam's eyes flicked back to the television. The news anchor said, "We're going to show the video from before. For viewers who are just tuning in, this is a reenactment of the events that took place this morning in Pikeville, which is roughly two hours north of Atlanta."

Sam watched the crude drawings awkwardly move across the screen—more of a simulation than a reenactment.

The anchor began, "At approximately six fifty-five this morning, the alleged shooter, Kelly Rene Wilson, walked into the hallway."

Sam watched the figure move to the center of the hallway.

A door opened. An old woman ducked as two bullets were fired.

Sam closed her eyes, but she listened.

Mr. Pinkman is shot. Lucy Alexander is shot. Two more figures enter the frame. Neither is identified by name. One male, the other female. The woman runs to Lucy Alexander. The man struggles with Kelly Wilson for the gun.

Sam opened her eyes. There was a bead of sweat on her forehead. She had gripped her hands so tightly that half-moon indentations cut into her palms.

Her cell phone started to ring. From the kitchen. Inside her purse.

Sam did not move. She watched the television. The anchor was interviewing a bald man whose bow tie indicated he was likely involved in the psychiatric profession.

He said, "Generally, you find that these types of shooters are loners. They feel alienated, unloved. Often, they are bullied."

Her phone stopped ringing.

Bow Tie continued, "The fact that the murderer in this instance is a woman—"

Sam turned off the television. The room faded to pitch-black, but she was used to maneuvering through the darkness. She checked to make sure Fosco was sleeping beside her. She tentatively reached out for the wine bottle and glass and took them into the kitchen, where the contents of both went down the sink.

Sam checked her phone. The call had come from an unknown number. Likely a telemarketer, though she'd had her number added to the do-not-call registry. Sam used her thumb to navigate the screens and block the number.

The phone vibrated in her hand, announcing a new email. She looked at the time. Hong Kong was open for business. If there was one constant in Sam's life, it was the steady, unrelenting volume of work to be done.

She didn't want to commit to retrieving her reading glasses unless there was an urgent message. She squinted, skimming down the list of new mails.

She left them all unopened.

Sam put the phone on the counter. She went about her nightly routine. She made sure all of Fosco's water bowls were full. She turned off the lights, pressed the appropriate buttons to close the blinds, checked to make certain that the alarm had been set.

She went into the bathroom and brushed her teeth. She took her nightly regimen of pills. In the closet, she changed into her pajamas. There was a very good novel on her bedside table, but Sam was eager to rest, to put the day behind her, to wake up tomorrow with a fresh perspective.

She climbed into bed. Fosco appeared from nowhere. He took his place on the pillow next to her head. She took off her glasses. She turned off the light. She closed her eyes.

Sam hissed out a low, steady stream of breath.

Slowly, she went through her nightly exercises, engaging, then releasing every muscle in her body, from the flexor digitorum brevis in her feet to the galea aponeurotica beneath her scalp.

She waited for her body to relax, for sleep to come, but there was a pronounced lack of cooperation. The silence in the room was too complete. Even Fosco was absent his usual sighs and licks and snores.

Sam's eyes opened.

She stared up at the ceiling, waited for the darkness to turn to gray, the gray to give way to shadows cast by the tiny edge of light that always sneaked between the blinds on the windows.

"Can you see?" Charlie had asked. "Sam, can you see?"

"Yes," Sam had lied. She could feel the freshly planted soil beneath her bare feet. Every step away from the farmhouse, away from the light, added one more layer of darkness. Charlie was a blob of gray. Daniel was tall and skinny, like a charcoal pencil. Zachariah Culpepper was a menacing black square of hate.

Sam sat up, swiveled her legs over the side of the bed. She pressed her hands into her thighs, working the stiff muscles. The radiant heat in the floor warmed the soles of her feet.

She could feel her heart beating. Slow and steady. The sinoatrial node, the atrioventricular node, the His-Purkinje network of fibers that sent impulses to the muscular walls of the ventricles, making them alternately contract and relax.

Sam stood up. She went back into the kitchen. She got her reading glasses out of her briefcase. She held her phone in her hand.

She opened the new email from Ben.

Charlie needs you.

CHAPTER EIGHT

Sam sat in the back seat of a black Mercedes, clenching and unclenching her hand around her phone as the driver merged onto Interstate 575.

Two decades of progress had done its damage to the North Georgia landscape. Nothing had been left untouched. Shopping centers had sprung up like weeds. Billboards peppered the landscape. Even the once-lush, wildflower-lined medians were gone. A massive, reversible toll lane cut through the center of the interstate, catering to all the pickup-driving John Boys who drove down to Atlanta every day to make money, then drove back at night and railed against the godless liberals who lined their pockets and subsidized their utilities, their healthcare, their children's lunches and their schools.

"We be another hour, maybe," Stanislav, the driver, relayed in his thick Croatian accent. "This construction—" He made a wide shrugging gesture. "Who knows?"

"That's fine." Sam stared out the window. She always requested Stanislav when she was in Atlanta. He was the rare driver who understood her need for silence. Or perhaps he assumed that she was a nervous passenger. He had no way of knowing that Sam was so used to being in the back seat of a black sedan that she seldom noticed the road.

Sam had never properly learned how to drive a car. When she had turned fifteen, Rusty had taken her out in Gamma's station wagon, but as with most family-oriented tasks, he had soon inundated her with work excuses that permanently forestalled Sam's lessons. Gamma had tried to take up the slack, but she was an incessantly picky driver, and an outright caustic passenger. Add to the mix that both Gamma and Sam were explosive, corrosive arguers, and in the end, they had agreed that Sam should start driver's ed during her fall semester in high school.

But then the Culpepper brothers had shown up in the kitchen.

While other girls Sam's age were studying for their learner's permit, she was busy trying to reestablish the connections between her toes, feet, ankles, calves, knees, thighs, buttocks, and hips with the hope of learning how to walk again.

Not that mobility was her only obstacle. The damage done to her eyes by Zachariah Culpepper was, to use *that word* again, mostly superficial. Her lingering sensitivity to light was an easily solvable issue. Her tattered eyelids had been stitched back together by a plastic surgeon. Zachariah's short, jagged fingernails had pierced the sclera, but not the choroid or the optic nerve, the retina or the cornea.

The thief of sight was a hemorrhagic stroke, subsequent to a congenital cerebral aneurysm rupturing during surgery, that had damaged some of the fibers responsible for transmitting visual information from Sam's eyes to her brain. Her vision corrected to 20/40, a threshold for driving in most states, but the peripheral vision in her right eye fell below twenty degrees of vision.

For legal purposes, Sam was considered blind.

Fortunately, there never seemed to be a need for Sam to drive herself. She took cars to and from the airport. She walked to work, or to the market, or to various appointments and social gatherings in her immediate neighborhood. If she needed to go uptown, she could hail a cab or ask Eldrin to book a car. She had never been one of those New Yorkers who claimed to love the city but couldn't wait to escape to the Hamptons or Martha's Vineyard the moment they were able to buy a second home. Sam and Anton had never even discussed the possibility. If they wanted to see open water, they could go to Palioxori or Korčula, not trap themselves in the cloistered equivalent of a Manhattan Disney beach vacation.

Sam's phone vibrated. She hadn't realized she was holding it so tightly until she saw her own sweat on the margins of the screen.

Ben had been sporadically updating her since Sam had emailed back last night. First, Rusty was in surgery, then he was out of surgery and in the ICU, then he was back in surgery for a bleed that had been missed, then he was back in the ICU again.

The latest update was the same she'd seen before the plane had taken off:

No change.

Sam looked at the time. Ben had tracked the Delta flight number that Sam had provided him. His email came ten minutes after the scheduled landing time. He had no idea that Sam had lied about the flight number as well as the flight itself. Stehlik, Elton, Mallory and Sanders had a corporate jet that was kept available for partners by level of seniority. Sam's name was not yet on the stainless-steel sign opposite the elevator doors, but the contracts had been signed, her buy-in had been wired, and the jet was made ready the moment she'd had Eldrin place the call.

But Sam had not left last night.

She had looked up the number of the early Delta flight to send to Ben. She had packed a bag. She had emailed the cat sitter. She had sat at her kitchen counter. She had listened to Fosco snore and grunt as he settled on the chair beside her, and she had cried.

What was she giving up to return to Pikeville?

Sam had promised Gamma she would never return.

Though if her mother had lived, if Gamma was still inhabiting the higgledy-piggledy farmhouse, surely Sam would have returned at Christmastime, perhaps even holidays in between. Gamma would have driven down for dinners in Atlanta when Sam had business in the city. Sam would have taken her mother to Brazil or New Zealand or wherever Gamma wanted to go. The break with Charlie would not have happened. Sam would have been a proper sister, sister-in-law, perhaps even an aunt.

Sam's relationship with Rusty would likely be the same, if not worse, because she would have to see him, but Rusty thrived on that type of adversity. Maybe Sam would have, too—in that other life, the one she would have lived had she not been shot in the head.

Sam would be able-bodied.

She could be running every morning rather than swimming her lackadaisical laps. She could walk without pain. Raise her hand in the air without wondering how high it would reach that day. She could trust her mouth to clearly articulate the words in her head. She could drive herself up the interstate. She could relish the freedom of knowing that her body, her mind, her brain, were whole.

Sam swallowed back the grief that sat at the base of her throat. She had not indulged herself in these *what-if* scenarios since leaving the Shepherd Spinal Center. If she allowed herself the luxury of sadness now, she would become paralyzed.

She looked down at her phone, skimmed up to Ben's first email. *Charlie needs you.*

He had found the one phrase that would make Sam respond.

But not quickly. Not without considerable equivocation.

Last night, after finally reading the email, Sam had hesitated. She had paced the apartment, her leg so weak that she had started to limp. She had taken a hot shower. She had steeped tea in her mug, tried to do her stretches, attempted to meditate, but a niggling inquisitiveness had chewed at the margins of all her procrastinations.

Charlie had never needed Sam before.

Instead of texting Ben the obvious questions—*Why? What's wrong?*—Sam had turned on the news. Half an hour had passed before MSNBC reported the stabbing. They had very little information to offer. Rusty had been found by a neighbor. He was lying prone at the end of the driveway. Mail was scattered on the

ground. The neighbor had called the police. The police had called
an ambulance. The ambulance had called a helicopter, and now,
Sam was returning to the one place to which she had promised her
mother she would never return.

Sam reminded herself that, technically, she was not going to be
in Pikeville. The Dickerson County Hospital was thirty minutes
away, in a town called Bridge Gap. When Sam was a teenager,
Bridge Gap was the big city, the place you'd go to if your boyfriend or a friend had a car and your parents were lenient.

Perhaps, when Charlie was younger, she had gone to Bridge
Gap with a boy or a group of friends. Rusty had certainly been
lenient; Gamma had always been the disciplinarian. Sam knew
that without Gamma's balancing check, Charlie had turned wild.
College saw the worst of it. There had been several late-night calls
from Athens, where Charlie was doing her undergrad at UGA. She
needed money for food, for rent, for the health clinic, and once, for
what had turned out to be a false pregnancy scare.

"Are you going to help me or not?" Charlie had demanded, her
aggressive tone cutting off Sam's as yet unuttered recriminations.

Judging by Ben, Charlie had managed to right herself. The tran-
sition would not have been an actual change so much as a rever-
sion to type. Charlie had never been a rebel. She was one of those
easygoing, popular girls, the sort who got invited to everything,
who effortlessly mixed with the crowd. She had a kind of natural
affability that had always eluded Sam even before the accident.

What was Charlie's life like now?

Sam didn't even know if her sister had children. She assumed
so. Charlie had always loved babies. She had babysat for half the
neighborhood before the red-brick house had burned down. She
was always taking care of stray animals, leaving pecans outside
for the squirrels, building bird feeders at Brownie meetings and
once erecting a rabbit hutch in the backyard, though, to Charlie's
utter disappointment, the rabbits seemed to prefer the neighbor's
abandoned doghouse.

What did Charlie look like now? Was her hair gray like Sam's? Was she still thin, muscular, from the perpetual motion of her life? Would Sam even recognize her own sister if she saw her?

When she saw her.

A sign welcoming them to Dickerson County flashed outside the window.

She should have told Stanislav to drive more slowly.

Sam thumbed to the browser on her phone. She reloaded the MSNBC homepage and found an updated story about Rusty. *Guarded condition.* Sam, even after a lifetime in and out of hospitals, had no idea what that meant. Better than critical? Worse than stable?

At the end of Anton's life, when he was finally hospitalized, there had been no updates on his condition, just the understanding that he was comfortable today, that he was in discomfort the next day, and then the solemn, unspoken understanding between them all that there would be no tomorrow.

Sam swiped up the *Huffington Post* in her browser to see if they had more details. Her breath caught in surprise when a recent photograph of Rusty appeared.

For reasons unknown, whenever she listened to her father's voicemails, Sam conjured an image of Burl Ives from the Luzianne Tea commercials: a robust, round man in a white hat and suit, a black string tie held together by some sort of gaudy silver medallion.

Her father was nothing like that. Not before, and certainly not today.

Rusty's thick black hair was mostly gray. His face had the texture if not color of beef jerky. He still had that lean look about him, as if he'd finally made his way out of a jungle. His cheeks were hollow. His eyes sunken. Photos had never done Rusty justice. In person, he was perpetually in motion, always fidgeting, gesturing with his hands like a Great Oz, so that you did not see the weak, old man behind the curtain.

Sam wondered if he was still with Lenore. Even as a teenager, Sam had understood why Gamma had taken such a dislike to the woman with whom Rusty spent most of his time. Had he given into the cliché and married his secretary after an appropriate period of mourning? Lenore had been a young woman when Gamma was murdered. Would there be a half sister or brother waiting at the hospital?

Sam dropped her phone back into her purse.

"Okay," Stanislav said. "We got one more mile, according to the Wave." He indicated his iPad. "You say two hours, then we go back?"

"Approximately," Sam said. "Maybe less."

"I get some lunch from a restaurant. The hospital cafeteria, that food's no good." He handed her a business card. "You text me. Five minutes, then I meet you out front."

Sam resisted the desire to tell him to wait in the car, engine running, wheels turned back toward Atlanta, and instead responded, "Okay."

Stanislav engaged the turn signal. He ran the butt of his palm along the steering wheel, taking a wide turn into the winding drive of the hospital.

Sam felt her stomach clench.

The Dickerson County Hospital was much larger than she remembered, or maybe the building had been added onto in the last thirty years. The Quinn family had been to the emergency room only once before the Culpeppers entered their lives. Charlie had fallen from a tree and broken her arm. This had happened for typical Charlie reasons; she had been trying to rescue a cat. Sam could recall Gamma lecturing over Charlie's screams during the car ride to the hospital—not about the idiocy of rescuing a creature whose every bundle of nerve and sinew equipped it with the ability to climb down a tree on its own—but about anatomical structure:

"The bone running from the shoulder to the elbow is the humerus.

This we call the upper arm, or, simply, the arm. The humerus connects with two bones at the elbow: the radius and the ulna, which are regarded as the forearm."

None of this information had abated the screaming. For once, Sam could not accuse Charlie of overreacting. Her broken humerus, or *arm*, as Gamma had called it, jutted up like a shark's fin from Charlie's torn flesh.

Stanislav pulled the Mercedes under the wide concrete canopy at the main entrance. He was a large man. The car shook as he hefted his frame from behind the wheel. He walked around the back of the car and opened the door for Sam. She had to lift her right leg to get out. She was using her cane today because there was no one she would meet who would not know what had happened.

"You text me, I come five minutes," Stanislav said, then got back into the car.

Sam watched him drive away, a peculiar tightness in her throat. She had to remind herself that she had his number in her purse, that she could call him back, that she had a credit card with no limit, a jet at her disposal, the ability to flee whenever she wanted.

And yet, she felt as if a straitjacket was tightening around her arms as the car moved farther away.

Sam turned. She looked at the hospital. Two reporters were on a bench beside the door, their press credentials hanging on lanyards around their necks, cameras at their feet. They looked up at Sam, then back down at their phones, as she made her way inside the building.

She scanned the area for Ben, half expecting to find him waiting. She only saw patients and visitors idling around the lobby. There was a help desk, but the color-coded arrows on the floor were clear enough to Sam. She followed the green line to the elevators. She ran her finger along the directory until she found the words ADULT ICU.

Sam rode up alone. She felt as if she had spent most of her life riding up or down in elevators while others took the stairs. The intercom dinged as she passed each floor. The car was clean, but smelled vaguely of sickness.

She stared straight ahead, forcing herself not to count the floors. The backs of the elevator doors were polished satin to hide fingerprints, but she could see the anamorphic outline of her lone figure: an aloof presence, quick blue eyes, short white hair, skin as pale as an envelope, and with a sharp tongue just as prone to inflicting tiny, painful cuts in inconvenient places. Even with the distortion, Sam could make out the thin line of her own disapproving lips. This was the angry, bitter woman who had never left Pikeville.

The doors opened.

There was a black line on the floor, much like the line on the bottom of the pool, that led to the closed doors of the Intensive Care Unit.

To Rusty.

To her sister.

To her brother-in-law.

To the unknown.

The stinging of a thousand hornets ran up and down her leg as Sam made her way down the long, forlorn hallway. The sound of her shoes slapping hospital tiles bongoed along with the slow thumps of her heart. Sweat had glued her hair to the nape of her neck. The twigs of delicate bones inside her wrist and ankle felt ready to snap.

Sam kept walking, choking down the antiseptic air, leaning into the pain.

The automatic doors opened before she reached them.

A woman blocked the way. Tall, athletic, long dark hair, light blue eyes. Her nose appeared to have been recently broken. Two dark bruises rimmed beneath each eye.

Sam pushed herself to move faster. The tendons cording through her leg sent out a high-pitched wail. The hornets moved into her chest. The handle of the cane was slippery in her hand.

She felt so nervous. Why was she nervous?

Charlie said, "You look like Mama."

"Do I?" Sam's voice shook in her chest.

"Except her hair was black."

"Because she went to the beauty parlor." Sam ran her hand through her hair. Her fingertips tripped over the furrow where the bullet had gone in. She said, "There was a Latin American study conducted by the University College of London that isolated the gene that causes gray hair. IRF4."

"Fascinating," Charlie said. Her arms were crossed. Should they hug? Should they shake hands? Should they stand here staring at one another until Sam's leg fell out from under her?

Sam asked, "What happened to your face?"

"What indeed?"

Sam waited for Charlie to acknowledge the bruises around her eyes, the nasty bump in her nose, but as usual, her sister did not seem inclined to explain herself.

"Sam?" Ben broke the awkward moment. He threw his arms around Sam, his hands firm on her back in a way that no one had held her since Anton had died.

She felt tears in her eyes. She saw Charlie watching and looked away.

"Rusty's condition is stable," Charlie said. "He's been in and out of it all morning, but they think he'll wake up soon."

Ben kept his hand at Sam's back. He told her, "You look exactly the same."

"Thank you," Sam mumbled, self-conscious.

"The sheriff's supposed to come by," Charlie said. "Keith Coin. You remember that dipshit?"

Sam did.

"They made some bullshit statement about using all their re- sources to find whoever stabbed Rusty, but don't hold your breath." She kept her arms tightly crossed over her chest. Same prickly, cocksure Charlie. "I wouldn't be surprised if it was one of his deputies."

"He's representing this girl," Sam said. "The school shooter."

"Kelly Wilson," Charlie said. "I'll spare you the long, tedious story."

Sam wondered at her choice of adjectives. Two people had been shot dead. Rusty had been stabbed. There did not seem to be an aspect to the story that was either too long or in any way tedious, but Sam reminded herself that she was not here to find out details.

She was here because of the email.

Sam asked Ben, "Could you give us a moment?"

"Of course." Ben's hand lingered at her back, and she realized that the gesture was because of her handicap, not out of a particular affection.

Sam stiffened. "I'm fine, thank you."

"I know." Ben rubbed her back. "I've gotta go to work. I'm around if you need me."

Charlie reached for his hand, but Ben had already turned to leave.

The automatic doors swung closed behind him. Sam watched his easy, loping gait through the windows. She waited for him to turn the corner. She hooked the cane on her arm. She motioned for Charlie to continue up the hallway to a row of plastic chairs.

Charlie went first, her feet pushing off from the floor with her usual physical confidence. Sam's stride was more tenuous. Without the cane, she felt as if she was walking the slanted floor of a fun house. Still, she made it to the chair. She put her hand flat to the seat and eased herself down.

She said, "What Rusty this cause."

Sam's eyes closed as the jumbled words reached her ears.

She said, "I mean—"

"They think it's because he's representing Kelly Wilson," Charlie said. "Someone in town isn't happy about it. We can rule out Judith Heller. She was here all night. She married Mr. Pinkman twenty-five years ago. Weird, right?"

Sam only trusted herself to nod.

"So, that leaves the Alexander family." Charlie quietly tapped her foot on the floor. Sam had forgotten that her sister could be as fidgety as Rusty. "There's no relation to Peter. You remember Peter from high school, right?"

Sam nodded again, trying not to chastise Charlie for falling back into her old habit of ending every sentence with the word "right," as if she wanted to eradicate the linguistic burden of Sam having to provide anything other than a nod or shake of the head.

Charlie said, "Peter moved to Atlanta, but he was hit by a car a few years ago. I read it on somebody's Facebook page. Sad, right?"

Sam nodded a third time, feeling an unexpected pang of loss at the news.

Charlie said, "There's another case Daddy was working on. I'm not sure who it involves, but he's been late more than usual. Lenore won't tell me. He annoys the shit out of her as much as anybody, but she keeps his secrets."

Sam's eyebrows went up.

"I know, right? How has she worked with him this long without killing him?" She gave a sudden laugh. "In case you're wondering, she was at home when Daddy was stabbed."

"Where?" Sam asked. She meant where was home for Lenore, but Charlie took the question differently.

"Mr. Thomas, the guy who lives down the street, found him at the end of the driveway. There wasn't a lot of visible blood except for a cut on his leg and some on his shirt. He bled mostly inside his abdomen. I guess that's how it is with those types of wounds." She pointed to her own belly. "Here, here, and here. Like they shiv you in prison—*pop-pop-pop*—which is why I think it might be related to this other case. Daddy has a way of pissing off convicts."

"No shit," Sam said, a crude but accurate consilience.

"Maybe you can get some information out of her?" Charlie stood up as the doors opened. She had obviously seen Lenore through the windows.

Sam saw her, too. She felt her mouth gape open.

"Samantha," Lenore said, her husky voice as familiar from Sam's childhood as the ringing of the kitchen phone announcing that Rusty would be late. "I'm sure your father will appreciate your being here. Was the flight okay?"

Sam was again reduced to nodding, this time by shock.

Lenore said, "I'm assuming you two are talking as if nothing ever happened and everything is fine?" She didn't wait for an answer. "I'll go check on your father."

She squeezed Charlie's shoulder before continuing up the hall. Sam watched Lenore tuck a dark blue clutch under her arm as she approached the nurses' station. She was wearing navy heels and a short matching skirt that hit too far above her knee.

Charlie said, "You didn't know, did you?"

"That she was—" Sam struggled for the correct words. "That—I mean, that she was—"

Charlie had her hand over her mouth. She shook with laughter.

"This isn't funny," Sam said.

Trapped air sputtered around Charlie's hand.

"Stop it. You're being disrespectful."

"Only to you," Charlie said.

"I can't believe—" Sam couldn't finish the thought.

"You were always too smart to know how stupid you are." Charlie could not stop smiling. "You really never put it together that Lenore's transgender?"

Sam returned to shaking her head. Her life in Pikeville had been sheltered, but Lenore's gender identity seemed self-evident. How had Sam missed that Lenore had been born a man? The woman was at least six-three. Her voice was deeper than Rusty's.

"Leonard," Charlie said. "He was Dad's best friend in college."

"Gamma hated her." Sam turned to Charlie, alarmed by a thought. "Was Mom transphobic?"

"No. At least, I don't think so. She dated Lenny first. They almost got married. I think she was mad about the . . ." Charlie's voice trailed off, because the blanks were easy to fill in. She said, "Gamma found out that Lenore was wearing some of her clothes. She wouldn't say which, but you know the first thing that came to mind when she told me was that it was her underwear. Lenore told me, I mean. Gamma never talked about it with me. You really didn't figure it out?"

Again, Sam could only shake her head. "I thought that Gamma thought they were having an affair."

"I wouldn't wish that on anyone," Charlie said. "Rusty, I mean. I wouldn't wish—"

"Girls?" Lenore's heels clicked against the tiles as she walked back toward them. "He's lucid, at least for Rusty. They say only two visitors at a time."

Charlie stood up quickly. She offered her arm to Sam.

Sam leaned heavily on her cane and pushed herself up. She was not going to let these people treat her like an invalid. "When will we be able to speak with his doctors?"

"They make their rounds in another hour," Lenore said. "Do you remember Melissa LaMarche from Mr. Pendleton's class?"

"Yes," Sam said, though she didn't know why Lenore remembered the names of one of Sam's friends and a teacher from high school.

"She's Dr. LaMarche now. She operated on Rusty last night."

Sam thought about Melissa, the way she had cried every time she scored less than perfect on a test. That was probably the kind of person you wanted operating on your father.

Father.

She had not attached that word to Rusty in years.

"You go first," Charlie told Lenore. Her eagerness to see Rusty had visibly dissipated. She stopped in front of a row of large windows. "Sam and I will go in after."

Lenore left them in silence.

At first, Charlie let the silence linger. She walked to the windows. She looked down at the parking lot. "Now's your chance."

To leave, she meant. Before Rusty had seen her. Before Sam got sucked back into this world again.

Sam asked, "Did you really need me here? Or was that Ben?"

"It was me, and Ben was nice enough to reach out because I couldn't, or couldn't bring myself to, but I thought that Dad was going to die." She leaned her forehead against the glass. "He had a heart attack two years ago. The one before that was mild, but this last one, he needed bypass surgery, and there were complications."

Sam said nothing. She had been left in the dark about Rusty's apparent heart condition. He had never missed a phone call. For all Sam knew, he had remained healthy all these years.

"I had to make a decision," Charlie said. "At one point, he couldn't breathe on his own, and I had to make the decision whether or not to put him on life support."

"He doesn't have a DNR?" Sam asked. The Do Not Resuscitate form, which specified whether or not a person wanted a natural death or CPR and cardiac support, was commonly drawn up alongside a will.

Sam saw the problem before Charlie could answer. "Rusty doesn't have a will."

"No, he doesn't." Charlie turned around, her back against the window. "I made the right choice, obviously. I mean, it's obvious now, because he lived and he was fine, but this time, when Melissa came out during surgery and said that they were having trouble getting the bleeding under control, and that his heartbeat was erratic, and that I might have to make the decision whether or not to take life-saving—"

"You wanted me here to kill him."

Charlie looked alarmed, but not because of Sam's bluntness. It was her tone, the hint of anger bubbling up around the words. She told Sam, "If you're going to get mad about this, we should go outside."

"So the reporters can hear?"

"Sam." Charlie looked anxious, as if she was watching the clock on a nuclear warhead start to tick down. "Let's go outside."

Sam squeezed her hands into fists. She could feel the long-forgotten darkness stirring inside of her. She took a deep breath, then another, then another until it folded itself back into a tight ball inside her chest.

She told her sister, "You have no idea, Charlotte, how wrong you are about my willingness or capacity to end someone's life."

Sam tilted against her cane as she walked toward the nurses' station. She glanced at the whiteboard behind the empty desk and located Rusty's room. She raised her hand to knock on the door, but Lenore opened it before her knuckles touched wood.

Lenore said, "I told him you were here. Wouldn't want him to have a heart attack."

"You mean another one," Sam said. She did not give Lenore time to respond.

Instead, she walked into her father's hospital room.

The air seemed too thin.

The lights were too bright.

She blinked against the headache that chewed at the back of her eyes.

Rusty's room in the ICU was a familiar, if more economized version of the private hospital suite in which Anton had died. There was no wood paneling or deep couch or flat-screen television or private desk where Sam could work, but the machines were all the same: the beeping heart monitor, the hissing oxygen supply, the grinding sound that the blood pressure cuff made as it inflated around Rusty's arm.

He looked much like his photograph, absent any color in his

face. The camera had never been able to capture the devil's glint in his eyes, the dimples in his rubbery cheeks.

"Sammy-Sam!" he bellowed, hacking out a cough at the end. "Come here, gal. Lemme see you up close."

Sam did not move closer. She felt her nose wrinkle. He reeked of cigarette smoke and Old Spice, two scents that had remained blissfully absent in her everyday life.

"Damn if you don't look like your mama." He gave a delighted laugh. "To what does your old pappy owe this pleasure?"

Charlie suddenly appeared on Sam's right. She knew this was Sam's blind side. There was no telling how long she had been there. She said, "Dad, we thought that you were going to die."

"I remain a constant disappointment to the women in my life." Rusty scratched his chin. Under the covers, his foot tapped out a silent beat. "I am happy to see that no fresh slings and arrows have been exchanged."

"Not so you can see." Charlie walked around to the other side of the bed. Her arms were crossed. She did not take his hand. "Are you okay?"

"Well." Rusty seemed to think about it. "I was stabbed. Or, in the vernacular of the streets, *cut*."

"The unkindest kind."

"Thrice in the belly, once in the leg."

"You don't say."

Sam tuned out their banter. She had always been a reluctant spectator of the Rusty and Charlie show. Her father, on the other hand, seemed to eat it up. He clearly still delighted in Charlie, a literal twinkle flashing in his eye when she engaged him.

Sam looked at her watch. She could not believe only sixteen minutes had passed since she had gotten out of the car. She raised her voice over the din, asking, "Rusty, what happened?"

"What do you mean what—" He looked at his stomach. Surgical drains hung from either side of his torso. He looked back at Sam, feigning shock. "'Oh, I am slain!'"

For once, Charlie didn't egg him on. "Daddy, Sam has a flight back this afternoon."

Sam was startled by the reminder. Somehow, she had momentarily let herself forget that she could leave.

Charlie said, "Come on, Dad. Tell us what happened."

"All right, all right." Rusty let out a low groan as he tried to sit up in bed. Sam realized that this was the first sign her father had given that he had been wounded.

"Well—" He coughed, a wet rattle shaking inside his chest. He winced from the exertion, then coughed again, then winced again, then waited to make sure it had passed.

When he was finally able, he directed his words toward Charlie, his most receptive audience. "After you dropped me at ye olde homestead, I had a bite to eat, maybe a little to drink, and then I realized that I hadn't checked the mail."

Sam could not think of the last time she had received mail at her home. It seemed like a ritual from another century.

Rusty continued, "I put on my walkin' shoes and headed out. Beautiful night, last night. Partly cloudy, chance of rain this morning. Oh—" he seemed to remember that morning had passed. "Did it rain?"

"Yes." Charlie made a rolling motion with her hand, indicating he should speed up the story. "Did you see who did it?"

Rusty coughed again. "That is a complicated question with an equally complicated answer."

Charlie waited. They both waited.

Rusty said, "All right, so, I walked to the mailbox to check my mail. Beautiful night. Moon high up in the sky. The driveway was giving off warmth saved up from the sun. Paints a picture, don't it?"

Sam felt herself nodding along with Charlie, as if thirty years had not passed and they were both little girls listening to one of their father's stories.

He seemed to relish the attention. Some color came back into his cheeks. "I came around the bend, and I heard something up above me, so I was looking up for that bird. Remember I told you about the hawk, Charlotte?"

Charlie nodded.

"Thought the old fella got himself a chipmunk again, but then—shazam!" He clapped together his hands. "I feel this hot pain in my leg."

Sam felt her cheeks redden. Like Charlie, she had jumped at the clap.

Rusty said, "I look down, and I have to twist around to see what's wrong, and that's when I spot it. There's a big ol' hunting knife sticking out of the back of my thigh."

Sam put her hand to her mouth.

Rusty said, "So there's me hitting the ground like a rock dropping into the water, because it hurts to have a knife stuck in the back of your thigh. And then I see this fella comes up, and he starts kicking me. Just kicking me and kicking me—in the arm, the ribs, the head. And mail is everywhere, but the point is, I'm trying to stand up, and I still got this knife in the back of my thigh. So the fella, he makes this one last kick at my head and I grab onto his leg with both arms and punch him in the hokey-pokey."

Sam felt her heart pounding in her throat. She knew what it was like to fight for your life.

"Then we struggle a little bit more, him hopping around 'cause I've got his leg, me trying to stay upright, and the fella seems to remember that knife's in my leg. So he grabs it, just yanks it out, and starts stabbing me in my belly." Rusty made a stabbing, twisting motion with his hand. "We're both tired out after this. Plumb tuckered. I'm limping away from him, holding in my own guts. He's standing there. I'm wondering can I make it back to the house, call the police, and then I see him pull out a gun."

"A gun?" Sam asked. Had he been shot, too?

"A pistol," Rusty confirmed. "One of those foreign models."

"For fucksakes, Dad," Charlie muttered. "Then did you drop a shipping container on his head?"

"Well—"

"That's how *Lethal Weapon 2* ends. You told me you watched it the other night."

"Did I?" Rusty seemed blameless, which meant there was much to blame.

And that Sam was an idiot.

"You asshole." Charlie stuck her hand on her hip. "What really happened?"

Sam felt her mouth start to move, but she could not speak.

Rusty said, "I was stabbed. It was dark. I didn't see him." He shrugged. "Forgive a man for trying to exploit the meager attentions of his two demanding daughters."

"That was all a lie?" Sam seized her purse between her hands. "All of it, pulled from a stupid movie?" Before she knew what she was doing, Sam swung the bag at her father's head. "You asshole," she hissed, echoing Charlie's words. "Why would you do that?"

Rusty laughed even as he held up his hands to block the blow.

"Asshole," she repeated, hitting him again.

Rusty flinched. His hand went to his stomach. "Don't make sense: you raise your arms and your belly hurts."

Sam said, "They cut through your abdominal muscles, you lying imbecile. It's called your core because it is the central, innermost foundation of your body's musculature."

"My God," he said. "It's like hearing Gamma."

Sam dropped her purse onto the floor before she hit him again. Her hands were shaking. She felt besieged by acrimony and acerbity and indignation and all of the other tumultuous feelings that had kept her away from her family for so long. "Good Christ in heaven," she practically screamed. "What the hell is wrong with you?"

Rusty listed on his fingers, "I was stabbed several times. I have a heart condition. I have a filthy mouth that I apparently passed on to my daughters. I guess the smoking and the drinking are two separate things, but—"

"Shut up," Charlie interrupted, her anger seemingly reignited by Sam's outburst. "Do you realize the kind of night we've all had? I slept in a God damn chair. Lenore was about ready to pull out her hair. Ben is—well, Ben will tell you he's fine, but he's not, Dad. He was really upset, and he had to tell me that you were hurt, and you know how shitty that was, and then he had to email Sam, and sure as fuck Sam doesn't want to be here ever, as in never." She finally stopped for breath. Tears filled her eyes. "We thought that you were going to die, you selfish old shit."

Rusty remained unmoved. "Death snickers at us all, my dear. The eternal footman will not hold my coat forever."

"Don't fucking Prufrock me." Charlie wiped her eyes with her fingers. She turned to Sam. "I can probably go online and try to change your flight to an earlier one." She told Rusty, "You're going to be in the hospital for at least another week. I'll have Lenore notify your clients. I can get continuances on—"

"No." Rusty sat up, his humor quickly retreating. "I need you to handle Kelly Wilson's arraignment tomorrow."

"What the—" Charlie threw her hands into the air, clearly exasperated. "Rusty, we've been over this. I can't be—"

"He means me," Sam said, because Rusty had not stopped looking at her since he had made the request. "He wants me to handle the arraignment."

A flash of jealousy lit up Charlie's eyes, though she had refused the task.

Rusty shrugged at Sam. "Tomorrow at nine. Easy peasy. In and out, maybe ten minutes."

"She's not licensed with the state bar," Charlie pointed out. "She can't—"

"She's licensed." Rusty winked at Sam. "Tell her I'm right."

Sam didn't ask her father how he knew she had passed the

Georgia bar exam. Instead, she looked at her watch. "My flight is already booked for later today."

"Plans can be altered."

"Delta will charge a change fee and—"

"I can float you a loan to cover it."

Sam brushed some imaginary lint off the sleeve of her six-hundred-dollar blouse.

They all knew this wasn't about the money.

Rusty said, "I just need a few days to get back on my feet, then I can jump into the case. It's a deep dive, my girl. There's a lot going on there. What say you help your old daddy make sure the big wheels keep on turnin'?"

Sam shook her head, though she knew that Rusty was probably Kelly Wilson's only chance at a zealous defense. Even if the standard was lowered to an obligatory defense, it would likely be impossible to find someone to take the job on short notice, especially given that her current lawyer had been stabbed.

Still, that was a Rusty problem.

Sam said, "I have work to do back in New York. I've got my own cases. Very important cases. We'll be at trial within the next three weeks."

Neither of them spoke. They both stared at her.

"What?"

Charlie said, quietly, "Sam, sit down."

"I don't need to sit down."

"You're slurring your words."

Sam knew that she was right. She also knew that she would be damned if she sat down over a simple case of exhaustion-induced dysarthria.

She just needed a moment.

She took off her glasses. She pulled a tissue from the box by Rusty's bed. She cleaned the lenses, as if the problem was a spot that could be easily wiped away.

Rusty said, "Baby, why don't you go downstairs with your sister, let her get some food in you, then we can talk about it when you feel better."

Sam shook her head. "I'm—"

"Nuh-uh," Charlie interrupted. "Not my job, mister. You tell her about your unicorn."

"Come on," he tutted. "She doesn't need to know that part right now."

"She's not an idiot, Rusty. She's going to ask eventually, and I'm not going to be the one to tell her."

"I'm right here." Sam put on her glasses. "Could you both stop talking as if I'm in another room?"

Charlie slumped against the wall. Her arms were crossed again. "If you do the arraignment, you're going to have to enter a plea of not guilty."

"And?" Sam asked. Seldom was a plea of guilty entered at an arraignment.

"I don't mean pro forma. Dad really thinks Kelly Wilson is not guilty."

"Not guilty?" Now Sam's auditory processing was shot. They had finally managed to short-circuit the last meaningful parts of her brain. "Of course she's guilty."

Charlie said, "Tell that to Foghorn Leghorn, JD, over there. He thinks Kelly is innocent."

"But—"

Charlie held up her hands in surrender. "Preacher/choir."

Sam turned to Rusty. If she was unable to ask the obvious question, it wasn't because of her injury. Her father had finally lost his mind.

He said, "Talk to Kelly Wilson yourself. Go to the police station after you eat. Tell them you're my co-counsel. Get Kelly alone in a room and talk with her. Five minutes, tops. You'll see what I mean."

"See what?" Charlie asked. "She murdered a grown man and

a little girl in cold blood. You want to talk about seeing? I was there less than a minute after it happened. I saw Kelly literally—literally—holding the smoking gun. I watched that little girl die. But Ironside over here thinks that she's innocent."

Sam had to take a moment to let the shock of Charlie's involvement sink in before she could ask her sister, "What were you doing there? At the shooting? How did you—"

"It doesn't matter." Charlie kept her focus on Rusty. "Think about what you're asking, Dad. What it means for her to get involved in this. You want Sam to get attacked by some revenge-driven maniac, too?" She snorted a derisive laugh. "Again?"

Rusty was immune to low blows. "Sammy-Sam, lookit, just talk to the girl. It'd help me to get a second opinion anyway. Even the great man you see before you is not infallible. I'd value your input as a colleague."

His flattery only annoyed her. "Do mass shootings fall under the purview of intellectual property?" she asked. "Or have you forgotten the kind of law that I practice?"

Rusty winked at her. "The Portland district attorney's office was a hotbed of patent infringement, was it?"

"Portland was a long time ago."

"And now you're too busy helping Bullshit, Incorporated, sue Bullshit, Limited, over some bullshit?"

"Everyone is entitled to their own bullshit." Sam did not let him move her off the point. "I'm not the sort of lawyer Kelly Wilson needs. Not anymore. Actually, not ever. I could be of more service to the prosecution, because that's the side on which I have always stood."

"Prosecution, defense—what matters is understanding the beats of a courtroom, and you've got that in your blood." Rusty pushed himself up again. He coughed into his hand. "Honey, I know you came all the way down here expecting to find me on my deathbed, and I promise you, on my life, that it'll get to that point eventually, but for now, I'm gonna say something to you that I have never said to you in your forty-four beautiful years on this earth: I need you to do this for me."

Sam shook her head, more out of frustration than disagreement. She did not want to be here. Her brain was exhausted. She could hear the sibilant slithering out of her mouth like a snake.

She said, "I'm going to leave."

"Sure, but tomorrow," Rusty said. "Baby, no one else is going to take care of Kelly Wilson. She's alone in the world. Her parents don't have the capacity to understand the trouble that she's in. She cannot help herself. She cannot aid in her own defense, and no one cares. Not the police. Not the investigators. Not Ken Coin." Rusty reached out to Sam. His nicotine-stained fingertips brushed the sleeve of her blouse. "They're going to kill her. They are going to jam a needle in her arm, and they are going to end that eighteen-year-old girl's life."

Sam said, "Her life was over the minute she decided to take a loaded gun to school and murder two people."

"Samantha, I do not disagree with you," Rusty said. "But, please, will you just listen to the girl? Give her a chance to be heard. Be *her* voice. With me laid up like this, you're the only person on earth I trust to serve as her counsel."

Sam closed her eyes. Her head was throbbing. The sound of machines grated. The lights overhead were too intense.

"Talk to her," Rusty begged. "I mean it when I say that I trust you to be her counsel. If you don't agree with the not-guilty plea, then go into the arraignment and throw down a flag for diminished capacity. That, at least, we can all agree on."

Charlie said, "That's a false choice, Sam. Either way, he gets you in court."

"Yes, Charlie, I am familiar with rhetological fallacies." Sam's stomach churned. She had not eaten in fifteen hours. She had not slept for longer than that. She was slurring her words—that is, when she could speak in complete sentences. She could not move without her cane. She felt angry, really angry, like she had not felt in years. And she was listening to Rusty as if he was her father rather than a man who would do anything, sacrifice anyone, for a client.

Even his family.

She picked up her purse from the floor.

Charlie asked, "Where are you going?"

"Home," Sam said. "I need this shit like I need another hole in my head."

Rusty's bark of laughter followed her out the door.

CHAPTER NINE

S am sat on a wooden bench in a large garden behind the hospital building. She took off her glasses. She closed her eyes.
She tilted her face toward the sun. She breathed in the fresh
air. The bench was in a walled-off area, a water fountain trickling
by the gated entrance, a sign reading SERENITY GARDEN—
ALL WELCOME mounted directly above another sign showing
a cell phone with a red line through it.

Apparently, the second sign was enough to keep the garden
empty. Sam alone sat in serenity. Or at least in an attempt to regain
her serenity.

A mere thirty-six minutes had passed between Stanislav abandoning her at the front doors and Sam abandoning Rusty in his
room. Another thirty minutes had passed since she had found
the Serenity Garden. Sam had no qualms about interrupting her
driver's lunch, but she needed time to compose herself. Her hands
would not stop shaking. She did not trust herself to speak. Her head
ached in a way that it had not in years.

She had left her migraine medication at home.

Home.

She thought of Fosco stretching his back into a reversed C as he
lolled on the floor. The sun streaming through the windows. The
warmth of the swimming pool. The comfort of her bed.

And Anton.

She allowed herself a moment to think about her husband. His big, strong hands. His laughter. His delight in new foods, new experiences, new cultures.

She could not let him go.

Not when it mattered. Not when he had asked her, pleaded with her, begged her to help him end the misery of his existence.

Initially, the fight was one that they had taken on together. They had traveled to MD Anderson in Houston, to the Mayo Clinic in Rochester, back to Sloan Kettering in New York. Each specialist, each world-renowned expert, had given Anton anywhere from a seventeen to twenty percent chance of survival.

Sam was determined he would best those percentages.

Photodynamic therapy. Chemotherapy. Radiation therapy. Endoscopy with dilation. Endoscopy with stent placement. Electrocoagulation. Anti-angiogenesis therapy. They removed his esophagus, raising his stomach and attaching it to the top of his throat. They removed lymph nodes. They performed more reconstructive surgery. A feeding tube was placed. A colostomy bag. Clinical trials. Experimental treatments. Nutritional support. Palliative surgery. More experimental treatments.

At what point had Anton given up?

When he had lost his voice, his actual ability to speak? When his mobility was so reduced that he lacked the strength to shift his frail legs in the hospital bed? Sam could not recall the occasion of his surrender, did not take notice of the change. He had told her once that he had fallen in love with her because she was a fighter, but in the end, her inability to quit had prolonged his suffering.

Sam opened her eyes. She put on her glasses. A wave of blue and white hovered just beyond the reaches of her narrowed right peripheral.

She told Charlie, "Stop doing that."

Charlie came into her line of sight. Her arms were crossed again. "Why are you out here?"

"Why would I be in there?"

"Good question." Charlie sat on the bench opposite her. She looked up into the trees as a light wind rustled the leaves.

Sam had always known she had inherited Gamma's striking features, that obtuse coldness that chilled so many people. Charlie's affable countenance stood in direct opposition to their mother's line. Her face, even with the bruises, was clearly still beautiful. She had always been so clever in the way that made people laugh rather than recoil. *Relentlessly happy*, Gamma had said. *The kind of person people just like*.

Not today, though. There was something different about Charlie, an almost palpable melancholy that seemed to have nothing to do with Rusty's condition.

Why did she really ask Ben to email Sam?

Charlie leaned back on the bench. "You're staring at me."

"Do you remember when Mama brought you here? You broke your arm trying to save that cat."

"It wasn't a cat," Charlie said. "I was trying to get my BB gun off the roof."

"Gamma threw it up there so you couldn't play with it anymore."

"Exactly." Charlie rolled her eyes as she slumped down onto the bench. She was forty-one years old, but she might as well have been thirteen again. "Don't let him talk you into staying."

"I hadn't planned on it." Sam looked for her cup. She had purchased some hot water at the cafeteria along with a sandwich she'd been unable to finish. She pulled a Ziploc bag from her purse. Her tea sachets were inside.

Charlie said, "We have tea here."

"I like this kind." Sam dipped the sachet into the water. She had a quiet moment of panic when she saw her bare ring finger. Then she remembered that she had left her wedding ring at home.

Charlie did not miss much. "What is it?"

Sam shook her head. "Do you have children?"

"No." Charlie did not return the question. "I didn't bring you here to kill Rusty. He's going to do that to himself eventually. His heart isn't good. The cardiologist basically said he's one strained bowel movement away from death. But he won't stop smoking. He won't cut back on the drinking. You know what a stubborn jackass he is. He won't listen to anybody."

"I can't believe he hasn't done you the courtesy of drawing up a will."

"Are you happy?"

Sam found the question both odd and abrupt. "Some days are better than others."

Charlie tapped her foot lightly against the ground. "Sometimes, I think about you all alone in that shitty, cramped apartment, and I just get sad."

Sam didn't tell her that the shitty apartment had sold for $3.2 million. Instead, she quoted, " 'Picture me with my ground teeth stalking joy.' "

"Flannery O'Connor." Charlie had always been good with quotes. "Gamma was reading *The Habit of Being*, wasn't she? I had forgotten all about it."

Sam had not. She could still recall her surprise when her mother had checked out the collection of essays from the library. Gamma had openly disdained religious symbolism, which ruled out most of the English canon.

"Dad says she was trying to be happy before she died," Charlie said. "Maybe because she knew she was sick."

Sam looked down at her tea. During Gamma's autopsy, the medical examiner had discovered that her lungs were riddled with cancer. Had she not been murdered, she likely would have been dead within the year.

Zachariah Culpepper had used this as part of his defense, as if a few more precious months with Gamma would have meant nothing.

"She told me to look after you," Sam said. "In the bathroom that day. She sounded so strident."

"She always sounded strident."

"Well." Sam let the string from the sachet hang over the edge of the cup.

Charlie said, "I remember how you used to argue with her. I could barely understand what either of you were saying." She made talking motions with her hands. "Dad said you were both like two magnets, always charging against each other."

"Magnets don't charge; they either attract or repel depending on the alignment of their north/south polarity. North to south, or south to north, attracts, whereas north to north or south to south repels." She explained, "If you charge them, I am assuming he meant with some type of electric current, you're only strengthening the magnets' polarity."

"Wow, you really proved your point."

"Don't be a smartass."

"Don't be a dumbass."

Sam caught her eye. They both smiled.

Charlie said, "Fermilab is working on neutron therapy protocols for cancer treatment."

Sam was surprised her sister followed that sort of thing. "I have some of her papers. Articles, I mean. They were published."

"Articles she wrote?"

"They're very old, from the 1960s. I could find references to her work in footnotes, but never the original material. There are two I was able to download from the International Database of Modern Physics." She opened her purse and found a thick stack of pages she had printed out this morning at Teterboro airport. "I don't know why I brought these," Sam said, the most honest words she had uttered to her sister since she'd arrived. "I thought you might want to have them since—" Sam stopped there. They both knew that everything else had been lost in the fire. Old home movies. Ancient report cards. Scrapbooks. Baby teeth. Vacation photos.

There was only one picture of Gamma that had survived, a candid shot of her standing in a field. She was looking back over her shoulder, staring not at the camera, but at someone standing off to the side. Three-quarters of her face was visible. A dark eyebrow was raised. Her lips were parted. The photo had been on Rusty's desk at his downtown office when the red-brick house was consumed by flames.

Charlie read the title of the first article. " 'Photo-transmutative Enrichment of the Interstellar Medium: Observational Studies of the Tarantula Nebula.' " She made a snoring sound, then thumbed to the second article. " 'Dominant P-Process Pathways in Supernova Envelopes.' "

Sam realized her mistake. "Maybe you can't understand them, but they're nice to have."

"They are nice. Thank you." Charlie's eyes scanned back and forth as she tried to decipher some meaning. "I only ever feel stupid when I realize how smart she was."

Sam had not remembered until this moment that she had felt that way her entire childhood. They might have been magnets, but they were of unequal power. Everything Sam knew, Gamma knew more.

"Ha," Charlie laughed. She must have read through a particularly dense line.

Sam laughed in turn.

Was this what she had missed over the years? These memories? These stories? This easiness with Charlie that Sam had thought died along with Gamma?

Charlie said, "You really do look like her." She folded the pages and put them beside her on the bench. "Dad still has the photo on his desk."

The photo.

Sam had always wanted a copy, but she was too proud to give Rusty the pleasure of doing her the favor.

She asked, "Does he really think I'll stand up and defend someone who shot two people with a gun?"

"Yes, but Rusty thinks he can talk anybody into anything."

"Do you think I should do it?"

Charlie considered her answer before speaking. "Would the Sam I grew up with do it? Maybe, though not out of any affinity for Rusty. She would be angry the same way I get angry when something isn't fair. And I guess it's not fair, because there's not another lawyer in a hundred miles who will treat Kelly Wilson like a human being rather than a burden. But what would the Sam you are now do?" She shrugged. "The truth is that I don't know you anymore. Just like you don't know me."

Sam felt a sting from the words, though they were all true. "That's fair."

"Was it fair to ask you to come?"

Sam was unaccustomed to not having a ready answer. "Why did you really want me here?"

Charlie shook her head. She didn't respond immediately. She picked at a loose thread on her jeans. She let out a heavy breath that whistled through her broken nose.

She said, "Last night, Melissa asked if I wanted her to take extraordinary measures. Which basically means, 'Let him die? Don't let him die? Tell me right now, this minute.' I panicked, but not from fear or indecision, but because it felt like I didn't have the right to decide on my own." She looked up at Sam. "The heart attacks felt like something that I had to fight against. I know he did it to himself with the smoking and drinking, but it was a situation where I felt there was an internal struggle, something organic, from within, and I had to help him fight it."

Sam recognized the feeling from Anton. "I think I understand."

Charlie's tight smile was disbelieving. "I guess if it comes down to the wire again, I'll lock you in a room with him and you can take him out with your purse."

Sam was not proud of that moment. "I used to tell myself that the one redeeming feature of my temper is that I have never struck anyone in anger."

"It's just Dad. I hit him all the time. He can take it."

"I'm serious."

"You almost hit me." Charlie's voice went up, a sign that she was forcing lightness into something dark. She was referring to the last time they had seen each other. Sam could remember the terror in Ben's eyes as he had stood between her and Charlie.

Sam said, "I'm sorry about that. I was out of control. I could have hit you if you stayed. I can't honestly say that wasn't a possibility, and I'm sorry."

"I know you're sorry." Charlie didn't say the words in a cruel way, which somehow made them more hurtful.

"I'm not like that anymore," Sam said. "I know it's hard to believe, given my earlier behavior, but there's something about being here that brings out the meanness in me."

"Then you should go back to New York."

Sam knew that her sister was right, but for now, just right now, in this scant moment of time with Charlie, she did not want to leave.

She took a sip of her tea. The water had gone cold. She poured it out on the grass behind the bench. "Tell me why you were at the school yesterday morning when the shooting started."

Charlie pressed together her lips. "Are you staying or going?"

"Neither should affect what you tell me. The truth is the truth."

"There are no sides. There's only right and wrong."

"That's a very neat logic."

"It is."

"Are you going to tell me about the bruises on your face?"

"Am I?" Charlie posed the question as a philosophical exercise. She crossed her arms again. She looked back up at the trees. Her jaw was tight. Sam could see the muscles cording through her neck. There was something so remarkably sad about her sister in that moment that Sam wanted to move to the bench beside her and hold her until Charlie told her what was wrong.

Charlie would be more likely to push her away.

Sam repeated her earlier question. "What were you doing at the school yesterday morning?" She didn't have children. There was no need for her to be there, especially before eight in the morning. "Charlie?"

Charlie's shoulder went up in a half-shrug. "Most of my cases are in juvenile court. I was at the middle school asking for a letter of recommendation from a teacher."

That sounded exactly like the kind of thing Charlie would do for a client, and yet, her tone had an edge of deception.

Charlie said, "We were in his room when we heard gunfire, and then we heard a woman screaming for help, so I ran to help."

"Who was the woman?"

"Miss Heller, if you can believe it. She was with the little girl by the time I got there. We watched her die. Lucy Alexander. I held her hand. It was cold. Not when I got there, but when she died. You know how quickly they turn cold."

Sam did.

"So." Charlie took a breath and held it for a moment. "Huck got the gun away from Kelly—a revolver. He talked her into giving it to him."

For no reason, Sam felt the fine hairs on the back of her neck straighten. "Who's Huck?"

"Mr. Huckabee. He was the teacher I was seeing. For the client. He taught Kelly—"

"Mason Huckabee?"

"I didn't catch his first name. Why?"

Sam could feel a shaking sensation churn through her body. "What does he look like?"

Charlie shook her head, oblivious. "Does it matter?"

"He's about your height, sandy brown hair, a little older than me, grew up in Pikeville?" Sam could tell from her sister's expression that she was correct. "Oh, Charlie. Stay away from him. Don't you know?"

"Know what?"

"Mason's sister was Mary-Lynne Huckabee. She was raped by that guy—what was his name?" Sam tried to remember. "Somebody Mitchell from Bridge Gap. Kevin Mitchell?"

Charlie kept shaking her head. "Why does everyone know this but me?"

"He raped her, and she hanged herself in the barn, and Dad got him off."

Charlie's shocked expression revealed a sudden awareness. "He told me to call Dad. Huck, Mason, whatever he's called. When Kelly was arrested, the police were being, well, the police. And Huck told me to call Dad to represent Kelly."

"I guess Mason Huckabee knows what kind of lawyer Rusty is."

Charlie looked visibly shaken. "I had forgotten about that case. His sister was in college."

"She was home for summer break. She drove down to Bridge Gap with friends to see a movie. She went to the bathroom, and Kevin Mitchell attacked her."

Charlie looked down at her hands. "I saw the pictures in Daddy's files."

Sam had seen them, too. "Did Mason recognize you? I mean, when you asked him for help with your juvenile offender?"

"We didn't talk much." Again, she gave a half-shrug. "A lot was going on. It happened really fast."

"I'm sorry that you had to see that. The little girl. With Miss Heller there, it must have brought back memories."

Charlie kept staring down at her hands, one thumb rubbing the joint of the other. "It was hard."

"I'm glad you have Ben to lean on." Sam waited for her to say something about Ben, to explain the awkward moment between them.

Charlie kept working the joint of her thumb. "That was funny, what you said to Dad, about another hole in your head."

Sam studied her sister. Charlie was a master at skirting around a topic. "I'm not usually given to crude language, but it seemed to sum up the mood."

"You sound so much like her. Look like her. Even stand like her." Charlie's voice got softer. "I felt this weird kind of thing in my chest when I saw you in the hall. For a split second, I thought you were Gamma."

"I do that sometimes," Sam admitted. "I'll see myself in the mirror and—" There was a reason she did not often look in the mirror. "I'm her age now."

"Oh, yeah. Happy birthday."

"Thanks."

Still, Charlie did not look up. She kept wringing her hands.

Their adult selves might very well be strangers, but there were certain things that age, no matter how cunning, could not wear away. The slope to Charlie's shoulders. The softness in her voice. The quiver in her lip as she fought back emotion. Her nose had been broken. There were bruises under her eyes. The easiness she had shared with Ben had become noticeably discordant. She was plainly hiding something, perhaps a lot of somethings, but just as plainly she had her reasons.

Yesterday morning, Charlie had held a dying little girl, and before midnight, she had learned that her father might die—not for the first time, undoubtedly not the last time—but this time, this one time in particular, she had gotten Ben to email Sam.

Charlie had not asked Sam here to help make a decision that she had already made once before.

And Charlie had not reached out to Sam directly, because even as a child, she was always asking for things that she wanted, never for the things that she needed.

Sam turned her face up to the sun again. She closed her eyes. She saw herself standing at the mirror inside the downstairs bathroom at the farmhouse. Gamma behind her. Their reflections echoing back from the glass.

"You have to put that baton firmly in her hand every time, no matter where she is. You find her. Don't expect her to find you."

Charlie said, "You should probably go."

Sam opened her eyes.

"You don't want to miss your flight."

Sam asked, "Did you talk to this Wilson girl?"

"No." Charlie sat up. She wiped her eyes. "Huck said that she's low functioning. Rusty puts her IQ in the low seventy range." She leaned toward Sam, elbows on her knees. "I've met the mother. She's not bright, either. Just good country people, since we're doing Flannery O'Connor today. Lenore put them up in a hotel last night. Inmates aren't allowed to have visitors until after they're arraigned. They must be frantic to see her."

"So it's at least diminished capacity," Sam said. "Her defense, I mean."

Again, Charlie shrugged with one shoulder. "That's really the only strategy in any of these mass shooting cases. Why else would someone do that if they weren't crazy?"

"Where is she being held?"

"Probably the city jail in Pikeville."

Pikeville.

The name felt like a shard of glass in her chest.

Charlie said, "I can't take the arraignment because I'm a witness. Not that Dad had any ethical qualms, but—" Charlie shook her head. "Anyway, Dad has this old law school professor, Carter Grail. He retired up here a few years ago. He's ninety, an alcoholic, hates everybody. He can fill in tomorrow."

Sam forced herself up from the bench. "I'll do it."

Charlie stood up, too. "No, you won't."

Sam found Stanislav's card in her purse. She retrieved her phone. She texted him: *Meet me out front.*

"Sam, you can't do this." Charlie nipped at her heels like a puppy. "I won't let you do this. Go home. Live your life. Be that less mean person."

Sam looked at her sister. "Charlotte, do you really think I've changed so much that I'm going to let my little sister tell me what to do?"

Charlie groaned at her obstinacy. "Don't listen to me. Listen to your gut. You can't let Rusty win."

Stanislav texted back: *FIVE MINUTES.*

"This isn't about Rusty." Sam put her purse on her arm. She found her cane.

"What are you doing?"

"My overnight bag is in the car." Sam had planned to stay at the Four Seasons and visit the Atlanta office tomorrow morning before heading back to New York. "I can have my driver take me to the police station or I can go with you. Your choice."

"What's the point of this?" Charlie followed her to the gate. "I mean, seriously. Why would you do anything for that stupid asshole?"

"You said it before. It's not fair that Kelly Wilson doesn't have someone on her side." Sam opened the gate. "I still don't like it when things aren't fair."

"Sam, stop. Please."

Sam turned to face her sister.

Charlie said, "I know that this is hard for you, that being back is like drowning in quicksand."

"I never said that."

"You don't have to." Charlie put her hand on Sam's arm. "I would've never let Ben send that email if I had known how much this would affect you."

"You mean because of a few slurred words?" Sam looked at the winding, paved path that led back to the hospital. "If I had listened to the doctors about my limitations, I would've died in that hospital bed."

"I'm not saying you can't do it. I'm asking if you should."

"It doesn't matter. I've made up my mind." Sam could think of only one way to end this conversation. She closed the gate on Charlie, telling her, "Last word."

CHAPTER TEN

Riding in the car with Charlie, Sam understood that she had never been a nervous passenger because she had never before been driven by her little sister. Charlie gave only a cursory glance in her mirrors before she changed lanes. She liberally used her horn. She talked to drivers under her breath, urging them to go faster, go slower, to move out of her way.

Sam sneezed violently. Her eyes were watering. Charlie's car, a sort of station wagon/SUV hybrid, smelled of damp hay and animals. "Do you have a dog?"

"He's on temporary loan to the Guggenheim."

Sam gripped the dashboard as Charlie swerved into another lane. "Shouldn't you leave your signal on for longer than that?"

"I think your verbal paraphasia is back," Charlie said. "You said 'shouldn't you,' when you meant, 'you should.'"

Sam laughed, which seemed inappropriate given their destination was the city jail.

Representing Kelly Wilson was secondary to finding out what was wrong with Charlie both physically because of the bruises and emotionally because of everything else, but Sam did not take lightly the job of representing the school shooter. For the first time in many years, she was nervous about talking to a client, and worse, walking into an unfamiliar courtroom.

She told Charlie, "My Portland cases were in family court. I've never sat across from an accused murderer before."

Charlie gave Sam a careful look, as if something might be wrong with her. "We both have, Sammy."

Sam waved off the concern. She was unwilling to explain how she had always put her life into categories. The Sam who had sat across from the Culpepper brothers at the kitchen table was not the same Sam who had practiced law in Portland.

She said, "It's been a long time since I've handled a criminal complaint."

"It's just an arraignment. It'll come back to you."

"I've never been on the other side."

"Well, the first thing you'll notice is the judge won't be kissing your ass."

"They didn't in Portland. Even the cops had 'fuck the man' bumper stickers."

Charlie shook her head. She had probably never been anywhere like it. "Usually, I have five minutes with my client before we're in court. There's not a lot to say. They generally did what they were charged with doing—buying drugs, selling drugs, using drugs, stealing shit or fencing shit so they can get more drugs. I look at their sheet and see if they qualify for rehab or some kind of diversion, and then I tell them what's going to happen next. That's what they usually want to know. Even if they've been in a courtroom a zillion times before, they want to know the sequence of events. What happens next? And then what happens? And then what? I tell them a hundred times, and each time they ask me again and again."

Sam thought that sounded a hell of a lot like Charlie's role during Sam's early recovery. "Isn't that tedious?"

"I always remind myself that they're freaked the hell out, and knowing what comes next gives them some sense of control." Charlie asked, "Why are you licensed in Georgia?"

Sam had wondered when this question would arise. "My firm has offices in Atlanta."

"Come on. There's a guy down here who handles the local stuff. You're the micromanaging asshole partner who flies down every few months and looks over his shoulder."

Sam laughed again. Charlie had more or less framed the dynamic. Laurens Van Loon was technically their point man in Atlanta, but Sam liked having the option to take over if needed. And she also liked walking into the bar exam and leaving with the certainty that she had passed without opening a book to study.

Charlie said, "The Georgia Bar Association has an online directory. I'm right above Rusty and he's right above you."

Sam thought about the three of their names appearing together. "Does Ben work with Daddy, too?"

"It's not 'too,' because I don't work with Dad, and no, he's an ADA under Ken Coin."

Sam ignored the inimical tone. "Doesn't that cause conflicts?"

"There are enough criminals to go around." Charlie pointed out the window. "They have good fish tacos here."

Sam felt an arch in her eyebrow. There was a taco truck on the side of the road, the same sort of thing she'd see in New York or Los Angeles. The line stretched at least twenty people deep. Other trucks had even longer lines—Korean barbecue, Peri-Peri chicken, and something called the Fusion Obtrusion.

She asked, "Where are we?"

"We passed the line into Pikeville about a minute ago."

Sam's hand reflexively went to her heart. She hadn't noticed the demarcation. She hadn't felt the expected shift in her body, the dread, the feeling of despondency, that she had assumed would announce her homecoming.

"Ben loves that place, but I can't stand it." Charlie pointed to a building with a distinct Alpine design to match the restaurant's name: the Biergarten.

The chalet was not the only new addition. Downtown was unrecognizable. Two- and three-story brick buildings had loft apartments upstairs and shops selling clothing, antiques, olive oils, and artisanal cheeses downstairs.

Sam asked, "Who in Pikeville would pay that much for cheese?"

"Weekenders, at first. Then people started moving up here from Atlanta. Retired baby boomers. Wealthy tech types. A handful of gay people. We're not a dry county anymore. They passed a liquor ordinance five or six years ago."

"What did the old guard think about that?"

"The county commissioners wanted the tax base and the good restaurants that come with alcohol sales. The religious nutjobs were furious. You could buy meth on any corner, but you had to drive to Ducktown for a watered-down beer." Charlie stopped for a red light. "I guess the nutjobs were right, though. Liquor changed everything. That's when the building boom really took off. Mexicans come up from Atlanta for the work. Tour buses pour into the Apple Shack all day. The marina rents boats and hosts corporate parties. The Ritz Carlton is building a golf resort. Whether you think that's good or bad depends on why you live here in the first place."

"Who broke your nose?"

"I've been told it's not really broken." Charlie took a right without engaging the turn signal.

"Are you not answering because you don't want me to know or are you not answering because you want to annoy me?"

"That is a complicated question with an equally complicated answer."

"I'm going to jump out of this car if you start quoting Dad."

Charlie slowed the car.

"I was teasing."

"I know." She pulled over to the side of the road. She put the gear in park. She turned to Sam. "Look, I'm glad you came down here. I know it was for a difficult and awful reason, but it's good to see you, and I'm happy that we've been able to talk."

"However?"

"Don't do this for me."

Sam studied her sister's bruised eyes, the shift in her nose where the cartilage had surely fractured. "What does Kelly Wilson's arraignment have to do with you?"

"She's an excuse," Charlie said. "I don't need you to take care of me, Sam."

"Who broke your nose?"

Charlie rolled her eyes in frustration. She said, "Do you remember when you were trying to help me learn the blind pass?"

"How could I forget?" Sam asked. "You were an awful student. You never listened to me. You kept hesitating, over and over."

"I kept looking back," Charlie said. "You thought that was the problem, that I couldn't run forward because I was looking back."

Sam heard echoes from the letter that Charlie had sent all those years ago—

Neither one of us will ever move forward if we are always looking back.

Charlie held up her hand. "I'm left-handed."

"So is Rusty," Sam said. "Though handedness is believed to be polygenic; there is a less than twenty-five percent chance that you inherited from Dad one of the forty loci that—"

Charlie made a loud snoring sound until Sam stopped speaking. She said, "My point is, you were teaching me to take the pass with my right hand."

"But you were the second handoff. That's the rule: the baton moves right hand, left hand, right hand, left hand."

"But you never thought to ask me what the problem was."

"You never thought to *tell* me what the problem was." Sam didn't understand the novelty of the excuse. "You would've failed in first or third. You're an inveterate false starter. You're terrible on bends. You had the speed to be a finisher, but you were always too much of a frontrunner."

"You mean I only ever ran as hard as I needed to in order to get there first."

"Yes, that is the definition of 'frontrunner.'" Sam felt herself becoming exasperated. "The second handoff played to all of your strengths: you're an explosive sprinter, you were the fastest runner on the team. All you needed was the handoff, and with enough practice, even a chimpanzee could master the twenty-meter takeover. I don't understand your issue. You wanted to win, didn't you?"

Charlie gripped the steering wheel. Her nose made that whistling sound again as she breathed. "I think I'm trying to pick a fight with you."

"It's working."

"I'm sorry." Charlie turned back in her seat. She put the car in gear and pulled onto the road.

Sam asked, "Is this over?"

"Yes."

"Are we fighting?"

"No."

Sam tried to silently play back the conversation, picking apart the various points at which she had been provoked. "No one made you join the track team."

"I know. I shouldn't have said anything. It was a gazillion years ago."

Sam was still irked. "This isn't about the track team, is it?"

"Fuck." Charlie slowed the car to a stop in the middle of the road. "Culpeppers."

Sam felt sick even before her brain had time to process exactly what the word meant.

Or *who*, to be specific.

"That's Danny Culpepper's truck," Charlie said. "Zachariah's youngest. They named him after Daniel."

Daniel Culpepper.

The man who had shot her.

The man who had buried her alive.

All of the air left Sam's lungs.

She could not prevent her eyes from following the line of Charlie's gaze. A gaudy black pickup truck with gold trim and spinning wheels took up the only two handicapped spaces in front of the police station. The word "Danny" was written in mirror gold script across the tinted back window. The cab was the extended kind that could accommodate four people. Two young women were leaning against the closed doors. They each held cigarettes between their stubby fingers. Red nail polish. Red lipstick. Dark eyeshadow. Heavy eyeliner. Bleach-blonde hair. Tight black pants. Tighter shirts. High heels. Sinister. Hateful. Aggressively ignorant.

Charlie said, "I can drop you behind the building."

Sam wanted her to. If there was a list of reasons she had left Pikeville, the Culpeppers were at the top. "They still think we lied? That there was some grand conspiracy to frame them both?"

"Of course they do. They even set up a Facebook page."

Sam had yet to disengage from life in Pikeville when Charlie was finishing high school. She had been provided with monthly updates about the treacherous Culpepper girls, their family's firmly held belief that Daniel had been home the night of the attacks, that Zachariah was working in Alabama, and that the Quinn girls, one of them a liar, the other mentally incapacitated, had framed them because Zachariah owed Rusty twenty thousand dollars in legal bills.

Sam asked, "Are those the same girls from high school? They look too young."

"Daughters or nieces, but they're all the same."

Sam shuddered just to be this near to them. "How can you stand to see them every day?"

"I don't have to if it's a good day." Charlie offered again, "I'll drop you around back."

"No, I'm not going to let them intimidate me." Sam folded her collapsible cane and shoved it into her purse. "They're not going to see me with this damn thing, either."

Charlie slowly drove the car into the parking lot. There were sheriff's cruisers and crime scene vans and black unmarked Town Cars in most of the spaces. She had to drive to the back, which put them over a dozen yards from the building.

Charlie turned off the engine. She asked, "Can you make the walk?"

"Yes."

Charlie didn't move. "I don't want to be a jerk—"

"Be a jerk."

"If you fall in front of those bitches, they'll laugh at you. They might try to do something worse, and I'll have to kill them."

"Use my cane if it comes to that. It's metal." Sam opened the door. She grabbed the armrest and heaved herself out.

Charlie walked around the car, but not to help. To join Sam. To walk shoulder to shoulder toward the Culpepper girls.

The wind picked up as they crossed the parking lot. Sam experienced a self-reflective moment of her own ludicrousness. She could almost hear spurs jangling as they crossed the asphalt. The Culpepper girls narrowed their eyes. Charlie lifted her chin. They could be in a western, or a John Hughes movie if John Hughes had ever written about aggrieved, almost middle-aged women.

The police station was housed in a squat, sixties-style government complex with narrow windows and a Jetsons-like roof that pointed to the mountains. Charlie had taken the last parking spot, which was the farthest away. To reach the sidewalk they would have to traverse a roughly forty-feet walk up a slight incline. There was no ramp to the elevated building, only three wide concrete stairs that led to another fifteen feet of boxwood-lined walkway, and then, eventually, the glass front doors.

Sam could handle the distance. She would need Charlie's help to ascend the stairs. Or the metal railing might be enough. The trick would be to lean on it while appearing to rest her hand. She would have to swing her left leg first, then pull her right, and then hope that the right could hold her unassisted weight as she somehow managed to swing her leg again.

She ran her fingers through her hair.

She felt the ridge of hard skin above her ear.

Her pace quickened.

The wind shifted back. Sam could hear the Culpepper girls' voices. The taller of the two flicked her cigarette in Charlie and Sam's direction. She raised her voice as she told her companion, "Looks like the bitch finally got the shit beat outta her."

"Both eyes. Means she had to be tole twice," the other cackled. "Next time you'uns go out, maybe you can fetch Precious over there a bowl of ice cream."

Sam felt the muscles in her right leg start to quiver. She looped her hand through Charlie's arm as if they were taking a walk in the park. "I had forgotten the sociolect of the native Appalachians."

Charlie laughed. She placed her hand over Sam's.

"What's that?" the tall girl said. "What'd she call you?"

The glass doors banged open.

They all recoiled from the loud sound.

A menacing-looking young man stomped down the walkway. Not tall, but thickly muscled. Here was the jangling sound: the chain linking his wallet to his belt swung at his side. His wardrobe ticked all the stereotypical redneck boxes, from his sweat-stained ball cap to the ripped-off sleeves of his red-and-black flannel shirt to his torn, filthy blue jeans.

Danny Culpepper, Zachariah's youngest son.

The spitting image of his father.

His boots made a heavy stomping sound as he jumped down the three stairs. His beady eyes homed in on Charlie. He made a gun sign with his hand and pretended to line her up in his sights.

Sam clenched her teeth. She tried not to relate the young man's stocky build to Zachariah Culpepper's. The hedonistic swagger. The way his thick lips smacked as he took a toothpick out of his mouth.

"Who we got here?" He stood in front of them, arms out to

his sides, effectively blocking their way. "You got a familiar look about you, lady."

Sam tightened her grip on Charlie's arm. She would not show fear to this animal.

"I gotcha." He snapped his fingers. "Seen your picture from my daddy's trial, but your head was all swoll up with the bullet still in it."

Sam dug her fingernails into Charlie's arm. She begged her leg not to collapse out from under her, for her body not to shake, for her temper not to annihilate this disgusting man outside of the police station.

She said, "Get out of our way."

He did not get out of their way. Instead, he started clapping his hands, stomping his foot. He sang, "Two Quinn gals standing in the lot. One got fucked, t'other got shot."

The girls yapped with laughter.

Sam tried to walk around him, but Charlie grabbed onto her hand, effectively nailing them both in place. Charlie told him, "It's hard to fuck a thirteen-year-old girl when your dick doesn't work."

The boy snorted. "Shit."

"I'm sure your dad can get it up for his buddies in prison."

The insult was obvious, but effective. Danny jammed his finger in Charlie's face. "You think I won't get my rifle and shoot off your ugly fucking head right here in front of this police station?"

"Make sure you get close," Sam said. "Culpeppers aren't known for their aim."

Silence cut a rift through the air.

Sam tapped her finger to the side of her head. "Lucky for me."

Charlie gave a startled laugh. She kept laughing until Danny Culpepper brushed past her, his shoulder bumping Charlie's.

"Fucking bitches." He told the two girls, "Get the fuck in, you wanna ride home."

Sam pulled at Charlie's arm to get her moving. She was afraid that Charlie would not take the win, that she would say something vitriolic that brought Danny Culpepper back.

"Come on," Sam whispered, tugging harder. "Enough."

Only when Danny was behind the wheel of his truck did Charlie allow herself to be led away.

They walked arm in arm toward the stairs.

Sam had forgotten about the stairs.

She heard the rumble of Danny Culpepper's diesel truck behind her. He kept racing the engine. Being run over would take less effort than mounting the stairs.

She told Charlie, "I don't—"

"I've got you." Charlie would not allow her to stop the forward motion. She slipped her arm under Sam's bent elbow, offering a sort of shelf to lean on. "One, two—"

Sam swung her left leg, leaned into Charlie to move her right, then her left took over and she was up the stairs.

The show was wasted.

Tires screeched behind them. Smoke filled the air. The truck peeled off in a cacophonous blend of engine grumble and rap music.

Sam stopped to rest. The front door was another five feet away. She was almost breathless. "Why would they be here? Because of Dad?"

"If I were in charge of the investigation into who stabbed Dad, the first suspect I would pick up is Danny Culpepper."

"But you don't think the police brought him in for questioning?"

"I don't think they're seriously looking into it, either because they've got bigger fish to fry with this school shooting or they don't care that somebody tried to kill Dad." Charlie explained, "Generally, the police don't let you drive yourself and your cousins to the station when you're being questioned for attempted murder. They bust down your door and drag you in by your collar and do everything they can to scare the shit out of you so that you know you're in trouble."

"So, Danny just happened to be here?"

Charlie shrugged. "He's a drug dealer. He's at the station a lot."

Sam searched her purse for a tissue. "Is that how he purchased that gauche truck?"

"He's not *that* good at selling drugs." Charlie watched as the truck squealed the wrong way up the one-way street. "Prices at the Gauche Truck Emporium are through the roof."

"I read that in the *Times*." Sam used the tissue to pat sweat from her face. She had no idea why she'd even spoken to Danny Culpepper, and there was not enough time left on earth to explain her words to him. In New York, Sam did everything possible to diminish her disability. Here, she seemed inclined to wield it as a weapon.

She returned the tissue to her purse. "I'm ready."

"Kelly had a yearbook," Charlie said, her voice low. "You know the thing where——"

"I know what a yearbook is."

Charlie nodded back toward the stairs.

Sam needed her cane, but she walked the ten feet back unaided. This was when she saw the sheet of bowed plywood laid across the sloped grass on the other side of the stairs. The handicapped ramp, she supposed.

"This godforsaken place," Sam muttered. She leaned against the metal railing. She asked Charlie, "What are we doing?"

Charlie glanced back at the doors as if she was afraid they would be overheard. She kept her voice to barely more than a whisper. "A yearbook was in Kelly's room, hidden on the top shelf of her closet."

Sam was confused. The crime had only happened yesterday morning. "Has Dad already received some of the discovery?"

Charlie's raised eyebrow explained the provenance.

Sam heaved out something between a sigh and a groan. She knew the kinds of shortcuts her father took. "What was in the yearbook?"

"A lot of nasty stuff about Kelly being a whore, having sex with football players."

"That's hardly anomalous to high school. Girls can be cruel."

"Middle school," Charlie said. "This was five years ago, when Kelly was fourteen. But it was more than cruel. The pages were filled. Hundreds of people signed on. Most of them probably didn't even know her."

"A Pikeville version of *Carrie* without the pig's blood." Sam realized the obvious. "Well, someone's blood was shed."

"Right."

"It's a mitigating factor. She was bullied, probably isolated. It could keep her off death row. That's good." Sam equivocated, "For Dad's case, I mean."

Charlie had more. "Kelly said something in the hallway before she gave Huck the gun."

"What?" Sam's throat hurt from trying to keep her voice down. "Why are you telling me this when we are standing outside of a police station instead of when we were inside the car?"

Charlie threw out her hand toward the doors. "There's only a fat guy behind a bulletproof window in there."

"Answer me, Charlotte."

"Because I was pissed off at you in the car."

"I knew it." Sam grabbed onto the railing. "Why?"

"Because you're here for me even though I told you that I don't need you, and you're lying like you always do out of this misplaced sense of duty to Gamma, and pretending that it's about this arraignment, and it just occurred to me when we walked up the steps that this isn't the bullshit tug-of-war between us. This is Kelly's life. She needs you to be on point."

Sam stiffened her spine. "I am always on point with clients. I take my fiduciary responsibilities very seriously."

"This is a lot more complicated than you think it is."

"Then give me the facts. Don't send me into that building where I'm going to get blindsided." She indicated her eye. "More than I already am."

"You've got to stop using that as a punchline."

She was probably right. "Tell me what Kelly said in the hall-way."

"This was after the shooting when she was sitting there. They were trying to get her to hand over the gun. I saw Kelly's lips move, and Huck heard it, but he didn't tell the GBI, but there was a cop standing there who heard her say it, too, and like I said, I saw it happen, but I didn't hear it, but whatever she said really upset him."

"Do you have a sudden aversion to proper pronouns?" Sam felt inundated by data fragments. Charlie was acting like she was thirteen again, flush with the excitement of telling a story. "This information was less important than complaining about being second position in the relay thirty years ago?"

Charlie said, "There's more about Huck."

"Okay."

Charlie looked away. Inexplicably, tears rimmed her eyes.

"Charlie?" Sam felt her own tears start to well. She could never abide seeing her sister in distress. "What is it?"

Charlie looked down at her hands. She cleared her throat. "I think Huck took the murder weapon from the scene."

"What?" Sam's voice went up in alarm. "How?"

"It's just a feeling. The GBI asked me about—"

"Wait, the Georgia Bureau of Investigation interviewed you?"

"I'm a witness."

"Did you have a lawyer?"

"I'm a lawyer."

"Charlie—"

"I know, I have a fool for a client. Don't worry. I didn't say anything stupid."

Sam did not argue the antithetical. "The GBI asked you if you knew where the murder weapon was?"

"In a roundabout way. The agent was good at playing her cards close to her chest. The weapon was a revolver, probably a six-shot. And then later, when I talked to Huck on the phone, he said they had asked him the same thing, only this time, it was the FBI asking, too: 'When did you last see the gun? Who had it? What happened to it?' Except I got the feeling that Huck had taken the gun. Just a feeling. Which I couldn't tell Dad, because if Dad found out, he would have Huck arrested. And I know he should be arrested, but he was trying to do the right thing, and with the FBI involved we're talking felony and . . ." She let out a heavy sigh. "That's it."

There were so many red flags that Sam couldn't keep up with all of them. "Charlotte, you cannot ever again speak with Mason Huckabee, on the phone or otherwise."

"I know that." Charlie hung her heels over the stair, stretching her calves, balancing herself on her two good legs. "Before you say it, I told Huck not to try to see me or call me, and to get a good lawyer."

Sam stared out at the parking lot. The sheriff's cruisers. The police cars. The crime scene vans. The Town Cars. This was what Rusty was up against, and now Charlie had managed to drag herself along for the ride.

Charlie asked, "Ready?"

"Can you give me a moment to compose myself?"

Rather than verbalizing her answer, Charlie nodded.

Charlie seldom just nodded. Like Rusty, she could never resist the urge to speak, to explain the nod, to expound upon the up and down movement of her head.

Sam was about to ask her what the hell else she was hiding when Charlie said, "What's Lenore doing here?"

Sam watched a red sedan make a quick turn into the parking lot. The sun glinted off the windshield as the car raced toward them. There was another sharp turn, then the tires skidded to a stop.

The window rolled down. Lenore waved for them to hurry. "The arraignment is scheduled to start at three."

"Motherfuck, that gives us an hour and a half, tops." Charlie quickly helped Sam down the stairs. "Who's the judge?"

"Lyman. He said he moved it up to avoid the press, but half of them are already lining up for seats." She motioned for them to get in the car. "He also appointed Carter Grail to stand in for Rusty."

"Shit, he'll hang Kelly himself." Charlie pulled open the rear door. She told Lenore, "Take Sam. I'll try to keep Grail away from Kelly and find out what the hell is going on. It's faster if I run."

Sam said, "Faster for—"

Charlie was gone.

"Grail's got a big mouth," Lenore said. "If Kelly talks to him, he'll spill to whoever listens."

"I'm sure that has nothing to do with why the judge appointed him." Sam had no choice but to get into Lenore's car. The courthouse, a large, domed building, was directly across from the police station, but the one-way street made the driving route more circuitous. Because of Sam's limited mobility, they would have to go up to the red light, then drive around the courthouse, then turn onto the street again.

Sam watched Charlie dart past a truck and leap over a concrete curb. She ran beautifully; arms tucked, head straight, shoulders back.

Sam had to look away.

She told Lenore, "This is a dirty trick. The hearing was scheduled for tomorrow morning."

"Lyman does whatever he wants." Lenore caught her eye in the mirror. "Cons call Carter 'the Holy Grail.' If he drinks before your trial, you're likely to get life."

"It's a chalice, actually. In Christian tradition."

"I'll send Indiana Jones a telegram." Lenore turned out of the parking lot.

Sam watched Charlie running across the courthouse lawn. She hurdled over a row of shrubs. There was a line out the door, but Charlie rushed past it, taking the steep stairs two at a time. "Can I ask you something?"

"Why not."

"How long has my sister been sleeping with Mason Huckabee?"

Lenore pursed her lips. "That wasn't the question I thought you would ask."

That wasn't a question that Sam thought she would ask, either, but it made a horrible kind of sense. The distance between Charlie and Ben. The way Charlie had teared up when she talked about Mason Huckabee.

Lenore asked, "You told Charlie who he is?"

Sam nodded.

"That oughtta make her feel like shit," Lenore added. "Even more than she already does."

"Not for want of defenders."

"You know a lot for somebody who's only been here five minutes."

Lenore looped around the courthouse and drove to the back of the building. She stopped in front of an area that was clearly the loading zone for deliveries.

She told Sam, "Go up the ramp. Elevator's on the right. Go down one floor to the sub-basement. That's the holding area. And listen," Lenore turned around to face her. "Rusty couldn't get a peep out of Kelly yesterday. Maybe she'll open up to a woman. Anything you can get would be better than what we've got now, which is zilch."

"Understood." Sam unfolded her cane. She felt sturdier on her feet as she got out of the car. Adrenaline had always been her ally. Anger ran a close second as she marched up a ramp intended for bulk toilet-paper deliveries and trash bins. The smell of rotting food from the dumpsters was noxious.

Inside, the courthouse was like every other courthouse Sam had entered, except there was an oversampling of good-looking men and women in camera-ready suits. Sam's cane got her to the front of the line. Two sheriff's deputies were stationed by the metal detector. Sam had to show her ID, sign in, put her purse and cane on the X-ray, show her legal credentials so that she could keep her phone, then wait for a female deputy to pat her down because the plate in her head set off the alarm when she walked through the metal detector.

The elevator was on the right. There were two sub-basement floors, but Lenore had told her to go down one floor, so Sam pressed the appropriate button and waited. The car was full of men in suits. She stood at the back. She leaned against the wall to take weight off her leg. When the doors opened, all of the men stepped aside so that she could leave the elevator first.

There were some things that Sam missed about the South.

"Hey." Charlie was waiting by the door. She held a tissue to her nose, which had started bleeding, likely from the run. She took a breath and words rushed out of her mouth. "I told Coin you're co-counsel. He's super-happy—not. So is Lyman, so try not to piss him off even more. I heard Grail didn't have a chance to talk to Kelly, but maybe check-see to make sure. She's been sick since they brought her over. Clogged the toilet. I hear it's a mess."

"What kind of sick?"

"Throwing up. I called over to the jail. She ate breakfast and lunch no problem. No one else is sick, so it's not food poisoning. She was horking when they brought her over about thirty minutes ago. She's not detoxing. It must be nerves. This is Mo." She indicated an older woman sitting behind the desk. "Mo, this is my sister, Samantha."

"Don't bleed on my desk, Quinn." Mo did not look up from her keyboard. She snapped her fingers for Sam's ID and credentials. She tapped some of the keys on her computer. She picked up the phone. She indicated a sign-in log.

The log was almost full. Sam signed her name on the last line below Carter Grail's. The time stamp said he'd spent less than three minutes with Kelly.

Charlie said, "Lyman's been here about twelve years. He retired up from Marietta. He's a super hard-ass about procedure. Do you have a dress or a skirt in your suitcase?"

"Whatever for?"

"Doesn't matter."

"Sure it doesn't." Mo put down the phone. She told Sam, "You've got seventeen minutes left. Grail drank away three. You'll have to talk to her in the cell."

Charlie slammed her fist on the counter. "What the fuck, Mo?"

"Charlie, I've got this." Sam addressed Mo. "If the room isn't available now, then you should inform the judge that we need to postpone the hearing until I have the necessary time to confer privately with my client."

Mo grunted. She glared at Sam, waiting for her to back down. When she did not, the woman said, "I thought you were supposed to be the smart one." She reached under her desk and pressed a buzzer. She winked at Sam. "Room's on the right. Sixteen minutes."

Charlie pumped her fist in the air, then sprinted toward the stairs. She was so light on her feet that she barely made a sound.

Sam moved her purse to her other shoulder. She leaned on her cane as she dragged through the door. She stopped in front of another door, effectively boxed in as the first door behind her closed. Another buzz, and the second door swung open in front of her.

Sam was besieged by the long-forgotten odors of a holding cell: putrid vomit mixed with an alkaline sweat, the ammonia of urine, the sewage stench from the one toilet that serviced roughly one hundred inmates a day.

Sam pushed herself off with her cane. Her shoes slapped brown puddles of water. No one had cleaned up the flooded toilet. There was only one inmate left in the holding cell, an older, toothless woman who was squatting on a long concrete bench. Her orange jumper bulked around her like a blanket. She moved slowly back and forth between her feet. Her rheumy eyes followed Sam as she walked toward the closed door on the right.

The knob turned before Sam could knock. The female deputy

who came out looked burly and brusque. She closed the door, her back pressed to the opaque glass. "You the second lawyer?"

"Third, technically. Samantha Quinn."

"Rusty's oldest."

Sam nodded, though she hadn't been asked a question.

"The inmate has puked approximately four times over the last half hour. I gave her a pack of orange crackers and one can of Coke served in a Styrofoam cup. I asked if she wanted medical attention. She declined. You've got fifteen minutes before I come back in." She tapped the watch on her wrist. "Whatever I hear when I come in is what I hear. You got me?"

Sam took out her phone. She set the timer for fourteen minutes.

"I'm glad we understand each other."

The woman opened the door.

The room was so dark that Sam's eyes could only slowly adjust. Two chairs. A metal table bolted to the floor. A flickering fluorescent light hanging crookedly from two furred lengths of chain.

Kelly Rene Wilson was slumped over the table. Her head was wrapped in the cocoon of her folded arms. When the door opened, she jumped up to standing, arms at her sides, shoulders straight, as if Sam had called a soldier to attention.

Sam said, "You can sit down."

Kelly waited for Sam to sit first.

Sam took the empty chair by the door. She rested her cane against the table. She reached into her purse for her notepad and pen. She changed out her glasses for her readers. "My name is Samantha Quinn. I'm your lawyer for the arraignment. You met my father, Rusty, yesterday."

Kelly said, "You talk funny."

Sam smiled. She sounded Southern to New Yorkers and she sounded like a Yankee to southerners. "I live in New York City."

"Because you're a cripple?"

Sam almost laughed. "No. I live in New York because I like it. I use a cane when my leg gets tired."

"My granddaddy had a cane but it was wood." The girl seemed matter-of-fact, but the *clink-clink* sound from her handcuffs indicated she was nervously bouncing her leg.

Sam said, "You don't have to be afraid, Kelly. I'm your ally. I'm not here to trip you up." She wrote Kelly's name and the date at the top of her notepad. She underlined the words twice. She felt the odd sensation of butterflies in her stomach. "Did you speak with Mr. Grail, the attorney who came to see you earlier?"

"No, ma'am, on account of I was sick."

Sam studied the girl. She spoke slowly, almost as if she was drugged. Judging by the *S* on the front of her orange jumper, they had given her an adult small, but the uniform was voluminous on her petite frame. Kelly looked wan. Her hair was greasy, speckled with pieces of vomit. As thin as she was, her face was round, angelic.

Sam reminded herself that Lucy Alexander's face had been angelic, too.

She asked Kelly, "Are you on any medication?"

"They give me liquids at the hospital yesterday." She showed Sam the bruised red dot near the crook of her right arm. "Through here."

Sam transcribed the exact words. Rusty would need to get the girl's hospital records. "You think they gave you fluids, but no medication?"

"Yes, ma'am, that's what I was told. On account of being shocked."

"In shock?" Sam clarified.

The girl nodded. "Yes, ma'am."

"You're not currently on or have not taken any illegal drugs?"

"Illegal drugs?" the girl asked. "No, ma'am. That wouldn't be right."

Again, Sam copied her words. "And how are you feeling now?"

"Okay, I guess. Not so poorly as before."

Sam looked at Kelly Wilson over the top of her reading glasses. The girl's hands were still clasped under the table, shoulders rolled in, making her look even smaller. Sam could see the red of the plastic chair peeking out on either side of the girl's back. "Are you okay, or are you okay, you guess?"

Kelly said, "I'm pretty scared. There's some mean people here."

"Your best strategy is to ignore them." Sam jotted down some general notes about Kelly's appearance, that she looked unwashed, unkempt. Her fingernails were chewed down. Her cuticles showed dried blood. "How's your stomach now?"

"It's just a little upset this time of day."

" 'This time of day.' " Sam made a notation and wrote down the time. "Were you sick yesterday?"

"Yes, ma'am, but I didn't tell nobody. When I get like that, it usually calms down on its own, but that lady out there was nice and give me some crackers."

Sam kept her gaze on her notepad. She did not want to look at Kelly because she felt an unwelcoming softening each time she did. The girl did not fit the image of a murderer, let alone a school shooter. Then again, perhaps Sam's past experiences with Zachariah and Daniel Culpepper had framed the wrong image in her mind. The fact was that anybody could kill.

She told Kelly, "I'm working with my father, Rusty Quinn, until he's feeling better. Did someone tell you that he's in the hospital?"

"Yes, ma'am. Them guards back at the jail were talking about it. How Mr. Rusty got stabbed."

Sam doubted the guards had anything good to say about Rusty. "So, did Mr. Rusty tell you that he works for you, not your parents? And that anything you say to him is private?"

"It's the law," she said. "Mr. Rusty can't tell nobody what I say."

"That's correct," Sam said. "And it's the same with me. We both took an oath of confidentiality. You can talk to me, and I can talk to Mr. Rusty about the things you tell me, but we can't tell anyone else your secrets."

"Is that hard, knowing everybody's secrets like that?"

Sam felt disarmed by the question. "It can be, but that's part of my job requirement, and I knew that I would have to keep secrets when I decided to become a lawyer."

"You gotta go to school for a lotta years to do that."

"I did." Sam looked at her phone. She normally charged by the hour; she was not accustomed to abbreviating her time. "Did Mr. Rusty explain to you what an arraignment is?"

"It ain't a trial."

"That's right." Sam realized that she was modulating her voice as if she was addressing a child. This girl was eighteen, not eight.

Lucy Alexander had been eight years old.

Sam cleared her throat.

She explained, "In most cases, the law requires an arraignment to take place within forty-eight hours of an arrest. Basically, this is when a case goes from being an investigation to a criminal case in court. There is a formal reading of a criminal charge or indictment in the presence of the defendant to inform the defendant, you, of the pending charges that have been filed against you, and afford you the opportunity to enter an initial plea into the record. I know that sounds like a lot, but soup-to-nuts, the entire process should take less than ten minutes."

Kelly blinked.

"Do you understand what I just told you?"

"You talk really fast."

Sam had worked hundreds of hours to normalize her speech, and now she had to concentrate in order to slow it down. She tried, "During the arraignment, there won't be any police officers or witnesses called. Okay?"

Kelly nodded.

"No evidence will be presented. Your guilt or innocence will not be assessed or determined."

Kelly waited.

"The judge will ask for your plea to be entered into the record. I will tell him your plea, which is not guilty. You can amend that later if you so desire." Sam paused. She had started to rev up again. "Then the judge, the prosecutor and I will discuss dates and motions and other business of the court. I will request those matters be taken up when my father, Mr. Rusty, has recovered, which will likely be within the next week. You need not speak during any part of this process. I will speak for you. Do you understand?"

Kelly said, "Your daddy told me not to talk to nobody, and I ain't. Not unless it was the guards and telling them I was feeling sick." Her shoulders rolled farther inward. "They was nice though, like I said. Everybody's been treating me real nice here."

"Except for some of the mean ones?"

"Yes, ma'am, there's been some mean ones."

Sam looked down at her notes. Rusty had been right. Kelly was too agreeable. She did not seem to understand the depth of trouble that she was in. The girl would have to be evaluated for mental competency. Sam was certain she could locate someone in New York who was willing to work pro bono.

"Miss Quinn?" Kelly asked. "Can I ask, do my mama and daddy know I'm in here?"

"Yes." Sam realized Kelly had been left in the dark for the last twenty-four hours. "Your parents aren't allowed to visit you in the jail until after the arraignment, but they are both very eager to see you."

"Are they mad about what happened?"

"They're worried about you." Sam could only go on assumptions. "They love you very much, though. You'll all get through this together. No matter what."

Kelly's lip quivered. Tears fell from her eyes. "I love them, too."

Sam sat back in her chair. She reminded herself of Douglas Pinkman, the way he had cheered for her at every track meet, even after she had moved up to high school. The man had been to more of Sam's events than her own father.

And now Sam was sitting across from the girl who had murdered him.

She told Kelly, "Your parents will be in the courtroom upstairs, but you aren't going to be able to touch them or talk to them other than to say hello." Sam hoped there were no cameras in the courtroom. She would have to make sure Kelly's parents were forewarned. "Once you're transferred back to the jail, you'll be able to visit with them, but remember anything you say to your parents, or anyone else, while you are in jail will be recorded. Whether it's in the visitation room or on the telephone, someone is always listening. Don't talk to them about what happened yesterday. Okay?"

"Yes, ma'am, but can I ask, am I in trouble?"

Sam studied her face for signs of guile. "Kelly, do you remember what happened yesterday morning?"

"Yes, ma'am. I killed them two people. The gun was in my hand."

Sam considered her affect, looking for signs of remorse.

There were none.

Kelly might as well have been describing events that had happened to someone else.

"Why did . . ." Sam thought about how to pose the question. "Did you know Lucy Alexander?"

"No, ma'am. I think she must'a been at the elementary school, 'cause she looked real little."

Sam opened her mouth and drew in some air. "How about Mr. Pinkman?"

"Well, I heard people say he wasn't a bad man, but I never got sent to the principal's office."

The randomness of the victims somehow made it worse. "So they both, Mr. Pinkman and Lucy Alexander, just happened to be in the hallway at the wrong time?"

"I guess," Kelly answered. "Like I said, the gun was in my hand, and then Mr. Huckabee put it down his pants."

Sam felt her heart shake inside of her chest. She looked at the timer on her phone. She made sure there was no shadow lingering at the door. She asked Kelly, "Did you tell my father what you just told me?"

"No, ma'am. I didn't say much to your daddy yesterday. I was upset 'cause they had me at the hospital, and plus my tummy was hurting like it does, and they were talking about keeping me overnight and I know that costs a lot of money to be there."

Sam closed her notepad. She capped her pen. She exchanged her readers for her regular glasses.

She was in a somewhat unique situation. A defense lawyer was not allowed to put a witness on the stand knowing that the witness was going to lie. This rule explained why attorneys never wanted their clients to tell them the whole truth. The whole truth seldom made for a good defense. Everything Kelly told Sam would be held in confidence, but Sam would never call or cross-examine a witness, so she would not have her hands tied. She could simply edit out the damaging facts when she relayed this conversation to Rusty and let him take care of the rest.

Kelly said, "My Uncle Shane passed in the hospital and his wife and them had to move out of their house 'cause the bills were too much."

"They won't charge you for the hospital stay."

She smiled. Her teeth were tiny white beads. "Do my parents know that? Because I think that'll come as a relief."

"I'll make sure they know."

"Thank you, Miss Quinn. I sure do appreciate all you and your daddy done for me."

Sam rolled the pen between her fingers. She remembered something from the news last night. "Do you know if the middle school has security cameras?"

"Yes, ma'am. They got one in each of the halls, except the one by the front office got hit and it don't get hardly anything past a certain point."

"It has a blind spot?"

"I don't know that it's got that, but it can't see everything past somewhere about the middle of the hall."

"How do you know it can't?"

She raised her thin shoulders up, then held them for a second before letting them drop back down. "It's just something everybody knows."

Sam asked, "Kelly, do you have many friends at school?"

"Acquaintances, you mean?"

Sam nodded. "Sure."

"I guess I know almost about everybody. I been at the school a real long time." She smiled again. "Not long enough to be a lawyer, though."

Sam felt herself smile back. "Do you have anyone you're particularly close to?"

Kelly's cheeks turned bright red.

Sam recognized that type of blush. She opened her notepad. "You can tell me his name. I won't repeat it to anyone."

"Adam Humphrey." Kelly was obviously eager to talk about the boy. "He's got brown hair and eyes and he's not real tall but he drives a Camaro. But we don't go together. Not like official or anything."

"Okay, how about friends who are girls? Do you have any of those?"

"No, ma'am. Not close like I'd bring 'em home with me." She remembered, "Except there was Lydia Phillips when I was in elementary school, only she moved away when her daddy got transferred on account of the economy."

Sam recorded the details in her pad. "Are there teachers you're close to?"

"Well, Mr. Huckabee used to help me with my history lessons, but he ain't done that in a while. Dr. Jodie said he'd let me do some extra work to make up for missing some classes last week, but he ain't give me that work yet. And Mrs. Pinkman's—"

Kelly quickly bowed her head.

Sam finished a line in her notes. She put down her pen. She studied the girl.

Kelly had gone still.

Sam asked, "Was Mrs. Pinkman helping you with English?"

Kelly did not answer. She kept her head down. Her hair covered her face. Sam could hear her sniff. Her shoulders began to shake. She was crying.

"Kelly," Sam said. "Why are you upset?"

" 'Cause Mr. Pinkman wasn't a bad man." She sniffed again. "And that girl was just a baby."

Sam clasped her hands together. She leaned her elbows on the table. "Why were you at the middle school yesterday morning?"

" 'Cause," she mumbled.

"Because why?"

" 'Cause I brung the gun from my daddy's glove box." She sniffed. "And I had it in my hand when I killed them two people."

The prosecutor in Sam wanted to press, but she wasn't here to break the girl. "Kelly, I know you're probably tired of hearing me say this, but it's important. You are never to tell anyone what you just told me. Okay? Not your parents, not friends, not strangers, especially not anyone you meet in jail."

"They ain't my friends, is what Mr. Rusty said." Kelly's voice was muffled behind the cascade of thick hair. "They might try to get me in trouble so they can get out of trouble theirselves."

"That's right. No one you meet in here is your friend. Not the guards, or your fellow inmates, or the janitor, or anyone else."

The girl sniffed. The handcuff chain was clinking under the table again. "I ain't talked to none of them. I just kept to myself, like I do."

Sam pulled the rest of the tissues from her purse and passed them to Kelly. "I'll speak with your parents before you see them and make sure they know not to ask you about what happened." Sam assumed that Rusty had given the Wilsons that speech already, but they were going to hear it from Sam before she left town. "Everything you told me about yesterday is between you and me. Okay?"

She sniffed again. "Okay."

"Blow your nose." She waited for Kelly to do as she was told, then said, "Tell me about Adam Humphrey. Did you meet him in school?"

Kelly shook her head. Sam could still not see her face. All she saw was the top of her head.

Sam asked, "Did you meet Adam when you were out? For instance, at a movie or at church?"

Kelly shook her head again.

"Tell me about the yearbook in your closet."

Kelly quickly looked up. Sam expected to see anger, but she saw fear. "Please don't tell nobody."

"I won't," Sam promised. "Remember, everything here is confidential."

Kelly kept the tissue in her hand as she wiped her nose with her sleeve.

Sam asked, "Can you tell me why people wrote those things about you?"

"They were bad things."

"I don't think the acts they were describing were bad. I think that the people who wrote those things were being unkind."

Kelly appeared baffled. Sam couldn't fault her. This was no time to lecture an eighteen-year-old spree killer on feminism.

She asked Kelly, "Why did they write those things about you?"

"I don't know, ma'am. You'd have to ask them."

"Were some of the things they said true?"

Kelly looked back down at the table. "Not like how they said, but maybe something similar."

Sam wondered at the turn of phrase. The girl was not so slow that she couldn't obfuscate. "Were you angry because they were picking on you?"

"No," she said. "I was hurt mostly, because them's private things and I didn't know most of them people. But I guess it was a long time ago. A lot of 'em could of graduated already."

"Has your mother seen the yearbook?"

Kelly's eyes went wide. This time, she looked scared. "Please don't show my mama."

"I won't," Sam promised. "Remember how I told you that anything you tell me will remain confidential?"

"No."

Sam felt a prick in her left eyebrow. "When I first walked into the room, I explained to you who I am, and that I work with my father, and that we have both taken an oath of confidentiality."

"No, ma'am, I don't remember that last part."

"Confidentiality means that I have to keep your secrets."

"Oh, well, okay, that's what your daddy said, too, about secrets."

Sam looked at the time. She had less than four minutes. "Kelly, I was told that yesterday morning, right after the shooting took place, when Mr. Huckabee was asking you to relinquish the revolver, you said something that Mr. Huckabee and perhaps a police officer heard. Do you remember what you said?"

"No, ma'am. I didn't much feel like talking after all that."

"You said something." Sam tried again, "The officer heard you. Mr. Huckabee heard you."

"Okay." Kelly nodded slowly. "I did say something."

Sam was surprised by how quickly the girl had changed her story. "Do you remember what you said?"

"I don't know. I don't remember saying it."

Sam felt Kelly's eagerness to please pushing out into the space between them. She tried approaching the question from a different angle, asking, "Kelly, in the hallway yesterday morning, did you tell Mr. Huckabee and the police officer that the lockers are blue?"

"Yes, ma'am." Kelly latched on to the suggestion. "They are blue."

Sam started nodding her head. "I know they're blue. But is that what you said at that point? Did you actually *say* that to them, that the lockers are blue? Is that what you told Mr. Huckabee and the policeman? That the lockers are blue?"

Kelly began nodding along. "Yes, I said that."

Sam knew the girl was lying. At that moment in time yesterday morning, Kelly Wilson had just shot and killed two people. Her former teacher was asking her to hand over the murder weapon. A policeman was undoubtedly pointing a gun at her head. Kelly had not stopped to note the school décor.

Sam asked, "You remember telling both of them that the lockers are blue?"

"Yes, ma'am." Kelly seemed so certain of the answer that she likely would have passed a lie-detector exam.

"Okay, so Mr. Huckabee was there," Sam said, wondering how far she could push the girl. "Mrs. Pinkman was there, too. Was anyone else there? Someone you didn't recognize?"

"There was a woman in a devil shirt." She indicated her chest. "The devil was wearing a blue mask, and it said the word 'Devils' on it."

Sam could still remember packing Charlie's things after her disastrous New York visit. Every T-shirt Charlie owned had some variation of the Duke Blue Devils logo.

Sam asked Kelly, "The woman in the Devils shirt. Did she hurt anybody?"

"No, ma'am. She was sitting there across from Mrs. Pinkman looking at her hands."

"Are you sure she didn't hurt anybody?" Sam made her voice firm. "This is very important, Kelly. You need to tell me if the woman in the Devils shirt hurt anyone."

"Well." Kelly studied Sam's face, looking for cues. "I don't know if she did, on account of I was sitting."

Very slowly, Sam began to nod again. "I think you saw the Devils woman hurt someone, even though you were sitting down. The evidence shows that you saw her, Kelly. There's no point in lying."

Kelly's uncertainty returned. "I don't mean to lie to you. I know you're trying to help me."

Sam made her voice firm. "Then admit the truth. You saw the woman in the Devils shirt hurt someone."

"Yes, ma'am." Kelly nodded, too. "Now that I think on it, maybe she hurt somebody."

"Did she hurt you?"

Kelly hesitated. She searched Sam's expression for guidance. "Maybe?"

"I can't use 'maybe' to help you, Kelly." Sam tried again, declaring, "You saw the woman in the blue Devils shirt hurt someone else who was in the hallway."

"Yes, ma'am." Kelly seemed more sure of herself now. She kept nodding her head, as if the motion informed her thinking. "That's what I saw."

Sam asked, "Did the Devils woman hurt Mrs. Pinkman?" She leaned forward. "Because Mrs. Pinkman was right there, Kelly. You told me as much not a few seconds ago. Do you think the Devils woman could have hurt Mrs. Pinkman?"

"I think so." Kelly continued to nod, because that was part of the pattern. She denied the statement, then she allowed that the statement might be true, then she accepted the statement as fact. All that Sam had to do was speak authoritatively, tell the girl the answer, nod a few times, then wait for the lie to be regurgitated back to her.

Sam said, "According to eye witnesses, Kelly, you saw exactly what the Devils woman did."

"Okay," Kelly said. "That's what I seen happen. That she hurt her."

"How did the Devils woman hurt Mrs. Pinkman?" Sam waved

her hands in the air, trying to think of examples. "Did she kick her? Did she punch her?"

"She slapped her with her hand."

Sam looked at the hand she had waved in the air, certain the motion had put the idea in Kelly's head. "You're sure you saw the Devils woman slap Mrs. Pinkman?"

"Yes, ma'am, it happened like you said. She slapped her across the face, and I could hear the noise all the way to where I was sitting in the hall."

Sam realized the enormity of the lie. Without thinking, she had implicated her own sister in assault. "So, what you're saying is that you saw with your own eyes when the Devils woman slapped Mrs. Pinkman across the face?"

Kelly continued to nod. There were tears in her eyes. She clearly wanted to please Sam, as if pleasing her would somehow unlock the secret to getting her out of this living nightmare.

Kelly whispered, "I'm sorry."

"It's all right." Sam didn't push her further, because the exercise had proven her point. Given the right kind of leading question, the right tone, Kelly Wilson probably would have said Charlie murdered Judith Pinkman with her own hands.

The girl was so suggestible, she could have been hypnotized.

Sam checked her phone. Ninety seconds remained, plus the one-minute buffer. "Did the police talk to you yesterday before Mr. Rusty did?"

"Yes, ma'am. They talked to me at the hospital."

"Did they read you your Miranda rights before they spoke with you?" Sam could tell she did not understand. "Did they say, 'You have the right to remain silent. You have the right to counsel.' Did they say any of that to you?"

"No, ma'am, not in the hospital, because I would'a remembered that from the TV."

Sam leaned across the table again. "Kelly, this is very important. Did you say anything to the police before you talked to my father?"

"This one older fella, he kept talking to me. He rode with me in the ambulance to the hospital, and then he stayed in my room to make sure I was okay."

Sam doubted the man was concerned about her well-being. "Did you answer any of his questions? Did he interrogate you?"

"I don't know."

"Were you handcuffed when he talked to you?"

"I ain't sure. In the ambulance, you mean?"

"Yes."

"Well, no, not then. Not that I remember."

"Do you remember exactly when you were handcuffed?"

"It was at some point."

Sam wanted to throw her pen across the room. "Kelly, it's very important that you try to remember. Did they interrogate you at the hospital before my father told you not to answer any questions?"

"I'm sorry, ma'am. I don't remember much from yesterday."

"But the older fella was always with you?"

"Yes, ma'am, except when he had to go to the bathroom, and then a police officer came and sat with me."

"Was the older fella in a police uniform?"

"No, ma'am. He was in a suit and a tie."

"Did he tell you his name?"

"No, ma'am."

"Do you remember when you were told your Miranda—When they said, 'You have a right to remain silent. You have a right to counsel?'" She waited. "Kelly, do you remember when you were told those words?"

Kelly could clearly see this was important. "Maybe in the police car on the way to the jail this morning?"

"But it wasn't at the hospital?"

"No, ma'am. It was sometime this morning, but I don't know what time exactly."

Sam sat back in the chair. She tried to think this through. If Kelly had not been read her Miranda rights until this morning, then anything she said before that time could technically be inadmissible in court. "Are you sure this morning was the first time they told you your rights?"

"Well, I know this morning it was the older fella that done it." She shrugged her thin shoulders. "Maybe if he did it before, you can see it on the videotape."

"What videotape?"

"The one they made of me at the hospital."

CHAPTER ELEVEN

S am sat alone at the defense table. Her purse was on the floor. Her cane was folded up inside. She studied her notes from the interview with Kelly Wilson, pretending as if she did not know that at least one hundred people were sitting behind her. Without question, the majority of the spectators were locals. The heat of their white-hot rage made sweat roll down her back.

One of them could be the person who had stabbed Rusty.

Judging by the furious whispering, Sam gathered that many of them would gladly stab her, too.

Ken Coin coughed into his hand. The county prosecutor was sitting with a veritable phalanx: a doughy, fresh-faced second chair, an older man with a brush-broom mustache, and the obligatory attractive young blonde woman. In New York, this type of woman would be wearing a well-cut suit and expensive heels. The Pikeville version had her looking more like a Catholic nun.

Ken coughed again. He wanted Sam to look at him, but she would not. A perfunctory handshake was all that she had allowed. Any gratitude that Coin believed was owed to him for killing Daniel Culpepper had been erased by his scurrilous behavior. Sam was not a resident of Pikeville. She would never return. There was no need to pretend she had any affinity for the dirty, underhanded bastard. Coin was the type of prosecutor who made all prosecutors look bad. Not only because of the cat-and-mouse he had played with the arraignment, but because of the videotape that had been made at the hospital.

Whatever was on the recording could hang Kelly Wilson.

There was no telling what the girl had said. Based on Sam's brief time with her, she did not doubt that Kelly Wilson could be talked into admitting that she had assassinated Abraham Lincoln. The legal issue, perhaps the most important motion that Rusty would argue, would be whether or not the film of Kelly should be admissible in court. If Kelly had not been read her Miranda rights before she answered questions on the record, or if it was clear that she did not understand her rights, then the video should not be shown to the jury.

Technically, that was how it was supposed to work.

But this was a legal matter. There were always workarounds.

Ken Coin would argue that Miranda did not matter because Kelly had voluntarily made the recorded statements. There was one giant legal hurdle in his way. In order for the video to be admissible, Coin had to prove that a *reasonable person*—fortunately, not Kelly Wilson herself—would assume that Kelly was *not* in police custody when the statements were recorded. If Kelly believed that she was under arrest, that handcuffs and fingerprint impressions and a mugshot were imminent, then she was entitled to the reading of her rights.

Ergo, no Miranda rights, no film shown to the jury.

At least that was how it was supposed to work.

There were other weak links in the system, including the mood of the judge. Very rarely did you find a completely impartial figure on the bench. They tended to lean toward the prosecution or the defense. No judge liked to be appealed, but as a case moved higher up the chain, it became increasingly more difficult for a defendant to argue that a mistake had been made.

No judge liked to reverse a lower judge.

Sam closed her notepad. She glanced behind her. The Wilsons sat with Lenore. Sam had talked with them for less than five minutes before the general public was allowed into the courtroom.

Cameras clicked as photographers caught Sam making eye contact with the killer's parents. Video cameras seemed to be banned from the courtroom, but there were plenty of reporters recording every moment with their pens.

This was not the appropriate setting for a reassuring smile, so Sam nodded to Ava, then to Ely. Both nodded back, their jaws clenched as they clung to one another. Their clothes were stiff with newness, the creases from hangers and folds pronounced on their arms and shoulders. The first thing they had asked Sam after establishing Kelly's disposition was when they would be able to return to their home.

Sam had been unable to provide a definitive answer.

The Wilsons took the lack of information with a type of resignation that seemed ingrained in their souls. They were clearly part of that forgotten swath of poor, rural people. They were accustomed to waiting for the system to play out, usually not in their favor. The hollowed looks in their eyes reminded Sam of the images of refugees in magazines. Perhaps there were parallels. Ava and Ely Wilson were completely lost, forced into an unfamiliar world, their sense of safety, their sense of peace, everything that they cherished from their life before, was gone.

Sam reminded herself that Lucy Alexander and Douglas Pinkman were gone, too.

Lenore leaned over and whispered something to Ava. The woman nodded. Sam noted the time. The hearing was about to begin.

Kelly Wilson's entrance was announced by the distant jingle of chains, as if Santa Claus and his sleigh were on the other side of the wall. The bailiff opened the door. Cameras clicked. Murmurs filled the courtroom.

Kelly was ushered in by four armed guards, each of them so large that the girl was lost in a sea of flesh. She was reduced to shuffling her feet because they had put her in four-point restraints. The guard on the right held her by the arm. His fingers overlapped. The man was so muscular he could have picked up Kelly one-handed and placed her in the chair.

Sam was glad that he was standing beside Kelly. The moment the girl saw her parents, her knees gave out. The guard kept her from falling to the floor. Kelly began to wail.

"Mama—" She tried to reach out, but her hands were chained to her waist. "Daddy!" she yelled. "Please!"

Sam was up and across the room before she could think about how she had managed to move so quickly. She grabbed Kelly's hands. "Look at me."

The girl would not look away from her parents. "Mama, I'm so sorry."

Sam squeezed Kelly's hands harder, just enough to cause pain. "Look at me," she demanded.

Kelly looked at Sam. Her face was wet with tears. Her nose was running. Her teeth chattered.

"I'm here," Sam said, holding firm to her hands. "You're okay. Keep looking at me."

"We all right?" the bailiff asked. He was an older man, but the hand resting on the butt of his taser was steady.

Sam said, "Yes. We're all right."

The guards unlocked the chains from Kelly's ankles, her wrists, her waist.

"I can't do this," Kelly whispered.

"You're okay," Sam insisted, willing her to be so. "Remember how we talked about people watching you."

Kelly nodded. She used her sleeve to wipe her nose, holding firm to Sam's hands.

Sam said, "You need to be strong. Don't upset your parents. They want you to be a big girl. All right?"

Kelly nodded again. "Yes, ma'am."

"You're okay," Sam repeated.

The chains hit the floor. One of the guards leaned down and gathered them in one hand.

Sam leaned into the girl's shoulder as they walked to the table. Sam sat down. The guard pushed Kelly down into the chair beside her.

Kelly looked back at her parents. "I'm okay," she told them, her voice quivering. "I'm okay."

The door opened to the judge's chamber.

The court clerk said, "All rise for Judge Stanley Lyman."

Sam nodded to Kelly, indicating that she should stand. As the judge walked to the bench, Kelly grabbed Sam's hand again. Her palms were soaked with sweat.

Stan Lyman appeared to be Rusty's age, absent the avuncular spring in his step. Judges were a varied breed. Some were confident enough to simply take their place at the bench. Others sought to establish their dominance the moment they entered the courtroom. Stan Lyman fell into the latter category. He scowled as he scanned the gallery, the overflowing prosecution table. His gaze stopped on Sam. He performed an almost mechanical assessment of every section of her body, as if processing her through an MRI. She had not been so thoroughly inspected by a man since her last physical.

He banged his gavel, his eyes still on Sam. "Be seated."

Sam sat, pulling Kelly down beside her. The unwelcome butterflies returned. She wondered if Charlie was watching from the gallery.

The clerk announced, "This is case number OA 15-925, Dickerson County versus Kelly Rene Wilson, for arraignment." She turned to Ken Coin. "Counsel, please state your name for the record."

Coin stood and addressed the judge. "Good afternoon, Your Honor. Kenneth C. Coin, Darren Nickelby, Eugene 'Cotton' Henderson, and Kaylee Collins for the county."

Lyman gave a stern nod. "Good afternoon."

Sam stood again. "Your Honor, Samantha Quinn for Miss Wilson, who is present."

"Afternoon." Lyman nodded again. "This arraignment will qualify as a probable cause hearing. Miss Quinn, if you and Miss Wilson will stand for arraignment."

Sam nodded for Kelly to stand beside her. The girl was shaking again. Sam did not hold her hand. Kelly would be in and out of courtrooms for the next several years. She needed to learn to stand on her own.

"Miss Quinn." Lyman stared down at Sam from the bench. He had gone off-script. "You will remove those sunglasses in my courtroom."

Sam was momentarily bewildered by the request. Her lenses had been darkened for so many years that she hardly remembered. "Your Honor, these are my prescription glasses. They're tinted for a medical condition."

"Come up here." He waved her to the bench. "Let me see them."

Sam felt the mad thumping of her heart in her chest. One hundred sets of eyes were on her back. Cameras were clicking. Reporters were noting every word. Ken Coin coughed into his hand again, but said nothing to vouch for her.

Sam left her cane in her purse. She burned with humiliation as she limped toward the judge. The cameras sounded like dozens of grasshoppers rubbing together their legs. The images they captured would be printed in newspapers, perhaps shown online where Sam's colleagues would see them. The stories that accompanied the photos would likely delve into why she needed her glasses. The locals in the gallery, the ones who had been around for years, would gladly provide the details. They were scrutinizing Sam's gait, trying to see how much damage the bullet had done.

She was a veritable freak at the circus sideshow.

At the bench, Sam's hand trembled as she removed her glasses. The harsh fluorescent light stabbed into her corneas. She told the judge, "Please be careful with them. I didn't bring a spare."

Lyman took the glasses, roughly, then held them up for inspection. "Were you not told to dress appropriately for my courtroom?"

Sam looked down at her outfit, the same variation on the black silk blouse and flowing black pants she wore every day. "I beg your pardon?"

"What are you wearing?"

"Armani," she told the judge. "May I have my glasses returned, please?"

He placed them on the bench with a hard tap. "You may take your place."

Sam checked the lenses for smudges. She slipped on the glasses. She turned back around. She searched for Charlie in the crowd, but all she could see were the vaguely familiar faces, older now, of people she recognized from her childhood.

The walk back was longer than the walk to the bench. She reached out for the table. At the last minute, she saw Ben sitting in the gallery directly behind Ken Coin. He winked at her, smiling his encouragement.

Kelly took Sam's hand as they stood together. She repeated Sam's encouragement back to her. "You're okay."

"I am, thank you." Sam let the girl hold her hand. She was too rattled to do otherwise.

Judge Lyman cleared his throat a few times. That he had seemingly realized the hell he'd put Sam through came as no consolation. She knew from experience that some judges covered their mistakes by punishing the lawyer from whom it had been elicited.

He said, "Miss Quinn, do you waive the full reading of the charges against Miss Wilson?"

Sam was tempted to tell him no, but the departure from the norm would only drag out the proceedings. "We do."

Lyman nodded to the clerk. "You may arraign Miss Wilson and advise her of her rights."

The clerk stood up again. "Kelly Rene Wilson, you have been

arrested on probable cause for two counts of murder in the first degree. Miss Quinn, are you prepared to enter a plea?"

Sam said, "We would ask the Court to enter the plea of not guilty."

There came a titter of shock from the ill-informed crowd. Lyman lifted up his gavel, but the noise died off before he brought it down.

The clerk said, "A not guilty plea is entered on behalf of the defendant to all counts." The woman turned to Kelly. Sam thought there was something familiar about her round face. Another schoolmate, long forgotten. She had not spoken up for Sam when the judge had demanded her glasses, either.

The clerk said, "Kelly Rene Wilson, you have a right to a public, speedy trial by jury. You have a right to counsel. You have a right against self-incrimination. These rights abide and stay with you throughout the proceeding."

"Thank you." Lyman lowered his hand. Sam told Kelly to sit. The judge said, "The first issue for me is, Mr. Coin, do you believe there will be a superseding indictment subsequent to convening a grand jury?"

Sam made a note in her pad as Ken Coin shuffled to the podium. Another one of his cheap tricks, trying to establish dominance. As with a child, the best thing to do was ignore him.

"Your Honor." Coin leaned his elbows on the podium. "There is a definite possibility."

Lyman asked, "Do you have a timetable?"

"Not definitely, Your Honor. Ballpark for convening is within the next two weeks."

"Thank you, Mr. Prosecutor, you may step back to the table." Lyman was an older judge; he knew the games lawyers played. "And the disposition of the defendant pending trial?"

Coin took his place behind the table as he addressed the judge. "We will hold the defendant either at the city or county jail, whichever is deemed the safest place for her."

"Miss Quinn?" the judge asked.

Sam knew there was no chance that Kelly Wilson would be given bail. She said, "I have no objection to the disposition at this time, Your Honor. Though, as to a previous matter, I would like to waive the right of Miss Wilson to have the charges heard by a grand jury." Kelly was already facing a probable cause finding for two counts of first-degree murder. Sam didn't want to open her up to further charges by convening a grand jury. "My client has no wish to slow down the process."

"Very well." Lyman made another note. "Mr. Coin, is it your intention to treat this as an open discovery case, meaning you will turn over evidence and such and not hold anything back?"

Coin held out his hands, a disciple to Christ. "Always, Your Honor. Unless there is some legal basis, open discovery has always been this office's policy."

Sam felt her nostrils flare. She reminded herself that the hospital tape would be Rusty's fight.

Lyman asked, "Are you satisfied with that, Miss Quinn?"

"I am for the moment, Your Honor. I am serving as co-counsel today. My father will be filing motions with the Court as soon as he is able."

Lyman put down his pen. For the first time, he looked at her without disapproval. "How is your father?"

"Eager to mount a vigorous defense for Miss Wilson, Your Honor."

Lyman twisted his lips to the side, clearly unsure of her tone. "Are you aware that this is a capital murder case, Miss Quinn, which means the prosecution may well seek the death penalty, as is its right?"

"Yes, Your Honor, I am."

"I'm unfamiliar with the customs where you're from, Miss Quinn, but down here, we take our capital cases very seriously."

"I'm from Winder Road, about six miles up the street, Your Honor. I am aware of the seriousness of these charges."

Lyman clearly did not like the giggles in the gallery. He asked Sam, "Why do I feel that you are not really operating in the capacity of co-counsel to your father?" He gestured broadly with his hand. "In other words, you have no intention of continuing your work through to the trial."

"I believe you put Mr. Grail in a similar position, Your Honor, but I assure you I am engaged in this case and intend to fully support Miss Wilson in any capacity that is required of me in aid of her defense."

"All right." He smiled, and Sam felt her blood run cold, because she had walked right into his trap. "Do you have any question or doubt in your mind about the defendant's ability to assist you or understand the nature of these proceedings?"

"I'm not raising that issue at this time, Your Honor."

Lyman would not let her off so easily. "Let's humor ourselves, Miss Quinn. Should you, as co-counsel, raise the issue in the future—"

"I would only do so on the basis of any scientific testing, Your Honor."

"Scientific testing?" He looked askance.

Sam said, "Miss Wilson has exhibited a vulnerability to suggestion, Your Honor, as I am certain the prosecution can confirm."

Coin jumped up. "Your Honor, I cannot—"

Sam talked over him. "Miss Wilson's verbal intellectual range is narrow for an eighteen-year-old. I would like to have assessed her memory encoding for visual-non-verbal communication, language functioning, any deficiencies in word and encoded information retrieval, and to quantify her emotional and intellectual quotient."

Coin huffed a laugh. "And you expect the county to pay for all that?"

Sam turned to look at him. "I was told you take your capital cases seriously down here."

There was a bubble of laughter from the crowd.

Lyman banged his gavel several times before they settled. Sam caught the slight lift of the corners of his mouth as he suppressed a smile. Judges rarely enjoyed themselves in the courtroom. This man had been on the bench so long that he likely thought he had seen everything.

"Your Honor," Sam said, testing the waters. "If I may raise another issue?"

He gave her an overly generous nod to illustrate the latitude he was allowing. "Why not?"

"Thank you, Your Honor," Sam said. "Miss Wilson's parents are eager to return to their home. A timeline from the prosecution as to when they expect to release the Wilson home would be welcomed."

Ken Coin jumped up from the table again. "Your Honor, as yet the county does not have an estimate for completion of said search of the Wilson abode." He seemed to realize he could not match Sam's formalized language. He flashed his teeth at the judge. "These things are very hard to predict, Judge. We need time for a thorough search, properly performed under the guidelines put forth in the warrant."

Sam kicked herself for not reading the warrant ahead of time.

Lyman said, "There is your answer, Miss Quinn, such as it is."

"Thank you, Your Honor." Sam watched him pick up the gavel. She mulled the judge's *such as it is* in her mind. She felt a rush of certainty, her instinct urging her that now was the time. "Your Honor?"

Lyman again laid down his gavel. "Miss Quinn?"

"As to discovery—"

"I believe that has been addressed."

"I understand that, Your Honor; however, there was a video recording made of Miss Wilson yesterday afternoon while she was being detained at the hospital."

"Your Honor." Coin was on his feet again. " 'Detained?' "

"In custody," Sam clarified.

"Oh, come on," Coin's tone dripped with disgust. "You can't—"

"Your Honor—"

Lyman held up his hand to stop them both. He sat back in his chair. He steepled together his fingers in thought. These moments happened often in the courtroom, where the judge stopped the proceedings to think through the intricacies of a request. Most times, they ended up kicking the problem down the road, asked for motions to be written, or simply said they would delay their decision to another time.

Sometimes, they threw the question back to the attorneys, which meant that you had to be prepared to succinctly argue the merits or run the risk of prejudicing the judge against your position for the remainder of the case.

Sam tensed, feeling as if she was locked into the starting block, staring down the open track. Lyman had mentioned discovery very early on, so he likely knew that Ken Coin was prepared to follow the letter, not the spirit, of the law.

Lyman gave Sam the nod.

She took off: "Miss Wilson was in the custody of a plainclothes police officer who accompanied her from the middle school to the hospital. He was in the ambulance with her. He stayed with her in her hospital room through the night. He rode with Miss Wilson in the police car that took her to the jail this morning, and he was present when she was Mirandized this morning. If I use the words 'detained' or 'in custody,' that is because any reasonable person—"

"Your Honor," Ken said. "Is this an arraignment or a special episode of *How to Get Away with Murder?*"

Lyman gave Sam a flinty look, but he also gave her more leeway. "Miss Quinn?"

"Pursuant to the prosecutor's stated position on open discovery, we request a copy of the hospital video be turned over to Miss Wilson posthaste so that she can evaluate how to proceed."

"'How to proceed,'" Coin echoed, as if the notion was ludicrous. "What Kelly Wilson said was—"

"Mr. Coin." Lyman's voice was raised loudly enough to project to the back of the room. He cleared his throat in the silence. He told Coin, "I would consider your words very carefully."

Coin demurred. "Yes, Your Honor. Thank you."

Lyman picked up his pen. He turned the barrel slowly, a stalling measure that was meant to further rebuke Coin. Even Kelly Wilson knew that you did not present evidence at an arraignment.

Lyman asked, "Mr. Coin, when can a copy of this hospital video be made available?"

Coin said, "We'll have to have the film converted, sir. It was made on an iPhone belonging to Sheriff Keith Coin."

"Your Honor?" Sam felt her teeth grit. Keith Coin was the very definition of male authority. Kelly would have jumped off a cliff for him. "Can I be clear—as you gathered, I've been away for a while. Sheriff Coin is Prosecutor Coin's brother?"

"You know he is, Samantha." Coin leaned toward the judge, his hand gripping the edge of the table. "Your Honor, I've been told we'll need to get somebody up from Atlanta to make sure the video transfer is done properly. There's a cloud or something involved. I'm no expert in these things. I'm just an ol' boy who misses the kind of phones that weighed twenty pounds and cost two bucks a month to rent from Ma Bell." He grinned at the judge, who was roughly his age. "Sir, these things take money and time."

"Spend the money, rush the time," Lyman said. "Miss Quinn, is there anything else?"

Sam felt the euphoria that came from knowing a judge was leaning her way. She decided to push her luck. "Your Honor, on the subject of video recordings, we would also ask for the footage from the security cameras at school to be turned over as quickly as possible so that our experts have time to analyze them."

Coin rapped his knuckles once on the table, clearly on his back foot. "That's gonna take a while, too, Your Honor. My own people haven't viewed that footage. We have a responsibility to the privacy of other folks at the school at the time of the shooting to make sure we are turning over only evidence that the defendant is entitled to per the rules of discovery."

Lyman appeared dubious. "You yourself have yet to view the footage taken from the middle school yesterday morning?"

Coin's eyes shifted. "My people have not, no sir."

"All of your people need to view it?"

"Experts, sir." Coin grasped at straws. "We need—"

"I'll put you out of your misery," Lyman said, obviously agitated. "For *your people* to view this footage would take one week? Two weeks?"

"I could not hazard a guess, Your Honor. The level of moving pieces is—"

"I'll expect your answer to my question by the end of the week." He picked up the gavel, ready to end the hearing.

Sam said, "If I may, Your Honor?"

He rolled the gavel in the air, urging speed.

"Could the prosecutor tell me if I need to retain an expert in auditory analysis as well? It's often time-challenging to locate qualified professionals."

Lyman said, "I have found in order to locate a courtroom professional, you need only drag a hundred-dollar bill through a university parking lot." He smiled as some of the reporters laughed at the purloined joke. "Mr. Coin?"

Coin looked down at the table. His hand was on his hip, suit coat unbuttoned, tie askew. "Your Honor."

Sam waited. Coin offered nothing else.

Lyman prodded, "Mr. Coin, your answer to the question of audio?"

Coin tapped the table with his index finger. " 'Was the baby killed?' "

No one answered.

" 'Was the baby killed?' " Coin tapped on the table again, one time for each word. " 'Was the *baby* killed?' "

Sam was not going to stop this, but she gave an obligatory, "Your Honor."

Lyman shrugged in confusion.

Coin said, "That is what Miss Quinn is after. She wanted to know what Kelly Wilson said in the hallway after she murdered a man and a child in cold blood."

Lyman frowned. "Mr. Coin. This is not the place."

" '*The Baby*—' "

"Mr. Coin."

"Was the name used by the Alexander parents to describe Lucy—"

"Mr. Coin."

"Called that by Barbara Alexander to her students. By Frank Alexander at the high school—"

"Mr. Coin, this is your last warning."

"Where Mr. Alexander was going to flunk Kelly Wilson." Coin turned to the crowd. "Kelly wanted to know: was *the Baby* killed."

Lyman banged his gavel.

Coin told Kelly, "Yes, *the Baby* was killed."

"Bailiff."

Coin looked back at the judge. "Your Honor—"

"Me?" Lyman feigned surprise. "I didn't realize you knew I was here."

There was no nervous laughter from the gallery. Coin's words had left their mark. The headlines had been set for the next few days.

Coin said, "My deepest apologies, Your Honor. I just came from little Lucy's autopsy and—"

"Enough!" Lyman's eyes found the bailiff's. The man stood at the ready. "As you said, Mr. Coin. This is an arraignment, not the *Get Away with Murder Show*."

"Yes, sir." Coin rested his fingertips on the table, bracing himself, his back to the crowd. "My apologies, Your Honor. I was overcome."

"And I am over your grandstanding." Lyman was visibly furious.

Sam pushed again. "Your Honor, am I to understand there is audio attached to the school security footage?"

"I believe that is understood by everyone in this courtroom, Miss Quinn." Lyman rested his cheek against his fist. He took a moment to consider the implications of what had just happened. The deliberations did not take long. "Miss Quinn, the prosecutor will deliver to your office and the court clerk by tomorrow, five o'clock sharp, the following timelines—"

Sam had her notepad and pen ready.

"The hasty release of the Wilson *abode* back into their custody. The release of the full, unedited videotape made at the hospital. The release of any and all security camera footage, unedited, in or around the middle school, the elementary school beside it and the high school across the street."

Coin opened his mouth, but rethought his objection.

Lyman said, "Mr. Coin, your timelines will astonish me with their speed and specificity. Am I correct?"

"Your Honor, you are correct."

The judge finally banged his gavel.

"All rise," the clerk called.

Lyman slammed the door behind him.

A collective breath was released in the courtroom.

The guards came for Kelly. They slowly prepared the restraints, generously allowing Kelly a few moments with her parents.

Coin did not offer the customary handshake. Sam barely noticed. She was too busy writing in her pad, recording for Rusty what exactly he could expect tomorrow afternoon because the court transcript would not be made ready for at least another week. There was a lot the judge had demanded; more than she had hoped for. Sam ended up having to write around some of the earlier notes she had taken when she spoke with Kelly.

Sam stopped writing.

She looked at the transcription, underlined—

It's just a little upset this time of day.

Sam turned the page. Then the next page. Her eyes skimmed down what Kelly Wilson had told her.

. . . Tummy was hurting like it does . . . Usually calms down on its own . . . Sick same time yesterday . . . Make up for missing classes last week . . .

"Kelly." Sam turned to the girl. Her feet were already chained. The guards were about to handcuff her, but Sam stepped in, drawing her into a close hug. The orange jumper bunched up under Kelly's arms. Her stomach pressed against Sam's.

Kelly whispered, "Thank you, Miss Quinn."

"You'll be okay," Sam told her. "Remember what I told you about not talking to anyone."

"Yes, ma'am. I'll keep to myself." She held out her thin wrists so that the guards could cuff together her hands. The chain was wrapped around her waist.

Sam resisted the need to tell them not to wrap the chain too tightly.

Lucy Alexander was not the baby that Kelly Wilson had been concerned about.

CHAPTER TWELVE

Sam carefully negotiated the steep loading ramp outside the courthouse. The stench of rotting food had dissipated, or perhaps she had become accustomed to the smell. She looked up at the sky. The orange sun grazed the distant mountaintops. Dusk was a few hours away. She had no idea where she was going to sleep tonight, but she had to speak to Rusty before she left town.

He needed to know that Kelly Wilson could be carrying the motive for her crimes in her belly.

Morning sickness did not always come in the morning. Sometimes, it came in the afternoon, but the key factor was that it came at roughly the same time every day, commonly during the first trimester. That would explain why Kelly was missing classes at school. It would also explain the round bump of her belly that Sam had felt when she had hugged the girl so tightly.

Kelly Wilson was several weeks pregnant.

Lenore's red car made a wide circle, stopping a few feet from the bottom of the ramp.

"Sammy!" Charlie jumped out of the front seat. "You were fucking fantastic in there! Oh my God!" She threw her hand around Sam's waist. "Let me help you."

"Give me a minute," Sam said. Her body was at that point where standing was easier than sitting down. "You could've warned me about the judge."

"I said he was a hard-ass," Charlie said. "But, Jesus, you made him smile. I've never seen him smile. And you had Coin sputtering like a broken sprinkler. That stupid asshole laid out his case right in the middle of the arraignment."

Lenore got out of the car.

Charlie was beaming. "Didn't my big sister play Ken Coin like a fucking fiddle?"

Lenore said, " 'I was impressed,' she said begrudgingly."

"That judge." Sam took off her glasses to rub her eyes. "I had forgotten—"

"That you look like a Victorian-era Dracula?"

"*Dracula* was set in Victorian times." Sam put on her glasses. "Rusty's top priority should be finding an expert to evaluate Kelly. Either she's deficient, or she's clever enough to pretend. She could be fooling us all."

Charlie huffed a laugh. "Dad maybe, but she can't fool you."

"Didn't you say that I was too smart to know how stupid I am?"

"You're right. We need an expert," Charlie said. "We'll also have to find someone who's good with false confessions. You know that hospital recording is going to show hope of benefit."

"Maybe." Sam was worried that Ken and Keith Coin were too clever to show their work. Hope of benefit, or any false inducement such as the promise of a lesser charge in exchange for a confession, was illegal. "I can find an expert in New York. Someone will need to comb the recordings to make certain they've been unedited. Does Rusty have an investigator?"

Lenore said, "Jimmy Jack Little."

Sam would not dither over the foolish name. "Jimmy Jack needs to locate a young man named Adam Humphrey."

"What's he looking for?" Lenore asked.

"Humphrey could be someone in whom Kelly confided."

"She was screwing him, or was he trying to screw her?"

Sam shrugged, because that was all she could really give without breaking privilege. "I don't think Kelly goes to school with him. Perhaps he graduated? The only detail I got was that he drives a Camaro."

"Classy," Charlie said. "Maybe he's in the yearbook? Either his photo or he wrote something down. Did Kelly say he was her boyfriend?"

"Undetermined," Sam said. Kelly Wilson might not fully understand the oath of confidentiality, but Sam did not take the pledge lightly. "Does Rusty know that Lucy Alexander's father was Kelly's teacher?" The man could be a second suspect in the paternity hunt. She asked Lenore, "If you could generate for Rusty a list of all of Kelly's teachers—"

"You know that's their angle," Charlie said. "Kelly was mad that Mr. Alexander was going to flunk her, so she took a gun to school and killed his daughter."

That wouldn't be their case if a positive pregnancy test came out.

Charlie opened her mouth to speak.

"Shush," Lenore nodded behind them.

Ben was coming down the ramp, hands in his pockets, hair tousled by the wind. He grinned at Sam. "You should be a lawyer when you grow up."

She smiled back. "I'll think about it."

"You were amazing." Ben squeezed her shoulder. "Rusty's going to be really proud of you."

Sam felt her smile soften. The last thing she had ever wanted was Rusty's approval. "Thank you."

"Babe," Charlie said. "Didn't my sister kill it?"

He nodded. "She killed it."

Charlie reached up to neaten his hair with her fingers, but Ben was already stepping back. He stepped forward again, but her hand went down. The uneasiness was back.

Sam tried, "Ben, can we all have dinner together?"

"I'm going to be busy putting my boss together after that shredding you gave him, but thank you for asking." His eyes darted toward Charlie, then back again. "But, hey, Sam. I didn't know about the video at the hospital. I was at the station all day yesterday. I found out about the arraignment half an hour before it started." He shrugged one shoulder, the same way Charlie did. "I don't play dirty like that."

Sam said, "I believe you."

"I'd better get back." Ben reached for Lenore's hand. "Make sure they get home safe."

He headed up the ramp, hands tucked deep into his pockets.

Charlie cleared her throat. She watched him with a longing that pierced Sam's heart. She had seen her sister cry more today than when they were children. Sam wanted to drag her sister after Ben and make Charlie beg for forgiveness. She was so damn obstinate. She never apologized for anything.

"Get in the car." Lenore climbed behind the wheel. She slammed the door.

Sam gave Charlie a questioning look, but she shrugged as she crawled across the back seat, leaving space for Sam.

Lenore was pulling away as Sam shut the door.

Charlie asked, "Where are we going?"

"Office." Lenore turned onto the main road. She sped through a yellow light.

"My car is at the police station," Charlie said. "Is there a reason we're going to the office?"

"Yes," was all Lenore would give.

This seemed to be enough for Charlie. She slumped down in the seat. She looked out the window. Sam guessed that she was thinking about Ben. The urge to grab Charlie, to shake some sense into her, was overwhelming. Why had her sister imperiled her marriage? Ben was the one good thing she had in her life.

Lenore turned down another side street. Sam finally got her bearings. They were on the bad side of town now, the place where the tourist dollars had stopped. Every building looked as derelict as it had thirty years ago.

Lenore held up a miniature Starship *Enterprise*. "Ben gave me this."

Sam had no idea why he would give Lenore a toy.

Charlie seemed to know. "He shouldn't have done that."

Lenore said, "Well, he did."

"Throw it away," Charlie said. "Put it in the blender."

Sam asked, "Can someone tell me—"

"It's a thumb drive," Charlie said. "And I'm guessing that it has something on it that will help our case."

"Exactly," Lenore said.

"Throw it the fuck away," Charlie said, enunciating each word. "He'll get in trouble. He'll get fired. Or worse."

Lenore tucked the thumb drive down the front of her bra.

"I'm not a part of this." Charlie held up her hands. "If you get Ben disbarred, I will never forgive you."

"Add it to the list." Lenore swung the car down another side street. The old stationery supply building had been slightly altered. The plate glass in the front was boarded over. Thick security bars striped the other windows. The gated entrance was new, too. Sam was reminded of the wild animal park at the San Diego Zoo as the gate buzzed open, ushering them into a walled sanctum behind the building.

"You're going to open the thumb drive?" Charlie asked.

"I'm going to open the thumb drive," Lenore said.

Charlie looked to Sam for help.

Sam shrugged. "He wanted us to have it."

"I fucking hate both of you." Charlie jumped out of the car. She had the security door open, then the regular door, before Sam could speak with her.

Lenore said, "We can open the file in my office."

Charlie stomped around a corner, turning on lights as she went.

Sam did not know whether to follow her sister or to give Charlie's anger time to burn itself out. She felt wary of her sister. She was so changeable—celebrating Sam's courtroom performance one minute, then denigrating her for doing her job the next. There was an undercurrent of misery flowing through Charlie that eventually pulled everything down.

"I'm this way." Lenore nodded toward the other side of the building.

Sam followed her up another long hallway that was tinged with the odor of Rusty's cigarettes. Sam tried to recall the last time she had been exposed to secondhand smoke. Probably in Paris before the indoor smoking ban.

They passed a closed door with Rusty's name on the sign outside. Sam would have guessed this was his office from the smell alone. The rays of nicotine radiating from the door offered a further clue.

Lenore said, "He hasn't smoked in the building for years. He brings it in on his clothes."

Sam frowned. She had so many things wrong with her body that she could not imagine why someone would purposefully damage themselves. If two heart attacks did not serve as a wake-up call, nothing would.

Lenore pulled a set of keys from her purse. She held her clutch under her arm as she unlocked the door. She turned on the lights. Sam narrowed her eyes as they protested against the sudden, bright light.

When her pupils finally adjusted, she was met with a welcoming, tidy space. Lenore's office was very blue. Light blue walls. Dark blue carpet. Pastel blue couch with throw pillows in various shades of blue. She said, "I like blue."

Sam stood by the couch. "It's very nice."

"You can sit down."

"I think it's better if I stand."

"Suit yourself." Lenore sat at her desk.

"My leg is—"

"No explanation needed." She leaned down and inserted the USB drive into her computer. She turned the monitor around so that Sam could see. "You want me to leave?"

Sam did not want to be perceived as any ruder than before. "I'll let you decide."

"I'll stay." Lenore clicked open the thumb drive. "One file. Just a series of numbers. Can you see?"

Sam nodded. The extension read .mov, which meant the file was video. "Go ahead."

Lenore clicked the file name.

The video opened.

She clicked the button to make it fill the screen.

The image could have been a photograph but for the numbers ticking in the corner: 07:58:47. A typical school hallway. Blue lockers. Tan tiled floor. The camera was tilted too far down. Only half of the hall was visible to the lens, about fifty feet of open space. The most distant point showed a thin slice of light that must have come from an open doorway. Posters were on the walls. Graffiti peppered the lockers. The entirety of the space was empty. The footage was grainy. The color was washed, more of a sepia tone.

Lenore turned up the volume on the speakers. "No sound."

"Look," Sam pointed to the monitor. As she'd watched, a piece of cinder block had spontaneously chipped away from the wall.

"Gunshot," Lenore said.

Sam looked at the round bullet hole.

A man ran into the hallway.

He had entered the scene from behind the camera. His back was to them. White dress shirt. Dark pants. His hair was gray, styled in a typical man's cut, short in the back, parted on the side.

He stopped, abruptly, hands out in front of him.

No, don't.

Lenore sucked air through her teeth as the man jerked violently once, then again, then again.

Blood misted into the air.

He collapsed to the floor. Sam saw his face.

Douglas Pinkman.

Shot once in the chest. Twice in the head. A black hole replaced his right eye.

A river of blood began to flow around his body.

Sam felt her hand cover her mouth.

Lenore said, "Oh God."

A small figure had rounded the corner. Her back was to the lens. Pigtails flopping on either side of her head.

Princess backpack, shoes that lighted up, arms swinging.

She came to an abrupt stop.

Mr. Pinkman. Dead on the floor.

Lucy Alexander fell quickly, landing on the incline of her backpack.

Her head lolled back. Her legs splayed. Her shoes pointed up at the ceiling.

The little girl tried in vain to raise her head. She touched her fingers to the open wound at her neck.

Her mouth was moving.

Judith Pinkman ran toward the camera. Her red shirt was a dull rust on the screen. She had her arms back, out to her sides, like a winged creature preparing to take flight. She passed her husband, then dropped to her knees beside Lucy.

"Look," Lenore said.

Kelly Wilson finally came into the frame.

Distant. Slightly out of focus. The girl was at the most remote reaches of the camera's lens. She was dressed in all black. Her greasy hair hung around her shoulders. Her eyes were wide. Her mouth hung open. She held the revolver in her right hand.

Like I said, the gun was in my hand.

Kelly sat down on the floor. The left half of her body was out of the camera's reach. Her back was to the lockers. The revolver stayed at her side, resting on the ground. She stared straight ahead.

Lenore said, "A hair shy of eleven seconds from the moment the bullet went into the wall." She pointed to the time in the corner. "I counted five shots total. One in the wall. Three in Pinkman. One in Lucy. That's not what the simulation had on the news. They said Judith Pinkman was shot at twice, missed both times."

Sam let herself look at Lucy again.

Judith Pinkman's mouth was open as she screamed up at the ceiling.

Sam read the grieving woman's lips.

Help me.

Somewhere in the school, Charlie was hearing the woman's pleas.

Lenore held up the box of Kleenex on her desk.

Sam took some tissues. She wiped her eyes. She blew her nose. She watched Judith Pinkman cradle her hand behind Lucy's head. She tried in vain to staunch the wound that had opened the little girl's neck. Blood seeped through her fingers as if she had squeezed a sponge. The woman was clearly sobbing, wailing from grief.

Charlie came out of nowhere, leaping into the frame.

She was running up the hallway, toward the camera, toward Lucy and Mrs. Pinkman. The expression on her face was one of complete panic. She barely gave Douglas Pinkman more than a glance. Her knees hit the floor. She was sideways to the camera, her face clearly visible. She clutched Lucy Alexander's hand. She spoke to the girl. She rocked back and forth as she tried to soothe both of them.

Sam had seen Charlie rock this way only once before.

"That's Mason," Lenore said. She blew her nose loudly.

Mason Huckabee had his back to the camera. He was clearly talking to Kelly, trying to coax away the gun. The girl was still seated, but she had slid farther down the hallway. Sam could no longer see her face. The only visible parts of Kelly's body were her right leg and the hand that held the revolver.

The butt of the weapon rested on the floor.

Mason went down to his knees. He leaned forward. His arm went out, palm open. He inched toward Kelly. Slowly, slowly. Sam could only imagine what he was saying. *Give me the gun. Just hand it to me. You don't have to do this.*

Mason knew Kelly Wilson, had been her teacher, her tutor. He would know that she could be talked down.

On screen, he kept moving closer, and closer until, without warning, Kelly raised the gun out of the frame.

Sam's stomach lurched.

Mason backed up quickly, putting distance between himself and Kelly.

"She turned the gun on herself," Lenore said. "That's why his hands are down instead of up."

Sam's gaze found Charlie again. She was beside Lucy, opposite Mrs. Pinkman. The older woman was looking up at the ceiling, eyes closed, clearly praying. Charlie sat cross-legged on the floor. Her hands were in her lap. She was rubbing together her fingers, staring at the blood as if she had never seen anything like it before.

Or perhaps she was thinking that she had seen something exactly like it before.

Charlie's head slowly turned. She looked off camera. A shotgun slid across the floor, stopping a few feet away. Charlie did not move. Another second passed. The shotgun was scooped up by a policeman. He ran down the hall. His bulletproof vest flapped at his waist. He dropped to one knee and jammed the butt of the shotgun into his shoulder.

The weapon was pointed at Mason Huckabee, not Kelly Wilson.

Mason was on his knees, his back to Kelly, blocking the man's shot.

All of this seemed lost on Charlie. She was looking back down at her hands, seemingly mesmerized by the blood. Her rocking had become less pronounced, more of a vibration moving through the body.

Lenore whispered, "My poor baby."

Sam had to look away from Charlie. She found Mason still on his knees. Now, his back was to Kelly Wilson. The shotgun was pointed at his chest.

The shotgun was pointed at his chest.

Sam's eyes skipped back to Charlie. She had not moved. She was still rocking. She looked to be in some type of fugue state. She did not seem to notice when a second police officer ran past her.

Sam followed the cop's quick progress down the hall. As with the other officer, his back was to the camera, but Sam could see the gun in his hand. He came to a stop a few feet away from the other cop with a shotgun.

Shotgun and revolver.

Revolver and shotgun.

Mason Huckabee had extended his hand toward Kelly, reaching over his left shoulder, offering his palm. He was talking to her, most likely still trying to coax the gun away.

The cops shook their weapons. Their stances were aggressive. Sam did not need to see their faces to know that they were shouting orders.

In contrast, Mason was calm, collected. His mouth moved slowly. His movements were almost catlike.

Sam's gaze returned to Charlie just as she looked up. The expression on her face was heartbreaking. Sam wanted to climb into the film and hold her.

"She moved back," Lenore said.

She meant Kelly. The girl was almost out of frame now. Only a patch of black from her jeans indicated Kelly was still there. Mason had moved back with her. His head, his left shoulder and left hand were completely gone. The angle of the camera had cut a diagonal line across his torso.

The cops did not move.

Mason did not move.

There was a puff of smoke from the cop's gun.

Mason's right arm recoiled.

The cop had shot him.

"Oh my God," Sam said. She could not see Mason's face, but his torso had only slightly twisted.

The cops appeared to be as surprised as Sam. They did not move, not for several more seconds, before slowly, they both lowered their weapons. They spoke to one another. The man with the shotgun unclipped the radio mic from his shoulder. The other turned around in the hall, looked at Charlie, then turned back.

He extended his hand to Mason.

Mason stood up. The second cop walked in the direction of Kelly Wilson.

Suddenly, the girl appeared on screen, face down, the cop's knee in her back. She had been tossed over like a sack.

Sam looked for the murder weapon.

Not in Kelly's hands or on her person.

Not on the floor near Kelly.

Not in the hands of the cop who had his knee in her back.

Mason Huckabee was standing, empty hands at his sides, talking to the cop with the shotgun. Blood had turned his shirt-sleeve almost black. He was talking to the cop as if they were discussing a bad call at a sporting event.

Sam scanned the ground at their feet.

Nothing.

No lockers had been cracked open.

None of the cops appeared to have tucked the revolver into the waistband of their pants.

No one had kicked the weapon across the floor.

No one had reached up to secrete it behind a ceiling tile.

Sam returned to Charlie. Her hands were empty. She still sat cross-legged on the floor, still looked dazed. Her head was turned away from the men. Sam noticed that a patch of blood swiped her cheek. She must have touched her face.

Her nose was not yet broken. Bruises did not encircle her eyes.

Charlie didn't seem to register the group of cops rushing down the hall. Their weapons were drawn. Their vests flapped open.

The monitor went black.

Sam stared at the blank screen for a few seconds more, even though there was nothing to see.

Lenore let out a long stream of breath.

Sam asked the only question that mattered. "Is Charlie okay?"

Lenore's lips pursed. "There was a time when I could tell you everything about her."

"But now?"

"A lot has changed in the last few years."

Rusty's heart attacks. Had Charlie been shaken by the sudden prospect of Rusty's death? It would be just like her to hide her fear, or to find self-destructive ways to take her mind off of it. Like sleeping with Mason Huckabee. Like alienating herself from Ben.

"You should eat," Lenore said. "I'll make you a sandwich."

"Thank you, but I'm not hungry," Sam said. "I need a place to make some notes for Dad."

"Use his office." Lenore took a key from her purse. She slid it over to Sam. "I'm going to transcribe this video, make sure we haven't missed anything. I want to pull that so-called reenactment from the news, too. I'm not sure where they're getting their information about the sequence, especially the gunshots, but they're wrong, based on this video."

Sam said, "In court, Coin indicated there was audio."

"He didn't correct Lyman," Lenore said. "My guess is there's an alternate source. The school can barely afford its electric bill. The cameras are probably decades old. They wouldn't pay to wire them for sound."

"A useless endeavor, considering the number of children who are typically in the hallway. Isolating one voice from the din would be challenging." She guessed, "A cell phone, maybe?"

"Maybe." Lenore shrugged as she returned to her computer. "Rusty will figure it out."

Sam looked down at the key on Lenore's desk. The last thing she wanted to do was sit in Rusty's office. Her father had been a hoarder before television popularized the disorder. She imagined there were boxes at the farmhouse that had not been unpacked since Gamma had brought them home from the thrift store.

Gamma.

Charlie had said that the photo—*the* photo of Gamma—was on Rusty's desk.

Sam walked back to her father's office. She could only get the door partway open before it caught against a pile of debris. The room was large, but the clutter brought down the scale. Boxes, papers, and files overflowed from almost every surface. Only a narrow path to the desk indicated anyone ever used the space. The stagnant air inside made Sam cough. She reached for the lights, then thought better of it. Her headache had only slightly receded since taking off her glasses in court.

Sam left her cane by the door. She carefully picked her way toward Rusty's desk, imagining that a virtual stroll through her father's convoluted brain would not be dissimilar. How on earth he managed to work in here was a mystery. She turned on the desk lamp. She opened the blinds to the filthy, barred window. Sam supposed the flat surface provided by a stack of depositions served as his writing table. There was no computer. A clock radio Gamma had given him when Sam was a child was the only acknowledgment of modernity.

The desk was walnut, a large expanse that Sam recalled had a green leather blotter. It was probably as pristine as the day it was made, preserved under piles of rubbish. She tested the sturdiness of Rusty's chair. The thing listed to the side because he was an inveterate leaner. When Sam thought of her father seated, he was always propped on his right elbow, cigarette in his hand.

Sam sat in Rusty's unsteady chair. The squeal from the height actuator assembly was loud and completely unnecessary. A simple can of spray lubricant could eradicate the noise. The arms could be tightened down with some Loctite on the bolts. Replacing the friction rings on the casters would probably improve the stability.

Or the fool could go online and order a new chair from Amazon.

Sam moved around papers and stacks of transcripts as she searched for *the* photo of Gamma. She wanted to slide the flotsam off the desktop, but she was sure that Rusty had a system to his madness. Not that Sam would ever let her desk get like this, but if anyone moved around her things, she would kill them.

Sam checked the top of the cluttered credenza, which held, among many other things, a pack of unopened yellow legal pads. She broke open the pack. She found her notes in her purse. She changed out her glasses. She wrote Kelly Wilson's name at the top of the yellow pad. She added the date. She made a list of items for Rusty to follow up on.

1. Pregnancy test
2. Paternity: Adam Humphrey? Frank Alexander?
3. Hospital video; security footage (audio?)
4. Why was Kelly at middle school? (victims were random)
5. List of tutors/teachers/class schedules
6. Judith Pinkman——?

Sam traced the letters of the woman's name.

During Sam's tenure at the middle school, the main floor outside the front office had been designated for the English department. Judith Pinkman was an English teacher, so that would explain why she was there when the shooting began.

Sam considered the security footage.

Mrs. Pinkman had appeared in the hallway after Lucy was shot in the neck. Sam believed less than three seconds passed from the time that the little girl was on her back, on the floor, and the time Judith Pinkman appeared at the end of the hallway.

Five gunshots. One in the wall. Three in Douglas Pinkman. One in Lucy.

If the revolver held six bullets, then why didn't Kelly use the last shot on Judith Pinkman?

"I think she was pregnant." Charlie was standing in the doorway, a plate with a sandwich in one hand, a bottle of Coke in the other.

Sam turned over her notes. She tried to keep her expression composed lest she give herself away. "What?"

"Back in middle school when all of that shit talk was going on. I think Kelly was pregnant."

Sam had a momentary sense of relief, but then she realized what her sister was saying. "Why do you think that?"

"I got it off Facebook. I've friended one of the girls from the school."

"Charlie."

"It's a fake account." Charlie put the plate on the desk in front of Sam. "This girl, Mindy Zowada, she's one of the bitches who was nasty in the yearbook. I prodded her a little, said that I'd heard some rumors that Kelly was loose in middle school. It took her about two seconds to spill that Kelly had an abortion when she was thirteen. Or, 'a abortion' as Mindy said."

Sam leaned her head against her hand. This information shed new light on Kelly Wilson. If the girl had been pregnant before, then surely she recognized the symptoms now. So why hadn't she told Sam? Was she playing dumb to gain Sam's sympathy? Could anything she'd said be trusted?

"Hey," Charlie said. "I tell you Kelly Wilson's deep, dark secret and all I get is a blank stare?"

"Sorry." Sam sat up in the chair. "Did you watch the video?"

Charlie didn't answer, but she knew about the audio problem. "I'm not sure about the cell phone theory. The sound would have to come from somewhere else. There's a lockdown procedure in case of an active shooter. The teachers do practice drills once a year. Everyone would've been in their rooms, doors shut. If someone made a call to 9-1-1, they wouldn't pick up the conversation in the hallway."

"Judith Pinkman didn't follow procedure," Sam said. "She ran into the hall after Lucy was shot." Sam turned over her pad and kept it angled away from Charlie as she added this to her notes. "She didn't run to her husband, either. She ran straight to Lucy."

"It was clear that he was gone." Charlie indicated the side of her face. Douglas Pinkman's jaw had been shot off almost completely. There had been a bullet hole in his eye cavity.

Sam asked, "So, was Coin lying when he let us believe there was audio of Kelly asking about 'the Baby'?"

"He's a liar, and I'm given to believe that liars always lie." Charlie seemed to think about it for a bit longer. "The cop could've told Coin. He was standing right there in the hallway when Kelly said whatever she said. It really affected him. He got angrier than before, and he was pretty fucking angry before."

Sam finished her notes. "Makes sense."

Charlie asked, "What about the murder weapon?"

"What about it?"

Charlie leaned back against a chair-shaped pile of junk. She picked at a string on her blue jeans, the same one she had picked at this morning.

Sam took a bite of the sandwich. She glanced out the dirty window. This day had been an exhaustively drawn-out one, and the sun had only now begun to set.

Sam pointed to the Coke. "Can I have some?"

Charlie unscrewed the cap. She set the bottle on top of Sam's overturned notes. "Are you going to tell Dad about Huck and the gun?"

"Why does it matter to you?"

Charlie did the half-shrug thing.

Sam asked, "What's going on between you and Ben?"

"Undetermined."

Sam washed down the peanut butter with a mouthful of Coke. Now would be the time to tell Charlie about Anton. To explain that she knew how marriages worked, understood the petty grievances that could build up. She should tell Charlie that it didn't matter. That if you loved someone, you should do everything you could to make it work because the person you adored more than anyone else in the world could complain of a sore throat one day and be dead the next.

Instead, she told her sister, "You need to make things right with Ben."

"I wonder," Charlie said, "how often you would speak if you eradicated the words 'you need' from your vocabulary."

Sam was too tired to argue a losing point. She took another bite of sandwich. She chewed slowly. "I was looking for the picture of Gamma."

"It's on his desk at home."

That fixed it. Sam was not going to the farmhouse.

"There's this." Charlie used her thumb and two fingers to edge a paperback out from under a file box, Jenga-style, without toppling the papers on top.

She handed the book to Sam.

Sam read the title aloud. " 'Weather Prediction by Numerical Process.' " The book appeared ancient but well-read. Sam thumbed through the pages. Pencil markings highlighted paragraphs. The text appeared to be as advertised; a guide to predicting the weather based on a specific algorithm that incorporated barometric pressure, temperature, and humidity. "Whose calculus is this?"

"I was thirteen," Charlie said.

"You weren't a moron." Sam corrected one of the equations. "At least, I didn't think you were."

"It was Gamma's."

Sam's pen stopped.

"She ordered the book before she died. It came a month after," Charlie said. "There's an old weather tower behind the farm."

"Is there really?" Sam had almost drowned in the stream underneath the tower because she was too weak to lift her head from the water.

"Anyway," Charlie said. "Rusty and I were going to fix up the instruments on the weather tower to surprise Gamma. We thought she'd get a kick out of tracking the data. NOAA calls it being a citizen scientist. There are thousands of people around the country who track for them, but computers take care of the reporting now. I guess the book proves she was one step ahead of us. As usual."

Sam flipped through the charts and arcane algorithms. "You know that this is physically unrealistic. The atmosphere has a delicate dynamical balance between the fields of mass and motion."

"Yes, Samantha, everyone knows that." Charlie explained, "Dad and I worked on the calculations together. We'd get the data from the weather equipment every morning, then plug it into the algorithm and predict the weather for the next day. Or at least, we tried to. It made us feel closer to her."

"She would've liked that."

"She would've been furious that I couldn't do the calculus."

Sam shrugged, because it was true.

She slowly paged through the book, not really paying attention to the words. She thought of Charlie when she was little, the way she would work at the kitchen table with her head bent, tongue between her lips, as she did her homework. She always hummed when she did her math. She whistled when she did art projects. Sometimes, she sang aloud lines that she read in books, but only if she thought she was alone. Sam would often hear her low, operatic warbling through the thin wall dividing their rooms. " 'Be worthy, love, and love will come!' " or " 'As God is my witness, I'll never be hungry again!' "

What had happened to that humming, whistling, singing Charlie?

Gamma's death, Sam's injury, had understandably quelled some of that joy, but Sam had seen that gleeful spark in Charlie when they were together that last time in New York. She was making jokes, teasing Ben, humming and singing and generally entertaining herself with her own noise. Her behavior back then reminded Sam of the way she would sometimes find Fosco alone in a room, purring to himself for his own pleasure.

So who was this profoundly unhappy woman that her sister had turned into?

Charlie was picking at the string on her pants again. She sniffed. She touched her fingers to her nose. "Jesus Christ. I'm bleeding again." She continued sniffing to no avail. "Do you have any tissue?"

Kelly Wilson had depleted Sam's supply. She looked around Rusty's office. She opened the desk drawers.

Charlie sniffed again. "Dad's not going to have Kleenex."

Sam found a roll of toilet paper in the bottom drawer. She handed it to Charlie, saying, "You should get your nose set before it's too late. Weren't you in a hospital all night?"

Charlie dabbed at the blood. "It really hurts."

"Are you going to tell me who hit you?"

Charlie looked up from examining the bloody toilet paper. "In the scheme of things, it's not a big deal, but somehow, it's grown into this *thing* and I really don't want to tell you."

"Fair enough." Sam glanced down into the drawer. There was an empty wire frame for files. Rusty had thrown a stack of letters on top of a dog-eared copy of a three-year-old volume of *Georgia Court Rules and Procedures*. Sam was about to close the drawer when she saw the return address on one of the envelopes.

Handwritten.

Angry, precise letters.

GEORGIA DIAGNOSTIC & CLASSIFICATION PRISON
PO BOX 3877
JACKSON, GA 30233

Sam froze.

The Georgia D&C.

Death-row inmates were housed at the facility.

"What's wrong?" Charlie asked. "Did you find something dead?"

Sam could not see the name above the address. Another envelope obscured the inmate's personal information, except for one half of the first letter.

Sam could see a curved line, possibly part of an *O*, possibly a hastily written *I*, or perhaps the edge of a capital letter *C*.

The rest of the name was covered by a bulk mailer advertising Christmas wreaths.

"Please don't tell me it's porn." Charlie walked around the desk. She stared down into the drawer.

Sam stared, too.

Charlie said, "Everything in here is Dad's private property. We have no right to look at it."

Sam reached into the drawer with her pen.

She pushed away the brightly colored mailer.

CULPEPPER, ZACHARIAH INMATE #4252619

Charlie said, "It's probably a death threat. You saw the Culpeppers today. Every time it looks like Zachariah might finally get an execution date—"

Sam picked up the letter. The weight was nothing, though she felt a heaviness in the bones of her fingers. The flap had already been ripped open.

Charlie said, "Sam, that's private."

Sam pulled out a single notebook page. Folded twice to fit inside the envelope. Blank on the back. Zachariah Culpepper had taken the time to tear off the tattered edges where the paper had been ripped from the metal spiral.

He had used those same fingers to shred apart Sam's eyelids.

"Sam," Charlie said. She was looking in the drawer. There were dozens more letters from the murderer. "We don't have a right to read any of these."

"What do you mean, 'right'?" Sam demanded. Her throat choked around the word. "I have a *right* to know what the man who murdered my mother is telling my father."

Charlie snatched away the letter.

She threw it back into the drawer and kicked it closed with her foot.

"That's perfect." Sam dropped the empty envelope onto the desk. She pulled at the drawer. It would not budge. Charlie had kicked the front panel past the frame. "Open it."

"No," Charlie said. "We don't need to read anything he has to say."

" 'We'," Sam repeated, because she was not the lunatic whose idea it was to pick a fight with Danny Culpepper today. "Since when has it ever been 'we' where the Culpeppers are concerned?"

"What the hell does that mean?"

"Nothing. It's pointless to discuss." Sam reached down and pulled on the drawer again. Nothing moved. Her fingers might as well be feathers.

Charlie said, "I knew you were still pissed at me."

"I'm not *still* pissed at you," Sam countered. "I am *newly* pissed at you, because you are acting like a three-year-old."

"Sure," Charlie agreed. "Whatever you say, Sammy. I'm a three-year-old. Fine."

"What the hell is going on with you?" Sam could feel her own anger feeding off Charlie's. "I want to read the letters from the man who murdered our mother."

"You know what they say," Charlie said. "You've been in town one day and you already heard it from the bastard's bastard himself: we lied. He's innocent. We're killing him because of some fucking legal bill that Dad would've never collected on anyway."

Sam knew that she was right, but that did not change her mind. "Charlie, I'm tired. Can you please open the damn drawer?"

"Not until you tell me why you stayed today. Why you did the arraignment. Why you're still here now."

Sam felt as if she had an anvil on either shoulder. She leaned against the desk. "Okay, you want to know why I stuck around today? Because I cannot believe how much you have screwed up your life."

Charlie snorted so hard that blood dripped from her nose. She wiped it away with her fingers. "Because your life is so fucking perfect?"

"You have no idea what—"

"You put a thousand miles between us. You never return Dad's phone calls, or Ben's emails, or call any of us, for that matter. You apparently fly down to Atlanta all the time, less than two hours away, and you never—"

"You told me not to reach out to you. 'Neither one of us will ever move forward if we are always looking back.' Those were your exact words."

Charlie shook her head, which only served to amplify Sam's irritation.

"Charlotte, you've been trying to pick this fight all day," Sam said. "Stop shaking your head as if I'm some kind of madwoman."

"You're not a madwoman, you're a fucking bitch." Charlie crossed her arms. "I told you we shouldn't look back. I didn't say we shouldn't look forward, or try to move forward together, like sisters are supposed to."

"Excuse me if I could not read between the lines of your poorly constructed invective on the status of our failed relationship."

"Well, you were shot in the head, so I'm sure there's a hole where your invective processing used to be."

Sam gripped together her hands. She was not going to explode. "I have the letter. Do you want me to send you a copy?"

"I want you to go to the copy store, duplex it for me, and then shove it up your tight Yankee ass."

"Why would I duplex a single-page letter?"

"Jesus Christ!" Charlie punched her fist into the desktop. "You've been here less than a day, Sam. Why is my miserable, pathetic little life suddenly such a huge concern for you?"

"Those are not my adjectives."

"You just pick at me." Charlie jabbed Sam's shoulder with her fingers. "Pick and pick like a fucking needle."

"Really?" Sam ignored the lightning strike of pain every time Charlie poked her shoulder. "*I* pick at *you*?"

"Asking me about Ben." She jabbed again, harder. "Asking me about Rusty." She jabbed again. "Asking me about Huck." She jabbed again. "Asking me about—"

"Stop it!" Sam yelled, slapping away her hand. "Why are you so fucking antagonistic?"

"Why are you so fucking annoying?"

"Because you were supposed to be happy!" Sam yelled, the sound of the truth like a shock to her senses. "My body is useless! My brain is—" She threw her hands into the air. "Gone! Everything I was supposed to be is gone. I can't see. I can't run. I can't move. I can't process. I have no sense of ease. I get no comfort—ever. And I tell myself every day—every single day, Charlotte—that it doesn't matter because you were able to get away."

"I did get away!"

"For what?" Sam raged. "So you can antagonize the Culpeppers? So you can turn into Rusty? So you can get punched in the face? So you can destroy your marriage?" Sam swept a pile of magazines onto the floor. She gasped at the pain that sliced up her arm. Her bicep spasmed. Her shoulder seized. She leaned against the desk, breathless.

Charlie stepped forward.

"No." Sam did not want her help. "You were supposed to have children. You were supposed to have friends who love you, and to live in your beautiful house with your wonderful husband, not throw it all away for some feckless asshole like Mason Huckabee."

"That's—"

"Not fair? Not right? That's not what happened with Ben? That's not what happened in college? That's not what happened whenever the fuck you felt like running away because *you* blame yourself, Charlie, *not me*. I don't blame you for running. Gamma wanted you to run. I *begged* you to run. What I blame you for is hiding—from your life, from me, from your own happiness. You think I'm closed off? You think I'm cold? You are *consumed* with self-hatred. You reek of it. And you think that putting everyone and everything in a separate compartment is the only way to pick up the pieces."

Charlie said nothing.

"I'm off in New York. Rusty's in his tilted windmill. Ben's over here. Mason's over there. Lenore's wherever the hell she is. That's no way to live, Charlie. You were not built for that kind of life. You're so clever, and industrious, and you were always so annoyingly, so relentlessly *happy*." Sam kneaded her shoulder. The muscle was on fire. She asked her sister, "What happened to that person, Charlie? You ran. *You got away*."

Charlie stared down at the floor. Her jaw was tight. Her breathing was labored.

So was Sam's. She could feel the rapid rise and fall of her chest. Her fingers trembled like the stuck second hand on a clock. She felt as if the world was spinning out of control. Why did Charlie keep pushing her? What was she trying to accomplish?

Lenore knocked on the open door. "Everything okay in here?"

Charlie shook her head. Blood dripped from her nose.

Lenore joked, "Should I call the cops?"

"Call a taxi." Charlie gripped the drawer handle. She heaved it open. The wood splintered. Zachariah Culpepper's letters scattered onto the floor. She said, "Go home, Samantha. You were right. This place makes you too mean."

CHAPTER THIRTEEN

S am sat across from Lenore at a booth in the otherwise empty diner. She slowly dipped her tea sachet into the hot water the waitress had brought to the table. She could feel Lenore watching her, but she did not know what to say.

"It'll be faster if I drive you to the hospital," Lenore offered.

Sam shook her head. She would wait for the taxi. "You don't have to stay with me."

Lenore held her coffee cup between her hands. Her nails were neatly trimmed and clear polished. She wore a single ring on her right index finger. She saw Sam looking and said, "Your mother gave me this."

Sam thought the ring looked like something her mother would wear—unusual, not particularly pretty, but striking in its own way. Sam asked, "Tell me about her."

Lenore held up her hand and studied the ring. "Lana, my sister, worked at Fermilab with her. They weren't in the same department, or even on the same level, but single gals weren't allowed to live on their own back then, so they were assigned housing together at the university. That was the only way my mother would let Lana work there, so long as she was kept away from the sex-mad male scientists."

Sam waited for her to continue.

"Lana brought Harriet home over Christmas break, and I ig-nored her at first, but then there was a night when I couldn't sleep, and I walked out into the backyard for some air, and there she was." Lenore raised her eyebrows. "She was looking up at the stars. Physics was her calling, but astronomy was her passion."

Sam felt sad that she had never known this about her mother.

"We talked all night. It was very rare for me to find someone who was that interesting. We sort of fell into dating, but there was never anything . . ." She shrugged off the details. "We were together for a little over a year, though it was a long-distance relationship. I was in law school with Rusty. Why that didn't work out is another story. But one summer, I took your father up to Chicago with me, and he swept her off her feet." She shrugged. "I bowed out. We were always more friends than lovers."

"But she was constantly mad at you," Sam said. "I could hear it in her voice."

"I kept her husband out late drinking and smoking instead of spending time with his family." Lenore shrugged again. "She always wanted a conventional life."

Sam could not imagine her mother wanting any such thing. "She was far from conventional."

"People always want what they can't have," Lenore said. "Harry never quite fit in, even at Fermi. She was too peculiar. She lacked the social graces. I suppose now they'd say she was somewhere on the spectrum, but back then, she was just considered too smart, too accomplished, too odd. Especially for a woman."

"So what was a normal life for her?"

"Marriage. A social construct. You girls. She was never so happy as when she had you. Watching your brain develop. Studying your reactions to new stimuli. She kept pages and pages of journals."

"You make me sound like a science project."

"Your mother loved projects," Lenore said. "Charlie was so different, though. So creative. So spontaneous. Harriet adored her; she adored you both, but she never understood anything about Charlie."

"Something we share." Sam drank her tea. The milk tasted off. She put down the mug. "Why don't you like me?"

"You hurt Charlie."

"Charlie seems quite capable of hurting herself."

Lenore reached into her purse and found the USB drive that Ben had given her. "I want you to take this."

Sam backed away, as if the thing posed a physical threat.

"Toss it somewhere in Atlanta." Lenore slid the Starship across the table. "Do it for Ben. You know what kind of trouble he could get into."

Sam did not know what to do but throw the thing into her own purse. She could not take the drive on the plane back to New York. She would have to find someone in the Atlanta office to destroy it.

Lenore said, "You can talk to me about the case, you know. Coin will never call me to the stand. I'd blow up any jury dressed like this."

Sam knew that she was right, just as she knew that the truth was wrong.

Lenore said, "The bullets are bothering me. The wild shot in the wall doesn't make sense. Kelly was able to hit Pinkman three times: once in the chest, twice in the head. That's either a lucky break or a damn good shot."

"Lucy." Sam touched the side of her neck. "That wasn't square on."

"No, but listen. You don't get to be a woman like me in Pikeville without making sure you know how to handle a gun. I couldn't hit those targets at the range, and that's with no pressure, no lives on the line. We're talking an eighteen-year-old girl standing in the hallway waiting for the bell to ring. Her adrenaline must have been through the roof. Either she's the coldest killer this town has ever run across or something else is going on."

"What could be the something else?"

"I have no idea."

Sam thought about Kelly's pregnancy. Adam Humphrey. The yearbook. These were pieces to a puzzle that she would likely never see come together.

She told Lenore, "I've never broken confidence before."

Lenore shrugged, as if it was nothing.

Sam felt guilty for even contemplating the breach, even more so because she was not confiding in her sister. Still, she finally admitted, "Kelly might be pregnant."

Lenore drank her coffee and said nothing.

"She mentioned Adam Humphrey when we spoke. I think he might be the father. Or Frank Alexander." Sam added, "Apparently, this is Kelly's second pregnancy. There was an earlier one in middle school that, according to gossip, was terminated. Charlie knows about that one. She doesn't know that Kelly might be pregnant now."

Lenore put down her cup. "Coin will say that it's Frank Alexander's, and Kelly murdered Lucy out of spite or jealousy."

"There's a simple test that will prove paternity."

"Rusty can make them wait until the kid is born. Undue burden. Those tests don't come without risk." She asked, "Do you think that Adam Humphrey or Frank Alexander talked Kelly into bringing a gun to school for some unknown reason? Or do you think she did it on her own?"

"The only thing I'm certain of is that Kelly Wilson is the last person we can rely on for the truth." Sam pressed her fingers into her temple, trying to smooth away some of the tension. "I've seen videos of false confessions before—in law school, on television, in documentaries. The West Memphis Three, Brendan Dassey, Chuck Erickson. We've all seen them, or read about them, but when you're sitting across from a person who is so suggestible, so eager to please, that they will literally follow you down any road—not even a winding road—it's quite unbelievable."

Sam tried to think back on her conversation with Kelly, to analyze it, to understand exactly what had happened. "I suppose it's some sort of confirmation bias that comes into play. You keep telling yourself that it's not possible for someone to be so slow, that they must be playing a trick on you, but the fact is, they don't have the mental acuity to fool you. They're too low functioning for that level of subterfuge, and if they were so high functioning that they were capable of deceiving you, then they wouldn't be stupid enough to implicate themselves in the first place." Sam realized that she was nattering on like Charlie. She tried to be more succinct. "I talked Kelly Wilson into saying that she witnessed Charlie slapping Judith Pinkman across the face."

"Good Christ." Lenore's hand covered her heart. She was likely offering up a prayer of thanks that a video proving otherwise was in their possession.

"It was so easy to get her to say it," Sam admitted. "I knew that she was tired, she was feeling sick, she was confused and scared and lonely. And in less than five minutes, I talked her into not only repeating what I'd said, but validating it, even making up fresh details, like that the slap was so loud that she could hear it down the hall; all in support of the lie I'd fed her." Sam shook her head, because she still could not believe it. "I've always known that I live in a different type of world from most people, but Kelly is at the bottom of the pile. I don't mean that to be cruel, or arrogant. It's simply a matter of fact. There's a reason girls like that get lost."

"You mean led astray?" Lenore suggested.

Sam shook her head again, unwilling to attach herself to any one theory.

"I already put Jimmy Jack on the Humphrey boy. He's probably got him tracked down by now."

"Lucy Alexander's father can't be entirely ruled out," Sam reminded her. "Just because we don't want Ken Coin to be right, that doesn't make it so."

"If anybody can get to the bottom of why this happened, it's Jimmy Jack."

Sam wondered if the net would be cast wide enough to include Mason Huckabee, but she knew better than to bring up her sister's lover to Lenore. Instead, she said, "Figuring out Kelly's motive won't bring back the victims."

"No, but it could keep a third victim off death row."

Sam pursed her lips. She was not wholly convinced that Kelly Wilson had been a victim. Low functioning or not, she had taken a gun to school and pulled the trigger enough times to brutally murder two innocent people. Sam felt fortunate that the girl's fate did not rest on her shoulders. There was a reason that juries were supposed to be impartial. Then again, the likelihood that an impartial jury would be found within one hundred miles of Pikeville was so remote as to be absurd.

"Your taxi will be here soon." Lenore looked for the waitress, holding up her hand for attention.

Sam turned around. The woman was sitting at the counter. "Excuse me?"

The waitress pushed herself up from the counter and returned to their table with visible reluctance. She sighed before asking Sam, "What?"

Sam looked at Lenore, who shook her head. "I'm ready to pay the bill."

The woman slapped the check down on the table. She picked up Lenore's mug between her thumb and index finger as if she was scared of contaminants.

Sam waited for the awful woman to leave. She asked Lenore, "Why do you live here? In this backward place?"

"It's my home. And there are still some good people here who believe in live-and-let-live." Lenore added, "Besides, New York lost the moral high ground during the last presidential election."

Sam gave a rueful laugh.

"I'm going to go check on Charlie." Lenore took a dollar bill out of her wallet, but Sam waved her off.

"Thank you," Sam said, though she could only guess at what Lenore had done for her family. Sam had always been so wrapped up in the agony of her own recovery that she had not given much consideration to what life had been like for Rusty and Charlie. Lenore had obviously filled some of the void left by Gamma.

Sam heard the bell over the door clatter as Lenore left. The waitress made a nasty remark to the cook. Sam considered correcting her, cutting her in two with a sharp comment, but she lacked the energy to fight any more battles today.

She went to the bathroom. She stood at the sink and performed a perfunctory wash as she dreamed of the shower at the Four Seasons back in Atlanta. Sixteen hours had passed since Sam had left New York. She'd spent almost twice as many hours awake. Her head had the dull ache of a rotting tooth. Her body was uncooperative. She looked at her tired, ragged face in the mirror and saw her mother's bitter disappointment.

Sam was giving up on Charlie.

There was no other option. Charlie would not speak to her, would not open her locked office door that Sam had knocked on repeatedly. This was not like the last time when Charlie had fled in the middle of the night, fearing for her safety. This was Sam begging, apologizing—for what, she did not know—only to be met with Charlie's stark silence. Finally, unhappily, Sam felt herself relent to what she should have known all along.

Charlie did not need her.

Sam used some toilet paper to wipe her eyes. She did not know if she was crying from the uselessness of her journey or from exhaustion. Twenty years ago, the loss of her sister had felt like a mutual agreement. Sam had exploded. Charlie had exploded back. There was a fight, an actual, drag-down fight, and they had both agreed in the end to walk away.

This latest break came more like a theft. Sam had grasped something good, something that felt true, in her hands, and Charlie had wrenched it away.

Was it because of Zachariah Culpepper?

Sam had the letters in her purse. Some of them, at least, because there were many, many more back at Rusty's. Sam had stood behind his desk opening envelope after envelope. They all held the same type of single, folded notebook paper, and had the same three words written on them with such a heavy hand that the pencil had embossed the paper:

YOU OWE ME.

One line, mailed hundreds of times, once a month to Rusty's office.

Sam's phone chirped.

She scrambled to find it in her purse. Not Charlie. Not Ben. There was a text message from the taxi company. The driver was outside.

Sam patted her eyes dry. She ran her fingers through her hair. She went back to the booth. She left a one-dollar bill on the table. She rolled her suitcase out to the waiting taxi. The man jumped out to help her load it into the trunk. Sam took her place in the back seat. She stared out the window as the man drove her through downtown Pikeville.

Stanislav was going to meet her at the hospital. Sam was reluctant to see her father, but she had a responsibility to Rusty, to Kelly Wilson, to turn over her notes, to share her thoughts and suspicions.

Lenore was right about the bullets. Kelly had shown remarkable firing accuracy in the hallway. She had managed to hit both Douglas Pinkman and Lucy Alexander from a considerable distance.

So why hadn't Kelly been able to shoot Judith Pinkman when the woman came out of her room?

More mysteries for Rusty to solve.

Sam rolled down the window in the taxi. She looked up at the stars dotting the sky. There was so much light pollution in New York that Sam had forgotten what the nighttime was supposed to look like. The moon was little more than a sliver of blue light. She took off her glasses. She felt the fresh air on her face. She let her eyelids close. She thought of Gamma looking at the stars. Had that magnificent, brilliant woman really craved a conventional life?

A housewife. A mother. A husband to take care of her; a vow to take care of him.

Sam's enduring memory of her mother was one of Gamma always searching. For knowledge. For information. For solutions. Sam remembered one of the many, anonymous days she had come home from school to find Gamma working on a project. Charlie was at a friend's. They were still living in the red-brick house. Sam had opened the back door. She dropped her bag on the kitchen floor. She kicked off her shoes. Gamma turned around. She had a marker in her hand. She had been writing on the large window that overlooked the backyard. Equations, Sam could see, though their meaning was elusive.

"I'm trying to figure out why my cake fell," Gamma had explained. "That's the problem with life, Sam. If you're not rising, you're falling."

The taxi bumped Sam awake.

For a panicked second, she was unsure of her surroundings.

Sam put on her glasses. Almost half an hour had passed. They were already in Bridge Gap. Four- and five-story office buildings sprouted up above cafés. Signs advertised concerts in the park and family picnics. They passed the movie theater where Mary-Lynne Huckabee had gone with her friends and ended up being raped in the bathroom.

Such violent men in this county.

Sam put her hand over her purse. The letters inside gave off a palpable heat.

YOU OWE ME.

Did Sam care what Zachariah Culpepper felt he was owed? Almost three decades ago, Rusty had argued for the man's life to be spared. If anything, Zachariah owed Rusty. And Sam. And Charlie. And Ben, if it came to that.

Sam unlocked her phone.

She pulled up a new email and typed in Ben's address. Her fingers could not decide on a combination of letters to press for the subject line. Charlie's name? A request for advice? An apology that she had not been able to fix what was broken?

That Charlie was broken was the only fact Sam saw with any clarity. Her sister had wanted Sam to come home for *something*. So that Sam would push Charlie into admitting something, giving away something, telling the truth about something that was bothering her. There was no other reason for the constant provocation, the lashing out, the pushing away.

Sam was familiar with the tactics. She had been so volatile after getting shot, infuriated by the weakness of her body, livid that her brain was not working as it had before, that there was not one person who was spared her temper. The steroids and antidepressants and anticonvulsants the doctors had prescribed only inflamed her emotions. Sam had felt furious most of the time, and the only thing that had made the anger lessen was to direct it outward.

Charlie and Rusty were the two targets she hit the hardest.

After rehab, the six months that Sam had lived at the farmhouse had been hell for everyone. Sam was never satisfied. She was always complaining. She had tortured Charlie, made her feel as if nothing she did was right. When anyone suggested therapy for her moods, Sam had screamed like a banshee, insisting that she was fine, that she was recovering, that she was *not fucking angry*—she was just tired, she was just annoyed, she just needed space, time, a chance to be alone, to get away, to recover her sense of self.

Finally, Rusty had allowed Sam to take the GED so that she could gain early acceptance to Stanford. It wasn't until Sam was at school, 2,500 miles away, that she had realized that her anger was not a creature solely confined to the farmhouse.

You could only ever see a thing when you were standing outside of it.

Sam was angry at Rusty for bringing the Culpeppers into their lives. She was angry at Charlie for opening the kitchen door. She was angry at Gamma for grabbing the shotgun. She was angry at herself for not listening to her gut when she stood in the bathroom, gripping the ball-peen hammer in her hand, and walked toward the kitchen instead of running out the back door.

She was angry. She was angry. She was so God damn, fucking angry.

Yet, Sam was thirty-one years old before she gave herself permission to say the words aloud. The blow-up with Charlie had opened the scab, and Anton, in his very deliberate way, had been the only reason that the wound had finally begun to heal.

Sam was at his apartment. New Year's Eve. On television, they watched the ball drop in Times Square. They were drinking champagne, or at least Sam was pretending to.

Anton had said, "It's bad luck if you don't take a sip."

Sam had laughed it off, because by that point, bad luck had followed her for more than half her life. Then she had admitted to him something that she had never before confessed to anyone else. "I worry all the time that I'll drink something, or take something, or move the wrong way, and it will cause a seizure, or a stroke, and break what's left of my mind."

Anton had not offered platitudes about the mysteries of life or advice on how to fix the problem. Instead, he had said, "Many people must have told you that you are lucky to be alive. I think you would have been lucky had you not been shot in the first place."

Sam had cried for almost a full hour.

Everyone constantly, incessantly, told her that she had been lucky to survive the shooting. No one had ever acknowledged that she had a right to be angry about *how* she must survive.

"Ma'am?" The taxi driver flipped up the turn signal. He pointed to the white sign up ahead.

The Dickerson County Hospital. Rusty would be in his room watching the news, likely trying to catch a glimpse of himself. He would know about Sam's courtroom performance. She felt her butterflies return, then chastised herself for caring about anything to do with Rusty.

Sam was only here to turn over her notes. She would say

goodbye to her father, probably the last time she would ever say goodbye in person, then head back to Atlanta where, tomorrow morning, she would wake up with her real life restored like Dorothy back in Kansas.

The driver stopped underneath the concrete canopy. He pulled Sam's suitcase from the trunk. He lifted up the handle. Sam was rolling the case toward the entrance when she smelled cigarette smoke.

" 'Oh, I am fortune's fool,' " Rusty bellowed. He was in a wheelchair, right elbow on the armrest, cigarette in his hand. Two IV bags were attached to a pole on the back of the chair. His catheter bag hung down like a chatelaine. He had stationed himself beneath a sign warning smokers to maintain a perimeter of one hundred feet from the door. He was twenty feet away, if that.

Sam said, "Those things are going to kill you."

Rusty smiled. "It's a balmy night. I'm talking to one of my beautiful daughters. I've got a fresh pack of smokes. All I need is a glass of bourbon and I'd die a happy man."

Sam waved away the smoke. "It's not so balmy with that smell."

He laughed, then started coughing.

Sam rolled her suitcase to the concrete bench by his chair. The reporters were gone, probably on to the next mass shooting. She sat on the far end of the bench, upwind from the smoke.

Rusty said, "I heard there was some rain-making at the arraignment."

Sam shrugged one shoulder. She had picked up the bad habit from Charlie.

" 'Was the baby killed?' " He made his voice quiver with drama. " 'Was the baby killed?' "

"Dad, a child was murdered."

"I know, darling. Believe me, I know." He took one last hit off his cigarette before stubbing it out on the bottom of his slipper. He dropped the butt into the pocket of his robe. "A trial is nothing but a competition to tell the best story. Whoever sways the jury wins the trial. And Ken's come right out the gate with a damn good story."

Sam quelled the urge to be her father's cheerleader, to tell him he could come up with the better story and save the day.

Rusty asked, "What'd you think of her?"

"Kelly?" Sam considered her answer. "I'm not sure. She could be smarter than we think. She could be lower functioning than any of us wants to believe. You can lead her anywhere, Dad. Anywhere."

"I've always preferred crazy to stupid. Stupid can break your heart." Rusty looked over his shoulder, checking to make sure they were alone. "I heard about the abortion."

Sam pictured her sister back in her office, calling Rusty to tattle. "You spoke to Charlie."

"Nope." Rusty leaned on his elbow, hand up, fingers spread, as if the cigarette were still there. "Jimmy Jack, that's my investigator, came up with it yesterday afternoon. We found some evidence from Kelly's middle-school days that pointed to something bad going on. Just rumors, you know. Kelly shows up plump one week, then she takes a vacation and comes back skinny. I confirmed the abortion with her mother last night. She was still real torn up about it. The baby daddy was a kid on the football team, long since left town. He paid for the abortion, or his family did. The mama took her down to Atlanta. Almost lost her job from taking the time off."

Sam said, "Kelly could be pregnant again."

Rusty's eyebrows went up.

"She's been throwing up the same time of day, every day. She's missed school. She's got a bump in her belly."

"She's started wearing dark clothes lately. The mama said she has no idea why."

Sam realized an obvious point she hadn't yet mentioned to Rusty. "Mason Huckabee has a connection to Kelly."

"He does."

Sam waited for more, but Rusty just gazed out into the parking lot.

She told him, "Lenore already has your investigator on this, but there's a boy named Adam Humphrey that Kelly has a crush on. You could also look at Frank Alexander, Lucy's father." She tried again, "Or Mason Huckabee."

Rusty scratched his cheek. For the second time, he ignored the man's name. "Her being pregnant—that's not good."

"It could help your case."

"It could, but she's still an eighteen-year-old girl with a baby in her belly and a lifetime of prison ahead of her." He added, "If she's lucky."

"I thought she was your unicorn."

"Do you know how many innocent people are in prison?"

"I'd rather not know." Sam asked, "Why do you think she's innocent? What else have you learned?"

"I have learned nothing, in general or in specific. It's this—" he pointed to his gut. "The knife just missed my intuition. It is still intact. It still tells me that there is more to this than meets the eye."

"My eyes have seen quite a lot," Sam said. "Did Lenore tell you that she managed to get her hands on the security footage?"

"I also heard that you and your sister almost resorted to fisticuffs in my office." Rusty covered his heart with his hands. "May the circle be unbroken."

Sam didn't want to make light of this. "Dad, what's wrong with her?"

Rusty stared out at the parking lot. Bright lights glared against the parked cars. " 'There ain't no sin and there ain't no virtue. There's just stuff people do.' "

Sam was certain Charlie would recognize the quote. "I've never understood your relationship with her. You two talk all the time, but you never say anything of substance." Sam imagined two roosters circling each other in the barnyard. "I guess that's why she was always your favorite."

"You were both my favorite."

Sam didn't buy it. Charlie had always been the good daughter, the one who laughed at his jokes, the one who challenged his opinions, the one who had stayed.

Rusty said, "A father's job is to love each of his daughters in the way they need to be loved."

Sam laughed out loud at the silly platitude. "How did you never win father of the year?"

Rusty chuckled along with her. "The one disappointment in my life is that I have never received one of those father of the year coffee mugs." He reached into the pocket of his robe. He found his pack of cigarettes. "Did Charlotte tell you about her personal involvement with Mason?"

"Are we finally going to talk about that?"

"In our own roundabout way."

Sam said, "*I* told her about Mason. She had no idea who he was."

Rusty took his time lighting the cigarette. He coughed out a few puffs of smoke. He picked a piece of tobacco off his tongue. "I could never again represent a rapist after that day."

Sam was surprised by the revelation. "You've always said that everyone deserves a chance."

"They do, but I don't have to be the one who gives it to them." Rusty coughed out more smoke. "When I looked at the photos of that girl, Mary-Lynne was her name, I realized something about rape that I had never understood before." He rolled his cigarette between his fingers. He looked at the parking lot, not Sam.

He said, "What a rapist takes from a woman is her future. The person she is going to become, who she is supposed to be, is gone. In many ways, it's worse than murder, because he has killed that potential person, eradicated that potential life, yet she still lives and breathes, and has to figure out another way to thrive." He waved his hand in the air. "Or not, in some cases."

"Sounds a lot like being shot in the head."

Rusty coughed as smoke caught in his throat.

He said, "Charlotte has always been a pack animal. She doesn't need to be the leader, but she needs to be in a group. Ben was her group."

"Why did she cheat on him?"

"It's not my place to tell you about your sister."

Sam could not keep talking in circles, though she knew that Rusty could gladly spin around all night. She pulled her notes from her purse. "I've got some other things you should follow up on. Kelly doesn't seem to know the victims. I'm not sure if that makes it better or worse." Sam knew it made things worse from her perspective. She had never become indifferent to the randomness of violence. "You're going to want to nail down the sequence and number of bullets fired. There seems to be some confusion."

Rusty talked through the list. "Pregnancy: question mark. Paternity: big question mark. Video: we got one, thanks to you-know-who, but we'll see if that ol' snake Mr. Coin follows the judge's order." He thumped the paper with his finger. "Yes, why indeed was Kelly at the middle school? Victims random." He looked at Sam. "You're sure she didn't know them?"

Sam shook her head. "I asked and she said no, but it's worth a follow-up."

"Follow-ups are my favorite things." He looked at the last line on the list. "Judith Pinkman. I saw her on the news earlier. Quite the conversion with this 'turn the other cheek' line." He folded the list back in two and put it in his pocket. "When Zachariah Culpepper was on trial, she wanted to flip the switch herself. This was back when they still electrocuted people. Remember everybody who committed a crime before May of 2000 was grandfathered in."

Sam had read about the methods of execution during law school. She had found the process barbaric until she imagined Zachariah Culpepper pissing himself the same way Charlie had as he awaited the first delivery of 1,800 volts.

Rusty said, "She wanted Gamma's murderer to be executed and she wants her husband's murderer to be spared."

Sam shrugged. "People mellow when they get older. Some people."

"I will take that as a compliment," Rusty said. "As to Judith Pinkman, I would say: 'It is better to be sometimes right than at all times wrong.'"

Sam decided now was as good a time as any to drop Charlie's problem back into Rusty's lap. "Kelly told me that Mason Huckabee put the murder weapon down the back of his pants. I'm assuming he walked it out of the building. You need to figure out why he took such a huge risk."

Rusty did not respond. He smoked his cigarette. He stared out into the parking lot.

"Dad," Sam said. "He took the murder weapon from the scene. He's either involved somehow or he's an idiot."

"I told you stupid breaks your heart."

"You came to that conclusion pretty quickly."

"Did I?"

Sam was not going to volley back his riddles. Rusty obviously knew something that he was not sharing. "You'll have to turn Mason in for the gun. Other than Judith Pinkman, he's probably Coin's strongest witness."

"I'll find another way."

Sam shook her head. "Excuse me?"

"I'll find another way to neutralize Mason Huckabee. No need to put a man in jail for making a stupid mistake."

"We'd have to let half of them out if that was the standard." Sam rubbed her eyes. She was too drained for this conversation. "Is this guilt on your part? Some sort of penance? I don't know if giving Mason a pass makes you a hypocrite or soft-hearted, because you're clearly trying to protect Charlie at the expense of your client."

"Probably both," Rusty admitted. "Samantha, I will tell you something very important: there is value in forgiveness."

Sam thought about the letters in her purse. She was not sure she wanted to know why her mother's murderer, the man who had tried to rape her sister, who had stood by while Sam was shot in the head, was reaching out to Rusty. In truth, Sam was afraid that her father had forgiven him, and that she could never forgive Rusty for having given Zachariah Culpepper's conscience a reprieve.

Rusty asked, "Have you ever been to an execution?"

"Why on earth would I attend an execution?"

Rusty stubbed out his cigarette. He slipped it into his pocket. He held out his arm to Sam. "Feel my pulse." He saw her expression. "Humor your old man before you get back on a plane home."

Sam pressed her fingers to the inside of his bony wrist. At first, she felt nothing but the thick line of his flexor carpi radialis. She moved her fingers around, then located the steady *tap-tap-tap* of blood pulsing through his veins.

She said, "Got it."

"When a person is executed," Rusty began. "You sit in the viewing area, and there's the family down front and a pastor and a reporter and then on the other side, there's you, the person who couldn't stop any of this from happening." Rusty put his hand over Sam's. His skin was rough and dry. She realized that this was the first time she had touched her father in almost thirty years.

He continued, "They pull back the drape, and there he is, this human being, this living, breathing creature. Is he a monster? Perhaps he has done monstrous deeds. But now, he is strapped down in a bed. His arms and legs, his head, are pinned so that he cannot make eye contact with any one person. He's staring up at the ceiling, where the tiles have been painted with white clouds and a blue sky. Cartoonish in nature, likely done by another inmate. This is the last thing this condemned man will ever see."

Rusty pressed her fingers closer against his wrist. His heart rate had accelerated.

"So what you notice is that his chest is pumping as he tries to control his breath. And that's when you feel it." He tapped the top of her fingers. "Dum-dum. Dum-dum. You feel your own blood pumping through your body. You feel your own breath swishing in and out of your lungs."

Without thinking, Sam had let her breathing match her father's.

"Then they ask him for his last words, and he says something about forgiveness, or hoping his death brings the family peace, or that he is innocent, but his voice is shaking, because he knows this is it. The red phone on the wall will not ring. He will never see his mother again. He will never hold his child. This is it. His death is nigh."

Sam pressed together her lips. She could not tell if her own heartbeat was matching the cadence of Rusty's or if she had let herself again get wrapped up in his words.

He said, "The warden nods the go-ahead. There's two men in the room. They each press separate buttons to deliver the drug cocktail. This is so no one knows for sure who killed him." Rusty was silent for a few seconds, as if he was watching the buttons being pressed. "You get a taste in your mouth, like a chemical, like you can taste the thing that's about to kill him. He tenses, and then slowly, surely, his muscles start to let go until he is completely, utterly without movement. And that's when you start to feel it, this sensation of tiredness, as if the drug is going into your own veins. And your head starts to nod. You're almost relieved, because you've been so tense the whole time, during the waiting time, and now it's finally seconds from being over." Rusty paused again. "Your heart slows. You feel your breaths start to taper off."

Sam waited for the rest.

Rusty said nothing.

She asked, "And then?"

"And then it's over." He patted her hand. "That's it. They shut the curtains. You leave the room. You get in your car. You go home. You have a drink. You brush your teeth. You go to bed, and you stare at the ceiling for the rest of your life the same way that condemned man stared at the ceiling tiles over his head." He held tight to Sam's hand. "This is what Zachariah Culpepper thinks about every second of his life, and he'll keep thinking about it every day until he's wheeled into that room and they open that curtain."

Sam pulled away from him. The skin of her hand felt tight, as if she'd been singed. "Lenore told you that we found the letters."

"I never was able to keep you girls out of my files." He gripped the arms of his wheelchair. He looked into the distance. "He's being punished. I know you wanted him to suffer. He is suffering. There is no need to pursue anything to do with that man. You need to go back to New York and forget about him. Live your life. That's how you get your revenge."

Sam shook her head. She should have seen this coming. She was infuriated with herself for always letting Rusty hide in her blind spot.

He said, "If you can't do it for yourself, do it for your sister."

"I've tried to help my sister. She doesn't want it."

Rusty grabbed her arm. "Listen to me, baby. You need to hear this, because it's important." He waited until she looked at him. "If you get Charlotte stirred up about Zachariah Culpepper right now, she will never, ever come back from the bad place that she's in."

"What does Zachariah think that you owe him?"

Rusty let her go. He sat back in his chair. "To borrow from Churchill, it is a riddle wrapped in a canard."

"A canard is an unfounded rumor or fable."

"Also, a winglike projection on an airplane. Or, in the French, *duck*."

"Rusty," Sam said. "He mails these letters to you, the same letter with the same message, the second Friday of every month."

"Is that so?"

"You know it's so," Sam said. "It's the same day you always call me."

"I am glad to know you look forward to my phone calls."

Sam shook her head. They both knew those were not her words. "Dad, why does he send you that same letter? What do you owe him?"

"I owe him nothing. On my life." Rusty held up his right hand as if he was swearing on a Bible. "The police know about the letters. It's just something he does. The miserable fuck has got an awful lot of time on his hands. It's easy to keep to a regular schedule."

"So there's nothing behind the letters? He's just an inmate on death row who feels you owe him something?"

"Men in that position often feel they are owed something."

"Please don't tell me there is value in forgiving him."

"There is value in *forgetting* him," Rusty clarified. "I have forgotten him so that I can move on with my life. My mind has rendered his existence immaterial; however, I will never forgive him for taking away my soulmate."

Sam was tempted to roll her eyes.

"I loved your mother more than anything else on this earth. Every day with her was the best day of my life, even if we were screaming at each other at the top of our lungs."

Sam remembered the screaming if not the adulation. "I've never understood what she saw in you."

"A man who did not want to wear her underwear."

Sam laughed, then felt bad for laughing.

"Lenny introduced us. Did you know that?" Rusty did not wait for a response. "He dragged me up north to meet this gal he was kind of dating, and the minute I saw her, I thought a God damn boulder had fallen out of the sky and conked me on the head. I simply could not take my eyes off of her. She was the most beautiful thing I had ever seen. Legs that went on for miles. Lovely curve of her hip." He grinned at Sam. "And of course, lest you think your daddy was a total poonhound, there was the enigma of her mind. My Lord, she knew things. Just blew me away with the breadth and depth of her knowledge. I had never in my life met a woman like that. She was like a cat." He pointed his finger at Sam. "Anyone ever say that about you?"

"I can't say that they have."

"Dogs are stupid," Rusty said. "This is a known fact. But

a cat—you have to earn a cat's respect every single day of your life. You lose it and—" He snapped his fingers. "That's what your mama was to me. She was my cat. She kept my compass pointing true north."

"Your metaphors are mixing."

"Cats sailed with the Vikings."

"To kill rats. Not to navigate the ship," Sam said. "Mama hated what you did."

"She hated the inherent risks in what I did. She hated the hours, without a doubt. But she understood that I needed to do it, and she always respected people who made themselves useful."

Sam heard Gamma's own voice in his words.

Rusty said, "*City of Portland v. Henry Alameda.*"

Sam felt a jolt of shock.

Her first case.

Rusty said, "I sat in the back with my teeth shining so bright I could've shown a cat how to sail a ship away from the rocky shore."

"But, Dad—"

"You were a natural, my girl. Just a damn fine prosecutor. Totally in charge of the courtroom. Never been more proud."

"Why didn't you—"

"I just wanted to check on you, see if you'd found your place." Rusty shook another cigarette out of his pack. "*Clinton Cable Corp. v. Stanley Mercantile Limited.*" He winked at her, as if it was nothing to recite the first patent complaint she had argued completely on her own. "That's your place, Samantha. You have found your way to be useful in this world, and you are undoubtedly the best in the game." He tossed the cigarette into his mouth. "I cannot say that I would've chosen that particular direction to point your remarkable brain, but you are truly in your element when you are discussing the tensile strength of a reinforced cable." He leaned over. He pointed his finger at her chest. "Gamma would have been proud."

Sam felt unwelcome tears in her eyes. She tried to conjure the image of the courtroom, to make herself turn around, to see her father sitting in the back row, but the memory would not come. "I never knew you were there."

"No, you did not. I wanted to see you. You didn't want to see me." He held up his hand to spare her the trouble of making an excuse. "It is a father's job to love his daughter in the way that she needs to be loved."

Instead of joking this time, Sam wiped away tears.

He said, "There's a picture of Gamma in my office that I want you to have."

Sam was surprised. Rusty had no way of knowing that she had spent part of her day thinking about the photo.

He said, "The picture is one you haven't seen before. I'm sorry about that. I always thought I would show it to you girls eventually."

"Charlie hasn't seen it?"

Rusty shook his head. "She has not."

Sam felt a strange lightness in her chest that he was telling her something that Charlie did not know about.

"Now." Rusty took the unlit cigarette out of his mouth. "When this photo was taken, Gamma was standing in a field. There was a weather tower in the distance. Not metal like the one at the farmhouse. It was wooden, an old, rickety thing. And your Gamma was looking at it when Lenny pulled out his camera. She was wearing these shorts." Rusty grinned. "My God, the time I spent with those legs . . ." He gave a low, disconcerting grumble. "Now, the picture you know about, that was taken the same day. We had a picnic spread out on the grass. I called her name, and she looked back at me with her eyebrow up, because I had said something devastatingly intelligent."

Sam smiled despite herself.

"But there's a second picture. My private photo. Gamma's facing the camera, but her head is turned slightly to the side because she's looking at me, and I am looking at her, and when Lenny and I got back home and we got the roll of film back from the Fotomat, I took one look at it, and I said, 'That's the moment when we fell in love.'"

Sam loved the story too much for it to be true. "Did Gamma agree with you?"

"My beautiful daughter." Rusty reached out. He cupped Samantha's chin in his hand. "I say without any guile that my interpretation of this critical moment was the only time in our lives that your mother and I were in complete agreement."

Sam blinked back more tears. "I'd like to see it."

"I will put it in the mail as soon as I am able." Rusty coughed into his hand. "And I will continue calling you, if you don't mind."

Sam nodded. She could not imagine her life in New York without his messages.

Rusty coughed again, a deep sound rattling in his lungs that did not stop him from trying to light his cigarette.

She said, "You know coughing is a sign of congestive heart failure."

He coughed some more. "It is also a sign of thirst."

Sam took the hint. She left her suitcase beside the bench and walked back into the hospital. The gift shop was by the front door. Sam found a bottle of water in the cooler. She waited in line behind an older woman who was intent on paying her bill with all the loose change from the bottom of her purse.

Sam drew in a breath and let it go. She could see Rusty outside. He was leaning on his right elbow again. The lit cigarette was held between his fingers.

The woman in front of Sam was scraping around for pennies. She made small talk with the cashier about her sick friend whom she was visiting upstairs.

Sam glanced around. The drive back to Atlanta would be another two hours. She should probably find something else to eat since she had been too upset to order anything at the diner. She was looking for a Kind Bar when she spotted a display of mugs in the back of the store. MOTHER OF THE YEAR. BEST FRIEND IN THE WORLD. STEPDAD OF THE YEAR. WORLD'S BEST DAD.

Sam picked up the BEST DAD mug. She rolled it in her hand.

She stood on her tiptoes so that she could see Rusty.

He was still leaning in his chair. Smoke curled up around his head. She put the mug back and chose the STEPDAD one because Rusty would think it was funny.

The penny counter was gone from the checkout. Sam found her credit card in her purse. She waited for the chip reader to process the charge.

The cashier said, "Visiting your stepdad?"

Sam nodded, because no normal person would find humor in the explanation.

"I hope he's better soon." The cashier ripped off the receipt and handed it to Sam.

She walked back through the lobby. The hospital doors slid open. Rusty was still by the bench. Sam held up the mug. "Look what I got."

Rusty did not turn to look.

Sam asked, "Dad?"

Rusty wasn't just leaning in his chair. He was listing to the side. His hand had dropped down. His lit cigarette had fallen to the ground.

Sam stepped closer. She looked into her father's face.

Rusty's lips were parted. His eyes stared blankly into the bright lights of the parking lot. His skin looked waxy, almost white.

Sam put her fingers to his wrist. To his neck. She pressed her ear to his chest.

She closed her eyes. She listened. She waited. She prayed.

Sam pulled herself away.

She sat down on the bench.

Her eyes blurred with tears.

Her father was gone.

CHAPTER FOURTEEN

S am woke up on Charlie's couch. She stared up at the white ceiling. Her head had not stopped aching since she had left New York. Last night, she had been unable to navigate the stairs to the guest bedroom. She had barely been capable of making it up the two steps into the house. Her body had started shutting down, her brain unwilling or incapable of fighting off the stress and the exhaustion and the unexpected despondency after finding Rusty dead in his wheelchair.

Normally, at the end of particularly bad days, Sam negotiated with herself about whether or not to add more pharmaceuticals to her daily cocktail of Celebrex for joint paint, Neurontin to ward off seizures, Paroxetine to treat chronic pain, and Cyclobenzaprine for muscle spasms. Did she really need another anti-inflammatory? Could she sleep without another muscle relaxer? Was the pain bad enough for half of an OxyContin, all of a Percocet?

Last night, her body had ached so badly that she had to keep herself from taking everything.

Sam turned her head away from the ceiling. She looked at the photographs lining Charlie's fireplace mantel. Sam had studied them more closely last night before the drugs had taken effect. Rusty sitting in a rocking chair, elbow propped, cigarette in hand, mouth open. Ben wearing a funny hat at a Devils basketball game. Various dogs that had likely passed away. Charlie and Ben standing together at the edge of what looked like a Caribbean beach. Suited up for skiing at the base of a snow-covered mountain. Standing beside a cable suspension for a bridge painted in the unmistakable red of the Golden Gate.

Proof that things had been better at some point in their lives.

Sam felt understandably drugged as she sat up on the couch. Her legs moved stiffly. Her head pounded. Her eyes would not focus. She stared at Charlie's giant television that took up most of the wall. The shadow of her reflection stared back.

Rusty was dead.

Sam had always assumed she would get the news while she was in a meeting, or when she landed in a different city, in a different world. She had assumed his death would elicit a sense of sadness, but a temporary one, the same way she had felt when Charlie had told her Peter Alexander, her old high school boyfriend, had been killed by a car.

Sam had not thought that she would find Rusty herself. That she would be the one required to deliver the news to her sister. That she would find herself so paralyzed by grief that she sat on the bench beside Rusty for half an hour before she could alert the hospital staff.

She had cried for the father she had lost.

She had cried for the father she had never known.

Sam found her glasses on the coffee table. She stretched her legs, starting with her ankles, moving into her calves, then her quads. Her back arched. She pushed her hands out in front of her, raised her arms over her head. When she was ready, she stood up. She performed more stretches until her muscles warmed and her limbs moved with only a modicum of discomfort.

There was no rug on the hardwood floor. Sam doubted Charlie had a yoga mat. She sat cross-legged beside the couch. She stared out at the backyard. The sliding door was cracked open to let in the morning breeze. The rabbit hutch, Charlie's long ago Brownie project, was still standing. Sam had been too overwhelmed with grief to comment on it last night, but she was glad to see that Charlie and Ben had built their home on the old lot where the red-brick house had been.

Not that Ben had stayed here last night. He'd gone upstairs for only a few minutes. Sam had heard the floorboards squeak as he walked into Charlie's room. There was no screaming. There was no crying. Ben had sneaked down the stairs and left the house without telling Sam goodbye.

Sam straightened her spine. She rested the backs of her hands on her knees. Before she could close her eyes, she spotted Charlie pushing a wheelbarrow through the yard. Sam watched her sister spread hay in the rabbit hutch while stray cats mewed at her feet. Bags of food were in the wheelbarrow. Kibble, birdseed, peanuts. Judging by the way Sam's eyes were watering, a dog had at some point lived in the house.

So this was how Charlie spent her time: feeding a menagerie.

Sam tried to push her sister's problems from her conscious. She was not here to fix Charlie, and even if she was, there was no way that Charlie would let her.

She closed her eyes. She pinched together her fingers. She considered the broken parts of her mind. The delicate folds of gray matter. The electrical current of synapses.

Rusty slumped in his wheelchair.

Sam could not clear her mind of the image. The way the left corner of his mouth had curved down. The total absence of his spirit, his spark, that had always been there. The sadness she had felt when Sam had realized that he was gone.

The need for comfort.

The need for Charlie.

Sam did not have her sister's phone number. She was too ashamed to admit this to the hospital staff. Instead, she had emailed Ben, then waited for him to email back. Again, the task of delivering bad news to Charlie had fallen on his shoulders. Her sister had not driven to the hospital, as Sam had expected. Charlie had sent Ben to pick up Sam. She had not come down the stairs when Sam arrived at her home. Sam might as well have been a stranger, though Charlie would never be so rude to someone who was not family.

"Are you having a stroke?" Charlie stood in the open doorway. Her eyes were swollen from crying. The bruises under her eyes had gone completely black.

Sam said, "I was trying to meditate."

"I tried that once. Irritated the shit out of me." She pushed off her boots. Hay was in her hair. She smelled of cat. Sam recognized the logo on her T-shirt from math club, the symbol PI with a snake curling around it. The Pikeville Pythons.

Sam adjusted her glasses. They had not been right since the judge had handled them in the courtroom. She stood up with less difficulty than she expected. She told Charlie, "A possum stared at me through the door all night."

"That's Bill." Charlie turned on the giant television. "He's my lover."

Sam leaned against the arm of the couch. This was exactly the kind of shocking thing Charlie used to say when she was ten. "Possums can transmit leptospirosis, E. coli, salmonella. Their scat can carry a bacteria that causes flesh-eating ulcers."

"We're not into the kinky stuff." Charlie flipped through the channels.

Sam said, "That's quite a television."

"Ben calls her Eleanor Roosevelt, because she's big and ugly but we still adore her." Charlie found CNN. She muted the sound. Captions scrolled up. Sam saw her eyes quickly scan the words.

"Why are you watching that?"

"I want to see if there are any stories about Dad."

Sam watched Charlie watch the news. There was nothing they could tell her sister that Sam could not provide. Without doubt, she knew more than the reporters. What their father had said. What he was likely thinking. That the police had been called. That Rusty's body had been left in the chair for over an hour. Because he had been stabbed, because his injuries had likely contributed to his death, the Bridge Gap Police Department had been called.

Fortunately, Sam had managed to remove her Kelly Wilson list from her father's robe pocket before the police had arrived. Otherwise, the girl's secrets would have been at Ken Coin's fingertips.

"Shit." Charlie unmuted the sound.

A voice-over was saying, ". . . exclusive interview with Adam Humphrey, a former student who attended Pikeville High School with Kelly Rene Wilson."

Sam watched a plump, pimply young man standing in front of a beat-up old Camaro. His arms were crossed. He was dressed as if for church, a white button-up shirt, skinny black tie and black pants. A smattering of hair suggested a goatee on his chin. His glasses had visible fingerprints.

Adam said, "Kelly was all right. I guess. There were things people said about her that weren't nice. But she was—okay, she was slow, all right? Up here." He tapped the side of his head. "But that's okay, you know? Not everybody can be on the honor roll or whatever. She was just a nice girl. Not real bright. But she tried."

The reporter came into the shot, microphone under his chin. "Can you tell me how you met her?"

"Ain't no telling. Maybe going back to elementary? Most of us know each other. This is a real small town. Like, you can't walk down the street without seeing people you know."

"Were you friends with Kelly Rene Wilson in middle school?" The reporter had the look of an animal that had smelled fresh meat. "There have been rumors about indiscretions during that time. I wondered if you—"

"Nah, man, I ain't gonna get into that." He tightened his crossed arms. "See, people are wanting to say bad things, like that she was bullied or whatever, and maybe there was some people who were mean to her, but that's life. Life in school, at least. Kelly knows that. She knew it back then, too. She's not stupid. People are saying she's stupid. Okay, she's not bright, I already said that, but she's not an idiot. It's just how things are when you're a kid. Kids are mean. Sometimes they get mean and stay mean, and sometimes it stops when they graduate, but you roll with it. Kelly rolled with it. So I don't know what set her off, but it ain't that. Not what you're saying. That's a falsehood."

The reporter said, "But with Kelly Rene Wilson, did you—"

"Don't be trying to John Wayne Gacy her, okay? It's just Kelly. Kelly Wilson. And what she did was a hateful thing. I don't know why she did it. I can't speculate or nothing. Nobody can, and nobody should, and if they try to, then they're a bunch of liars. What happened is just what happened, and nobody but Kelly knows why, but you—you people on the TV—y'all gotta remember it's just Kelly. Folks that went to school with her, too. It's just Kelly."

Adam Humphrey walked off. The reporter did not let the absence of an interview subject slow him down. He told the anchor back in the studio, "Ron, as I said before, the typical profile of a shooter is male, a loner, generally bullied, isolated, and with an ax to grind. With Kelly Rene Wilson, we're presented with a different possibility, that of a young girl who was ostracized for her sexual promiscuity, who, according to sources close to the Wilson family, terminated an unplanned pregnancy, which in a small town—"

Charlie muted the set. "Unplanned pregnancy. She was in middle school. It's not like she kept a fucking fertility calendar."

Sam said, "Adam Humphrey would be a good character witness. He clearly didn't want to denigrate her like some of her other friends have."

"Friends don't denigrate you," Charlie said. "I bet you could get Mindy Zowada on TV and she'd talk about love and forgiveness, but you read the shit she's posting on Facebook and you'd think she was two seconds away from grabbing a pitchfork and a burning torch and heading to the jail to pull some kind of Frankenstein shit."

"People understandably feel that she's a monster. She murdered—"

"I know who she murdered." Charlie looked down at her hands as if she still expected to find Lucy's blood on them. "That Humphrey kid better get a good lawyer. This 'femme fatale' angle is going to catch on quick. They're going to hog-tie him to Kelly whether he had anything to do with her or not."

Sam refrained from commenting. She felt guilty for unburdening herself to Lenore at the diner last night when she would not break privilege for her own sister; however, unlike Lenore, Charlie would definitely be called to the witness stand. Sam did not want to put her sister in the position of having to choose between perjuring herself or providing evidence that might cause a jury to vote for execution.

This was one of the many reasons Sam did not practice criminal law. She did not want to have her words lead to the literal difference between life and death.

Sam changed the subject, asking Charlie, "What now? I assume we have to make arrangements for Dad."

"He already took care of that. He pre-funded everything, told the funeral director how he wants it to go."

"He could do all that but couldn't draw up a will or a DNR?"

"Rusty always wanted to make a good exit." Charlie looked at the clock on the wall. "The service starts in three hours."

Sam felt sucker-punched by the news. She had assumed she would be looking for a hotel today. "Why so quickly?"

"He didn't want to be embalmed. He said it was beneath his dignity."

"Surely one day wouldn't matter?"

"He wanted it to be fast so that you didn't feel like you had to come, or for you to feel guilty because you couldn't make it." Charlie turned off the television. "It's not like him to let something drag out."

"Unless it was one of his stupid stories."

Charlie shrugged rather than making a pithy comment.

Sam followed her into the kitchen. She sat down at the counter. She watched Charlie tidy the counters and load the dishwasher. She said, "I don't think he suffered."

Charlie took two mugs down from the cabinet. She poured coffee into one. She added tap water to the other and put it in the microwave. "You can leave after the funeral. Or before. I don't think it matters. Dad won't know, and you don't care what people here think."

Sam ignored the pointed remark. "Ben was very kind to me before he left last night."

"Where's your tea?" Charlie retrieved Sam's purse from the bench by the door. "It's in here, right?"

"Side pocket."

She found the Ziploc in Sam's purse and slid it across the counter. "Can we acknowledge that Ben's not living here without actually having to have a conversation about it?"

"I think we've been doing that for a while." Sam pulled out a tea sachet. She tossed it to Charlie. "Do you have milk?"

"Why would I have milk?"

Sam shrugged and shook her head at the same time. "I didn't forget that you're lactose intolerant. I thought maybe Ben—" She saw the futility in a drawn-out explanation. "Let's try to get through the day without arguing again. Or continuing the argument from yesterday. Or whatever it is we're doing."

The microwave beeped. Charlie found a potholder. She put the mug on the counter. She pulled a saucer from the cabinet. Sam studied the back of her shirt. Charlie had put her math club handle in iron-on letters on the back of her shirt: Lois Common Denominator.

Sam asked, "What's going to happen to Kelly Wilson? Will that alcoholic, Grail, get the case?"

Charlie turned around. She placed the mug in front of Sam. The saucer was on top for unknown reasons. "There's a guy in Atlanta,

Steve LaScala. I think I can get him to take over. He might call you for your impressions."

"I'll leave you my number."

"Ben has it."

Sam put the saucer on the bottom. She dipped the tea bag in and out of the water. "If this LaScala won't do it pro bono, then I'll pay him."

Charlie snorted. "That's gonna be over a million bucks."

Sam shrugged. "It's what Dad would want me to do."

"Since when do you do what Dad wants you to do?"

Sam felt their temporary peace start to tear at the margins. "Dad loved you. It was one of the last things he talked about."

"Don't start that."

"He was worried about you."

"I'm sick of people being worried about me."

"On behalf of people, we're sick of it, too." Sam looked up from the mug. "Charlie, whatever is bothering you, it's not worth it. This anger you have. This sadness."

"My father is dead. My husband left me. The last few days have been the shittiest days I've had since you were shot and Mama died. I'm sorry I'm not happy and peppy for you, Sam, but my give-a-fuck is broken." Charlie drank her coffee. She looked out the kitchen window. Birds had flocked to the feeder.

This was the time, perhaps the last opportunity, for Sam to tell her sister about Anton. She wanted Charlie to know that she understood what it meant to be loved, and what a crushing responsibility that love could sometimes be. They could trade secrets the way they had when they were little—*I'll tell you about that boy I have a crush on if you tell me why Gamma put you on restriction for three days.*

Sam said, "Rusty told me that the letters from Zachariah Culpepper were nothing. The police know about them. He's just desperate. He's trying to get a rise out of us. Don't let him win."

"I think you forfeit your participation trophy when you're on death row." Charlie put down her coffee. She crossed her arms. "Go ahead. What else did he say?"

"He talked to me about the death penalty."

"Did he make you put your fingers on his wrist?"

Sam felt hoodwinked yet again. "How did he never get run out of town for selling fake band instruments?"

"He didn't want me to go to Culpepper's execution. If the state ever gets around to doing its job." Charlie shook her head, as if the death of a man was a mild inconvenience. "I'm not sure if I want to go. But nothing Rusty says, said, is going to influence my decision."

Sam hoped that was not true. "He told me about a photo of Mama."

"*The* photo?"

"A different one, one he says that neither of us has seen."

"I find that hard to believe," Charlie said. "We used to go through all of his stuff. He had no privacy."

Sam shrugged. "He said it was in his office at home. I'd like to get it before I leave."

"Ben can take you by the HP after the funeral."

The farmhouse. Sam did not want to go, but she would not leave town without having at least one piece of her mother to take back to New York. "I can help you cover that." Sam indicated the bruises on Charlie's face. "For the funeral."

"Why would I want to cover it?"

Sam could not think of a good reason. No one would likely be at the funeral, at least no one Sam wanted to see. Rusty had hardly been a popular figure in town. Sam would make an appearance, then she would go to the farmhouse, then she would wait for Stanislav to drive up from Atlanta and leave this place as fast as she could.

That was, if she could manage to find the energy to stand. The muscle relaxer was still in her system. She could feel the drug weighing her down. Sam had been awake less than fifteen minutes and she could have just as easily gone back to sleep.

She picked up the mug of tea.

"Don't drink that." Charlie's cheeks were flush. "It's got boob sweat."

"It's got—"

"Boob sweat," Charlie said. "I ran the tea bag under my bra when you weren't looking."

Sam put down the mug. She should have been irritated, but she laughed. "Why would you do that?"

"Don't expect me to explain myself," Charlie said. "I don't know why I'm acting like a kid again, pestering you, trying to annoy you, trying to get your attention. I see myself doing it and I fucking hate it."

"Then stop."

She groaned out a heavy sigh. "I don't want to fight, Sam. Dad wouldn't want that, especially not today."

"Actually, Dad loved arguments."

"Not the hurtful kind."

Sam drank some tea. She needed the caffeine too much to care what was in it. "So, what now?"

"I guess I'm going to go cry in the shower and then get ready for my father's hastily arranged funeral."

Charlie rinsed her coffee mug in the sink. She loaded it into the dishwasher. She wiped her hands on a towel. She started to leave.

"My husband died." Sam had pushed out the words so fast that she wasn't sure Charlie had heard them. "His name was Anton. We were married for twelve years."

Charlie's lips parted in surprise.

"He died thirteen months ago. Esophageal cancer."

Charlie's mouth moved as she tried to think what to say. She settled on, "I'm sorry."

"It was tannins," Sam said. "In wine. They're—"

"I know what tannins are. I thought that kind of cancer was caused by HPV."

"His tumor tested negative." Sam offered, "I can send you the research."

"Don't," Charlie said. "I believe you."

Sam wasn't sure she quite believed herself anymore. Her druthers were always to apply logic to a problem, but as with the weather, life existed in a delicate dynamical balance between the fields of mass and motion.

In essence, sometimes shit happened.

She told Charlie, "I want to go to the funeral home with you, but I don't think I can stay. I don't want to see the people who will come. The hypocrites. The sightseers. People who would cross the street when they saw Dad coming and never, ever understood that he was trying to do good."

"He didn't want a service," Charlie said. "Not a formal one. There's a visitation, and then he wanted everybody to head over to Shady Ray's."

Sam had forgotten about her father's favorite bar. "I can't sit around listening to a bunch of old drunks regaling each other with courthouse stories."

"That was one of his favorite things to do." Charlie leaned against the counter. She looked down at her feet. There was a hole in her sock. Sam could see her big toe sticking out.

Charlie said, "We talked about his funeral the last time. Before the open-heart surgery. Just me and Dad. That's when he made all of these plans. He said he wanted people to be happy, to celebrate life. It sounded nice, right? But now that I'm in the middle of it, all I can think is what a stupid asshole he was to assume I would feel like celebrating when he was dead." She brushed away tears. "I can't decide if I'm in shock or if what I'm feeling is normal."

Sam could offer no expertise. Anton had been a scientist from a culture that did not romanticize death. Sam had stood by the furnace and watched his wooden coffin slide into the flames.

Charlie said, "I remember going to Gamma's funeral. *That* was shock. It was so unexpected, and I was terrified that Zachariah would get out. That he would come back for me. That his family would do something. That you would die. That they would kill you. I don't think I let go of Lenore's hand the entire time."

Sam had still been in the hospital when her mother was buried. She was certain Charlie had told her about the funeral, just as she was certain that her brain had not been able to retain the information.

Charlie said, "Dad was good that day. Present. He kept making sure I was okay, catching my eye, interrupting when the wrong person said the wrong thing. It was kind of like you said. Some hypocrites. Some sightseers. But there were other people, like Mrs. Kimble from across the street, and Mr. Edwards from the real estate office. They told these stories, like strange things Gamma had said, or how she had known how to solve a weird problem, and it was really nice to see that other part of her. The adult part of her."

"She never fit in."

"Every place always has somebody who doesn't fit in. That's what makes them fit in." Charlie looked at the clock. "We should get ready. The faster we can do this, the faster it'll be over."

"I can stay." Sam sensed her wariness. "For the funeral. I can stay if—"

"Nothing has changed, Sam." Charlie did her half-shrug. "I still need to figure out what I'm going to do with my wasted, unhappy life, and you still need to leave."

CHAPTER FIFTEEN

Sam watched Charlie pace around the front lobby of the funeral home. The building was modern on the outside, but the inside was decorated more in the style of a fussy old woman. They seemed to operate with the same efficiency. There were two funerals taking place in the chapels on either side of the lobby. Two identical black hearses awaited their passengers outside. Sam recalled the funeral home's logo from a billboard she had passed on the way into Pikeville. The ad showed a happy-go-lucky-looking teen beside the ominous words, *Slow down! We don't need the business.*

Charlie passed by Sam, arms swinging, mouth set. She was wearing a black dress and heels. Her hair was pulled back. She had worn no makeup, done nothing to cover her grief. She mumbled under her breath, "Who ever heard of waiting in line at a damn funeral home?"

Sam knew that her sister was not looking for an answer. They had been asked to wait less than ten minutes ago. Competing music came from behind closed doors on opposite sides. One service seemed to be winding down while the other started. They would soon be overcome with mourners.

"Unbelievable," Charlie muttered, pacing past her again.

Sam felt her phone buzz. She looked down at the screen. Before leaving Charlie's, she had texted Stanislav, asking him to meet her at the farmhouse. The driver had been well compensated for each trip, but she still read a curt tone in his reply: *Will return ASAP.*

The ASAP threw her. Sam was suddenly possessed by the

desire to tell him to take his time. She had arrived in Dickerson County wanting nothing more than to leave, but now that she was here, she found herself overcome by inertia.

Or perhaps obstinance was a better choice of word.

The more Charlie told her to leave, the more rooted Sam felt to this cursed place.

A side door opened. Sam had assumed the room was a closet, but the older gentleman in a suit and tie came out drying his hands on a paper towel. He leaned back in and threw the towel in the trash.

"Edgar Graham." He shook Sam's hand first, then Charlie's. "I'm sorry that we kept you waiting."

Charlie said, "We've been here almost twenty minutes."

"Again, my apologies." Edgar indicated the hall. "Ladies, this way, please."

Sam took the lead. Her leg was cooperating today, just a tinge of pain reminding her that the détente was likely temporary. She heard Charlie muttering behind her, but the words were too low to make out.

Edgar said, "Your husband dropped by with the requested attire this morning."

"Ben?" Charlie sounded surprised.

"Through here." Edgar stepped ahead of them so that he could hold open the door. The sign said BEREAVEMENT COUNSELING. There were four club chairs, a coffee table, and boxes of Kleenex discreetly placed behind potted plants around the room.

Charlie glared at the sign on the door. Sam could feel a flinty heat coming off of her sister. Usually, they fed off each other, whatever emotion Charlie was feeling becoming amplified inside of Sam. Now, Charlie's panic, her anger, served to make Sam calmer.

This was what she was here for. She could not solve Charlie's problems, but right now, in this moment, she could give her sister what she needed.

Edgar said, "You can make yourself comfortable in here. We've got a full house today. I'm sorry we weren't expecting you."

Charlie asked, "You weren't expecting us for our father's funeral?"

"Charlie," Sam said, trying to rein her in. "We came unannounced. The funeral doesn't start for another two hours."

Edgar offered, "We generally open visitation an hour before the service."

"We're not having a service." Charlie asked, "Whose funeral is in the other chapel? Is it Mr. Pinkman?"

"No, ma'am." Edgar had stopped smiling, but he appeared unruffled. "Douglas Pinkman's service is scheduled for tomorrow. We have Lucy Alexander the following day."

Sam felt unexpectedly relieved. She had been so focused on Rusty that she had not remembered that there were two more bodies that would require burial.

Edgar indicated a chair to Sam, but she did not sit. He said, "Currently, your father is downstairs. When the service in our Memory Chapel is completed, we'll bring him upstairs and place him on the podium at the front of the room. I want to assure you that—"

"I want to see him now," Charlie said.

"He's not prepared."

"Did he forget to study for a test?"

Sam rested her hand on Charlie's shoulder.

Edgar said, "I apologize that my meaning was unclear." He kept his hands on the back of the chair, his preternatural coolness intact. He explained, "Your father has been placed in the casket that he chose, but we need to move him to the podium, set up the flowers, prepare the room. You want the first time to see him to be—"

"That's not necessary." Sam squeezed Charlie's shoulder to keep her silent. She knew what her sister was thinking—*Don't tell me what I want.* She said, "I'm sure you've got something lovely planned, but we'd like to see him now."

Edgar gave a smooth nod. "Of course, ladies. Of course. Please allow me a moment."

Charlie didn't wait for the door to close behind him. "What a condescending prick."

"Charlie—"

"The worst thing you could say right now is that I sound like Mother. Jesus." She pulled at the neck of her dress. "It feels like it's a hundred degrees in here."

"Charlie, this is grief. You want to control things because you feel out of control." Sam worked to take the lecture out of her tone. "You need to learn how to deal with this because what you are feeling is not going to stop after today."

"*You need*," Charlie repeated. She took a tissue from the box beside the chair. She mopped sweat from her brow. "You'd think with all of these dead people, they'd keep the air down low." She paced the small room. She kept moving her hands, shaking her head, as if she was having some kind of private conversation with herself.

Sam sat in the chair. This was her chickens coming home to roost, watching her sister's manic, frantic energy manifest itself in rage. Charlie was right that she sounded like their mother. Gamma had always struck out when she felt threatened, the same way that Sam had, the same way that Charlie was doing now.

Sam offered, "I have some Valium in my purse."

"You should take it."

Sam tried again, "Where's Lenore?"

"So she can calm me down?" Charlie walked over to the window. She bent open the metal blinds to look out at the parking lot. "She won't come to this. She'd want to kill everybody here. What do you use on your neck?"

Sam touched her fingers to her neck. "What?"

"I remember Gamma's neck was getting crepey. Like, the skin was starting to wrinkle. Even though she was only three years older than I am now."

Sam did not know what to do but carry on the conversation. "She was out in the sun all of the time. She never used sunscreen. None of her generation did."

"Don't you worry about it? I mean, you're fine now, but—" Charlie looked in the mirror by the window. She pulled at the skin of her neck. "I put lotion on it every night, but I think I need to get a cream."

Sam opened her purse. The first thing she saw was the note she had given Rusty. The odor of cigarette smoke lingered on the paper. Sam resisted doing something melodramatic, like holding the note to her face so she could remember what her father smelled like. She found her hand cream beside Ben's USB drive. "Here."

Charlie looked at the label. "What's this?"

"It's what I use."

"But it says 'for hands.'"

"We can Google something." Sam reached for her phone. "What do you think?"

"I think . . ." Charlie took a short breath. "I think I'm losing my shit."

"It's more likely you're having a panic attack."

"I'm not panicking," Charlie said, but the tremble in her voice indicated otherwise. "I feel dizzy. Shaky. I might throw up. Is that a panic attack?"

"Yes." Sam helped her sit down in the chair. "Take some deep breaths."

"Jesus." She put her head down between her knees. "Oh Jesus."

Sam rubbed her sister's back. She tried to think of something that would take away the pain, but grief defied logic.

"I didn't believe he would die." Charlie grabbed her hair in her hands. "I mean, I knew it would happen, but I didn't think it would. Like, the opposite of when you buy a lottery ticket. You're saying, 'Of course I'm not going to win,' but then you actually *do* think you *might* win, because why else would you buy the damn ticket?"

Sam kept rubbing her back.

"I know I still have Lenore, but Dad was—" Charlie sat up. She took a jittery breath. "I always knew that, no matter what, if I had a problem, I could take it to him and he wouldn't judge me, and he would make a joke about it so it didn't hurt so much and then we would figure out how to solve it together." She covered her face with her hands. "I hate him for not taking care of himself. And I love him for living his life on his own terms."

Sam was familiar with both sensations.

"I didn't know that Ben brought his clothes." She turned to Sam, alarmed. "What if he asked to be dressed up like a clown?"

"Charlie, don't be silly. You know he would've chosen something from the Renaissance."

The door opened. Charlie stood up.

Edgar said, "Our Memory Chapel is clearing out. If you would give me another moment, I could place your father in a more natural setting."

"He's dead," Charlie said. "None of this is natural."

"Very well." Edgar tucked down his chin. "We've temporarily placed him in our showroom. I've put out two chairs for your comfort and reflection."

"Thank you." Sam turned to Charlie, expecting her to complain about the chairs or make a sharp comment about reflection. Instead, she found her sister crying.

"I'm here," Sam said, though she did not know if that was a comfort.

Charlie bit her lip. Her hands were still clenched into fists. She was trembling.

Sam peeled open Charlie's fingers and held on to her hand.

She nodded to Edgar.

He walked to the other side of the small room. Sam had not noticed a discreet door built into the wood paneling. He turned the latch, and she saw the brightly lit showroom.

Charlie would not move on her own, so Sam gently led her

toward the door. Though Edgar had called this the showroom, Sam had not been expecting to find an actual showroom. Shiny caskets painted in dark earth tones lined the walls. They were tilted at a fifteen-degree angle, their lids opened to display the silk liners. Spotlights illuminated silver and gold handles. An assortment of pillows was in a spinning rack. Sam wondered if mourners checked the softness before making their decision.

Charlie was unsteady on her high heels. "Is this what it was like when your—"

"No," Sam said. "Anton was cremated. They put him in a pine box."

"Why didn't Daddy do that?" Charlie looked down at a jet-black display casket with black satin lining. "I feel like we're in a Shirley Jackson story."

Sam turned, remembering Edgar. She mouthed the words, "Thank you."

He bowed out of the room, closing the door behind him.

Sam looked back at Charlie. She had come to a standstill. All of her bluster was gone. She was staring at the front of the room. Two folding chairs draped in pastel blue satin covers. A white casket with gold handles on a stainless-steel cart with big, black wheels. The lid was open. Rusty's head was tilted up on a pillow. Sam could see the peppered gray of his hair, the tip of his nose, and a flash of bright blue from his suit.

Charlie said, "That's Dad."

Sam reached for her sister's hand again, but Charlie was already moving toward their father. Her deliberate stride tapered off quickly. She stuttered to a stop. Her hand went to her mouth. Her shoulders began to shake.

She told Sam, "It's not him."

Sam understood what she meant. This was clearly their father, but just as clearly it was not. Rusty's cheeks were too red. His wild eyebrows had been tamed. His hair, normally sticking up in every direction, was combed into something resembling a pompadour.

Charlie said, "He promised me he would look handsome."

Sam wrapped her arm around Charlie's waist.

"When we talked about it, I told him I didn't want an open casket, and he promised me that he would look handsome. That I would want to see how good he looked." She told Sam, "He doesn't look good."

"No," Sam said. "He doesn't look like himself."

They stared down at their father. Sam could not remember a time that she had not seen Rusty in motion. Lighting a cigarette. Throwing out a dramatic hand. Tapping his toes. Snapping his fingers. Nodding his head as he hummed or clicked his tongue or whistled a tune that she did not recognize, yet could not get out of her brain.

Charlie said, "I don't want anyone to see him like this." She reached up to close the lid.

Sam gave a hushed, "Charlie!"

She pulled on the lid. The lid did not move. "Help me close it."

"We can get—"

"I don't want that creepy asshole back in here." Charlie pulled with both hands. The lid moved perhaps five degrees before it stopped. "Help me."

"I'm not going to help you."

"What was your list? You can't see, you can't run, you can't process? I don't recall you saying your useless body couldn't help close the fucking lid on your own father's coffin."

"It's a casket. Coffins are tapered at the head and foot."

"For fucksake." Charlie dropped her purse on the floor. She kicked off her shoes. She used both hands to pull down on the lid, practically hanging from it.

There was a creak of protest, but the casket remained open.

Sam said, "It won't simply close. That would be a safety hazard."

"You mean, it could kill him if the lid slammed shut?"

"I mean it could hit you in the head or break your fingers." She leaned over Rusty to examine the brass barrel hinges. A cloth-covered strap and loop assembly kept the lid from over-opening, but no apparent mechanism controlled the closing. "There must be some kind of release."

"Jesus Christ." Charlie hung from the lid again. "Can't you just help me?"

"I am trying—"

"I'll do it myself." Charlie walked around to the back of the casket. She pushed from behind. The table moved. One of the front wheels was unlocked. Charlie pushed harder. The table moved again.

"Hold on." Sam checked the exterior of the casket for some kind of lever or button. "You're going to—"

Charlie jumped up, pushing down on the lid with all of her weight.

Sam said, "You're going to knock it off the table."

"Good." Charlie pushed again. Nothing moved. She banged her palm against the lid. "Fuck!" She banged it again, this time with her closed fist. "Fuck! Fuck! Fuck!"

Sam ran her fingers inside the edge of the silk liner. She found a button.

There was a loud click.

The pneumatic pump hissed as the lid slowly closed.

"Shit." Charlie was breathless. She leaned her hands on the closed casket. She closed her eyes. She shook her head. "He leaves us with a metaphor."

Sam sat down in the chair.

"You're not going to say anything?"

"I'm reflecting."

Charlie's laugh was cut off by a sob. Her shoulders trembled as she cried. Her tears fell onto the top of the casket. Sam watched them roll down the side, bend around the stainless-steel table, then drop onto the floor.

"Shit," Charlie said, using the back of her hand to wipe her nose. She found a box of tissues behind the handle display. She blew her nose. She dried her eyes. She sat down heavily in the chair beside Sam.

They both looked at the casket. The gaudy, gold handles and fil-igree corner guards. The bright white paint had a sparkling finish, as if glitter had been mixed into the clear coat.

Charlie said, "I can't believe how ugly that thing is." She threw away the used tissue. She snagged another from the box. "It looks like something Elvis was buried in."

"Do you remember when we went to Graceland?"

"That white Cadillac."

Rusty had charmed the attendant into letting him sit behind the wheel. The paint on the Fleetwood had been the same bright white as the casket. Diamond dust had brought out the sparkle.

"Dad could talk anybody into letting him do anything." Char-lie wiped her nose again. She sat back in the chair. Her arms were crossed.

Sam could hear a clock ticking somewhere, a kind of metronome that synched with the beating of her heart. Her fingers still held the memory of the *tap-tap-tap* of Rusty's blood rushing through his veins. She had spent two days begging Charlie to unburden her-self, but her own sins weighed far heavier.

Sam said, "I couldn't let him die. My husband. I couldn't let him go."

Charlie silently worked the tissue in her fingers.

"He had a DNR, but I didn't give it to the hospital." Sam tried to take a deep breath. She felt the weight of Anton's death restrict-ing her chest. "He couldn't speak for himself. He couldn't move. He could only see and hear, and what he saw and heard was his wife refusing to let the doctors turn off the machines that were extending his suffering." Sam felt the shame boiling in her stomach like oil. "The tumors had spread to his brain. There's only so much volume inside the skull. The pressure was pushing his brain down into his spine. The pain was excruciating. They had him on morphine, then Fentanyl, and I would sit there by his bed and watch the tears roll from his eyes and I could not let him go."

Charlie kept working the tissue, wrapping it around her finger.

"I would've done the same thing here. I could've told you that from New York. I was the wrong person to ask. I couldn't put my own needs, my desperation, aside for the only man I have ever loved. I certainly could not have done the right thing by Dad."

Charlie started to pull apart the layers of tissue.

The clock kept ticking.

Time kept moving forward.

Charlie said, "I wanted you here because I wanted you here."

Sam had not meant to stir up Charlie's guilt. "Please don't try to make me feel better."

"I'm not," Charlie said. "I hate that I made you come here. That I've put you through this."

"You didn't force me to do anything."

"I knew that you would come if I asked. I've known that for the last twenty years, and I used Dad as an excuse because I couldn't take it anymore."

"Couldn't take what?"

Charlie wadded the tissue into a ball. She held it tight in her hands. "I had a miscarriage in college."

Sam remembered the hostile phone call from all those years ago, Charlie's angry demand for money.

Charlie said, "I was so relieved when it happened. You don't realize when you're that young that you're going to get older. That there's going to come a time when you're not relieved."

Sam felt her eyes start to water at the piercing undertone of anguish in her sister's words.

Charlie said, "The second miscarriage was worse. Ben thinks it was the first, but it was the second." She shrugged off the deception. "I was at the end of my first trimester. I was in court, and I felt this pain, like cramps. I had to wait another hour for the judge to call a recess. I ran to the bathroom, and I sat down, and I had this feeling of blood rushing out of my body." She stopped to swallow. "I looked in the toilet and it was—it was nothing. It didn't look like anything. A really bad period, a glob of something. But it didn't feel right to flush it. I couldn't leave it. I crawled out from under the stall so I could leave the door locked. I called Ben. I was crying so hard he couldn't understand what I was saying."

"Charlie," Sam whispered.

Charlie shook her head, because there was more. "The third time, which Ben thinks was the second time, was worse. I was at eighteen weeks. We were outside, raking leaves in the yard. We had already started to put together the nursery, you know? Painted the walls. Looked at cribs. I felt the same kind of cramping. I told Ben I was going to get some water, but I barely made it to the bathroom. It just came out of me, like my body couldn't wait to get rid of it." She used the tips of her fingers to brush away tears. "I told myself it was never going to happen again, that I wasn't going to risk it, but then it happened again."

Sam reached over. She held tight to her sister's hand.

"This was three years ago. I stopped taking my birth control. It was stupid. I didn't tell Ben, which made it worse because I was tricking him. I was pregnant in a month. And then another month passed, and then I hit the three-month mark, and then it was six months, seven, and we were so fucking excited. Dad was walking on air. Lenore kept giving hints about names."

Charlie pressed her fingers to her eyelids. Tears streamed down. "There's this thing called Dandy-Walker syndrome. It sounds so stupid, like an old-timey dance, but basically, it's a group of congenital brain malformations."

Sam felt an ache inside her heart.

"They told us late on a Friday. Ben and I spent the whole weekend reading about it on the Internet. There'd be this one great story about a kid who was smiling, living his life, blowing out the candles on his birthday cake, and we'd say, 'Okay, well, that's—

that's fantastic, that's a gift, we can do that,' and then there'd be another story about a baby who was blind and deaf and had open-heart surgery and brain surgery and died before his first birthday, and we'd just hold each other and cry."

Sam squeezed Charlie's hand.

"We decided that we couldn't give up. It's our baby, right? So we went to see a specialist at Vanderbilt. He did some scans, and then he took us into this room. There weren't any pictures on the wall. That's what I remember. The rest of the place had babies everywhere. Photos of families. But not in this room."

Charlie stopped to dry her eyes again.

Sam waited.

Charlie said, "The doctor told us that there was nothing we could do. The cerebrospinal fluid was leaking. The baby didn't have . . . organs." She took a shaky breath. "My blood pressure was high. They were worried about sepsis. The doctor gave us five days, maybe a week, before the baby died, or I died, and I just—I couldn't wait. I couldn't go to work and eat dinner and watch TV knowing that—" She clasped Sam's hand. "So we decided to go to Colorado. That's the only place we could find where it's legal."

Sam knew she was talking about abortion.

"It's twenty-five grand. Plus flights. Plus the hotel room. Plus taking off work. We didn't have time to take out a loan, and we didn't want anyone to know what we were using it for. We sold Ben's car. Dad and Lenore gave us money. We put the rest on credit cards."

Sam felt a crushing sense of shame. She should have been there. She could have given them the money, flown with Charlie on the plane.

"The night before we were supposed to leave, I took a sleeping pill, because what did it matter, right? But I woke up with this burning pain. It wasn't like before with the cramps. I felt like I was being ripped apart. I went downstairs so I wouldn't wake up Ben. I started throwing up. I couldn't make it to the bathroom. There was so much blood. It looked like a crime scene. There were pieces I could see. Pieces of—" Charlie shook her head, unable to say the rest. "Ben called an ambulance. I've got a scar, like a C-section, but no baby to show for it. And when I finally came home, the rug was gone. Ben had cleaned up everything. It was like it had never happened."

Sam thought about the bare floor in Charlie's living room. They had not replaced the rug in three years. She asked, "Did you talk to Ben about it?"

"Yeah. We talked about it. We went to therapy. We got past it."

Sam could not believe that was true.

Charlie said, "It was my fault. I never told Ben, but every time, it was my fault."

"You can't believe that."

She used the back of her hand to rub her eyes. "I saw Dad do this closing argument once. He talked about how people always obsess about lies. Damn lies. But no one really understands that the real danger is the truth." She looked up at the white casket. "The truth can rot you from the inside. It doesn't leave room for anything else."

Sam tried, "There's no truth in blaming yourself. Nature has its own design."

"That's not the truth I'm talking about."

"Then tell me, Charlie. What's the truth?"

Charlie leaned over. She put her head in her hands.

"Please," Sam pleaded. She couldn't stand her own uselessness. "Tell me."

Charlie inhaled deeply, drawing air between the gap in her hands. "Everybody thinks I blame myself for running away."

"Don't you?"

"No," she said. "I blame myself for not running faster."

WHAT REALLY HAPPENED TO CHARLIE

"Run!" Sam shoved her away. *"Charlie, go!"*

Charlie fell back onto the ground. She saw the bright flash of the gun firing, heard the sudden explosion of the bullet leaving the barrel.

Sam spun through the air, almost somersaulting into the gaping mouth of the grave.

"Shit," Daniel said. "Christ. Jesus Christ."

Charlie scrambled away, crab-like, on her hands and heels, until her back hit a tree. She pushed herself up. Her knees shook. Her hands shook. Her whole body was shaking.

"It's okay, sweetpea," Zach told Charlie. "Stay right there for me."

Charlie stared at the grave. Maybe Sam was hiding, waiting to spring up and run. But she wasn't springing up. She wasn't moving, or talking, or shouting, or bossing everybody around.

Zach told Daniel, "You cover this bitch up. Lemme take the little one off for a minute."

If Sam could talk right now, she would be yelling, furious at Charlie for just standing there, for blowing this chance, for not doing what Sam always told her to do.

Don't look back . . . trust me to be there . . . keep your head down and—

Charlie ran.

Her arms flailed. Her bare feet struggled for purchase. Tree limbs slashed at her face. She couldn't breathe. Her lungs felt like needles were stabbing into her chest.

She heard Sam's voice—

Breathe through it. Slow and steady. Wait for the pain to pass.

"Get back here!" Zach yelled. The air shook with a steady *thud-thud-thud* that started to vibrate inside of Charlie's chest.

Zachariah Culpepper was coming after her.

She tucked her arms into her sides. She forced the tension from her shoulders. She imagined her legs were pistons in a machine. She tuned out the pinecones and sharp rocks gouging into her bare feet. She thought about the muscles that were helping her move—

Calves, quads, hamstrings, tighten your core, protect your back.

Zach was getting closer. She could hear him like a steam engine bearing down.

Charlie vaulted over a fallen tree. She scanned left, then right, knowing she shouldn't run in a straight line. She needed to locate the weather tower, to make sure she was heading in the right direction, but she knew if she looked back she would see Zach, and that seeing him would make her panic even more, and if she panicked even more, she would stumble, and if she stumbled, she would fall.

And then he would rape her.

Charlie veered right, her toes gripping the dirt as she altered direction. At the last minute, she saw another fallen tree. She flung herself over it, landing awkwardly. Her foot twisted. She felt her anklebone touch earth. Pain sliced up her leg.

She kept running.

Her feet were sticky with blood. Sweat dripped down her body. She scanned ahead for light, any indication of safety.

How much longer could he keep running? How much farther could she go?

Sam's voice came back to her—

Picture the finish line in your head. You have to want it more than the person behind you.

Zachariah wanted something. Charlie wanted something more—to get away, to get help for her sister, to find Rusty so he could figure out a way to make it all better.

Suddenly, Charlie's head jerked back.

Her feet flew out in front of her.

Her back slammed into the ground.

She saw her breath *huff* out of her mouth like it was a real thing.

Zach was on top of her. His hands were everywhere. Grabbing her breasts. Pulling her shorts. His teeth clashed against her closed mouth. Charlie scratched at his eyes. She tried to bring up her knee into his crotch but she couldn't bend her leg.

Zachariah sat up, straddling her. He worked his belt back

through the buckle. His weight was too much. He was pushing the air out of her.

Charlie's mouth opened. She had no breath left to scream. She was dizzy. Vomit burned up her throat.

Her shorts were wrenched down. He flipped her over like she was nothing. She tried again to scream, but he shoved her face into the ground. Dirt filled her mouth. He grabbed her hair in his fist. She felt a tearing deep inside her body as he ripped into her. His teeth bit down on her shoulder. He grunted like a pig as he raped her behind. She smelled rot from the earth, from his mouth, from what he was pushing inside of her.

Charlie squeezed her eyes shut.

I am not here. I am not here. I am not here.

Every time she convinced herself that this wasn't happening, that she was in the kitchen at the red-brick house doing her homework, that she was running the track at school, that she was hiding in Sam's closet listening to her talk on the phone to Peter Alexander, Zachariah did something new and the pain wrenched her back into reality.

He was not finished.

Charlotte's arms flopped uselessly as he turned her over. He shoved inside of her from the front. She was finally numb. Her mind went blank. She was aware of things, but as if from a remove: Her body shifting up and down as he started to thrust. Her mouth hanging open. His tongue jamming down her throat. His fingers digging into her breasts like he was trying to rip them away from her body.

She looked up. Past his ugly, contorted face.

Past the bowed trees. Their crooked limbs.

The night sky.

The moon was blue against the dark expanse.

Stars were scattered, indistinct pinholes.

Charlie closed her eyes. She wanted darkness, but she saw Sam twisting through the air. She could hear the *thump* of her sister's body hitting the grave like it was happening all over again. And then she saw Gamma. On the kitchen floor. Back to the cabinet.

Bright white bone. Pieces of heart and lung. Cords of tendon and arteries and veins and life spilling out of her gaping wounds.

Gamma had told her to run.

Sam had ordered her to get away.

They would not want this.

They had sacrificed their lives for Charlotte, but not for this.

"No!" Charlotte screamed, her hands turning into fists. She pounded into Zach's chest, swung so hard at his jaw that his head whipped around. Blood sprayed out of his mouth—big globs of it, not like the tiny dots from Gamma.

"Fucking bitch." He reared back his hand to punch her.

Charlotte saw a blur out of the corner of her eye.

"Get off her!"

Daniel flew through the air, tackling Zach to the ground. His fists swung back and forth, arms windmilling as he beat his brother.

"Motherfucker!" he yelled. "I'll fucking kill you!"

Charlotte backed away from the men. Her hands pressed deep into the earth as she forced herself to stand. Blood poured down her legs. Cramps made her double over. She stumbled. She spun around in a circle, blind as Sam had been. She couldn't get her bearings. She didn't know which way to run, but she knew that she had to keep moving.

Her ankle screamed as she ran back into the woods. She didn't look for the weather tower. She didn't listen for the stream, or try to find Sam, or head toward the HP. She kept running, then walking, then she felt so exhausted that she wanted to crawl.

Finally, she gave into it, collapsing to her hands and knees.

She listened for footsteps behind her, but all she could hear was her own heavy breaths panting out of her mouth.

Blood dripped between her legs. His *stuff* was in there, festering, decaying her insides. Charlotte threw up. Bile hit the ground and splattered back into her face. She wanted to lie down, to close her eyes, to go to sleep and wake up in a week when this was all over.

But she couldn't.

Zachariah Culpepper.

Daniel Culpepper.

Brothers.

Charlotte would see them both dead. She would watch the executioner strap them to the wooden chair and put the metal hat on their heads with the sponge underneath so that they wouldn't catch on fire and she would look between Zachariah Culpepper's legs to watch the urine come out when he realized that he was going to be electrocuted to death.

Charlotte got up.

She stumbled, then she walked, then she jogged and then, suddenly, miraculously, she saw a light.

The second farmhouse.

Charlotte reached out her hand as if she could touch it.

She swallowed back a sob.

Her ankle could barely hold her as she limped through the freshly plowed fields. She kept her eyes on the porch light, using it as a beacon, a lighthouse that could guide her away from the rocks.

I am here. I am here. I am here.

There were four steps up the back porch. Charlotte stared at them, trying not to think of the steps at the HP, the way she had run up them two at a time just a few hours ago, kicked off her shoes, peeled off her socks, and found Gamma cursing in the kitchen.

"Fudge," Charlie whispered. "Fudge."

Her ankle buckled on the first step. She held on to the shaky railing. She blinked at the porch light, which was bright white, like a flame. Blood had dripped into her eyes. Charlotte used her fists to rub it away. The welcome mat had a plump, red strawberry on it with a smiling face, arms and legs.

Her feet left dark prints on the mat.

She raised her hand.

Her wrist had a springiness, like the rubber band on a paddle ball.

Charlotte had to steady one hand with the other so that she could knock on the door. A bloody, wet impression of her knuckles was left on the painted white wood.

In the house, she heard a chair scrape back. Light footsteps across the floor. A woman's chipper voice asked, "Who could that be knocking so late?"

Charlotte did not answer.

There were no locks that clicked, no chain that slid back. The door opened. A blonde woman stood in the kitchen. Her hair was pinned back in a loose ponytail. She was older than Charlotte. Pretty. Her eyes went wide. Her mouth opened. Her hand fluttered to her chest, as if she had been hit by an arrow.

"Oh—" the woman said. "My God. My God. Daddy!" She reached for Charlotte, but she didn't seem to know where to touch her. "Come in! Come in!"

Charlotte took one step, then another, then she was standing inside the kitchen.

She shivered, though the space was warm.

Everything was so clean, so brightly lit. The wallpaper was yellow with red strawberries. A matching border rimmed the tops of the walls. The toaster had a knitted cozy with a strawberry stitched onto the side. The kettle on the stove was red. The clock on the wall, a cat with moving eyes, was red.

"Good Lord in Heaven," a man whispered. He was older, bearded. His eyes were almost perfectly round behind his glasses.

Charlotte stepped away until her back was against the wall.

He asked the woman, "What the hell happened?"

"She just knocked on the door." The woman was crying. Her voice trilled like a piccolo. "I don't know. I don't know."

"That's one of the Quinn girls." He opened the curtains. He looked outside. "Are they still out there?"

Zachariah Culpepper.

Daniel Culpepper.

Sam.

The man reached his hands to the top of the cabinet. He pulled down a rifle, a box of bullets. "Give me the phone."

Charlotte started to shake again. The rifle was long, its barrel like a sword that could cut her open.

The woman reached for the cordless phone on the wall. She knocked it to the ground. She scooped it up. Her hands were still fluttering, their motions chaotic, uncontrollable. She raised the antenna. She handed the phone to her father.

He said, "I'll call the police. Lock the door behind me."

The woman did as she was told, her fingers clumsy as she tried to turn the latch. She clasped together her hands. She looked at Charlotte. She took a quick breath. She glanced around the room. "I don't know what . . ." She put her hand to her mouth. She was looking at the mess on the floor.

Charlotte saw it, too. Blood was pooling around her feet. It was coming from her insides, sliding down her legs, past her knees, her ankles, steady and slow like the trickle that came from the farmhouse faucet if you didn't hit it hard enough with the hammer.

She moved her foot. The blood followed her. She remembered learning about snails, the way they left a slick slime behind them.

"Sit down," the woman said. She sounded steadier now, more sure of herself. "It's okay, sweetheart. You can sit down." She gently pressed her fingers to Charlotte's shoulder, guided her to the chair. "The police will come," she said. "You're safe now."

Charlotte did not sit down. The woman did not look like she felt safe.

"I'm Miss Heller." She knelt down in front of Charlotte. She brushed back her hair. "You're Charlotte, is that right?"

Charlotte nodded.

"Oh, angel." Miss Heller kept stroking her hair. "I'm sorry. Whatever happened to you, I'm so sorry."

Charlotte felt a weakness in her knees. She did not want to sit, but she had to. The pain was like a knife jamming into her insides. Her bottom ached. She could feel something warm coming out of her front like she was peeing herself again.

She asked Miss Heller, "Can I have some ice cream?"

The woman said nothing at first. Then she stood. She gathered a bowl, some vanilla ice cream, a spoon. She placed it all on the table.

The smell brought a surge of bile into Charlotte's throat. She swallowed it back down. She picked up the spoon. She ate the ice cream, shoving it into her mouth as fast as she could.

"Slow down," Miss Heller said. "You'll make yourself sick."

Charlotte wanted to be sick. She wanted him out of her. She wanted to cleanse herself. She wanted to kill herself.

"Mama, what would happen if I ate two bowls of ice cream? Really big ones."

"Your intestines would burst and you would die."

Charlotte devoured a second bowl of ice cream. She used her hands because the spoon was not big enough. She reached for the container, but Miss Heller stopped her. She looked aghast.

She asked Charlotte, "What happened to you?"

Charlotte was winded from eating so fast. She could hear her breath whistling through her nose. Her shorts were wet with blood. The strawberry cushion on the chair was completely saturated. She felt the dripping between her legs but she knew that it was not just blood. It was *him*. It was Zach Culpepper. He had left his stuff inside of her.

The vomit roiled up again. This time, she couldn't stop it. Charlotte slapped her hand to her mouth. Miss Heller picked her up by the waist. She ran down the hall, carrying Charlotte to the bathroom.

Charlotte threw up so hard that she thought her stomach would come out of her mouth. She gripped the cold sides of the toilet. Her eyes bulged. Her throat burned. Her intestines felt as if razors were inside. She yanked down her shorts. She sat on the toilet. She felt a torrent of fluid rush from her body. Blood. Feces. *Him.*

Charlotte cried out from the pain. She folded at the waist. She opened her mouth. She screamed out an anguished wail.

She wanted her mother. She *needed* her mother.

"Oh, sweetheart." Miss Heller was on the other side of the door. She was kneeling down again. Charlotte could hear her voice coming through the keyhole. " 'He said unto them, "Let the little children come unto me, and do not hinder them, for the kingdom of God belongs to such as these." ' "

Charlotte squeezed shut her eyes. Tears flowed. She breathed through her open mouth. She heard the heavy drops of blood hitting water. It would not end. This was never going to end.

"Sweet baby," Miss Heller said. "Let God carry this burden."

Charlotte shook her head. Her blood-soaked hair slapped at her face. She kept her eyes closed. She saw Sam spinning, somersaulting through the air.

The mist as the bullet entered her brain.

The heavy spray of blood as Gamma's chest exploded.

"My sister," Charlotte whispered. "She's dead."

"What's that, baby?" Miss Heller had cracked open the door. "What did you say?"

"My sister." Charlotte's teeth were chattering. "She's dead. My mother's dead."

Miss Heller held on to the doorknob as she sunk to the floor.

She said nothing.

Charlotte looked down at the white tiles at her feet. She could see black spots in her vision. Blood dripped from her open mouth. She rolled off some toilet paper. She held it to her nose. The bone felt broken.

Miss Heller came into the room. She turned on the sink faucet.

Charlotte tried to wipe herself. She could feel strips of flesh hanging down between her legs. The blood would not stop. It was never going to stop. She pulled up her shorts, but a wave of dizziness kept her from standing.

She sat back down on the toilet. She stared at the framed picture of a strawberry patch on the wall.

"It's all right." Miss Heller wiped Charlotte's face with a wet cloth. Her hands trembled along with her voice. "'But unto you that fear my name shall the Sun of righteousness arise with healing in his wings; and ye shall go forth, and grow up as—'"

A loud knock shook the back door. Banging. Screaming.

Miss Heller's hand went to Charlotte's chest, keeping her still.

"Judith!" the old man yelled. "Judith!"

The back door splintered open.

Miss Heller grabbed Charlotte again, picking her up by the middle. Charlie felt her feet leave the ground. She braced her hands against the woman's shoulders. Her ribs felt crushed as Miss Heller ran down the hall.

"Charlotte!"

The word was pained, like the sound you would hear from a dying animal.

Miss Heller skidded to a stop.

She turned around.

Her grip around Charlotte's waist slowly released.

Rusty was standing at the end of the hallway. He leaned heavily against the wall. His chest was heaving. He gripped a handkerchief in his hand.

Charlotte felt her feet touch the ground. Her knees folded, unable to support her weight.

Rusty staggered down the hallway. His shoulder bumped the wall, then the other wall, then he was on his knees and then he was holding Charlotte.

"My baby," he cried, enveloping her body in his. "My treasure."

Charlotte felt the slow release of her muscles. Her father was like a drug. She became a rag doll in his arms.

"My baby," he said.

"Gamma—"

"I know!" Rusty wailed. She felt his chest shake as he struggled to control his sorrow. "I know, sweetheart. I know."

Charlotte began to sob; not from the pain, but from fear because she had never seen her father cry.

"I've got you." He rocked her. "Daddy's here. I've got you."

Charlotte was crying so hard that she couldn't open her eyes. "Sam—"

"I know," he said. "We'll find her."

"They buried her."

Rusty let out a howl of despair.

"It was the Culpeppers," Charlotte said. Knowing their names, telling them to Rusty, was the only thing that had kept her moving. "Zach and his brother."

"It doesn't matter." He pressed his lips to the top of her head. "We got an ambulance coming. They're going to take care of you."

"Daddy." Charlotte lifted her head. She put her mouth close to his ear. She whispered, "Zach put his thing inside of me."

Rusty's arms slowly fell away. It was like the air had been let out of him. His mouth dropped open. He crumbled to the floor. His eyes scanned back and forth as he looked at Charlotte's face. His throat worked again. He tried to speak, but all that came out was a whimper.

"Daddy," she whispered again.

Rusty put his fingers to her mouth. He bit his lip, like he didn't want to speak, but he had to.

He asked, "He raped you?"

Charlotte nodded.

Rusty's hand dropped like a stone. He looked away. He shook his head. His tears had turned into two rivers running down the sides of his face.

Charlotte felt the shame of his silence. Her father knew the things that men like Zachariah Culpepper did. He could not even look at her.

"I'm sorry," Charlotte said. "I didn't run fast enough."

Rusty's eyes went to Miss Heller, then finally, slowly back to Charlotte. "It's not your fault." He cleared his throat. He said it again. "It's not your fault, baby. Do you hear me?"

Charlotte heard him, but she did not believe him.

"What happened to you," Rusty said, sounding strident. "It's not your fault, but we can't tell anybody else, okay?"

Charlotte could only stare. You didn't have to lie if something wasn't your fault.

Rusty said, "It's a private thing, and we're not going to tell anybody, okay?" He looked up at Judith Heller again. "I know what lawyers do to girls who are raped. I'm not going to put my daughter through that hell. I won't let people treat her like she's damaged." He wiped his eyes with the back of his hand. His voice became stronger. "They'll hang for this. Those two boys are murderers, and they'll die for it, but please don't let them take my daughter with them. Please. It's too much. It's just too much."

He waited, his eyes on Miss Heller. Charlie turned around. Miss Heller looked down at her. She nodded.

"Thank you. Thank you." Rusty rested his hand on Charlotte's shoulder. He looked at her face again, saw the blood and bone and sticks and leaves that had become glued to her body. He touched the ripped seam of her shorts. His tears started to flow again. He was thinking about what had been done to her, what had been done to Sam, to Gamma. He dropped his face into his hands. His sobs turned into howls. He fell against the wall, racked by grief.

Charlotte tried to swallow. Her throat was too dry. She could not clear the taste of sour milk. She was torn up inside. She could still feel the steady flow of blood sliding down the inside of her leg.

"Daddy," Charlotte said. "I'm sorry."

"No." He grabbed her, shook her. "Don't ever apologize, Charlotte. Do you hear me?"

He seemed so angry that Charlotte dared not speak.

"I'm sorry," Rusty stuttered out. He got up on his knees. He wrapped his hand around the back of her head, pressed his face to her face, their noses touching. She could smell cigarette smoke and his musky cologne. "You listen to me, Charlie Bear. Are you listening?"

Charlotte stared into his eyes. Red lines spoked out from the blue irises.

He said, "It's not your fault. I am your daddy, and I am telling you that none of this is your fault." He waited. "Okay?"

Charlotte nodded. "Okay."

Rusty whimpered out another breath. He swallowed hard. He was still openly weeping. "Now, do you remember all those boxes your mama brought home from the thrift store?"

Charlotte had forgotten about the boxes. No one would be around to unpack them now. It was just Charlotte and Rusty. There would never be anyone else.

"Listen to me, baby." Rusty cupped his hands to her face. "I want you to take what that nasty man did to you, and I want you to put it in one of those boxes, okay?"

He waited, clearly desperate for her to agree.

Charlotte let herself nod.

"All right," he said. "All right. Well, then your daddy's gonna get some tape, and we're gonna tape up that box together, sweetheart." His voice warbled again. His eyes desperately searched hers. "Do you hear me? We're gonna close up that box and tape it shut."

Again, she nodded.

"Then we're gonna put that mean ol' box on a shelf. And we're gonna leave it there. And we're not gonna think about it or look at it until we're good and God damn ready, okay?"

Charlotte kept nodding, because that's what he wanted.

"Good girl." Rusty kissed her cheek. He pulled her close to his chest. Charlotte's ear folded against his shirt. She could feel his heart thumping beneath the skin and bone. He had sounded so frantic, so afraid.

He asked, "We're gonna be okay, aren't we?"

He held her so tight that she couldn't nod, but Charlotte understood what her father wanted. He needed her to flip on her logical switch, but for real this time. Gamma was gone. Sam was gone. Charlotte had to be strong. She had to be the good daughter who took care of her father.

"Okay, Charlie Bear?" Rusty kissed the top of her head. "Can we do that?"

Charlotte imagined the empty closet in the bachelor farmer's bedroom. The door hung open. She saw the box on the floor. Brown cardboard. Packing tape sealed it closed. She saw the label. TOP SECRET. She watched Rusty hefting the box onto his shoulder, sliding it onto the top shelf, pushing it back until shadows placed it in darkness.

"Can we do that, baby?" He begged, "Can we just close that box?"

Charlie imagined herself shutting the closet door.

She said, "Yes, Daddy."

She would never open the box again.

CHAPTER SIXTEEN

Charlie could not look at Sam. She kept her head buried in her hands. She stayed bent over in the chair. She had not thought about her promise to Rusty in decades. She had been the good daughter, the obedient daughter, putting her secret on a shelf, letting the dark shadows of time obscure the memories. Their Devil's Pact had never felt like the part of the story that mattered, but she could see now that it mattered almost more than anything else.

She told Sam, "I guess the moral of the story is that bad things happen to me in hallways."

Charlie felt Sam's hand on her back. All that she wanted in the world right now was to lean into her sister, to put her head in Sam's lap, and let Sam hold her while she cried.

Instead, she stood up. She found her shoes. She rested her hip against Rusty's casket as she put them on. "It was Mary-Lynne. I thought Lynne was her last name. Not Huckabee." She felt nauseated when she recalled Huck's cold reaction when he learned that Charlie was Rusty Quinn's daughter. "Do you remember the pictures of her in the barn?"

Sam nodded.

"Her neck was stretched at least a foot; that's what I remember. That she looked like a giraffe, almost. And the expression on her face—" Charlie wondered if she'd had the same agonized expression when Rusty had found her in the hallway. "We thought you were dead, we knew Mama was dead. He didn't say, but I know that he was afraid that I would hang myself, or find some way to kill myself, like Mary-Lynne." Charlie shrugged. "He was probably right. It was just too much."

Sam kept silent for a moment. She had never been given to fidgeting, but she smoothed out the leg of her pants. "Did the doctors believe that was the cause of your miscarriages?"

Charlie almost laughed. Sam always wanted the scientific explanation.

She told her sister, "After the second one, which was really the third, I went to a fertility expert in Atlanta. Ben thought I was at a conference. I told the doctor what happened—what really happened. I laid it out for her, things that even Dad didn't know. That he'd used his hands. His fists. His knife."

Sam cleared her throat. Her expression, as always, was obscured by her dark glasses. "And?"

"And she ran tests and did scans and then she said something about the thinness of this wall or scarring on that tube and she drew this diagram on a sheet of paper but I said, 'Give it to me straight.' And she did. I have an inhospitable womb." Charlie laughed bitterly at the phrase, which sounded like something you'd read on a travel review site. "My uterine environment is not suitable for hosting a fetus. The doctor was amazed I'd managed to get so far into my second trimester."

Sam asked, "Did she say it was because of what happened?"

Charlie shrugged. "She said it could be, but there was no way to know for sure. I dunno, a guy jams the handle of a knife up your twat, it makes sense that you can't have babies."

"The last time," Sam said, always zeroing in on the deductive fallacy. "You said Dandy-Walker is a syndrome, not resultant of a uterine malformation. Is there a genetic component?"

Charlie couldn't go down this road again. "You're right. That was my last time. I'm too old now. Any pregnancy would be considered too high risk. The clock has ticked down."

Sam took off her glasses. She rubbed her eyes. "I should have been here for you."

"And I should have never asked you to come." She smiled, remembering something Rusty had said two days ago. "Our familiar impasse."

"You need to tell Ben."

"There's that *you need* again." Charlie blew her nose. She had not missed Sam's bossy older sisterness over the years. "I think it's too late for me and Ben." The words sounded flippant, but after her disastrous attempts at seduction, she had to stop denying the possibility that her husband would not come back. Charlie couldn't even work up the courage to ask him to stay last night because she was too afraid he would tell her no again.

She said, "Ben was a saint when it happened. Every time. I really mean that. I just don't understand where all that goodness comes from. Not his mother. Not his sisters. God, they were all awful. They wanted to know every detail, like it was gossip. They practically set up their own hotline. And you don't know what it's like to be pregnant, and buying baby furniture, and planning your maternity leave, and being big as a Mack Truck, then a week later you go to the grocery store and everybody who was smiling at you before can't even look you in the eye." Charlie asked, "I'm assuming you don't know what that's like?"

Sam shook her head.

Charlie was not surprised. She could not see her sister risking the physical toll a child would take on her body.

Charlie said, "I turned into such a bitch. I would hear myself—I can hear myself now, ten minutes ago, yesterday, every fucking day before that—and think, *Shut up*. Let it *go*. But I don't. I can't."

"And adoption?"

Charlie tried not to bristle at the question. Her baby had died. It wasn't like a dog, where you could get a new one a few months later to take away the loss. "I kept waiting for Ben to bring it up, but he kept saying he was happy with me, that we were a team, that he loved the idea of the two of us growing old together." She shrugged. "Maybe he was waiting for me to bring it up. Like the Gift of the Magi, but with a toxic uterus."

Sam put on her glasses. "You say that it's already over with Ben. What do you lose if you tell him what happened?"

"It's what I gain," Charlie said. "I don't want his pity. I don't want him to stay with me because he feels an obligation." She leaned her hand on the closed casket. She was talking to Rusty as much as Sam. "Ben would be happier with someone else."

"Utter bullshit," Sam said, her tone clipped. "You have no right to decide on his behalf."

Charlie felt like Ben had already decided. She could not blame him. She was hard-pressed to believe any forty-one-year-old man would be unhappy with a limber twenty-six-year-old. "He's so great with kids. He loves them so much."

"So do you."

"But he's not the one keeping me from having children."

"What if he was?"

Charlie shook her head. It didn't work like that. "Do you want a minute alone?" She indicated the casket. "To say goodbye?"

Sam frowned. "To whom would I be speaking?"

Charlie crossed her arms. "Can I have a minute?"

Sam's eyebrow arched up, but she managed for once to withhold her opinion. "I'll be outside."

Charlie watched her sister leave the room. Sam wasn't limping as much today. That, at least, was a relief. Charlie could not stand seeing her back in Pikeville, so out of her element, so unprotected. Sam could not turn a corner, she could not walk down the street, without everyone knowing exactly what had happened.

Except for Judge Stanley Lyman.

If there had been a way for Charlie to run up to the bench and slap the bastard across the face for humiliating her sister, Charlie would have risked being arrested.

Sam had always worked so hard to hide the things that were wrong with her, but you did not have to do more than study her for a few minutes to notice the peculiarities. Her posture, always too stiff. The way she walked with her arms tight to her sides rather than letting them swing freely. The way she held her head at an angle, always wary of her blindside. Then there was her precise, maddeningly didactic way of speaking. Sam's tone had always been sharp, but after being shot, it was as if every word was folded around the corner of a straight edge. Sometimes, you could hear a hesitation as she searched for the correct word. More rarely, you heard the sound of her breath as she pushed out sound, using her diaphragm the way the speech pathologist had trained her.

The doctors. The pathologists. The therapists. There had been a whole team surrounding Sam. They all had opinions, recommendations, warnings, and none of them understood that Sam would defy them all. She was not a normal person. She had not been that way before being shot, and she certainly was not that way during her recovery.

Charlie could remember one of the doctors telling Rusty that the damage to Sam's brain could shave off as many as ten IQ points. Charlie had almost laughed. Ten points would be devastating for any normal human being. For Sam, it meant that she went from being a genius-level prodigy to just really, really fucking smart.

Sam was seventeen years old, two years on from the gunshot, when she was offered a full scholarship to Stanford.

Was she happy?

Charlie could hear Rusty's question echoing in her head.

She turned around to face her father's hideous casket. She rested her hand on the lid. The paint had chipped in the corner, which she supposed was what happened when you hung on it like a demented, foul-mouthed monkey.

Sam did not seem happy, but she seemed content.

In retrospect, Charlie should have told her father that contentedness was the more laudable goal. Sam was thriving in her legal practice. Her temper, once a roiling tempest, finally seemed to be under control. The anger she had carried around like a brick in her chest was clearly gone. Of course, she was still pedantic and annoying, but that came with being their mother's child.

Charlie tapped her fingers on the casket.

The irony was not lost on Charlie that both she and her sister had failed miserably in matters of life and death. Sam had not been able to ease her husband's suffering. Charlie had not been able to provide a place of safety for her growing child.

"And here they come again," Charlie mumbled as tears filled her eyes. She was sick of crying. She didn't want to do it anymore. She didn't want to be a bitch anymore. She didn't want to feel sad anymore. She didn't want to be without her husband anymore.

As hard as it was to hold on to things, it was even harder to let them go.

She pulled over one of the reflecting chairs. She yanked off the baby-blue satin cover, because this was not a teenage girl's sweet sixteen party.

Charlie sat down on the hard plastic.

She had told Sam her secret. She had opened the box.

Why did she not feel different? Why had things not miraculously changed?

Years ago, Rusty had dragged Charlie to a therapist. She was sixteen. Sam was living in California. Charlie had started acting out in school, dating the wrong boys, screwing the wrong boys, slicing the tires on the cars that the wrong boys drove.

Rusty had probably assumed that Charlie would tell the truth about what had happened, just as Charlie had assumed that Rusty would expect her to leave that part out.

Hello, familiar impasse.

The therapist, an earnest man in a sweater vest, had tried to take Charlie back to that day, to the kitchen in the farmhouse, to that damp room where Gamma had left a pot of water on the stove to boil while she had gone down the hallway in search of Sam.

The man had told Charlie to close her eyes and picture herself at the kitchen table, her hands working the folds of the paper plate as she tried to turn it into an airplane. Instead of hearing a car in the driveway, he told her to imagine Jesus walking through the door.

He was a Christian therapist. Well-meaning, undoubtedly sincere, but he thought that Jesus was the answer to a lot of things.

"Keep your eyes closed," he had told Charlie. "Picture Jesus lifting you up."

Instead of Gamma grabbing the shotgun. Instead of Sam being shot. Instead of Charlie running through the woods to Miss Heller's house.

Charlie had kept her eyes closed as instructed. She had sat on her hands to keep them still. She could remember swinging her legs, pretending to play along, but she saw Lindsay Wagner, not Jesus Christ, coming to her rescue. The Bionic Woman used her super strength to punch Daniel Culpepper in the face. She karate-kicked Zachariah in the balls. She moved in slow motion, her long hair swinging as the *chuh-chuh-chuch-chuh* bionic sound played in the background.

Charlie had never been particularly good at following instructions.

Though, she seethed with humiliation to think that the frumpy licensed social worker with a bad haircut that Ben had dragged her to had been right about at least one thing. Something horrible that had happened to Charlie almost three decades ago was screwing up her life now.

Had screwed it up, because her husband was gone, her sister was flying back to New York in a few hours and Charlie was going to go home to an empty house.

It wasn't even her week to take care of the dog.

Charlie stared at her father's casket. She didn't want to think about Rusty lying inside the cold, metal box. She wanted to remember him smiling. Winking at her. Tapping his feet. Beating out a staccato on the nearest table. Telling one of his bullshit stories that he had told thousands of times before.

She should have taken more pictures of him.

She should have recorded his voice so she wouldn't forget the inflections, the annoying way he would stress the wrong words.

There had been times in her life that Charlie had prayed that Rusty would just please, for the love of God, shut the fuck up, but now, all she wanted in the world was to hear his voice. To listen to one of his yarns. To recognize one of his obscure quotes. To feel that moment of clarity when she realized that the story, the odd line, the seemingly innocuous observation, was actually advice, and that the advice was usually, aggravatingly, worth taking.

Charlie reached out to her father.

She placed her palm flat to the side of the casket. She felt stupid for doing this, but she had to ask, "What do I do now, Daddy?"

Charlie waited.

For the first time in forty-one years, Rusty did not have the answer.

CHAPTER SEVENTEEN

Charlie walked around the Memory Chapel with a glass of wine in her hand. Only her father would specify that alcohol be served at his funeral. There was hard liquor at the bar, but at noon, it was too early for most, which was the first problem with Rusty's speedy funeral plans. The second problem was one that Sam had spotted early on: the sightseers, the hypocrites.

Charlie felt bad for painting some of her former friends with this same brush. She couldn't blame them for choosing Ben over her. She would have chosen Ben, too. In a week or a month or maybe next year, their silent presence, their kind nods and smiles, would mean something, but right now, all she could concentrate on was the assholes.

The townsfolk who had reviled Rusty for his liberal do-gooder ways were out in force. Judy Willard, who had called Rusty a murderer for representing an abortion facility. Abner Coleman, who had called him a bastard for representing a murderer. Whit Fieldman, who had called him a traitor for representing a bastard. The list could go on, but Charlie was too disgusted to go through it.

The worst offender was Ken Coin. The pustulant cocksucker stood at the center of a group of minions from the district attorney's office. Kaylee Collins was front and center. The young woman who was probably cheating with Charlie's husband didn't seem to get that she might not be wanted here. Then again, the entire legal community was treating this as a social occasion. Coin was obviously telling a story about Rusty, some kind of courtroom antic her father had pulled. Charlie watched Kaylee throw back her head and laugh. She tossed her long, blonde hair out of her eyes. She did that intimate thing that women do where they reach out and touch a man's arm in a way that only the man's wife could tell was inappropriate.

Charlie drank her wine, wishing it was acid she could throw in the woman's face.

Her phone started to ring. She walked toward an empty corner, answering it right before voicemail picked up.

"It's me," Mason Huckabee said.

Charlie turned her back to the room, guilt manifesting itself in shame. "I told you not to call me."

"I'm sorry. I had to talk to you."

"No, you didn't," she told him. "Listen to me very carefully: What happened between us was the worst mistake of my life. I love my husband. I am not interested in you. I don't want to talk to you. I don't want anything to do with you, and if you call me again, I will slap you with a restraining order and make sure the state board of education knows that you've got a record against you for harassing a woman. Is that what you want?"

"No. Christ. Dial it back, okay? Please?" He sounded desperate. "Charlotte, I need to talk to you face-to-face. This is really important. Bigger than both of us. Bigger than what we did."

"That's where you're wrong," she assured him. "The biggest thing in my life is my relationship with my husband, and I am not going to let you get in the way of that."

"Charlotte, if you could—"

Charlie ended the call before he could spread any more of his bullshit.

She dropped her phone back into her purse. She neatened her hair. She finished her glass of wine. She got another from the bar. Half of it was gone before she felt the shaking stop. Thank God Mason had only called on the phone. If he'd come to the funeral, if the town had seen them together, if Ben had seen them, Charlie would have melted into a pool of self-disgust and hate.

"Charlotte." Newton Palmer, another shiftless lawyer in a room full of them, gave her a practiced look of condolence. "How are you doing?"

Charlie finished her wine to drown out the curses. Newton was one of those prototypical old white men who ran most of the small towns in America. Ben had once said that all they had to do was wait for racist, sexist old bastards like Newton to die. What he hadn't realized was that they kept making new ones.

Newton said, "I saw your father at a Rotary breakfast last week. Virile as ever, but he said the most humorous thing."

"That's Dad. Humorous." Charlie pretended to listen to the man's stupid Rotary story as she looked for her sister.

Sam was trapped, too, by Mrs. Duncan, her eighth-grade English teacher. Sam was nodding and smiling, but Charlie could not imagine her sister having much patience for idle conversation. Sam's sense of otherness was more pronounced in the crowd. Not because of her disabilities, but because she was clearly not of this place, or maybe not even of this time. The dark glasses. The regal tilt to her head. The way Sam dressed did not exactly help her blend in, even at a funeral. She was dressed in all black, but the wrong black. The kind of black that was only available to the one percent. Standing next to her ancient teacher, Sam looked like a silk bag of money by the proverbial sow's ear.

"It's like watching your mother." Lenore was wearing a tight black dress and heels that were higher than Charlie's. She smiled at Newton. "Mr. Palmer."

Newton blanched. "Charlotte, if you'll excuse me."

Lenore ignored him, so Charlie did, too. She pressed her shoulder into Lenore's as they both watched Sam. Mrs. Duncan was still talking her ear off.

Lenore said, "Harriet wanted so badly to connect with people, but she never quite solved the equation."

"She connected with Dad."

"Your father was an aberration. They were two singular people who functioned best when they were together."

Charlie leaned closer into her arm. "I didn't think you'd come."

"I couldn't resist taunting these hateful bastards one last time. Listen—" Lenore took a deep breath, as if preparing herself for something difficult. "I think I'm going to retire to Florida. Be among my people—bitter old white women living on fixed incomes."

Charlie smoothed together her lips. She couldn't cry again. She couldn't make Lenore feel guilty for doing what she needed to do.

"Oh, sweetheart." Lenore wrapped her arm around Charlie's waist. She put her mouth to Charlie's ear. "I am never going to leave you. I'm just going to be somewhere else. And you can come visit me. I'll make a special bedroom for you, with pictures of horses on the walls, and kittens and possums."

Charlie laughed.

Lenore said, "It's time for me to move on. I've fought the good fight long enough."

"Dad loved you."

"Of course he did. And I love you." Lenore kissed the side of her head. "Speaking of love."

Ben was making his way through the crowd. He held up his hands as he darted around an old man who looked like he had a story to tell. Ben said a few hellos to people he knew, constantly moving forward, easily detaching himself from hangers-on. People always smiled when they saw Ben. Charlie felt herself smiling, too.

"Hey." He smoothed down his tie. "Is this a girls-only thing?"

Lenore said, "I was just about to antagonize your boss." She kissed Charlie again before sidling over to Ken Coin.

The district attorney's group broke away, but Lenore trapped Coin like a cheetah with a baby warthog.

Charlie told Ben, "Lenore's going to retire to Florida."

He did not seem surprised. "Not much left for her with your dad gone."

"Just me." Charlie couldn't think about Lenore leaving. It hurt too much. She asked Ben, "Did you pick out Dad's suit?"

"That was all Rusty." He said, "Hold out your hand."

Charlie held out her hand.

He reached into his coat pocket. He pulled out a red ball. He placed it in her palm. "You're welcome."

Charlie looked down at the red clown nose and smiled.

Ben said, "Come outside."

"Why?"

Ben waited, patient as ever.

Charlie put down the glass of wine. She tucked the clown nose into her purse as she followed him outside. The first thing she noticed was the thick smog of cigarette smoke. The second thing she noticed was that she was surrounded by cons. Their ill-fitting suits could not hide the prison tattoos and lean muscle that came from hours of pumping iron in the yard. There were dozens of men and women, maybe as many as fifty.

These were Rusty's real mourners—smoking outside, like the bad kids behind the gym at school.

"Charlotte." One of the men seized her hand. "I wanna tell you how much your daddy meant to me. Helped me get my kid back."

Charlie felt herself smile as she shook the man's rough hand.

"Helped me find a job," another man said. His front teeth were rotted, but the fine comb marks in his oily hair showed that he had made an effort for Rusty.

"He was all right." A woman flicked a cigarette toward the overflowing ashtray by the door. "Made my dickhead ex-husband pay child support."

"Come on," another guy said, likely the dickhead ex-husband.

Ben winked at Charlie before going back inside. An assistant district attorney wasn't popular with this crowd.

Charlie shook more hands. She tried not to cough from all of the smoke. She listened to stories about Rusty helping people when no one else seemed inclined to do so. She wanted to go back inside and get Sam, because her sister would want to hear what these people had to say about their complicated, irascible father. Or maybe Sam wouldn't *want* to. Maybe she would *need* to. Sam had always been so starkly drawn to black and white. The gray areas, the ones that Rusty seemed to thrive in, had always mystified her.

Charlie laughed to herself. The paradox was not lost on her that after unburdening to Sam her deepest, darkest sins, Charlie felt that the most important thing Sam could take back home with her was the knowledge that their father had been a good man.

"Charlotte?" Jimmy Jack Little blended in well with the cons. He had more tattoos than most of them, including a sleeve that he'd gotten during a prison stint for bank robbery. His black fedora put him in another place and time. He seemed perpetually angry, like it was to his utter disappointment that he was not one of the good guys being corrupted by a bad doll in a 1940s noir novel.

"Thanks for coming." Charlie hugged his neck, something she had never done before and probably would never do again. "Dad would've been happy you were here."

"Yeah. Well." He seemed overcome by the physical contact. He took his time lighting his cigarette, restoring his sense of macho toughery. "Sorry about the old shit. I expected him to go down in a blaze of bullets."

"I'm glad he didn't," Charlie said, because her father had been stabbed two days ago. Being shot to death was too close a possibility for her to joke about.

"This Adam Humphrey punk." Jimmy Jack picked some tobacco off his lip. "Not sure I got a bead on him. Could be he was buttering her biscuit, but kids today, girls and boys, they can be friends without the boom-chicka-wow-wow." He shrugged away the inexplicableness the way he would shrug off self-driving cars and Tivo. "Now, Frank Alexander, him I know from a couple years back. Guy had a DUI that Rusty helped disappear."

"Dad worked with the Alexander family?" Charlie realized her voice was too loud. She whispered, "What happened?"

"Pay-as-you-go as far as ol' Russ was concerned. Nothing unusual about their interaction. What happened was, Frank was burping his worm in the wrong mole hole. Got a little sauced with the gal at the no-tell motel, then came home to the wifey stinking of another chick's perfume. Or tried to go home. Cops slapped him with a DUI Less Safe."

Charlie knew this meant Frank Alexander's breathalyzer had been below the legal limit, but he was still charged with the DUI because the officer deemed his driving was impaired.

She asked, "The girlfriend, was she a student?"

"A real estate agent, a lot older than the wife, which doesn't make a hell of a lot of sense, because why? I mean, she's got money, sure, but chicks ain't classics, like cars. You want the soap at the end of your rope to be fresh, am I right?"

Charlie did not want to open up a discussion on the finer points of cheating. "So, what happened to Frank Alexander?"

"He did some community service, went to DUI school. The judge rolled the charge off his record so he could keep his teaching license. I've got some sources saying that the real problems were back home. Wife wasn't too happy about the old girlfriend. I mean, shit, why go older?"

Charlie asked, "Was there talk of divorce?"

Jimmy Jack shrugged. "Maybe they didn't have a choice. DUIs are a rich man's game. The legal bills. The cash money for the drunk classes. The fines. The fees. You know that shit sets you back eight, nine grand easy."

Charlie knew that was a lot of money for anybody, but the Alexanders were both schoolteachers with a young child. She doubted they had that kind of cash lying around.

Jimmy Jack said, "Nothing says 'I love you' like realizing you're gonna be eating ramen noodles for the rest of your life."

"Or maybe they love each other and they wanted to work it out because they had a kid?"

"That's real pretty talk coming from you, doll." He'd smoked his cigarette down to the filter. He tossed it into a planter by the door. "Guess it don't matter now. Rusty's not gonna pay me to track down this shit from the grave."

"Whoever takes over the case will need someone on the ground."

He winced, as if the thought caused him injury. "Dunno if I got it in me to work for a lawyer who's not your dad. Present company excluded. But shit, lawyers don't pay their bills and they just basically suck as human beings."

Charlie did not disagree.

He winked at her. "All right, dolly, go back to listening to these dirtbags. Those dickholes inside didn't know your dad. Not good enough to hold a cup of his piss if you ask me."

Charlie smiled. "Thank you."

Jimmy Jack clicked his tongue as he gave her a wink. Charlie watched him work his way through the crowd. He slapped a few backs, did a few fist bumps as he made his way toward the doors and, presumably, the open bar. He tipped his fedora to the woman who had gotten her kids back. She put her hand on her hip, and Charlie got the impression that neither of them were going to be alone tonight.

A car horn beeped.

They all looked out at the parking lot.

Ben was behind the wheel of his truck. Sam sat beside him.

The last time a boy had beeped a car horn at Charlie, Rusty had put her on restriction for crawling out her bedroom window in the middle of the night.

Ben beeped the horn again. He waved Charlie over.

She made her excuses to the group, though she assumed that

many of them had at one point in their lives run toward a truck idling in a parking lot.

Sam got out, her hand resting on the open door. Charlie could hear the truck's muffler belching from thirty feet away. Ben's Datsun was twenty years old, the only thing they could afford after the canceled trip to Colorado. They had sold his SUV for the loan payoff. A week later, the buyer was not amenable to selling it back to them. Rusty and Lenore had offered to let them keep the loaned money, but Charlie couldn't bring herself to do it. The clinic in Colorado had refunded the wire within days. The problem was the other bills: the flight and hotel cancellations, surcharges on their credit cards for cash advances, then the post-miscarriage hospital bills, surgical bills, specialist bills, anesthesiology bills, radiology bills, doctors' bills, pharmacy bills, and a ton of co-pays and an avalanche of no-pays. At the time, the debt was so crushing that they'd been lucky they could afford to pay cash for the piece-of-shit truck.

They had spent an entire weekend scraping the giant Confederate flag decal off the back window.

Sam said, "Ben offered to help me escape. I couldn't take being in that crowd for much longer."

"Me, either," Charlie said, though she would rather congregate with known felons than suffer through what she assumed was Sam's lame attempt at matchmaking.

Charlie had an awkward moment over the gearshift, which jutted out of the hump in the floor. She started to hike up her dress to straddle it, but Ben had made it clear the other night that he did not want his knob between her legs.

"You okay?" Ben asked.

"Sure." Charlie ended up sitting sidesaddle, knees clenched together, legs at an angle, like Bonnie Blue Butler before the fall.

The door groaned on rusty hinges as Sam pulled it shut. "A spray lubricant would alleviate that noise."

Ben said, "I tried some WD-40."

"That's a solvent, not a lubricant." She told Charlie, "I thought we could spend some time together at the farmhouse."

Charlie did a double take. She could not imagine why her sister would want to spend two seconds at that detestable place. The night before Sam had left for Stanford, she had made a not completely unfunny joke about the most efficient way to burn it to the ground.

Ben shifted the gear into drive. He made a tight U-turn around a cluster of parked cars. BMWs. Audis. Mercedes. Charlie hoped none of Rusty's mourners boosted them.

"Shit," Ben muttered.

Two police cars were parked on the median by the exit. Charlie recognized Jonah Vickery, Greg Brenner, and most of the other cops from the middle school. They were waiting to do the funeral escort, leaning against their cruisers, smoking cigarettes.

They recognized Charlie, too.

Jonah made circles with his fingers and put them to his eyes. The rest of the gang joined in, laughing like hyenas as they made raccoon eyes in honor of Charlie's bruises.

"Fuckers." Ben grabbed the handle and rolled down the window.

"Babe," Charlie said, alarmed.

He leaned out the window, fist raised. "Motherfuckers."

"Ben!" Charlie tried to pull him back in. He was almost yelling. What the hell had gotten into her passive husband? "Ben, what are—"

"Go fuck yourselves." Ben flipped them the bird with both hands. "Assholes."

The cops were no longer laughing. They stared Ben down as the truck pulled out onto the highway.

"Are you crazy?" Charlie demanded. She was supposed to be the unhinged one. "They could beat your ass."

"Let them."

"Let them kill you?" Charlie asked. "Jesus, Ben. They're dangerous. Like sharks. With switchblades."

Sam said, "Surely not switchblades? They're illegal."

Charlie felt a strangled groan die in her throat.

Ben rolled the window back up. "I'm so sick of this fucking place." He wrenched the gearshift into third, then pushed it into fourth as he sped up the highway.

Charlie stared at the empty road ahead.

He had never been sick of this place before.

"Well." Sam cleared her throat. "I love living in New York. The culture. The arts. The restaurants."

"I couldn't live up north," Ben said, as if entertaining the thought. "Maybe Atlanta."

Sam said, "I'm sure the public defender's office would be happy to have you."

Charlie glared at her sister, mouthing a *"What the fuck?"*

Sam shrugged, her expression unreadable.

Ben loosened his tie. He unbuttoned his collar. "I've done my time for the greater good. I want to join the dark side."

Charlie could almost feel her mind boggling. "What?"

"I've been thinking about it for a while," Ben said. "I'm tired of being a poor civil servant. I want to make some money. I want to own a boat."

Charlie pressed together her lips, the same as she had done when Lenore told her she was moving to Florida. Ben was generally easygoing about most things, but Charlie had learned that his mind, once made up, was not likely to change. He had clearly made up his mind about changing careers. Maybe he had made up his mind about leaving. There was something different about him. He seemed relaxed, almost giddy, like a great burden had been lifted from his shoulders.

Charlie assumed that the burden was her.

Sam offered, "We have some Atlanta firms we work with in

cases of criminal litigation. I could certainly write some letters of recommendation."

Charlie glared at her sister again.

"Thanks. I'll let you know after I do some research." Ben unknotted his tie. The material made a *thwip* sound as he pulled it through his collar. He tossed it behind the seat. "Kelly confessed on the hospital tape."

"Jesus!" Charlie's voice was high enough to break glass. "Ben, you can't tell us that."

"You've still got spousal privilege and her—" He laughed. "God, Sam, you scared the shit out of Coin. I could practically hear the crap coming out of his ass when you started to parry with the judge."

Charlie grabbed his arm. "What is wrong with you? You could get fired for—"

"I resigned last night."

Charlie let her hand drop.

Sam asked Ben, "The video—"

"Shit," Charlie whispered.

Sam said, "What do you think? Is she guilty?"

"Without a doubt, she's guilty. Forensics backs it up. She tested positive for gunpowder residue on her hand, the sleeve of her shirt, and around her shirt collar and right breast, exactly where you'd expect to find it." Ben chewed at the tip of his tongue. At least part of him still knew what he was doing was ethically wrong. "I don't like the way they got her to admit it. I don't like the way they do a lot of things."

Sam said, "Kelly can be talked into anything."

Ben nodded. "They didn't Mirandize her. Even if they did, who knows if she understands what a right to remain silent is."

"I think she's pregnant."

Charlie's head whipped around. "Why do you think that?"

Sam shook her head. She was talking to Ben. "Do you know what happened to the gun?"

"No." Ben asked, "Do you?"

"I do," Sam said. "Did Kelly say if she knew the victims?"

Ben provided, "She knew that Lucy Alexander was Frank Alexander's daughter, but I think that information came after the fact."

"About the Alexanders," Charlie jumped in. "Jimmy Jack told me that Frank got caught cheating on his wife a few years ago. He was pulled over for a DUI and the story came out."

"Ah," Sam said. "So, he's done it before. Was it a student?"

"No, a real estate agent. Wealthy, but older, which is apparently the wrong way to do it." Charlie added, "Dad represented Frank for the DUI. Jimmy Jack said it was routine."

"It was," Ben said. "Coin already looked into it. His focus is on the fact that Kelly had Frank for algebra. Frank was going to fail her. You heard the theory yesterday. Coin thinks a girl who has the IQ of a turnip is so worried and ashamed about failing algebra that she took a gun to school and killed two people. The wrong school, by the way."

"That's an interesting point," Sam said. "Why was Kelly at the middle school?"

"Judith Pinkman was tutoring her for some kind of English proficiency test."

"Ah," Sam repeated, as if pieces were finally clicking into place.

Ben added, "But Judith said she wasn't supposed to meet Kelly that week. She had no idea Kelly was even in the hall until she heard the gunshots."

Sam asked, "What else did Judith tell you?"

"Not much more. She was really upset. I mean, that sounds like an obvious thing because her husband was dead and then there was the stuff that happened with Lucy and probably seeing Charlie—" Ben glanced at Charlie, then back at the road. "Judith was really shaken. They had to sedate her just to get her into the ambulance. I guess that's when it hit her, like, the second she walked out of the building. She became hysterical, but like in the real sense of the word. Just completely overcome with grief."

"Where was Judith when the shooting started?"

Ben said, "In her room. She heard the gun go off. She was supposed to lock the door and hide in the corner at the back of her classroom, but she ran out into the hallway because she knew the first bell was about to ring and she wanted to warn the kids not to come. I mean, if she could do it without being shot. She wasn't thinking about her own safety, she said." He looked at Charlie again. "There was a lot of that going around."

Sam told him, "Boats are very expensive to maintain."

"I'm not looking for a yacht."

"There's insurance, docking fees, taxes."

Charlie could not listen to her estranged sister talk to her estranged husband about boats. She stared blankly at the road. She tried to work out what had just happened. Ben resigning—that was something she couldn't deal with right now. She concentrated instead on the conversation with Sam. Ben had prattled on like a jailhouse snitch. Sam had been more circumspect. Kelly pregnant. The gun missing. Charlie had been at the school when the shooting occurred, she had been a witness to part of what played out, but she was more in the dark than either of them.

Ben leaned over to look at Sam. "You should take over the Wilson case."

Sam laughed. "I couldn't afford the pay cut."

He slowed down for a tractor on the road. The farmer was taking up both lanes. His combine was down. Ben beeped the horn twice and the man edged over enough for him to pass on the median.

Ben and Sam resumed their idle boat chatter. Charlie found herself going back to Sam's questions, trying to see where they led. Sam had always been faster at solving puzzles. Faster at most things, to be honest. She was certainly better in the courtroom. Charlie had been in awe yesterday, and she had also called it right the first time. Sam had looked like the quintessential Victorian Dracula, from her stylish clothes to her air of entitlement, to the way she had unhinged her jaw and swallowed Ken Coin like a plump rat.

Sam asked, "How many bullets were fired?"

Charlie waited for Ben to answer, but then she realized Sam was talking to her. "Four? Five? Six? I don't know. I'm a really bad witness."

Ben said, "There's five on the tape. One in—"

"The wall, three in Pinkman, one in Lucy." She leaned back over to look at Ben. "How about near Mrs. Pinkman's room? Anything near her door?"

"I have no idea," he admitted. "The case is only two days old. They're still doing the forensics. But there's another witness. He said that he counted six shots, total. He's been in combat. He's pretty reliable."

Mason Huckabee.

Charlie looked down at her hands.

"What about the audio?"

"There's a really shaky cell phone call from the front office, but that was made after the shooting stopped. The audio you want came from an open mic on the cop in the hallway. That's where Coin got the thing about 'the baby.'" Ben added, "None of the gunshots were captured. We—at least I—don't have the coroner's report. There could be one more bullet inside the bodies."

Sam said, "I think I want to look at that video again."

"I can't access it. I was kind of frank in my resignation letter," Ben said. "I'm pretty sure I won't get a referral."

Charlie wanted to crawl under the covers in her bed and go to sleep. They had a mortgage. They had a car payment. Health insurance premiums. Car insurance. Property taxes. All the bills from three years ago.

"I'll be your referral." Sam had her hand deep in her purse, a leather bag that would likely pay for all of their bills. She pulled out Ben's *Enterprise* USB. "Does Dad have a computer?"

"He's got a great TV," Ben said. They had bought Rusty the

same model that they had at home. This had been four years ago, before Colorado. Before the boat.

Ben slowed the truck. They were at the HP, but he didn't turn into the driveway. Blood had stained the red clay an oily black. This was where her father had fallen the night he'd walked to the end of the driveway to get the mail.

Ben said, "They think the uncle stabbed Rusty."

"Faber?" Sam asked.

"Rick Fahey." Charlie remembered Lucy Alexander's uncle from the press conference. "Why do they think it's him?"

Ben shook his head. "I'm way out of the loop on that one. I heard some gossip at the office, then Kaylee was complaining about getting called out late the night Rusty was stabbed."

"So they needed someone to talk to a possible suspect," Charlie said, pretending that the way he'd casually dropped the name of the woman Charlie thought he was cheating with hadn't driven a knife into her own gut. "I think Dad saw whoever did it."

"I do, too," Sam said. "He spun a yarn to me about how there is value in forgiveness."

"Can you imagine," Charlie said. "If Dad had lived, he probably would've offered to represent Fahey."

No one laughed because they all knew that it was possible.

Ben put the gear in first. He made the turn into the driveway, driving slowly to avoid the ruts.

The farmhouse came into view, paint chipping, wood rotting, windows crooked, but not otherwise altered since the Culpeppers had knocked on the kitchen door twenty-eight years ago.

Charlie felt Sam shift in her seat. She was steeling herself, strengthening her resolve. Charlie wanted to say something that would bring her comfort, but all she could do was hold on to Sam's hand.

Sam asked, "Why no security bars and gates here? The office is a fortress."

"Dad said that lightning doesn't strike twice." Charlie felt the lump come back into her throat. She knew that the overabundant security at the office was for her sake, not Rusty's. Of the handful of times she had been to the HP over the years, she had inevitably stayed out in her car, laying on her horn for Rusty to come out because she did not want to go inside. Maybe if she had visited more, her father would have taken better measures to keep the place secure.

Ben said, "I can't believe I was here last weekend, talking to him on the porch."

Charlie longed to lean against him, to put her head on his shoulder.

"Brace yourselves," Ben said. The wheels bounced into a pothole, then hit a deep rut, before smoothing out. He started to pull to the parking pad by the barn.

"Go to the front door," Charlie said. She did not want to go through the kitchen.

"'Goat fucker,'" Sam said, reading the graffiti. "The suspect knew him."

Charlie laughed.

Sam did not. "I never thought I would come back here."

"You don't have to." Charlie offered, "I could go inside and look for the photo."

The set to Sam's jaw said she was determined. "I want us to find it together."

Ben looped the truck around to the front porch. The grass was mostly weeds. A kid from down the street was supposed to keep it mowed, but Charlie was ankle-deep in dandelions when she stepped out of the truck.

Sam held her hand again. They had not touched each other this much when they were children.

Except for that day.

Sam said, "I remember that I was sad about losing the red-brick house, but I also remember that it was a good day." She turned to Charlie. "Do you remember that?"

Charlie nodded. Gamma had wafted in and out of irritations, but everything had felt like it was starting to smooth out. "This could have been our home."

Ben said, "That's all kids want, right? To have a safe place to live." He seemed to remember himself. "I mean, safe before or—"

"It's all right," Charlie told him.

Ben tossed his suit jacket back into the truck. He grabbed his laptop from behind the seat. "I'll go inside and work on the TV."

Sam placed the USB drive in his hands. She told him, "Make sure I get that back so I can have it destroyed."

Ben gave her a salute.

Charlie watched him bolt up the stairs. He reached above the edge of the door frame for the key and let himself in.

Even from the yard, Charlie could smell the familiar odor of Rusty's unfiltered Camels.

Sam looked up at the farmhouse. "Still higgledy-piggledy."

"I guess we'll sell it."

"Did Dad buy it?"

"The bachelor farmer was a bit of a peeping Tom. And a foot fetishist. And he stole a lot of lingerie." Charlie laughed at Sam's expression. "He had a lot of legal bills when he died. The family deeded the house to Rusty."

Sam asked, "Why didn't Dad sell it years ago and rebuild the red-brick house?"

Charlie knew why. There had been a lot of bills from Sam's recovery. The doctors, the hospitals, the therapists, the rehab. Charlie was familiar with the crushing weight of an unexpected illness. Not much time or energy was left for rebuilding anything.

She told Sam, "I think it was mostly inertia. You know Rusty wasn't one for change."

"You can have the house. I mean—not that you asked, but I don't need the money. I just want Mom's photo. Or a copy of it. Of course I'll make one for you. Or for me. You can have the original if—"

"We'll figure it out." Charlie tried to smile. Sam was never rattled, but she was clearly rattled now. "I can do this for you, you know."

"Let's go." Sam nodded toward the house.

Charlie helped her up the stairs, though Sam did not ask. Ben had left the door open. She could hear him opening more windows to help air the place out.

They would be better off sealing it, like Chernobyl.

The bulk of Charlie's inheritance filled the front room. Old newspapers. Magazines. Copies of the *Georgia Law Review* dating back to the 1990s. File boxes from old cases. A prosthetic leg Rusty had taken as payment from a drunk everyone knew as Skip.

"The boxes," Sam said, because some of Gamma's thrift store finds had never been unpacked. She peeled back the dry tape on a cardboard box marked EVERYTHING $1 EA and took a purple Church Lady shirt off the top.

Ben watched from behind the TV set. He said, "There's another box in the den. You could probably make a fortune from that stuff on eBay." He looked at Charlie. "No *Star Trek*. Just *Star Wars*."

Charlie couldn't believe she had managed to disappoint her husband even as far back as when she was thirteen. "Gamma picked everything out, not me."

His head ducked behind the set. He was trying to hook up the components that Rusty had unplugged, claiming all of the blinking lights were going to give him seizures.

Sam said, "Okay, I think I'm ready."

Charlie did not know what she was ready for until she saw Sam looking into the long hallway that ran down the length of the house. The back door with its opaque window was at the far end. The kitchen was at the top. This was where Daniel Culpepper had stood when he had watched Gamma leave the bathroom.

Charlie could still remember her own trek down the hallway in search of the toilet, the way she had screamed "Fudge" for her mother's benefit.

There were five doors, none of them laid out in any way that made sense. One door led to the creepy basement. One led to the chifforobe. Another led to the pantry. Yet another led to the bathroom. One of the middle doors inexplicably led to the tiny downstairs bedroom where the bachelor farmer had died.

Rusty had turned this room into his office.

Sam went first. From behind, she seemed impervious. Her back was straight. Her head was held high. Even the slight hesitation in her gait was gone. Her only tell was that she kept her fingers touching the wall as if she needed to make sure she had access to something steady.

"The back door." Sam pointed toward the door. The frosted glass was cracked. Rusty had attempted to repair it with yellow masking tape. "You have no idea how many times I've woken up over the years dreaming about running out that door instead of walking into the kitchen."

Charlie said nothing, though she'd had the same kinds of dreams herself.

"All right." Sam wrapped her hand around the doorknob to Rusty's office. She opened her mouth and inhaled deeply, like a swimmer about to put her head underwater.

The door opened.

More of the same, but draped with the clinging odor of stale nicotine. The papers, the boxes, the walls, even the air had a yellow tint. Charlie tried to open one of the windows but paint had sealed it shut. She realized that her wrist felt sprained from banging on her father's casket. She was not having a good day with inanimate objects.

"I don't see it," Sam said, anxious. She was at Rusty's desk. She pushed some papers around, stacked others together. "It's not here." She looked at the walls, but they were adorned with drawings from Charlie's school projects. Only Rusty would tape on his wall an eighth grader's rendering of the anatomy of a dung beetle.

"There's this one," Charlie said, spotting the flimsy black metal frame that had held *the* photo for almost fifty years. "Shit, Dad." Rusty had let the sun bleach out their mother's face. Only the dark holes of her eyes and mouth were evident under the black mop of her hair.

"It's ruined." Sam sounded devastated.

Charlie felt sick with guilt. "I should've taken this from him a long time ago and had it preserved, or whatever you're supposed to do. I'm so sorry, Sam."

Sam shook her head. She dropped the picture back on the file. "That's not the photo he meant. Remember, he said there was a different one that he kept from us." She started moving around papers again, checking behind manuscript boxes and bound depositions. She seemed distressed. The picture was obviously important on its own, but this was also one of the last things that Rusty had spoken to Sam about.

Charlie took off her shoes so she didn't catch the heels on something and break her neck. The next year of her life was going to be wasted going through all of this shit. She might as well start now.

She hefted away some boxes from a shaky folding table. A row of unaccompanied red checkers spilled onto the floor. They managed to hit a pristine piece of bare hardwood. The sound was like jacks scattering.

She asked Sam, "Do you think he'd keep it in his filing cabinets?"

Sam looked wary. There were five wooden filing cabinets, all with heavy bar locks on them. "Can we find the keys in this mess?"

"He probably had them on him when they took him to the hospital."

"Which means they're in evidence."

"And we don't know anyone at the DA's office who could help us because my husband apparently told them all to fuck off." She thought of Kaylee Collins, and silently added, *Maybe not all of them.*

She asked Sam, "Dad was sure that you and I have never seen this picture before?"

"I told you this already. He said that he kept it to himself. That it captured the moment that he and Gamma fell in love."

Charlie felt the poignancy of her father's remark. His language had always been so annoyingly baroque that she had sometimes lost sight of the meaning. "He did love her," she told Sam.

"I know," she said. "I let myself forget that he lost her, too."

Charlie looked out the window. She had cried enough to last the rest of her life.

Sam said, "I can't leave without finding it."

"He could've been making it up," Charlie said. "You know how he loved to spin stories."

"He wouldn't lie about this."

Charlie kept her mouth shut. She wasn't so sure about that.

Ben asked, "Did you check the safe?" He was standing in the hall with a bunch of colored cables looped over his shoulders.

Charlie rubbed her eyes. "When did Dad get a safe?"

"When he figured out that you and Sam were reading everything he brought home." He pushed away a pile of boxes with his foot, revealing a floor safe that came up to the middle of his thigh. "Do you know the combination?"

"I didn't know he had a safe," Charlie reminded him. "Why would I know the combination?"

Sam knelt down. She studied the dial. "It would be a set of numbers that are relevant to Dad."

"What's the price on a carton of Camels?"

"I've got an idea." Sam spun the dial a few times. She stopped at the number two, then turned back to the number eight, then back to seventy-six.

Charlie's birthday.

Sam tried the handle.

The safe did not open.

Charlie said, "Try your birthday."

Sam spun the dial again, stopping at the correct numbers. She pulled on the handle. "Nope."

"Gamma's birthday," Ben suggested.

Sam entered the numbers. No luck. She shook her head, as if she had figured out the obvious. "Rusty's birthday."

She worked the dial quickly, entering Rusty's date of birth.

She tried the handle.

Again, nothing.

Sam looked at Ben. "Your birthday's next."

Charlie said, "Try 3-16-89."

The day the Culpeppers had shown up at the kitchen door.

Sam let out a slow breath. She turned back around. She spun the dial right, then left, then right again. She rested her fingers on the handle. She looked up at Charlie. She tried the handle.

The safe opened.

Charlie knelt down behind Sam. The safe was packed tight, just like everything else in Rusty's life. At first, all she smelled was musty old papers, but then there was something else, almost like a woman's perfume.

Sam whispered, "I think that's Mama's soap."

"Rose Petal Delight," Charlie recalled. Gamma bought it at the drug store. Her only vanity.

"I think it's coming from these." Sam had to use both hands to extricate a stack of envelopes wedged against the top.

They were tied with a red ribbon.

Sam smelled the letters. She closed her eyes like a cat purring in the sun. Her smile was beatific. "It's her."

Charlie smelled the envelopes, too. She nodded. The scent was faint, but it was Gamma's.

"Look." Sam pointed to the address, which was made out to Rusty, care of the University of Georgia. "This is her handwriting." Sam ran her fingers over the perfect, Palmer Method print of their mother. "The postmark is from Batavia, Illinois. That's where Fermilab is. These must be love letters."

"Oh," Ben said. "Yeah, you maybe don't want to read those."

"Whyever not?"

"Because they were really in love."

Sam was beaming. "But, that's wonderful."

"Is it?" Ben's voice went up to a register he probably hadn't used since puberty. "I mean, do you really wanna read a pack of scented letters your dad kept tied with a red string that are from way back when he and your mom just met and were probably—" He tucked his fingers into his open fist. "Think about it. Your dad could be a real horn dog."

Charlie felt queasy.

Sam said, "Let's put aside that decision for the moment." She placed the letters on top of the safe. She wedged her hand back inside and slid out a postcard.

Sam showed Charlie the aerial photo of the Johnson Space Center.

Gamma had worked with NASA before going to Fermilab.

Sam turned over the card. Again, their mother's neat handwriting was unmistakable.

Charlie read aloud the message to Rusty, " 'If you can see things out of whack, then you can see how things can be in whack.' —Dr. Seuss."

Sam gave Charlie a meaningful look, as if their mother was offering marital advice from the grave.

Charlie said, "Obviously, she was trying to communicate with Dad on his level."

"Obviously." Sam was smiling the same way she had on Christmas mornings. She had always opened presents so maddeningly slow, commenting on the wrapping paper, the amount of tape used, the size and shape of the box while Charlie tore through her gifts like a Chihuahua on methamphetamine.

Sam said, "We need to go through all of this very carefully." She made herself more comfortable on the floor. "I hope that we'll find the photo today, but if not, or I guess either way, do you mind if I take all of this back to New York? Some of it is very precious. I can catalog everything and—"

"It's fine," Charlie said, because she knew that Gamma and Sam had always spoken in their own, impenetrable language.

And also that she would never make a catalog.

"I'll bring them back," Sam promised. "You can meet me in Atlanta, or I can come up here."

Charlie nodded. She liked the idea of seeing her sister again.

"I can't believe Daddy kept this." Sam was holding one of her track and field ribbons. "He must have had it in his office. Otherwise, it would've burned in the fire. And—oh my goodness." She had found a pile of old school assignments. "Your paper on transcendentalism. Charlie, do you remember Gamma got into a two-hour argument with your teacher? She was so livid that he'd marginalized Louisa May Alcott. Oh—and look, my old report card. He was supposed to sign it."

Ben whistled for Charlie's attention. He was holding up a blank sheet of paper. "Your dad kept my drawing of a rabbit in a snowstorm."

Charlie grinned.

"Oh, wait." He took a pen off the desk and drew a black dot in the center of the page. "It's a polar bear's asshole."

She laughed, and then she wanted to cry because she missed his humor so much.

"Charlie," Sam said, delighted. "I think we hit the jackpot. Do you remember Mother's notebooks?" She was reaching into the safe again. This time, she brought out a large, leather-bound journal. She opened the cover.

Instead of diary pages filled with equations, there were blank checks.

Charlie looked over Sam's shoulder again. Spiral bound. Three rows to a sheet, torn stubs where older checks had been written. The account was drawn on Bank of America, but she did not recognize the company name. "Pikeville Holding Fund."

Sam paged through the check stubs, but the usual information—the date, the amount, and the person to whom the check was made payable—were blank. She asked Charlie, "Why would Dad have a business checking account for a holding company?"

"His escrow account is under Rusty Quinn, esquire," Charlie said. Most litigators had non-interest-bearing holding accounts into which settlement funds were deposited. The lawyer took his cut, then paid out the rest to the client. "But this doesn't make sense. Lenore does all of Dad's bookkeeping. She took over when he forgot to pay his electric bill and the power was cut off."

Ben rifled through a pile of unopened mail on Rusty's desk. He found an envelope and held it up. "Bank of America."

"Open it," Charlie said.

Ben extracted the one-page statement. "Holy crap. Over three hundred grand."

"Dad never had a client who got that kind of payout."

Ben said, "There's only one withdrawal last month, check number zero-three-four-zero for two thousand dollars."

Sam said. "Normally the first check number in an account starts with triple-zero one." She asked, "On what day was the last check written?"

"It doesn't say, but it was cashed four weeks ago."

"The second Friday of every month."

"What?" Charlie looked down at the checkbook. "Did you find something?"

Sam shook her head. She closed the leather cover.

Ben said, "Not to go all Scooby-Doo and the Gang, but do you want to try the pencil trick? Rub the lead over the blank checks that were underneath the ones he wrote? Rusty was quite the bearer-downer when he had a pen in his hand."

"That's brilliant, babe." Charlie stood to look for a pencil on the desk.

"We'll need to get official copies," Sam said. "A pencil rubbing won't tell us anything."

"It'll tell us who he wrote the checks to."

Sam held the journal to her chest. "I have several accounts with Bank of America. I can call them tomorrow and ask for copies. We'll need to get Dad's death certificate. Charlie, are you sure he didn't have a will? We really should look for it. A lot of older people draw up wills, but they don't tell their children."

Charlie froze. She felt sweat break out on the back of her neck. A car was making its way toward the house. The familiar bump when the front wheel hit the pothole. The crunching of rubber against packed red clay.

Sam said, "That's probably Stanislav, my driver. I told him to meet me here." She looked at the clock on Rusty's desk. "He made good time. I should find a box to put all of this in."

Charlie said, "Ben—"

"I'll go." Ben walked down the hallway.

Charlie stood in the hall, tracking his progress to the kitchen. He looked out the window. His hand encircled the doorknob. Her heart did a weird trembly thing inside of her chest. She did not want Ben in the kitchen. She did not want him to open the door.

Ben opened the door.

Mason Huckabee stood on the side porch. He looked up at Ben, surprised. He was wearing a black suit with a blue tie and a camouflage ball cap.

Ben did not speak to the man. He turned around. He walked back down the hall.

Charlie felt sick. She ran to meet Ben. She blocked his way, her hands touching either side of the wall. "I'm sorry."

Ben tried to go around.

Charlie held firm. "Ben, I didn't ask him here. I don't want him here."

Ben wasn't going to push her out of his way. He stared at her. He chewed the tip of his tongue.

"I'll get rid of him. I've been trying to get rid of him."

Sam called from the office, "Ben, can you help me pack this stuff?"

Charlie knew that Ben was too much of a gentleman to tell her no.

She reluctantly let him pass. She ran toward the kitchen, practically galloping down the hallway.

Mason waved to her, because he had a clear line of sight to the back of the house. He had the sense not to smile as she got closer. He said, "I'm sorry."

"You're going to be fucking sorry," Charlie whispered, her voice hoarse. "I wasn't bullshitting you about that restraining order. It'll take me two minutes to blow up your entire fucking life."

"I know that," he said. "Look, I'm sorry. I'm really sorry. I just want to talk to you and your sister."

Charlie ignored the desperation in his tone. "I don't care what you want. You need to leave."

Sam said, "Charlie, let him in."

Charlie turned around. Sam stood in the hallway. She was touching the wall with her fingers again. "In here," she told Mason, then walked into the living room before Charlie could tell her no.

Mason stepped into the kitchen without being invited. He stood inside the doorway. He took off his ball cap. He worked it between his hands. He looked around the room, clearly unimpressed. Rusty had not changed anything since the day they had moved in. The rickety chairs, the chipped table. The only thing missing was the air conditioner that had been in the window. There had been no way to get the pieces of Gamma out of the fan.

"This way." Charlie scanned the empty hallway for Ben. The door to Rusty's office was closed. Ben's truck hadn't left. He had not opened the back door. He must be in Rusty's office wondering why his wife was such a whore.

"I'm sorry about your father," Mason said.

Charlie spun around. "I know who you are."

Mason looked alarmed.

"I didn't know when I met you, clearly, but then my sister told me about your sister, and—" She struggled to find the right words. "I'm very sorry for what happened to her. And to you and your family. But what you and I did, that was a one-time mistake, a huge mistake. I'm in love with my husband."

"You said that before. I understand. I respect that." Mason nodded to Sam. She had made a space to sit on a straight-back chair. The footage from the school security camera was paused on the TV set beside her. Ben had figured out how to make it work.

Mason stared at the massive screen. "Who's going to be Kelly's lawyer now?"

Sam said, "We'll find someone from Atlanta."

"I can pay," he said. "My family has money. My parents do. Did. They had a trucking company."

Charlie remembered the signs from her childhood. "Huckabee Hauling."

"Yeah." He looked at the paused footage again. "Is that from the other day?"

Charlie did not want to open the conversation. "Why are you here?"

"It's just—" He cut himself off. Instead of offering an explanation for his continued, unwanted presence, he said, "Kelly tried to kill herself. That shows remorse. I read about it on the Internet, that remorse matters in death penalty cases. So you could use that during her trial to make the jury give her life, or maybe life with a chance of parole. They know that, right?"

"Who knows that?" Sam asked.

"The police. The prosecutor. You guys."

Charlie told him, "They'll say it was a cry for help. She gave up the gun. She didn't pull the trigger."

"She did," he said. "Three times."

"What?" Sam stood up from the chair.

Charlie said, "You can't lie about this. People were there."

"I'm not lying. She put the gun to her chest. You were twenty feet away. You had to see it, or at least hear it." He told Sam, "Kelly pressed the muzzle to her chest, and she pulled the trigger three times."

Charlie had absolutely no recollection of any of this.

"I heard the clicks," he said. "I bet Judith Pinkman did, too. I'm not making this up. She really tried to kill herself."

Sam asked, "Then why didn't you just take away the gun?"

"I didn't know if she'd reloaded. I'm a Marine. You always assume a weapon is hot unless you can clearly visualize the empty chamber."

"Reloaded," Sam repeated, giving weight to the word. "When the shooting began, how many shots did you hear?"

"Six," he said. "One, then there was a pause, then there were three real quick in a row, then there was a shorter pause, then another shot, then a quick pause, then another shot." He shrugged. "Six."

Sam sat back down. She reached into her purse. "You're sure about that?"

"If you've been in close-quarters combat as many times as I have, you learn really fast to count the bullets."

She had her notepad in her lap. "And Kelly's revolver holds six shots?"

"Yes, ma'am."

Charlie asked, "Was it empty when you took it?"

Mason glanced nervously at Sam.

She said, "Now would be a good time to explain why you stuck it down the back of your pants."

"Instinct." He shrugged, as if committing a felony was inconsequential. "The cop wouldn't take it, so I just stowed it, temporarily, like you said, in the waist of my pants. And then none of the cops asked me about it, or searched me for it, and then I was out the door and in my truck before I realized it was still there."

Sam did not poke holes in the thin story. Instead, she asked, "What did you do with the gun?"

"I took it apart and dropped it around the lake. The deepest parts."

Again, she let him off the hook. "Is it possible to tell whether a gun is loaded just by looking at it?"

"No," Mason said. "I mean, a nine-mill, the slide will go back, but you can pop the catch and—"

Charlie interrupted, "With a revolver, once the bullets are fired, the shells stay in the cylinder."

"They do," Mason confirmed. "All six of them were left in the cylinder, so she hadn't reloaded."

Charlie said, "Which means that she knew the gun was empty when she clicked the trigger three times."

"You don't know that," Mason insisted. "Kelly probably thought—"

"Verify the sequence for me, please." Sam slid the pen out of her notepad. She started writing as she spoke. "One shot, long pause, three quick shots, then a short pause, then another shot, then another short pause, then another shot. Right?"

Mason nodded.

She said, "There was another shot fired after Lucy Alexander was hit in the neck."

"Into the floor," Mason said. "I mean, that's what I'm assuming."

Sam arched her brow.

He explained, "I saw a bullet hole in the floor, right around here." He pointed to the right side of the screen. "It wouldn't be on the video because of the camera angle. It's closer to the door. More like where Kelly ended up when they cuffed her."

Charlie asked, "What did the hole look like?"

"The tile was chipped away, but there was no stippling, so it was probably fired from a distance of at least two, three feet. It was oval, too. Like a tear drop, so it was shot down and at an angle." He held out his hand, finger, and thumb in the shape of a weapon. "So, at her waist, maybe? She's shorter than I am, but the angle wasn't that steep. You'd have to string it." Mason shrugged. "I'm not really an expert. I took a class as part of my continuing ed during my service."

Sam said, "She didn't want to kill Judith Pinkman, so she shot the last bullet into the floor."

Mason shrugged again. "Maybe. But she knew the Pinkmans from way back, and that didn't keep her from killing Doug."

"She knew them?" Sam asked.

"Kelly was the water girl for the football team. That's when those rumors started about her and one of the players. I'm not one hundred percent on what happened, but Kelly missed a couple'a three weeks of school and the kid left town, so—" He shrugged off the rest, but he must have been talking about the rumors that had spurred half the school to denigrate Kelly Wilson in her own yearbook.

Sam clarified, "Douglas Pinkman was the coach of the football team, so he would know Kelly Wilson from her stint as a water girl."

"Right. She did two seasons, I think, along with another girl from the special ed group. The county office sent down this edict that we were supposed to integrate the special kids into more extracurricular programs: marching band, cheerleading, basketball, football. It was a good idea. I think it really helped some of them. Obviously not Kelly, but—"

"Thank you." Sam went back to her notes. She turned the pages slowly, making notations with her pen. She hadn't dismissed Mason so much as found something more interesting.

Mason looked at Charlie for some kind of explanation.

Charlie could shrug, too. "What did you want to talk to us about?"

"Yeah." He worked his hat between his hands. "Do you mind if I use your bathroom first?"

She couldn't believe he was dragging this out. "It's back down the hall."

He nodded before leaving, like they were in an English drawing room.

Charlie turned to Sam, who was still focused on her notes. "Why are you talking to him? We need to get him out of here."

"Can you look at this and tell me what you see?" Sam pointed to the right side of the screen. "I don't trust my eyes. Does this shadow look odd to you?"

Charlie heard Mason open the door to the bathroom, then close it. Thank God he hadn't accidentally found Rusty's office.

Charlie told Sam, "Please help me get rid of him."

"I will," Sam said. "Just look at the video."

Charlie stood in front of the giant set. She studied the paused footage. She could see that the camera was angled down, only capturing half of the hallway. The famous blind spot that Mason had told her about. The overhead lights were on, but a weird shadow came from the right-hand side of the hallway. Narrow, long, almost like a spider's leg.

"Wait," Charlie said, but not because of the video. "How did he know where the bathroom is?"

"What?"

"He just walked right to it and opened the door." Charlie felt a prickling sensation in her spine. "No one guesses the right door, Sam. There are five of them, and none of them make any sense. You know that. It's pretty much a joke that no one can figure them out." Charlie's heart started throbbing at the base of her throat. "Do you think Mason knew Dad? That he's been here before? Like a lot of times before, so he knows where the bathroom is without being told?"

Sam opened her mouth. She closed it.

"You know something," Charlie guessed. "Did Dad tell you—"

"Charlie, sit down. I don't know anything for certain at the moment, but I'm trying to work it out."

Sam's calmness made her anxious. "Why do you want me to sit down?"

"Because you're hovering over me like a military drone."

"You couldn't say something delicate, like a hummingbird?"

"Hummingbirds are quite vicious, actually."

"Chuck!" Ben yelled.

Charlie felt her heart lurch. She had never heard him scream so loudly before.

"Chuck!" Ben yelled again.

His footsteps pounded up the hall. He overshot the living room. He doubled back, frantic.

"Are you okay?" Ben looked over his shoulder, up and down the hall. "Where is he?"

Charlie said, "Ben, what—"

"Where the fuck is he!" Ben screamed so loudly that she put her hands to her ears. "Mason!" He slammed his fist into the wall. "Mason Huckabee!"

The bathroom door creaked open.

"You fucker!" Ben screamed, storming back down the hall.

Charlie ran after him. She skidded to a stop as Ben tackled Mason to the floor.

Ben's fists started to swing. Mason held up his arms, covering his face. Charlie was filled with horror as she watched her husband beat another man.

"Ben!" She had to do something. "Ben—stop!"

Sam grabbed Charlie by the waist, holding her back.

"I have to—" Charlie stopped. She didn't know what to do. Mason would kill Ben. He was a trained soldier. "Sam, we have to—"

"He's not fighting back," Sam said, almost as if she was narrating a documentary. "Look, Charlie. He's not fighting back."

She was right. Mason lay on the floor, his hands covering his face, as he absorbed every blow to his head, his neck, his chest.

"You coward!" Ben screamed. "Show me your fucking face!"

Mason took away his hands.

Ben landed a solid blow across Mason's jaw. Charlie heard teeth crack. Blood spewed from Mason's mouth. He lay there, hands out to the side, and took the beating.

Ben did not let up. He punched him again, then again, then again.

"No," Charlie whispered.

Blood spattered the wall.

Mason's eyebrow opened against the edge of Ben's wedding band.

His lip was split.

The skin of his cheek was rent.

Mason still just lay there, taking it.

Ben hit him again.

Again.

"I'm sorry," Mason said, slurring the word. "I'm sorry."

"You fucking—" Ben reared back his elbow, his whole body twisting, then slammed his fist into Mason's jaw.

Charlie watched the skin on Mason's cheek ripple like the wake behind a boat. She heard a sharp crack, a bat hitting a ball. Mason's head whipped to the side.

His eyelids fluttered.

Blood dribbled from his mouth, his nose.

He blinked again, but he did not move. His gaze stayed on the wall. Blood dripped down the dusty baseboard and pooled onto the hardwood floor.

Ben sat back on his heels. He was panting from exertion.

"I'm sorry," Mason said. "I'm sorry."

"Fuck your sorry." Ben spat in his face. He fell to the side, his shoulder hitting the wall. His hands dropped to his sides. Blood dripped from his knuckles. He wasn't screaming anymore. He was crying. "You—" he tried again, his voice breaking. "You let him rape my wife."

CHAPTER EIGHTEEN

Charlie felt her vision blur. Panic gripped her throat. She could only hear the screaming inside her head.

Ben knew.

She asked Sam, "Did you tell him?"

"No," Sam said.

"Don't lie to me, Samantha. Just tell me."

"Charlie," Sam said. "You're focusing on the wrong thing."

There was only one wrong thing. Her husband knew what had happened to her. He had beat a man nearly senseless because of it. He had spat on him, he had told him—

You let him rape my wife.

Let him.

Charlie felt a rush of air leaving her lungs. Her hand slapped to her mouth as bile swirled up her throat.

"It was him," Ben said. "Not Daniel."

"In the woods?" Charlie asked, her vocal cords straining around the question. She saw Zachariah Culpepper's hideous face. She had punched him so hard that his head had whipped around. Blood had come out of his mouth. And then Daniel Culpepper had tackled him to the ground and started beating him the way that Ben had just beaten Mason Huckabee.

Except it had not been Daniel Culpepper in the woods.

Charlie said, "You tackled Zachariah." She had to swallow before she could add, "You were too late."

"I know." Mason rolled over onto his back. He covered his eyes with his hand. "In the house. In the woods. I was always too late."

Charlie felt her knees turn rubbery. She leaned her shoulder into the wall. "Why?"

Mason moved his head side to side. He was breathing hard. Blood bubbled out of his nose.

"Tell them," Ben said, fists clenched.

Mason wiped his nose with the back of his hand. He looked at Ben, then Sam, then Charlie. Finally, he answered, "I hired Zach to help me take care of Rusty. I gave him everything I'd saved up for college. I knew that he owed Rusty money, but——" He stopped, his voice cracking. "You guys were supposed to be at track practice. We were gonna take Rusty, drive him down the access road, and get rid of him. Zach would get three grand on top of wiping away his legal bills. I would get my revenge . . ." He looked at Sam again, then Charlie. "I tried to stop Zach when your dad wasn't here, but he——"

"You don't have to tell us what he did." Sam's words were so strained that they were almost inaudible in the open space.

Mason covered his face again. He started to cry.

Charlie listened to his dry sobs and wanted to punch him in the throat.

Mason said, "I was going to take the fall for your mom. I said that out in the woods. Five times, at least. You both heard me. I never wanted any of it to happen." His voice cracked again. "When your mom was shot, it was like I was numb, like, I couldn't believe it. I just felt sick, and shaky, and I wanted to do something but I was scared of Zach. You know what he's like. We were all scared of him."

Charlie felt rage pumping through every artery in her body. "Don't you *we* any of this, you pathetic prick. There was no *we* in the kitchen except me and Sam. *We* were forced out of our house. *We* were led into the woods at gunpoint. *We* were terrified for our lives. *You* shot my sister in the head. *You* buried her alive. *You* let that monster chase me through the woods, rape me, beat me, take away everything—*everything*—from me. That was you, Mason. That was all you."

"I tried—"

"Shut up." Charlie clenched her fists as she stood over him. "You might tell yourself that you tried to stop it, but you didn't. You let it happen. You helped it happen. *You* pulled that trigger." She stopped, trying to catch her breath. "Why? Why did you do it? What did we ever do to you?"

"His sister," Sam said. Her voice had a deathly kind of calmness. "That's what he meant about getting his revenge. Mason and Zachariah showed up the same day Kevin Mitchell walked on the rape charge. We assumed it was about Culpepper's legal bills when it was really about Mason Huckabee being mad enough to kill but too scared to do it with his own hands."

Charlie's tongue turned into lead. She had to lean against the wall again to keep from falling down.

Mason said, "I was the one who found my sister. She was in the barn. Her neck was—" He shook his head. "She was tortured by what that bastard did to her. She couldn't get out of bed. She just cried all the time. You don't know what it's like to feel that useless, that helpless. I wanted someone to be punished. Someone had to be punished."

"So you came looking for my father?" Charlie felt the now-familiar vibration in her hands. It spread up her arms, into her chest. "You came here to kill my father, and you—"

"I'm sorry." Mason started crying again. "I'm sorry."

Charlie wanted to kick him. "Don't you fucking cry. You shot my sister in the head."

"It was an accident."

"It doesn't matter!" Charlie yelled. "You shot her! You buried her alive!"

Sam's arm went out. She blocked Charlie from standing over Mason, beating him the same way Ben had.

Ben.

Charlie looked at her husband. He was sitting on the floor, back to the wall. His glasses were blood-streaked, crooked on his face. He kept flexing his hands, opening the wounds, encouraging more blood to flow.

Sam asked, "Why was Rusty writing checks to Zachariah Culpepper's son?"

Charlie was so shocked she could not make her mouth form a question.

Sam explained, "The check numbers. Twelve checks a year for twenty-eight years, four months, would be a total of three hundred forty checks."

"That's the most recent check number," Charlie remembered.

"Right," Sam confirmed. "And then there's the balance. You started at one million, correct?"

She was asking Mason.

Slowly, reluctantly, Mason nodded.

Sam said, "If you start at one million and subtract two thousand dollars a month for twenty-eight years and change, that leaves you with approximately three hundred twenty thousand dollars." She told Mason, "Everything began to click into place when you told us that your parents had money. Back in 1989, no one else in Pikeville had that kind of wealth and especially that kind of reach. They traded your freedom for one million dollars. That would've been a lot back then. More than Culpepper would ever see in his abbreviated lifetime. He bargained away his dead brother for his unborn son."

Mason looked up at her. He slowly nodded.

Sam asked, "What was my father's part in this? Did he set up the deal between you and Culpepper?"

"No."

"Then, what?" Sam demanded.

Mason rolled to his side. He pushed himself up. He sat with his back toward the door. The masking tape Rusty had used on the window made a sort of lightning bolt above his head. "I didn't know about any of it."

Ben glowered at Mason. "You're gonna rot in hell for dragging Rusty into your bullshit."

"It wasn't Rusty. Not at first." Mason winced as he touched his jaw. "My parents set up the arrangement. The night it happened, I walked home. Six miles. Zach took my shoes, my jeans, because they had his blood on them. I was half-naked, covered in blood, by the time I got home. I confessed to both of them. I wanted to go to the police. They wouldn't let me. I found out later they sent a lawyer to talk to Zach."

"Rusty," Ben said.

"No, someone from Atlanta. I don't know who." Mason worked his jaw. The joint popped. "They left me out of it. I had no choice."

Sam said, "You were a seventeen-year-old man. I'm certain you had a car. You could've gone to the police on your own, or waited until you turned eighteen."

"I wanted to," Mason insisted. "They locked me in my room. Four guys came. They drove me to a military academy up north. I joined the Marines as soon as I was old enough." He wiped blood out of his eye. "I was in Afghanistan, Iraq, Somalia. I kept volunteering. I wanted to earn it, you know? I wanted to use my life to help other people. To redeem myself."

Charlie bit her lip so hard that she felt the skin start to open. There was no redemption, no matter how many countries he had pinned on his stupid world map.

Mason said, "I put in my twenty years. I moved back home. I went to school. I thought it was important to give back here, in this town, to these people."

"You bastard." Ben stood up. His hands were still clenched.

He walked down the hall. Charlie was afraid that he was going to continue out the back door, but he stopped at Mason's iPhone. He slammed his heel into the glass, breaking it into tiny pieces.

Ben lifted his shoe. Glass clinked down from the sole. He said, "Daniel Culpepper was murdered because of you."

"I know," Mason said, but he was wrong.

Charlie was the one who unleashed Ken Coin on Daniel.

She told Mason, "He called you 'brother.'"

Mason shook his head. "He called a lot of people brother. It's just something guys do."

"It doesn't matter," Ben said. "Neither one of them should have been here in the first place. Whatever happened after that is on them."

"It is," Mason agreed. "It's on me. All of it's on me."

Sam asked, "How did your clothes and your gun end up at Daniel's trailer?"

Again, Mason shook his head, but it wasn't hard to come up with the answer. Ken Coin had planted the evidence. He had framed an innocent man and let a guilty one go free.

Mason said, "My mom told me about the arrangement after my dad died. I was stationed in Turkey, trying to do right by people. I came home for the funeral. She was worried something would happen and Zach would renege on his part of the deal."

Sam said, "To be clear, the deal was that Zach would keep silent about Daniel's innocence—and your guilt—in exchange for two thousand dollars a month to be paid by your parents to his son, Danny Culpepper?"

Mason nodded. "I didn't know. Not until my mother told me. Eight years had gone by. Culpepper was still on death row. He kept getting out of his execution dates."

Charlie clenched her jaw. Eight years after the murder. Eight years after Sam clawed out of her grave. Eight years after Charlie was ripped apart.

Sam had been starting her master's at Northwestern. Charlie

was applying to law school, praying that she could make a fresh start.

Sam asked, "How did my father get roped into this?"

"I went to him to confess," Mason said. "Here, in this house. We sat in the kitchen. I don't know why, but in a way it made it easier to sit at the table and unburden myself. The scene of the crime. I got sick just letting it all out, every piece of the truth. I told him how I was torn up about Mary-Lynne, how I paid Zach to help me get my revenge. When you're young like that, you see things so clearly. You don't understand how the world works. That there are consequences you can't predict. That bad choices, bad deeds, can corrupt you." Mason was nodding, as if to agree with himself. "I wanted to explain to Rusty what happened, *why* it happened, man to man."

"You're not a man," Charlie told him, sickened by the thought of Mason and Rusty sitting in the kitchen where Gamma had died, that the setting had brought Mason absolution rather than pain. "You're an attempted murderer. You're an accomplice to rape. To the murder of my mother. To abduction. Kidnapping. Breaking and fucking entering." She could not let herself think about all the girlfriends he'd had, the parties he'd attended, the birthdays, the New Year's Eve celebrations, while Sam got out of bed every morning praying that she could fucking walk. She told Mason, "Joining the Marines does not make you a good man. It makes you a coward for running away."

Charlie's voice was so loud that she heard her words echo up the hallway.

Ben said, "Rusty had him sign a confession." He looked at Sam, not Charlie. "I found it in the safe."

Charlie looked up at the ceiling. She let her tears fall. She would never forgive herself for making Ben find out from a piece of paper.

Mason said, "I *wanted* to sign the confession. I wanted to come forward. I was sick with it, the lies, the guilt."

Sam held on to Charlie's arm as if to keep them both rooted in place. "Why didn't Dad turn you in?"

"He didn't want another trial," Mason said. "You guys were living your lives, getting past it."

"Getting past it," Charlie mumbled.

Mason continued, "Rusty didn't want it dredged up again, to make you come home, to make Charlie go on the stand. He didn't want her to have to—"

"Lie," Sam finished.

The box, sealed for so long, placed high on the closet shelf. Rusty had not wanted to force Charlie to choose between lying under oath and opening up the box for the world to see.

The Culpepper girls.

The torture those nasty bitches had put her through—still put her through. What would they say, what would they do, if proof came out that they had been right about Daniel's innocence all along?

They *had* been right.

Charlie had pointed her finger at the wrong man.

Sam asked, "Why did my father write the checks?"

Mason said, "That was one of Rusty's stipulations. He wanted Zach to know that he knew, that somebody else could blow up the deal, cut off the money to Danny, if Zach didn't keep his mouth shut."

"That put a target on his back," Charlie said. "Culpepper could've had him killed."

Mason shook his head again. "Not if he wanted the checks to keep going to his son."

"Do you think he really cared about his son?" Sam asked. "Culpepper was taunting him. Did you know that? Every month, he sent Rusty a letter telling him *You owe me*. Just to rub it in. To remind Rusty that he could tear apart all of our lives, rob us of our peace, our sense of safety, at any moment."

Mason said nothing.

470 | KARIN SLAUGHTER

Sam demanded, "Do you know what kind of stress you caused our father? Lying to us. Hiding the truth. He wasn't built for that kind of deception. He'd already lived through his wife being murdered, his daughter almost dying, Charlie being——" She shook her head. "Rusty's heart was already weak. Did you know that? Do you know how much your lies, your guilt, your cowardice, contributed to his bad health? Maybe that's why he drank so much, to chase away the bad taste of his own complicity. Complicity that you drew him into. He had to live with that every day, every month when he wrote that check, every time he called me——"

Sam finally broke. She took off her glasses. She pressed her fingers to her eyelids. She said, "He was protecting us all of those years because of you."

Mason leaned his head between his knees. If he was crying again, Charlie did not care.

Ben asked, "Why are you here? Did you think you could talk them out of turning you in?"

"I came to confess," Mason said. "To tell you I'm sorry. That I have tried every day since then to make up for what I did. I've got medals." He looked up at Sam. "I've got combat medals, a purple heart, a——"

"I don't care," Sam said. "You've had twenty-eight years of your life to plead guilty. You could have walked into any police station, confessed, and taken your punishment, but you were afraid you would end up with life in prison, or on death row, the same as Zachariah Culpepper."

Mason did not answer, but the truth was self-evident.

Charlie said, "You knew we never told anybody about what really happened in the woods. That's how you got my father on your side, isn't it? You blackmailed him. My secret for yours."

Mason wiped blood from his mouth. He still said nothing.

Charlie said, "You sat in that kitchen where my mother was murdered, and you told my father that you would use your family's money to fight a murder conviction, no matter who it hurt, no matter what came out during the trial. Sam would've been dragged back down here. I would've been forced to testify. You knew Daddy wouldn't let that happen to us."

Mason only asked, "What are you going to do now?"

"It's what you're going to do," Sam said. "You've got exactly twenty minutes to drive to the police station and confess on the record, without a lawyer, to lying to the police and taking Kelly Wilson's gun from the scene of a double homicide or so help me I will take your written confession to attempted murder and conspiracy to commit murder straight to the chief of police. This town doesn't forget, Mason. Your excuse that you were just standing there, that it was an accident, still constitutes felony murder. If you don't do exactly as I say right now, you'll end up in a cell beside Zachariah Culpepper, where you should've been for the last twenty-eight years."

Mason wiped his hands on his pants. He reached for his broken phone.

Ben kicked it away. He opened the back door. "Get out."

Mason stood up. He did not speak. He turned and walked out of the house.

Ben slammed the door so hard that a new crack spread up the window.

Sam put her glasses back on. She asked Ben, "Where is the confession?"

"On the safe by the letters."

"Thank you." Sam did not go to the office.

She walked into the living room.

Charlie hesitated. She didn't know whether or not to follow Sam. What could she say to her sister that could possibly make either of them feel better? The man who had shot Sam in the head, who had buried her alive, had just walked out their back door with nothing but a threat to make him do the right thing.

Ben turned the latch on the deadbolt.

Charlie asked him, "Are you all right?"

He took off his glasses, wiped the blood from the lenses. "I've never been in a real fight before. Not where I managed to hit anybody."

"I'm sorry. I'm sorry that you were upset. I'm sorry that I lied. I'm sorry that you had to read about what happened instead of me telling you myself."

"There's nothing in the confession about what Zachariah did to you." Ben slid his glasses back on. "Rusty told me."

Charlie was speechless. Rusty had never betrayed a confidence.

Ben said, "Last weekend. He didn't tell me Mason was involved, but he told me everything else. He said that the worst sin he had ever committed against anybody in his life was making you keep it a secret."

Charlie rubbed her arms, unable to fight off a sudden chill.

Ben said, "What happened to you—I'm sorry, but I don't care."

Charlie felt his disregard as an almost physical pain.

"I said that wrong." Ben tried to explain, "I'm sorry it happened, but it doesn't matter. I don't care that you lied. I don't care, Chuck."

"It's why—" Charlie looked down at the floor. Fittingly, Mason Huckabee had left a trail of blood on his way out of the house.

"It's why what?" Ben was standing in front of her. He tilted up her chin. "Chuck, just say it. Holding it in is killing you."

He already knew. He knew everything. And still, she struggled to give voice to her own failures. "The miscarriages. They were because of what happened."

Ben rested his hands on her shoulders. He waited for her to look him in the eye, then said, "When I was nine years old, Terri kicked me in the nuts, and I peed blood for a week."

Charlie started to speak, but he shook his head, telling her not to.

"When I was fifteen, I got punched in the junk by a jock. I was just hanging with my nerd herd, minding my own business, and he punched my balls so hard I thought they went up my asshole."

Ben pressed his finger to her lips so she could not interrupt.

"I keep my cell phone in my front pocket. I know I'm not supposed to because it scrambles your sperm, but I do it anyway. And I can't wear boxers. You know I hate the way they bunch up. And I masturbated a lot. I mean, some now, but when I was a kid, I was Olympic-ready. I was the only member of the Starfleet Club in my school, and I collected comic books, and I played triangle in the band. No girl would look at me. Not even the ones with acne. I jerked myself off so much that my mom took me to the doctor because she was worried I would get blisters."

"Ben."

"Chuck, listen to me. I dressed up as red shirt ensign from *Star Trek* for my senior prom. There wasn't a theme. I was the only guy who wasn't in a tux. I thought I was being ironic."

Charlie finally smiled.

"Obviously, I was not meant to procreate. I have no idea why I ended up with someone as hot as you, or why we couldn't—" He didn't say the words. "It's just the card we drew, babe. We don't know if it's something that happened to me or something that happened to you or plain old natural selection, but that's the way it is, and I am telling you that I don't care."

Charlie cleared her throat. "Kaylee could give you children."

"Kaylee gave me gonorrhea."

Charlie should have felt wounded, but the first emotion that registered was concern. Ben was allergic to penicillin. "Did you have to go to the hospital?"

"I spent the last ten days going to Ducktown so no one here would find out."

Now she felt the wound. "So, this was recent."

"The last time was almost two months ago. I thought I was just having trouble peeing."

"You didn't think that was a sign that you should go to the doctor?"

"Eventually, obviously," he said. "But that's why I didn't—the other night. I tested clean, but it didn't feel right to not tell you. And I was there to check on you because I was worried. I didn't need a file. There was no plea deal that went south."

Charlie did not care about the lie. "How long did it last?"

"It didn't last. It was four times, and it was fun at first, but then it was just sad. She's so young. She thinks Kate Mulgrew got her start on *Orange Is the New Black*."

"Wow," Charlie said, trying to make a joke so she didn't cry. "How did she manage to get through law school?"

Ben tried to joke, too. "You were right about being on top. It's a lot of work."

Charlie felt nauseated. "Thanks for the image."

"Try never being able to sneeze again."

Charlie chewed the inside of her cheek. She should have never told him the details. She sure as hell wished she had not heard his.

He said, "I'm going to go pack up that stuff for Sam."

Charlie nodded, but she didn't want him to go, not even down the hall.

He kissed her forehead. She leaned into him, smelling his sweat and the wrong detergent he was using on his shirts.

He said, "I'll be in your dad's office."

Charlie watched his goofy, loping gait as he walked away.

He hadn't left the house.

That had to be something.

Charlie didn't immediately go to Sam. She turned around. She looked into the kitchen. The door was hanging open. She could feel the breeze coming through. She tried to adjust her memory to that moment when she had opened the door, expecting to find Rusty, instead seeing two men, one in black, one wearing a Bon Jovi T-shirt.

One with a shotgun.

One with a revolver.

Zachariah Culpepper.

Mason Huckabee.

The man who had been too late to stop Charlie's rapist was the same man she'd had frenzied sex with in the parking lot of Shady Ray's.

The same man who had shot her sister in the head.

Who had buried Sam in a shallow grave.

Who had beaten Zachariah Culpepper, but not before he had torn Charlie into a million tiny pieces.

"Charlie?" Sam called.

She was sitting in the straight-back chair when Charlie entered the living room. Sam was not throwing things or fretting or doing that slow boil that she did when she was ready to go off. Instead, she had been studying something in her notepad.

Sam said, "Quite a day."

Charlie laughed at the understatement. "How did you figure it out so fast?"

"I'm your big sister. I'm smarter than you are."

Charlie could offer no evidence to the contrary. "Do you think Mason will go to the police station like you said?"

"Did it seem likely to you that I wouldn't follow through on my threat?"

"It seemed likely that you would've killed him if someone had put a knife in your hand." Charlie winced at the thought, but only because she didn't want Sam to have literal blood on her hands. "He didn't just lie to the GBI. He lied to an FBI agent."

"I'm sure the arresting officer will happily explain to him the difference between a misdemeanor and a felony."

Charlie smiled at the neat trick, which could mean years in federal prison as opposed to monitored probation with weekends at the county jail. "Why are you so calm right now?"

Sam shook her head, puzzled. "Shock? Relief? I always felt that Daniel got away with something, that he hadn't suffered enough. In a strange way, it brings me some satisfaction to know that Mason was tormented. And also that he's going to go to prison for at least five years. Or at least he'd better unless the prosecutors want me hounding their very existence."

"You think Ken Coin will do the right thing?"

"I don't think that man has ever done the right thing in his life." Her lips curved into a private smile. "Maybe there's a way to knock him off his perch."

Charlie didn't ask her to explain how that miracle would come about. Men like Coin always managed to weasel their way back on top. "I'm the person who pointed the finger at Daniel. I said that Zachariah called the second man his brother."

"Don't put that on yourself, Charlie. You were thirteen years old. And Ben was right. If Mason and Zachariah hadn't been here in the first place, none of it would have happened." She added, "Ken Coin is the one who took it upon himself to frame and murder Daniel. Don't forget that."

"Coin also stopped the investigation into finding the real shooter." Charlie felt sick when she considered the unknowing part she had played in the cover-up. "How hard would it be to figure out that the rich kid who was suddenly shipped off to military school in the middle of the night was involved?"

"You're right. Zachariah would have flipped on Mason without inducement," Sam said. "I want to care about Daniel, even about Mason, but I just can't. I feel like it's behind me now. Is that strange?"

"Yes. No. I don't know." Charlie sat in Rusty's cleared-out space on the couch. She tried to examine her emotions, to explore how she felt about everything Mason had told them. She realized that there was a feeling of lightness in her chest. She had expected to feel unburdened after telling Sam the truth about what happened in the woods, but it hadn't come.

Until now.

"What about Dad?" Charlie asked. "He hid this from us."

"He was trying to protect us. Like he always did."

Charlie raised her eyebrows at her sister's sudden conversion to Rusty's side.

Sam said, "There is value in forgiveness."

Charlie wasn't so sure about that. She slumped back into the couch. She looked up at the ceiling. "I feel so tired. The way cons feel when they confess. They just go to sleep. I can't tell you how many times I've been in the middle of an interview and they start snoring."

"It's relief," Sam told her. "Am I wrong for not feeling guilty that Daniel was a victim in this just as much as we were?"

"If you're wrong, then so am I," Charlie admitted. "I know Daniel didn't deserve to die like that. I can tell myself he's a Culpepper and he would've eventually ended up behind bars or six feet under, but he should've been allowed the luxury of making his own choices."

"Apparently, Dad got past it," Sam said. "He spent most of his life working to exonerate guilty men, but he never cleared Daniel's name."

" 'Nothing is more deceitful than the appearance of humility.' "

"Shakespeare?"

"Mr. Darcy to Bingley."

"Of all people."

"If it wasn't his pride, it was his prejudice."

Sam laughed, but then she turned serious. "I'm glad Dad didn't tell us about Mason. I think I could handle it now, but back then?" She shook her head. "I know this sounds horrible, because the decision obviously haunted Dad, but when I consider where my mind was eight years after being shot, I think that making me come back here to testify would have killed me. How's that for hyperbole?"

"Pretty accurate, if you include me." Charlie knew that a trial would have accelerated her own downward trajectory. She would not have gone to law school. She would not have met Ben. Neither she nor Sam would be here talking to each other. She asked, "Why do I feel like I can handle it better now? What's changed?"

"That is a complicated question with an equally complicated answer."

Charlie laughed. This was Rusty's real legacy. They were going to sit around quoting a dead man quoting dead people for the rest of their lives.

Sam said, "Dad must have known that we would find the confession in the safe."

Charlie easily spotted one of Rusty's high-stakes gambles. "I bet he thought he'd outlive Zachariah Culpepper's execution date."

"I bet he thought he'd figure out how to fix it on his own."

Charlie thought they were probably both right. There was not a plate that Rusty would not try to spin. "When I was little, I thought Dad was driven to help people because he had this burning sense of justice. And then I got older and I thought it was because he loved the idea of himself as the scrappy, asshole hero fighting the good fight."

"And now?"

"I think he knew that bad people did bad things, but he still believed that they deserved a chance."

"That's a very romanticized way to look at the world."

"I was talking about Dad, not me." Charlie felt sad that they were talking about Rusty in the past tense. "He was always searching for his unicorn."

"I'm glad you brought that up," Sam said. "I think he found one."

CHAPTER NINETEEN

Charlie stood with her nose a few inches from the television screen. She scrutinized the right-hand corner of the paused school security footage for so long that her eyes started blurring in and out. She took a step back. She blinked to clear her vision. She studied the entirety of the image. The long, empty hallway. The vivid blue lockers rendered navy by the ancient camera. The lens was angled down, capturing the hallway roughly to the middle point. Her eyes went back to the corner. There was a door, possibly closed, a millimeter out of frame, but clearly there. The light from the window cast a shadow onto something that was reaching into the hallway.

Charlie asked, "Is it Kelly's shadow?" She pointed past the TV, as if they were both standing in the hallway rather than Rusty's living room. "She would've been standing here, right?"

Sam kept her own counsel. She had her head turned, using her good eye to view the image. "What do you see?"

"This." Charlie pointed to the shadow reaching into the hall. "It's a blurry, hairy line, like a spider's leg."

"There's something strange about it." Sam narrowed her eyes, clearly seeing something that Charlie could not. "Don't you think there's something strange?"

"I can try to make it bigger." Charlie went to Ben's laptop, but then remembered she had no idea what she was doing. She hit random keys. There had to be a way to do this.

Sam said, "Let's get Ben to help."

"I don't want Ben to help." Charlie leaned down to read the menu icons. "We left it in a really good—"

"Ben!" Sam called.

"Don't you have a flight to catch?"

"The plane won't leave without me." Sam used her hands to frame the upper-right section of the footage. "It's not right. The angle doesn't work."

"What angle?" Ben asked.

"This." Charlie pointed to the shadow. "It looks like a spider's leg to me, but Sherlock Holmes over here sees a hound in the Baskerville."

"More like a Study in Scarlet," Sam said, but still did not explain herself. "Ben, can you make this upper-right corner larger?"

Ben performed some magic on the laptop and the corner of the frame was isolated, then enlarged to fill the television. Because her husband was not a tech wizard in a Jason Bourne movie, the image did not sharpen, but became more blurred.

"Oh, I see it." Ben pointed to the furry spider's leg. "I thought it was a shadow, but—"

"There wouldn't be one," Sam said. "The lights are on in the hallway. They're on in the classroom. Absent a third light source, shadows would be cast backward from the door, not to the front."

"Okay, yeah." Ben started to nod. "I thought it was coming out of the open door, but it looks like it's pointing in."

"Correct," Sam said. She had always been good at puzzles. This time, she had apparently figured out the solution before Charlie even understood there was a puzzle to be solved.

"I can't see anything," Charlie admitted. "Can't you just tell me?"

Sam said, "I think it's better if you both independently validate my suspicion."

Charlie wanted to throw her out the window like a sack of bull-shit. "Do you really think this is the time for the Socratic method?"

"Sherlock or Socrates. Pick one and stay with it." Sam asked Ben, "Can you correct for color?"

"I think so." Ben opened another program on his laptop, a purloined copy of Photoshop he'd used to insert Captain Kirk into their Christmas cards two years ago. "Let me see if I remember how to do this."

Charlie crossed her arms, making sure Sam knew she was displeased, but Sam was watching Ben too closely to take notice.

There was more tapping, more tracking, and then the colors on the screen were saturated, almost too much. The blacks were up so far that gray spots bubbled through the midnight fields.

Charlie suggested, "Use the blue on the lockers as a color guide. They're close to the same blue as Dad's funeral suit."

Ben opened the color chart. He clicked on random squares.

"That's it," Charlie said. "That's the blue."

"I can clean it up more." He sharpened the pixels. Smoothed out the edges. Finally, he zoomed in as close as he could without distorting the image into nothing.

"Holy shit," Charlie said. She finally got it.

Not a leg, but an arm.

Not one arm, but two.

One black. One red.

A sexual cannibal. A slash of red. A venomous bite.

They had not found Rusty's unicorn.

They had found a black widow.

Charlie sat in Ben's truck, hands sweaty on the wheel. She looked at the time on the radio: 5:06 PM. Rusty's funeral would be winding down by now. The drunks at Shady Ray's would be spent of their stories. The stragglers, the sightseers, the hypocrites, would be whispering gossip into their phones, posting snipey tributes on Facebook.

Rusty Quinn was a good lawyer, but—

Charlie filled in the blank with the things that only the people who really knew Rusty understood:

He had loved his daughters.

He had adored his wife.

He had tried to do the right thing.

He had found his mythical creature.

A harpy, Sam had said, referring to the half-woman, half-bird from Roman and Greek mythology.

Charlie was sticking with her spider analogy because it better fit the situation. Kelly Wilson had gotten caught up in a carefully spun web.

The heat in the truck was on, but Charlie felt herself shudder from the cold. She reached down for the keys. She turned off the engine. The truck shook as it came to a stop.

She angled the rearview mirror to look at her face. Sam had helped her cover the bruises. She had done a good job. No one would guess that Charlie had been punched in the face two days ago.

Sam had almost punched her again.

She didn't want Charlie to do this. Ben certainly did not.

Charlie was doing it anyway.

She smoothed out her funeral dress as she got out of the truck. She put on her heels, balancing against the steering wheel. She found her cell phone on the dash. She closed the door quietly, listening for the click of the latch.

She had parked away from the farmhouse, hiding the truck around a bend. Charlie walked carefully, avoiding the pocks in the red clay. The house came into view. Any similarities to the HP were slight. Colorful plants and evergreens filled the front yard. The clapboard was painted bright white, the trim a stark black. The roof looked new. An American flag hung from a swiveling bracket by the front door.

Charlie didn't go to the front. She rounded the side of the house.

She could see the old back porch, the floor freshly painted robin's egg blue. The kitchen curtains were closed. Not yellow with red strawberries anymore, but white damask.

There were four steps up to the porch. Charlie stared at them, trying not to think of the steps at the HP, the way she had run up them two at a time all those years ago, kicked off her shoes, peeled off her socks, and found Gamma cursing in the kitchen.

Fudge.

Her heel caught on a knotty hole in the first step. She held on to the sturdy railing. She blinked at the porch light, which even in the early dusk was bright white, like a flame. Sweat had dripped into her eyes. Charlie used her fingers to wipe it away. The welcome mat had a lattice design on it, rubber and coir fibers that reminded her of the grass that grew in the fields behind the farmhouse. A cursive *P* was in the center of the design.

Charlie raised her hand.

Her sprained wrist still felt tender.

She rapped three times on the door.

In the house, she heard a chair scrape back. Light footsteps across the floor. A woman's voice asked, "Who is it?"

Charlie did not answer.

There were no locks that clicked, no chain that slid back. The door opened. An older woman stood in the kitchen. Hair more white than blonde, pinned in a loose ponytail. Still pretty. Her eyes went wide when she saw Charlie. Her mouth opened. Her hand fluttered to her chest, as if she had been hit by an arrow.

Charlie said, "I'm sorry I didn't call first."

Judith Pinkman pressed together her chapped lips. Her lined face looked windburned from crying. Her eyes were swollen. She cleared her throat. "Come in," she told Charlie. "Come in."

Charlie stepped into the kitchen. The room was cold, almost frigid. The strawberry theme was no more. Dark granite countertops. Stainless-steel appliances. Eggshell white walls. No cheerful, dancing fruit bordering the ceiling.

"Sit down," Judith said. "Please."

There was a cell phone beside a glass of ice water on the table. Dark walnut, heavy matching chairs. Charlie sat on the opposite side. She put her own phone on the table, facedown.

Judith asked, "Can I get you something?"

Charlie shook her head.

"I was going to have some tea." Her eyes darted to the glass of water on the table. Still, she asked, "Would you like some?"

Charlie nodded.

Judith took the kettle off the stove. Stainless steel, like everything else. She filled it at the kitchen sink, saying, "I'm very sorry about your father."

"I'm sorry about Mr. Pinkman."

Judith glanced over her shoulder. She held Charlie's gaze. The woman's lips were trembling. Her eyes glistened, as if her tears were as constant as her sorrow. She turned off the faucet.

Charlie watched her return the kettle to the stove, turn the knob on the Wolf range. There were several clicks, then a *whoosh* as the gas ignited.

"So." Judith hesitated, then sat down. "What brings you here today?"

"I wanted to check on you," Charlie said. "I haven't seen you since the whole thing with Kelly."

Judith smoothed together her lips again. She clasped her hands on the table. "That must have been hard for you. I know it brought back some memories for me."

Charlie said, "I want you to know how much I appreciate what you did for me that night. That you took care of me. Made me feel safe. That you lied for me."

Judith's lips were trembling when she smiled.

"That's why I'm here," Charlie told the woman. "I never talked about it when Daddy was alive."

Her mouth opened. The tension drained from her eyes. She smiled kindly at Charlie. This was the caring, generous woman that Charlie remembered. "Of course, Charlotte. Of course. You can talk to me about anything."

Charlie said, "Back then, Dad had this case, this rapist he represented, and the man got off, but the girl hanged herself in her family's barn."

"I remember that."

"I've been wondering, do you think that's why Dad wanted to keep it secret? Was he worried that I would do something like that?"

"I—" She shook her head. "I don't know. I'm sorry I can't answer you. I think that he had just lost his wife, and he thought his oldest daughter was dead, and he saw what happened to you and . . ." Her voice trailed off. "People say that God won't give you more than you can handle, but sometimes, I don't think that's true. Do you?"

"I'm not sure."

"The verse is in Corinthians. 'God is faithful, and He will not let you be tempted beyond your ability, but with temptation, He will provide the way of escape, that you may be able to endure it.'" She said, "It's the second part that makes me wonder. How do you *know* the way of escape? It might be there, but what if you don't recognize it?"

Charlie shook her head.

"I'm sorry," Judith apologized. "I know your mother didn't believe in God. She was too smart for that."

Charlie knew that Gamma would have taken the observation as a compliment.

"She was so clever," Judith said. "I was a bit afraid of her."

"I think a lot of people were."

"Well." Judith drank some ice water.

Charlie watched the woman's hands, looking for that telltale tremble, but there was nothing.

"Charlotte." Judith put down the glass. "I'm going to be honest with you about that night. I've never seen a man so broken as your father was. I hope I never do again. I'm not sure how he managed to go on. I'm really not. But I know that he loved you unconditionally."

"I never doubted that he did."

"That's good." Judith used her fingers to wipe condensation from the glass. "My father, Mr. Heller, he was devout, and loving, and he provided for me, and he supported me, which, Lord knows a first-year schoolteacher needs support." She chuckled quietly. "But after that night, I understood that my father did not cherish me the way that your father cherished you. I don't blame Mr. Heller for that. What you and Rusty had was something special. So, what I guess I am telling you is, that no matter what your father's motivations were for asking you to lie, it came from a place of deep and abiding love."

Charlie expected to feel tears, but none came. She was finally cried out.

Judith said, "I know that Rusty is gone, and that a parent's death makes you think about a lot of things, but you shouldn't be angry with your father for asking you to keep it secret. He did it with the best of intentions."

Charlie nodded at what she knew was the truth.

The kettle started to whistle. Judith stood. She turned off the stove. She went to a large cabinet that Charlie remembered from before. It was tall, almost floor to ceiling. Mr. Heller had kept his rifle on top, obscured by the crown molding. The white wood had been painted dark blue in the interim. Judith opened the doors. There were decorative mugs hanging from hooks beneath the shelves. Judith selected two mugs from either side of the rack. She closed the doors and went back to the stove.

"I've got peppermint and chamomile."

"Either is fine." Charlie looked at the closed cabinet doors. There was a sentence painted in script underneath the molding. Light blue, but not in enough of a contrast against the dark blue to make the words stand out. She read aloud, " 'He settles the childless woman in her home as the mother of happy children.' "

At the counter, Judith's hands went still. "From the Psalms: 113:9. But that's not the King James version." She poured hot water into the mugs.

Charlie asked, "What's the King James version?"

" 'He maketh the barren woman to keep house, and to be a joyful mother of children. Praise ye, the Lord.' " She found two spoons in a drawer. "I'm not barren, though, so I like the other version."

Charlie felt a cold sweat come over her. "I guess in some ways you're the mother of your kids at school."

"You're exactly right." Judith sat down, passing one of the mugs to Charlie. "Doug and I spent more than half of our lives taking care of other people's children. Not that we don't enjoy it, but when we're home, we enjoy the quiet even more."

Charlie turned the handle of the mug around, but she did not pick it up.

"I'm barren," Charlie said, the word feeling like a rock in her throat.

"I'm so sorry." Judith stood up from the table. She brought back a carton of milk from the fridge. "Do you want sugar?"

Charlie shook her head. She wasn't going to drink the tea. "You never wanted children?"

"I love other people's children."

Charlie said, "I heard that you were helping Kelly study for some kind of exam."

Judith put the milk on the table. She sat back down.

"You must have felt betrayed," Charlie said. "For her to do that."

Judith watched the steam rise from the tea.

"And she knew Mr. Pinkman," Charlie said, not because Mason Huckabee had told them, but because Sam had shown Charlie her notes where she had recorded Kelly Wilson's exact words:

"I heard people say he wasn't a bad man, but I never got sent to the principal's office."

Kelly had managed to finagle her way past Sam's question. The girl had not said that she did not know Douglas Pinkman. She had said that he was not known to be a bad man.

Charlie said, "I saw the security footage from the school."

Judith's eyes snapped up, then back down to the mug. "There was a reenactment on the news."

"No, this was the actual security footage from the camera above the front office."

She picked up her mug. She blew on her tea before taking a sip.

"At some point, the camera was pushed down. The angle stops about two feet away from your classroom door."

"Does it?"

Charlie asked, "Do you think Kelly knew about the camera? That whatever happened directly outside your door wasn't recorded?"

"She never mentioned it. Have you asked the police?"

Charlie had asked Ben. "The kids knew that the camera didn't catch the back end of the hall, but they didn't know the exact cut-off point. But the strange thing was, Kelly knew. She was standing just shy of the camera's range when she started shooting. Which is odd, because how would she know where to stand unless she's been inside the room where the security cameras are?"

Judith shook her head, seemingly bewildered.

"You've been in that room, right? Or at least seen inside it?"

Again, the woman feigned ignorance.

"The monitors were kept in a closet right beside your husband's office. The door was always open, so anyone who went inside could see it." Charlie added another detail. "Kelly said she had never been sent to the principal's office. It's curious that she knew the blind spot without ever having seen the monitors."

Judith put down the mug. She placed her palms flat on the table.

"'Thou shalt not lie,'" Charlie said. "That's a Bible verse, right?"

Judith's lips parted. She breathed out, then in again before she spoke. "It's part of the Ten Commandments. 'Thou shalt not bear false witness against thy neighbor.' But I think you're looking for Proverbs." She closed her eyes. She recited, " 'These six things the Lord doth hate; yea, seven are an abomination unto him: a proud look, a lying tongue, and hands that shed innocent—' " Her throat worked. " 'That shed innocent blood.' " She paused again before finishing, " 'An heart that deviseth wicked imaginations, feet that be swift in running to evil, a false witness that speaketh lies and he that soweth discord among brethren.' "

"That's quite a list."

Judith looked down at her hands, still spread flat to the table. Her nails were clipped close. Her fingers were long and thin. They cast a narrow shadow on the top of the polished walnut table.

Like the spider's leg that Sam had seen inching its way into the camera's frame.

Ben had been able to work more wizardry on his laptop once he realized what they were all staring at. It was like an optical illusion. Once you understood what your eyes were seeing, you could never again see the image otherwise.

In that paused frame, the camera had caught Kelly Wilson holding the revolver, just as she had confessed to Sam, but as with a lot of Kelly Wilson's statements, there was more to the story.

Kelly had worn black that day.

Judith Pinkman had worn red.

Charlie remembered thinking how the woman's shirt was soaked through with Lucy Alexander's blood.

The sepia tone of the recording had almost blended the two dark colors, but once Ben had finished on his laptop, the truth was there for all to see.

The black-sleeved arm had a red-sleeved arm alongside it.

Two arms pointing toward the classroom door.

Two fingers wrapped around the trigger.

"The gun was in my hand."

Kelly Wilson had told Sam at least three times during the interview that she was holding the revolver when Douglas Pinkman and Lucy Alexander were murdered.

What the girl had failed to mention was that Judith Pinkman's hand was holding it there.

Charlie said, "They tested Kelly for gunshot residue at the hospital. It was on her hand, all over her shirt. Exactly where you'd expect to find it."

Judith sat back in her chair. Her eyes stayed on her own hands.

Charlie said, "The residue is like talcum powder, if that's what you're worried about. It washes off with soap and water."

"I know it does, Charlotte." Her voice was scratchy, like the sound a record makes when the needle first hits the vinyl. "I know it does."

Charlie waited. She could hear a clock ticking somewhere. She felt a slight breeze snaking out from the edges of the closed kitchen door.

Judith finally looked up. Her eyes glistened in the overhead light. She studied Charlie for a moment, then asked, "Why is it you? Why didn't the police come?"

Charlie did not realize that she was holding her breath until she felt the strain in her lungs. "Do you want it to be the police?"

Judith looked up at the ceiling. Her tears began to fall. "I guess it doesn't matter. Not anymore."

Charlie said, "She was pregnant."

"Again," Judith said. "She had an abortion in middle school."

Charlie braced herself for a polemic about the sanctity of life, but Judith did not offer one.

Instead, the woman stood up. She pulled a paper towel from the roll. She wiped her face. "The father was a boy on the football team. Several boys had their fun, apparently. She was naïve. She had no idea what they were doing to her."

"Who was the father this time?"

"You're going to make me say it?"

Charlie nodded. She was a recent convert to giving voice to the truth.

"Doug," she said. "He fucked her in my room." Charlie must have reacted to the *fuck*, because she said, "I'm sorry for the language, but when you see your husband screwing a seventeen-year-old girl in the classroom where you teach middle schoolers, that's the first word that comes to mind."

"Seventeen," Charlie repeated. Douglas Pinkman had been an administrator. Kelly Wilson was a student in the same school system. What he had done was commit statutory rape. Fucking had nothing to do with it.

Judith said, "That's why the camera was angled down. Doug was smart about it. He was always smart about it."

"There were other students?"

"Anything he could stick it into." She balled the paper towel into her hand. She had become visibly angry. For the first time, Charlie was worried Sam and Ben had been right about how dangerous this could be.

Charlie asked, "That's why this happened, because Kelly got pregnant?"

"It wasn't for the reason you're thinking. I'm sorry, Charlotte. You clearly wanted children, but I didn't. I never did. I love them, I love how their minds work, I love how funny and interesting they can be, but I love it more when I can leave them at school, come home and read a book and enjoy the silence." She tossed the paper towel into the trash can. "I'm not some desperate woman who couldn't have a child so she snapped. Not having a child was a choice. A choice I thought Doug agreed with, but—" She shrugged. "You never know how bad your marriage is until it's over."

Charlie guessed, "He wanted a divorce?"

Judith laughed bitterly. "No, and I didn't want one, either. I had learned to live with his perpetual midlife crisis. He wasn't a pedophile. He didn't go after the young ones."

Charlie wondered at how easily the woman dismissed the fact that Kelly Wilson had the emotional intelligence of a child.

Judith said, "Doug wanted us to keep the baby. Kelly was going to drop out of school anyway. There was no way she could graduate. He wanted us to give her some money, make her go away, and raise the baby together."

Of all the things Judith could have said, Charlie had never suspected this was what had finally broken her. "What changed his mind about wanting a kid?"

"Feeling his mortality? Wanting to leave a legacy? Just so damn arrogant and selfish and stupid?" She huffed out an angry breath. "I'm fifty-six years old. Doug was about to turn sixty. We should be planning our retirement. I didn't want to raise some other woman's—some teenager's—baby." She shook her head, clearly still furious. "Not to mention Kelly's mental deficits. Doug wasn't just expecting me to raise a child for the next eighteen years. He wanted us to be stuck with it for the rest of our lives."

Any sympathy Charlie could have felt evaporated with those words.

Judith asked, "What else did Kelly tell you?" She shook her head. "It doesn't matter. I was going to play the martyr; the poor widow accused of being complicit by a cold-blooded simpleton. Who would believe her over me?"

Charlie said nothing, but she knew that, without the footage, no one would have believed the girl.

"So." Judith angrily wiped away her tears. "Is this the part where I tell you how I did it?" She pointed to Charlie's phone. "Make sure it's still recording."

Charlie turned over the phone, though she trusted that Ben had set it up properly. The phone was not only recording, it was transmitting the audio back to his laptop.

Judith said, "The affair started a year ago. I saw them through the window in my classroom. Doug thought I had left. He stayed to lock up—at least, that's what he said. I went back for some papers. As I said, he was screwing her on one of the desks."

Charlie pressed her back to the chair. Judith seemed to be getting angrier with each word.

"So, I did what any obedient wife would do. I turned around. I went home. I prepared dinner. Doug came home. He told me he got hung up with a parent. We watched TV together and I seethed. I seethed all night."

"When did you start tutoring Kelly?"

"When she started dressing like a witch again." Judith braced the heels of her hands on the counter. "That's what she did the last time. She started wearing black, like the Goths, to hide her belly. I knew the moment I saw her in the hall that she was pregnant again."

"Did you confront Doug?"

"Why would I do that? I'm just the wife. I'm just the woman who cooks his meals and irons his clothes and bleaches the stains out of his underwear." Her voice had a grinding undertone, like a clock being overwound. "Do you know what it's like to not matter? To live in the same house with a man for almost your entire adult life and feel like you're nothing? That your wishes, your desires, your plans, are irrelevant? That any burden, no matter how great, can be thrown at you and because you're a good woman, a God-fearing, Christian woman, and you'll just take it with a smile because your husband, the man who is supposed to be your protector, is the master of the house?"

Judith had clasped her hands together so hard that the knuckles were white. She told Charlie, "Of course you don't. You've been coddled, you've been cherished, all of your life. Even losing your mother, your sister almost dying, your father being reviled by everyone in the state, made people love you more."

Charlie's heart pounded in her throat. She did not realize that she had stood up from the chair until she felt her back against the wall.

Judith didn't seem to notice the effect she was having. "You can talk Kelly into anything, did you know that?"

Charlie did not move.

"She's so sweet. And fragile. And tiny. She's like a child. She really is. But the more time I spent with her, the more I hated her." She shook her head. Her hair was coming unpinned. Her eyes had a wild look. "Do you know how that feels, to hate an innocent kid? To focus all of your rage on someone who doesn't know what they're doing, what's happening to them, because you realize that you can see your own stupidity reflected in their behavior? That you see how your husband controls them, cheats on them, uses them, abuses them, the same way that he does with you?"

Charlie scanned the room. She saw the knives in the wooden block, the drawers full of utensils, the cabinet that likely still had Mr. Heller's rifle on top.

"I'm sorry," Judith said, visibly working to calm herself. She followed Charlie's gaze to the top of the cabinet. "I thought I was going to have to make up a story about how Kelly had stolen it. Or give her the money and pray that she could follow the instructions to buy one."

Charlie said, "Her dad kept a revolver in his car."

"She told me he used it to shoot squirrels. Holler people eat them sometimes."

"It's greasy," Charlie said, trying to keep her calm. "I have a client who cooks it in stew."

Judith gripped the back of the chair. Her knuckles were white. "I'm not going to hurt you."

Charlie forced out a laugh. "Isn't that what people say before they hurt someone?"

Judith pushed away from the chair. She leaned against the counter again. She was still angry, but she kept working to control it. "I shouldn't have said that about your tragedy. I apologize."

"It's all right."

"You're saying that because you want me to keep talking."

Charlie shrugged her shoulder. "Is it working?"

Her laugh was filled with disgust.

Ben had said that Judith Pinkman had been hysterical when the paramedics had taken her out the middle-school doors. They'd had to sedate her to get her into the ambulance. She had stayed at the hospital all night. She had gone on camera to plead for Kelly's life. Even now, her eyes were swollen from crying. Her face was haggard with grief. She was telling Charlie the truth, the brutal, unvarnished truth, though she knew that she was being recorded.

She wasn't bargaining, she wasn't pleading, she wasn't trying to make some kind of trade. This was how a person behaved when they felt true remorse for their actions.

Judith said, "Kelly wouldn't pull the trigger on her own. She promised me that she would, but I knew that she wasn't like that. She was too kind, and she was too trusting, and she would've been a horrible shot, so I stood behind her in the hall, and I wrapped my hand around hers, and I fired a shot into the wall to get Doug's attention." She tapped her fingers to her mouth as if to remind her voice to stay calm. "He came running out, and I shot him three times. And then—"

Charlie waited.

Judith pressed her hand to her chest. Her anger had gone completely cold.

She admitted, "I was going to kill Kelly. That was the plan: shoot Doug, then murder Kelly and say that I stopped her from slaughtering more children. Town hero. I'd get Doug's pension, his social security. No messy divorce. More time to read my books, right?"

Charlie wondered if she had planned on shooting Kelly in the stomach to make sure her baby was dead, too.

Judith said, "I managed to hit Doug in all the right places. The coroner told me that any one of the three shots was fatal. I guess he thought that would be a comfort." Her eyes glistened again. She swallowed, her throat making an audible sound. "But Kelly wouldn't let go of the gun. I don't think she knew the rest of the plan, that I was going to kill her. I think she panicked when she saw that Doug was dead. We struggled. The trigger was pulled. I don't know if it was me or her, but the bullet ricocheted into the floor."

Judith breathed through her mouth. Her voice was raspy.

She continued, "We were both shocked that the gun had gone off, and Kelly turned, and I—I don't know. I don't know what happened. I panicked. I saw movement out of the corner of my eye, and I pulled the trigger again and—" She was cut off by a whimper. Her lips had turned white. She was trembling. "I saw her. I saw her when—while—my finger pulled the trigger. It happened so slowly, and my brain recognized it, I remember thinking, 'Judith, you're shooting a child,' but I couldn't stop it. My finger kept pulling back, and—"

She could not say the words, so Charlie did.

"Lucy Alexander was shot."

Judith's tears flowed like water. "I team-teach with her mother. I used to see Lucy at meetings, dancing around in the back of the room. She would sing to herself. She had such a sweet voice. I don't know, maybe it would've been different if I hadn't known her, but I knew her."

Charlie could not help but think that the woman had known Kelly Wilson, too.

Judith said, "Charlotte, I'm so sorry that I made you a part of this. I had no idea you were in the building. I would've done it the next day, or next week. I never would have knowingly put you in that situation."

Charlie was not going to thank her.

"I wish I could explain what came over me. I thought that Doug and I were—I don't know. He wasn't the great love of my life, but I thought that we cared for each other. Respected each other. But after that many years, everything is entangled. You'll see when you get there. Finances, retirement, benefits, cars, this house, savings accounts, tickets we bought for a cruise this summer."

"Money," Charlie said. Rusty had thousands of quotes about man's destructive desires for sex and money.

"It wasn't just the money," Judith said. "When I confronted Doug about the pregnancy, and he presented his brilliant plan for us to become geriatric parents, like it was nothing to take on that kind of commitment—and it wasn't, not for him. He wasn't going to be the one getting up at three in the morning to change diapers. I know it seems incredible that that was what finally did it, but it was the last straw."

She searched Charlie's eyes as if she expected agreement.

Judith said, "I let myself hate Kelly because that was the only way I could talk myself into doing it. I knew that she was pliable. All I had to do was whisper in her ear—wasn't she a bad girl for what she let Doug do to her? Wasn't she going to hell for what happened in middle school? Couldn't she punish Doug for his transgressions? Couldn't she stop him from hurting other girls? I was amazed by how little time it took to convince another human being that she was nothing." Judith repeated, "Nothing. Just like me."

Charlie's hands were sweating. She wiped them on her dress.

"There's another verse you probably know, Charlotte. I'm sure you heard it in a movie or read it in a book. 'Therefore all things whatsoever ye would that men should do to you, do ye even so to them: for this is the law and the prophets.'"

"The Golden Rule," Charlie said. "Do unto others as they do unto you."

"I did to Kelly what Doug did to me. That's what I told myself. That's how I justified my actions, and then I saw Lucy and I realized . . ." Judith held up her index finger, as if to start counting. "A *proud look* through the window of my room." She held up another finger, listing her sins. "A *lying tongue* to my husband, to Kelly." Another finger went up. "*Wicked imaginations* about murdering both of them. *Running toward evil* when I put that gun in her hand. *False witness* to the police about what happened. *Sowing discord* to you, to Mason Huckabee, to the entire town." She gave up counting and held up all of her fingers. " '*Hands that shed innocent blood.*' "

Judith stood there, her hands in the air, palms out, fingers spread.

Charlie did not know what to say.

"What will happen to her?" Judith asked. "To Kelly?"

Charlie shook her head, though she knew that Kelly Wilson would go to prison. Not to death row, probably not for the rest of her life, but low IQ or not, the girl was right: the gun was in her hand.

Judith said, "I need you to leave, Charlotte."

"I—"

"Take your phone." She tossed the phone to Charlie. "Send the recording to that woman at the GBI. Tell her she can find me here."

Charlie fumbled to catch the phone. "What are you—"

"Leave." Judith reached her hand up to the top of the cabinet. She didn't have her father's rifle. She had a Glock.

"Jesus." Charlie stumbled back.

"Please leave." Judith dropped the empty magazine from the gun. "I told you, I'm not going to hurt you."

"What are you going to do?" Charlie's heart quivered as she asked the question.

She knew what the woman was planning to do.

"Charlotte, go." Judith found a box of bullets and scattered them onto the table. She started to load the magazine.

"Jesus," Charlie repeated.

Judith paused her work. "I know how ridiculous this is going to sound, but please stop taking the Lord's name in vain."

"Okay," Charlie said. Ben was listening. He was probably on his way, running through the woods, jumping over trees, pushing limbs aside, trying to find Charlie.

All she had to do was keep Judith talking.

"Please," Charlie begged. "Please don't do this. I have questions to ask you about that day, about what—"

"You need to forget about it, Charlotte. You need to do what your daddy told you and put it in a box and leave it there, because I am telling you right now that you don't ever want to remember what that horrible man did to you." Judith jammed the magazine into the gun. "Now, I really need for you to go."

"Oh, Judith, please don't do this." Charlie felt her voice shake. This couldn't happen. Not in this kitchen. Not to this woman. "Please."

Judith pulled back the slide, loading a bullet into the chamber. "Leave, Charlotte."

"I can't—" Charlie held out her hands, reaching toward Judith, toward the gun. "Please don't do this. This can't happen. I can't let you—"

Bright white bone. Pieces of heart and lung. Cords of tendon and arteries and veins and life spilling out of her gaping wounds.

"Judith," Charlie cried. "Please."

"Charlotte." Her voice was firm, like a teacher in front of the classroom. "You are to go outside immediately. I want you to get in your truck, and drive to your father's house and call the police."

"Judith, no."

"They're used to handling these sorts of things, Charlotte. I know that you think you are, but I can't take that on my conscience. I just can't."

"Judith, please. I am begging you." Charlie was so close to the gun. She could lunge for it. She was younger, faster. She could stop this.

"Don't." Judith placed the gun behind her on the counter. "I told you that I'm not going to hurt you. Don't make me go back on my word."

"I can't!" Charlie was sobbing. She felt like razors were pumping through her heart. "I can't leave you here to kill yourself."

Judith opened the kitchen door. "You can and you will."

"Judith, please. Don't put this burden on me."

"I'm lifting your burden, Charlotte. Your father is gone. I'm the last person who knows. Your secret dies with me."

"It doesn't need to die!" Charlie screamed. "I don't care! People already know. My husband. My sister. I don't care. Judith, please, please don't—"

Without warning, Judith charged toward her. She grabbed Charlie around the middle. Charlie felt her feet leave the ground. She braced her hands against the woman's shoulders. Her ribs felt crushed as she was carried across the kitchen and thrown out onto the porch.

"Judith, no!" Charlie scrambled to stop her.

The door slammed in her face.

The lock clicked.

"Judith!" Charlie yelled, banging her fist on the door. "Judith! Open the—"

She heard a loud crack echo inside the house.

Not a car backfiring.

Not fireworks.

Charlie fell to her knees.

She pressed her hand to the door.

A person who has been up close when a gun is fired into another human being never mistakes the sound of a gunshot for something else.

WHAT HAPPENED TO SAM

Sam alternated her arms in the water, cutting a narrow channel through the warm waters of the swimming pool. She turned her head every third stroke and drew in a long breath. Her feet fluttered. She waited for the next breath.

Left-right-left-breathe.

She performed a perfect flip-turn against the wall of the pool, keeping her eyes on the black line guiding her lane. She had always loved the calmness, the simplicity, of the freestyle stroke; that she had to concentrate just enough on swimming so that all extraneous thoughts floated away.

Left-right-left-breathe.

Sam saw the mark at the end of the line. She coasted until her fingers touched the wall. She kneeled on the floor of the pool, breathing heavily, checking her swimmer's watch: 2.4 kilometers at 154.2 seconds per 100 meters, so 38.55 seconds per 25-meter length.

Not bad. Not as good as yesterday, but she had to make peace with the fact that her body worked at its own speed. Sam tried to tell herself that accepting this truth was progress. Still, as she got out of the pool, her competitive streak niggled at the edge of her encouragements. The desire to jump back in, to improve her time, was only dampened by a dull throb down her sciatic nerve.

Sam quickly showered off the salt water. She dried herself with the towel, her wrinkled fingers catching on the Egyptian cotton. She examined the furrows in her fingertips; her body's response to being submerged for so long.

She kept on her prescription goggles as she rode up in the elevator. At the lobby floor, an older man got on, newspaper under one arm, wet umbrella in his hand. He chuckled when he saw Sam.

"A beautiful mermaid!"

She tried to match his ebullient grin. They talked about the bad weather, that a storm working its way up the coast was expected to bring even heavier rains to New York by the afternoon.

"Almost June!" he said, as if the month had somehow sneaked up on him.

Sam felt caught a bit unawares herself. She could not believe that only three weeks had passed since she had left Pikeville. Her life had easily gone back to normal since then. Her schedule was the same. She saw the same people at work, conducted the same meetings and conference calls, studied the same sanitary storage bin schematics in preparation for trial.

And yet, everything felt different. Fuller. Richer. Even doing something as mundane as getting out of bed came with a sense of lightness that had eluded her since—well, if she was being honest, since she had woken up in the hospital twenty-eight years ago.

The elevator bell dinged. They had reached the old man's floor.

"Happy swimming, beautiful mermaid!" He waved his paper in the air.

Sam watched him walk down the hall. He had a jaunty step that reminded her of Rusty, especially when he began to whistle, then loudly jangled his keys to the beat.

As the elevator doors closed, Sam whispered, " 'Exit, pursued by a bear.' "

The wavy chrome that lined the doors showed a woman in ridiculous goggles, smiling to herself. Slim build. Black one-piece suit. She ran her fingers through her short, gray hair to help it dry. Her finger caught the edge of the scar where the bullet had entered her brain. She seldom thought of that day anymore. Instead, she thought of Anton. She thought of Rusty. She thought of Charlie and Ben.

The elevator doors opened.

Dark clouds showed through the floor-to-ceiling windows that lined her penthouse apartment. Sam heard car horns and cranes and the usual din of activity muffled behind the triple-paned glass.

She walked to the kitchen, turning on lights as she went. She exchanged her goggles for her glasses. She put out food for Fosco. She filled the kettle. She prepared her tea infuser, mug and spoon, but before boiling the water, she went to the yoga mat in her living room.

Sam took off her glasses. She ran through her stretches too quickly. She was anxious to start her day. She tried to meditate, but she found herself unable to clear her mind. Fosco, finished with his breakfast, took advantage of the break in routine. He dolphined his head into her arm until she gave in. Sam scratched underneath his chin, listening to his soothing purrs, and wondered as she often did whether she should adopt another cat.

Fosco nipped at her hand, indicating he'd had enough.

She watched him saunter off, then fall onto his side in front of the windows.

Sam put on her glasses. She returned to the kitchen and turned on the kettle. Rain slanted outside the windows, saturating the lower end of Manhattan. She closed her eyes and listened to the tinny splatter of thousands of raindrops hitting the glass. When she opened her eyes again, she saw that Fosco was staring out the windows, too. He was curved into a backward C, front legs stretched toward the glass, enjoying the heat coming up from the kitchen tiles.

They both watched the rain beat down until the kettle gave a low whistle.

Sam poured her mug of tea. She set the egg timer to three and a half minutes to allow the leaves to steep. She got yogurt from the fridge and mixed in granola with a spoon from the drawer. She took off her regular glasses and put on her reading glasses.

Sam turned on her phone.

There were several work emails, but she opened the one from Eldrin first. Ben's birthday was next week. Sam had asked her assistant to come up with a clever message that would please her brother-in-law. Eldrin had suggested—

That's the tribble with getting older!

Tribble in paradise!

Yesterday, all my tribbles seemed so far away . . .

Sam frowned. She didn't know if *tribble* was inappropriate or too young for a forty-four-year-old woman to send to her sister's husband.

She tapped open her phone's browser to research the word. Charlie's Facebook page was already on the screen. Sam visited her sister's page twice a day because that was the most reliable way to find out what Charlie and Ben were up to—Looking at houses together in Atlanta. Interviewing for new jobs. Trying to find someone who knew whether or not it was advisable to relocate rabbits from the mountains to the city.

Instead of searching for *tribble*, Sam reloaded Charlie's page. She shook her head at a new photo her sister had posted. Another stray had been found. The mutt was splotched like a bluetick hound, but with stubby dachshund legs. He was standing in the backyard, knee-deep in grass. One of Charlie's friends, a person going by the dubious handle of Iona Trayler, had posted a snarky rejoinder about how Charlie's husband needed to mow the grass.

Poor Ben. He had spent hours with Charlie excavating Rusty's offices and the main floors of the HP, boxing and donating and listing on eBay various magazines, articles of clothing and, unbelievably, a prosthetic leg that had sold for sixteen dollars to a man in Canada.

They had never found the photograph of Gamma. There was *the* photo, the washed-out, sun-bleached picture that Rusty had let fade into nothing on his desk, but the photograph he had told Sam about, the one that he claimed captured the moment he and Gamma had fallen in love, was nowhere to be found. Not in the safe. Not in Rusty's files. Not in the cabinets. Not anywhere in the downtown office or the HP.

Sam and Charlie had finally decided that the mythical image was likely one of Rusty's tall tales, embellished for the sake of the listener, founded in very little fact.

Still, the loss of this phantom photo had opened up an ache inside of Sam. For years, she had scoured the academic and scientific world looking for the products of her mother's brilliant mind. The thought had not occurred to her until three weeks ago how foolish she had been to have never once searched for her mother's face.

Sam could look in a mirror and see the similarities. She could share memories with Charlie. But except for two dry academic papers, there was no proof that their mother had been a vital, vibrant human being.

The NASA postcard they had found in Rusty's safe had given Sam an idea. The Smithsonian, in cooperation with the Johnson Space Center, maintained detailed records of every stage of the space race. Sam had put out feelers for a researcher or a historian to perform a proper investigation into whether or not the archives contained photographs of Gamma. She had already gotten several responses. There seemed to be a renaissance within the STEM fields to acknowledge the long-forgotten contributions of women and minorities to the scientific advancements of mankind.

The search would be finding a proverbial needle in the haystack, but Sam felt to the core of her being that a photograph of Gamma existed in NASA's or even Fermilab's records. For the first time in her life, she found herself believing that there was such a thing as fate. What had happened in the kitchen almost three decades ago was not the end of it. Sam knew that she was meant to see her mother's face again. All that it would take was money and time, two things Sam had in abundant supply.

The egg timer buzzed.

Sam poured milk into her hot tea. She stared out the window, watching the rain pelt the glass. The sky had turned darker. The wind had picked up. Sam could feel the slight shift of the building as it rocked against the coming storm.

Oddly, Sam found herself wondering what the weather was like in Pikeville.

Rusty would have known. Apparently, he had kept up the weather project that he had started with Charlie. Ben had found piles of forms in the barn where for twenty-eight years Rusty had almost daily notated wind direction and speed, air pressure, temperature, humidity, and precipitation. They had no idea why Rusty was still tracking the information. The weather station Ben had installed on the tower wirelessly reported the data back to NOAA.

Maybe what it boiled down to was that Rusty had been a creature of habit. Sam had always thought that she was more like her mother, but at least in this one regard, she was certainly like her father.

The daily laps in the pool. The mug of tea. The yogurt and granola.

One of Sam's many small regrets was that she had not preserved that last message Rusty had left on her birthday. The boisterous greeting. The weather update. The arcane bit of history. The discordant sign-off.

She missed his laughter most of all. He had always been impressed by his own cleverness.

Sam was so lost in thought that she did not hear her phone ring. The stuttered vibrations of the device shook her back to the present. She slid the bar across the screen. She put the phone to her ear.

"She signed the deal," Charlie said by way of greeting. "I told her we could try to get it knocked down a few more years, but Lucy Alexander's parents have been pushing pretty hard and the Wilsons just want it over with, so she's at ten years, minimum security, eligible for monitored parole in five if she's on good behavior, which of course she will be."

Sam had to silently repeat Charlie's words back in her head before she fully understood them. Her sister was talking about Kelly Wilson. Sam had hired a lawyer from Atlanta to help work out a plea deal. With Ken Coin's abrupt resignation and the recording that Charlie had made of Judith Pinkman being considered tantamount to a deathbed confession, the state prosecutor had been eager to make the Kelly Wilson case go away.

Charlie said, "Coin would've never made that deal."

"I bet I could've talked him into it."

Charlie laughed appreciatively. "Are you ever going to tell me how you got him to quit?"

"It's an interesting story," Sam said, but did not tell the story. Charlie still refused to explain how her nose had been broken, so

Sam still refused to explain how she had used Mason's confession to intimidate Coin into stepping down.

Sam said, "Parole in five years is a good deal. Kelly will be in her early twenties when she gets out. Her child will be young enough for them to bond with each other."

"It rankles," Charlie said, and Sam knew she did not mean Kelly Wilson or her unborn child or even Ken Coin. She was talking about Mason Huckabee.

The FBI had done a full-court press against Mason for lying to a federal agent, tampering with evidence, obstruction of justice, and accessory to a double murder after the fact. Despite his voluntary confession to the Pikeville police, Mason Huckabee had, unsurprisingly, hired a really good, really expensive lawyer who'd pled him down to six years without a chance of parole. The Atlanta Federal Pen was not an easy place to serve time, but over the last few weeks, both Charlie and Sam had found themselves wondering if they should follow through on Sam's threat to release Mason's written confession.

Sam said what she always said: "It's good for us to let this go, Charlie. Dad would not have wanted us to tie up our lives for the next five, ten, twenty years, hounding Mason Huckabee through the criminal justice system. We need to move on with our lives."

"I know," Charlie admitted, but with obvious reluctance. "It just pisses me off that he only got one more year than Kelly. I guess that's a lesson about lying to a federal agent. But, you know, we could always go after him before his release. Who knows where we'll be in six years? There's no statute of limitations on—"

"Charlie."

"All right," she said. "Maybe he'll get shivved in the shower or someone will put glass in his food."

Sam let her sister talk.

"I'm not saying he should be murdered or anything, but, like, he loses a kidney or his stomach is shredded or, hey, better yet, he's forced to shit into a bag for the rest of his life." She took a quick pause for breath. "I mean, okay, the living conditions in prisons are deplorable and healthcare is a joke, and they feed them, basically, rat turds, but aren't you kind of glad that he could get something as stupid as an infected tooth and die a miserable, painful death?"

Sam waited to make sure she was finished. "Once you and Ben are living in Atlanta, starting your new lives, it won't matter as much. That's your revenge. Enjoy your life. Appreciate what you have."

"I know," Charlie repeated.

"Be useful, Charlie. That's what Mama wanted."

"I know," she said, sighing out the words for a third time. "Let's change the subject. Since I'm catching you up on the Pikeville crime report, they had to let Rick Fahey go."

Lucy Alexander's grieving uncle. The man who had more than likely stabbed Rusty.

Sam said what Charlie must have known. "Absent a confession, they have no proof against him."

"I keep telling myself that Dad saw him that night, and that he knew it was Fahey, but he decided to let it go, so we should let it go."

Sam chose not to patronize her sister with Rusty's line about the value in forgiveness. "Isn't this exactly what you said you wanted to do—learn to let things go?"

"Yeah, well, I thought you were learning not to be a pain in my ass."

Sam smiled. "I want to send you a check for cleaning—"

"Stop." Charlie was too stubborn to take Sam's money. "Look, we were thinking of taking a vacation before we start our new jobs. Swing down to Florida for a few days to make sure Lenore is settling in, then maybe fly up to see you?"

Sam felt her smile strain at her cheeks. "You won't accept my money but you'll accept free room and board?"

"Exactly."

"I'd like that." Sam looked around her apartment. Suddenly,

it felt too sterile. She needed to buy things like pillows and hang some artwork and maybe add some color before Charlie got here. She wanted her sister to know that she had made herself a home.

Charlie said, "Okay, I've got to go stew and complain about this to Ben until I wear myself out. Check your email. We found something crazy in the basement."

Sam cringed. The basement had been the bachelor farmer's domain. "Is this another weird thing that's going to freak me out?"

"Check your email."

"I just checked it."

"Check it again, but when we're off the phone."

"I can look while we're—"

Charlie had hung up.

Sam rolled her eyes. There was a downside to having her little sister back in her life.

She clicked the home button on her phone. She opened her email. She dragged down the screen with her thumb. The circle spun as the emails reloaded.

Nothing new appeared at the top. Sam reloaded the emails again.

Still nothing.

She took off her glasses. She rubbed her eyes. She ran through all the troubling bachelor farmer surprises they had already found in the basement: assorted lingerie, various shoes, but only left ones, and a clock of a naked woman that had a perverted Tweety Bird effect.

Fosco jumped onto the counter. He sniffed the empty bowl of yogurt, clearly disappointed. Sam scratched his ears. He started to purr.

Her phone chirped.

Charlie's email had finally arrived.

Sam skimmed the listing: *this message has no content*.

"Charlie," she mumbled. Sam opened the email, mentally preparing a wry response, only to find that the message was not empty.

A file was attached at the bottom.

Tap to download.

Sam's thumb hovered over the icon.

The file name was above her nail.

Instead of tapping the screen, she put the phone down on the counter.

She leaned over, pressing her forehead to the cold marble. Her eyes closed. Her hands clasped together in her lap. She slowly breathed in, filling her lungs, before she breathed out again. She listened to the pelting rain. She waited for the butterflies in her stomach to float away.

Fosco nudged her cheek. He purred exuberantly.

Sam took another deep breath. She sat back up. She scratched Fosco's ears until he'd had enough and jumped down.

She put on her glasses. She picked up her phone. She looked at the email, the name of the file.

Gamma.jpg

If Charlie had been Rusty's creature, Sam had felt herself entirely Gamma's own. As a child, Sam had spent so many hours watching her mother, studying her, wanting to be like her—to be interesting, to be smart, to be good, to be right; but after Gamma's death, whenever Sam tried to summon her mother's face, she found herself unable to fill in the corresponding expressions—a smile, a look of surprise, a look of puzzlement, of dubiousness, of curiosity, of encouragement, of delight.

Until now.

Sam tapped the file. She watched the image load onto her phone.

She covered her mouth with her hand. She did nothing to stop her tears.

Charlie had found the photograph.

Not *the* photo, but the mythical photograph from Rusty's love story.

Sam stared at the image for minutes, for hours, for as long as it took to make her memories become whole.

As Rusty had described, Gamma was standing in a field. The red picnic blanket was on the ground. In the distance, there was an old weather tower; wood, not like the metal tower back home. Gamma's body was turned toward the camera. Her hands rested on her slim hips. One of her legs, admittedly beautiful, was bent at the knee. She was clearly trying not to give Rusty the satisfaction of laughing at something foolish he had said. An eyebrow was raised. Her white teeth showed. Freckles dotted her pale cheeks. She had a slight dimple in her chin.

Sam could not deny her father's assessment of the critical moment that had been captured on film. The vivid blue of Gamma's eyes undoubtedly showed a woman falling in love, but there was something else; a set to her mouth, an awareness of the coming challenges, a willingness to learn, a hope for convention, for children, for family, for a full, useful life.

Sam knew that this was exactly how Gamma would've wanted to be remembered: head straight, shoulders back, teeth ground, forever stalking joy.

ACKNOWLEDGMENTS

Thanks to Kate Elton, my friend and editor, who has been with me since my second book. Also to Victoria Sanders, friend and agent, who has been with me since before the before. Then there's Team Slaughter, who keep the trains running on time: Bernadette Baker-Baughman, Chris Kepner, Jessica Spivey, and the great Oz, Diane Dickensheid. Thanks also to my film agent, Angela Cheng Caplan, friend and advocate.

At William Morrow, much appreciation goes to Liate Stehlik, Dan Mallory, Heidi Richter, and Brian Murray.

There are too many other folks to list at Harper divisions around the world, but thanks especially to the folks in Norway, Denmark, Finland, Sweden, France, Ireland, Italy, Germany, the Netherlands, Belgium, and Mexico, with whom I've had the honor of spending so much time.

And now I'd like to thank the experts: Dr. David Harper, who patiently answers my medical questions (with illustrations!) so that I sound smarter than I actually am.

On the legal side of things: Alafair Burke, a Stanford Law graduate, a former prosecutor in Portland, a current law professor and also a remarkably gifted author, who despite juggling ten million balls in the air still managed to answer my urgent texts about legal procedure. Thanks also to the following for free legal advice: Aimee Maxwell, Don Samuel, Patricia Friedman, Judge Jan Wheeler, and Melanie Reed Williams. You have all made me at once glad I have your numbers and terrified that I will ever need them.

At the GBI, deputy director Scott Dutton was kind enough to walk me through procedure, and as always, deputy director (ret.) Sherry Lange, assistant special agent in charge (ret.) Dona Robinson, and APD sergeant (ret.) Vickye Prattes were enormously helpful. I always feel a tinge of guilt when I write about cops behaving badly because I have the great honor of knowing so many good ones. Thanks to Speaker David Ralston for making the introductions. Director Vernon Keenan, I hope you notice that I always make y'all the good guys.

My pal and fellow author Sara Blaedel helped me with the Danish bits. Brenda Allums and her merry band of coaches helped me calculate times and distances and many other things that I know nothing about.

I'm always grateful to Claire Schoeder for her travel services and friendship. Thanks very much to Gerry Collins and Brian for showing me around Dublin. Anne-Marie Diffley offered a wonderful tour of Dublin Trinity College. Ms. Antonella Fantoni in Florence and Ms. MariaLuisa Sala in Venice made history come alive with their joy and exuberance for these wonderful cities. And also, their joy and exuberance for wine.

My heartfelt thanks to the women who shared their stories and their losses with unflinching character and grace. Jeanenne English spoke with me about TBI. Margaret Graff reluctantly delved back into physics to help me with some passages. Chiara Scaglioni at HarperCollins Italy helped me come up with a fancy wine name. Melissa LaMarche made a generous donation to the Gwinnett Public Library in exchange for having her name appear in this novel. Bill Sessions first mentioned to me the Flannery O'Connor quote that I felt so perfectly captured the dilemma of the accomplished woman. I am sorry I have to thank him posthumously; he was a gifted storyteller and an amazing teacher.

Lewis Fry Richardson's 1922 *Weather Predictions by Numerical Process* provided a helpful reference. The forward in the 2007, second edition, written by Peter Lynch, Professor of Meteorology at

University College Dublin, gave additional insight into the work. Any mistakes are of course my own.

Last thanks always goes to my daddy, who makes sure I don't starve and/or freeze to death while I am writing, and to DA, my heart, who always welcomes me back home to the restful pied-monts of Mount Clothey.

This story is for Billie—sometimes, your world turns upside down, and you need somebody to show you how to walk on your hands before you can find your feet again.

ALSO BY KARIN SLAUGHTER

THE GOOD DAUGHTER
A Novel
"Fiction doesn't get any better than this."
—Jeffery Deaver

PRETTY GIRLS
A Novel
"Stunning. . . . Certain to be a book
of the year." —Lee Child

THE KEPT WOMAN
A Novel
"Exciting . . . an intense look at the nature of loss
and control, and how love can taint both."
—*Publishers Weekly*

BLINDSIGHTED
The First Grant County Thriller
"A debut of rare quality that grips like a vise
from the first page." —Val McDermid,
author of *A Place of Execution*

KISSCUT
A Grant County Thriller
"Engrossing . . . [with] meticulous
characterizations." —*People*

A FAINT COLD FEAR
A Grant County Thriller
"Simply one of the best thriller writers
working today." —Gillian Flynn, bestselling
author of *Gone Girl*

INDELIBLE
A Grant County Thriller
"Her characters, plot, and pacing are unrivaled
among thriller writers." —Michael Connelly

LIKE A CHARM
A Novel in Voices
"Riveting." —*Washington Post*